NIGHTMARISH DREAMS

WINTER LAWRENCE

NIGHTMARISH DREAMS
Copyright © 2022 by Winter Lawrence

ISBN: 978-1-955784-22-1

Published by Satin Romance
An Imprint of Melange Books, LLC
White Bear Lake, MN 55110
www.satinromance.com

Published in the United States of America.

Cover Design by Caroline Andrus

For Cory

A Note to Readers...

Hi, there, and thanks for taking some of your valuable time to read my book. I appreciate it more than you'll ever know. Before you dig in, though, I wanted to make sure everyone knows this is a work of fiction, and a highly dramatized one at that. When I started writing this book way back in 2013, all I knew was that it had to have a happy ending—sort of, anyway. At the very least, I wanted the main character to overcome his addictions. In order for me to do that, though, I had to stretch the fabric of reality a bit so everything fit together perfectly. In other words, I had to create highly romanticized versions of Hollywood, police procedures, and occultism. It was meant to come off as campy and theatrical, and so I wanted to emphasize that this is not an entirely accurate account of how Hollywood, Satanism, or addictions works. It's just a book, and one I intended as a tribute to Cory Monteith.

You see, my family and I are huge *Glee* fans, and when Cory passed away, we were inexplicably devastated by the news. Clearly, we never had the pleasure of knowing him, yet his loss cast a huge shadow over our family, and so I did the only thing I could: I wrote a book for him—one where he beats his demons. It seemed the least I could do given that he's brought so many years of joy into our lives. And so in honor of Cory, 100% of the author's proceeds will go toward non-profit organizations that are dedicated to helping young adults overcome their substance abuse issues.

Those we love truly never leave us. There are things that death cannot touch.

— Jack Thorne

Cast of Characters

Prologue

Cory

The final stop of the day for our charity event is at the Los Angeles branch of the Society for the Prevention of Cruelty to Animals. I've always liked animals, but when I was growing up I always made sure to keep them as far away from my house as possible, otherwise my father would beat them mercilessly just for the fun of it. I know, because aside from my mother, I was his favorite punching bag.

As the cast of *Copper Creek* exits the huge tour bus the studio had rented for our day-long charity event, I catch glimpses of nearby buildings as I head down the aisle. If I remember correctly from the "briefing" we had this morning when we met up at the studio, I'm sure they said the spcaLA is next door to the Long Beach Animal Care Services.

For a shelter, it's pretty ritzy, though I hadn't imagined that the studio was going to send us into the ghetto. *Copper Creek* is a cheesy teenage romantic drama, but the ratings are promising enough that the studio signed us for a second season—and rumor has it that *my* character, Ethan Green, has garnered enough attention to warrant an upgrade to potential lover status with the female lead.

It's still all so surreal and unbelievable.

I mean, I'd like to think of myself as a man's man, but I still get a little choked up when I think about it. This is some real-life Cinderella shit, though. I'm still so mind-blown by it that I can't wrap my brain around it. But I did it. I made it big. Me. Cory Hudson. The used and abused child of an alcoholic asshole. The orphan who bounced from foster home to homeless shelters all over the middle of nowhere New York. I made it. *I'm* a Hollywood heartthrob.

As I step off the bus, I watch the press swarm after Dee Armstrong, the female lead who my character is going to get involved with in season two. She's definitely the star of the show, no doubt because she's an adored child actress who's from an elite Hollywood family, but she's also a good actress, and I'm actually a little nervous about working with her. As of right now, we've only had one scene together, and it was of her fantasizing about being with my character. It was beyond awkward to film, but she had been graceful about it, and apparently our on-screen chemistry is what convinced the powers that be to bump up my status—that, and the fan response to Ethan Green. Apparently my character is the underdog—the poor stable boy who would never have a chance with the beautiful heiress of a horse farm.

It's all so damn cheesy, but it's paying the bills, and while I haven't really experienced the fame part yet, my agent keeps telling me it's coming. Once all the episodes air, people will really start to recognize me. Until then, I just watch as reporters and paparazzi yell questions at the other cast members. My time will come. I can feel it. So until then, I'll just enjoy the perks, like the star-studded treatment we get inside the animal shelter.

The director is there to greet us, as well as a slew of other staff members and volunteers. We take pictures and sign autographs, and then we talk about wildfires, which is how this whole "Good Samaritan" thing got started. Some big-wig at the studio thought it was the perfect opportunity for the show to get some good PR if we tag-teamed with the major nonprofits in the Los Angeles area. Apparently, he was right, and so we go through the motions of caring—again—and make our rounds through the facility.

In one room, I play with puppies. In another, with senior dogs. In the next area, there are a ton of dog runs, and each of the cast members is assigned a dog we walk outside. My dog is cute; an old fella by the name of Liam who has a bit of a limp. He's easy going and photogenic, so we take lots of pictures together. Then I'm shepherded into a cat room. It's a huge space with lots of free-roaming cats who have ample trees and condos to climb. I'd like to think of myself as a dog kind-of-guy, but after a long day of visiting with veterans, seniors, and disaster victims, the cats are a welcome respite, so I linger behind to play with a few.

When I notice a lone volunteer waiting to guide me back to the group, I start to make my way over to her, but I stop short when I notice a small room tucked off in the corner. The door has a large window so there's a clear view of a woman sitting in a rocking chair. She's bottle feeding the smallest kitten I've ever seen. Intrigued, I walk that way. At first, the woman is so focused on stroking the little kitten and holding the bottle just so that she doesn't notice me or the volunteer, but when she finally looks up, her eyes go wide.

I have to say, it's a little flattering.

I push open the door with a smile. The woman is speechless, so I walk over and kneel beside her, though my attention is on the kitten.

"How old is it?" I inquire.

"I..." she stammers, clearly caught off guard, which thankfully doesn't hinder her ability to continue feeding the hungry kitten. "Ah..."

It's my first time with an awestruck fan, but I get the sense it's best to help in moments like these.

"Was it rescued during the wildfires?" I hedge, hoping to get her talking.

The woman, who's probably in her early twenties, nods, because apparently she's still speechless. At this point, it's getting a little awkward, especially because the woman's long, dark hair and big, light brown eyes are sort of mesmerizing. She's hot, and definitely not the kind of chick I'd expect to find nursing kittens at an animal shelter, though I remind myself that not all people are so set on survival mode or jaded that they can't naturally be altruistic. And hot chicks can volunteer too. They aren't all airheaded bimbos.

"Are you a fan of the show?" I ask as I move close to a row of nearby kennels. There are a bunch of equally tiny kittens tucked away in each.

"The show?" the woman asks.

I peer over my shoulder and study her face. She seems genuinely confused. *"Copper Creek,"* I say, sure that given her reaction, the title will help snap her out of her stupor.

The woman, though, shakes her head. "I...I don't have a television..."

"Oh..." I say, since now I'm speechless too.

"A-hem," the other volunteer chimes in. "Penny is one of our devout volunteers..." the woman pulls the door open and motions to a sign beneath the window. "And these kittens are actually under quarantine, so this room is usually off limits." The volunteer, whose name I can't recall, is motioning in a clear sign that indicates she wants me to get the hell out.

I gladly oblige. "It was nice to meet you," I say to the silently sexy and strange volunteer, and then I follow the other volunteer through the building until we regroup with the cast. We gather in the parking lot for another photo op and on my way back to the bus, a reporter stops me. She's cute, and she asks me a bunch of very specific, on-point questions about my character and my future with the show, because she suspects that I'm going to become a key player in the *Copper Creek* saga. Her enthusiasm is contagious and somehow, in the midst of our conversation, I try to convince her to adopt Liam. The reporter, who's name I discover is Chelsea, is nearly about to cave and go inside when the silent and sexy volunteer walks over to us.

4

"Hello, again, Ethan." Her voice is low, yet smooth like velvet. With trembling hands, she extends the headshot photo that the studio had handed out to each organization we appeared at today.

I pull a Sharpie out of my inner jacket pocket and take the picture. "And whom shall I make it out to?" I inquire, a bit light-headed and giddy for the request.

"To Penny," she says as she runs her finger along the top of the photo. Then she slides her finger to the bottom of the image. "Love always, Ethan."

For a fraction of a second, I hesitate, not sure if it's normal to autograph a picture of myself with my character's name, but then I do as she asks, and I'm rewarded with a dazzling smile.

Penny stares down at the picture for a long moment before she looks back up at me. "Ethan..."

She's at a loss for words beyond that though, and thankfully I don't have to personally deal with the second awkward moment on my own because the intern who's been shepherding us around all day starts screaming for us to board the bus. Relieved for the reprieve, I wave a goodbye to Penny and then I set my sights on Chelsea.

"You'll adopt him, won't you?"

"I'll think about it," she says, but there's a bit of a glimmer in her eye that makes me hopeful. "See you around, Hollywood."

"Hopefully at the dog park," I say as coolly as I can, the nickname giving me that heady, intoxicating feeling again.

Chelsea just laughs and walks off. Penny continues to stand there, staring after me. I give her a curt wave and then hurry to board the bus. With so many cast and crew members, it takes a few minutes for me to finally get settled back in. When I do, I drop back against my seat and recount the day. It all seems like a blur now, but this last leg of the trip made it feel like it was all worth it. The one fan and reporter somehow validating all the hard work I've put into my career. I think this is really it. The start of the fame and fortune I've sought for so long.

As the bus begins to pull away from its spot, I glance out the window and notice that Penny is still standing exactly where I left her, except now she's turned toward the bus. The windows are tinted, so I'm sure she can't see me, per se, but she stands there and watches us for at least as long as I can see her, which is a bit unnerving, but something I'm sure I'll eventually get used to.

Five Years Later

Chapter 1

Penelope

Los Angeles, California
January 20th, Saint Agnes Eve

Breaking into Destiny O'Rourke's house was a rather simple endeavor. Unfortunately, as I was leaving, I tripped some kind of sensor—probably an added feature she had recently installed after the last time I broke in. I drive along the twisty mountain roads of the Hollywood Hills, checking my rearview mirror often, expecting to see flashing lights and sirens any minute even though I had chosen to steal the non-descript Honda because I knew it wouldn't draw much attention. Not that I really expected to be followed, as I had made sure to lock up the house after I left, and I had only taken one thing. Its importance is insurmountable to me, but I doubt Destiny will even notice its gone.

I'm nearly at Griffith Park when I see the flashing lights. As a courtesy, I turn on the hazard lights and pull to the shoulder. Three cop cars blow past me, heading up the mountain at breakneck speeds. When the last car passes, I smile as I disengage the hazards and continue along to the park. After ditching the car at one of the visitors' parking lots, I hike the mile to my Range Rover and then make it to my house in Glendale in no time flat.

Just as I exit the freeway, I notice a billboard sign advertising *Copper Creek,* my favorite television show. My heart skips a beat as my eyes lovingly follow along the bolded black letters that read: **Cory Hudson as Ethan Green,** the larger-than-life picture of him engrossing me so thoroughly that I run the red light. A horn honks, snapping me out of my musing. I slam on the brakes and wince as a bright flash of light momentarily blinds me. *Dammit.* I'm sure the stupid photo-enforced camera just snapped a picture.

Thankfully, I make it home without further incident, but the second I pull into my driveway, my neighbor's annoying Chihuahua begins to bark. Normally, I'm an animal lover, but this particular dog has spent years getting on my bad side. Mrs. Reich has doggy doors on her front and back doors, since her yard has a chain-linked fence around its entire perimeter. That gives her dog free reign to come outside at all hours of the night to harass me. He barks. Growls. Snarls. And on more than one occasion, he's slipped under the fence and bitten me. So while I usually love animals, I hate this guy, and as his incessant barking follows me to the door, I have to force myself to stay calm. *Focus.* I take several soothing breaths as I place my bag on the kitchenette table.

Once centered, I unzip the small backpack and retrieve the sole item within: a 5X7 frame containing a picture of Destiny and Ethan. My left eye begins to twitch and I grind my teeth.

How dare that bitch keep a picture of them on her nightstand?

I rip the back of the frame off, remove the photo, and take a moment to admire Ethan. He looks older in this picture compared to the huge billboard photo I admired moments ago, but he's still breathtaking in the tuxedo that he had worn to the

MTV Music Awards. The single-breasted charcoal jacket with matching vest and tie did an amazing job of accenting his beautiful turquoise eyes, and the tuxedo's custom fit hugged the contours of his divine physique beautifully. He always looks amazing, but Destiny had the audacity to wear a skimpy, repugnant dress even though she was up to win a Grammy that night. Even worse was that she had chopped her long blonde hair into a way-too-short pixie style that wasn't at all flattering and made it look like Ethan had accompanied a prepubescent boy to the awards ceremony.

Ugh! I will never wear anything unbecoming when we're finally together.

Repulsed by the dress and crop-cut, and further infuriated that Ethan is even with her, I crease the picture down the center and gently tear it along the seam. If only it was this simple to separate them in real life.

Soon you'll be mine.

I kiss his image then place his half of the photo on the table. I'll add it to my ever-growing collection later. For now, I walk down the hallway with Destiny's image held firmly within my grip. When I get to the master bedroom door, I slide the picture into my back pocket and then, with careful intent, I remove the security pin from the uppermost part of my sanctuary door. It's rigged with C4 because it is my most cherished place—*the* sacred space where I first communed with my Dark Father—and so I would sooner see it destroyed than ever allow it to be violated by another.

Once safely inside, I flick on the light and smile as the overhead light illuminates the room. All is as it should be; the beautiful black hand-carved altar rests within the large pentagram that's drawn onto the carpet in the center of the room. More importantly, the one and only picture I have of *my* late Ethan is hanging on the far wall. As I move toward the delicate frame, my heart rate accelerates. He was so beautiful.

I run my finger along the glass. *I miss you.*

The rapid pounding of my heart begins to wane as sorrow creeps up my spine. I hate that everything between us ended so badly, but I have a second chance now because *my* Ethan has come back to me. His spirit somehow reincarnating itself into Cory Hudson's body, taking over the persona of Ethan Green, a man who—even down to the name—is just like my late Ethan. Granted, *my* Ethan rarely drank or partied. And he never had a desire to perform or pursue a career in acting. He was a humble, sweet man. Ethan Green, on the other hand, is wilder—almost as if he's *my* Ethan's alter ego. Yet they share so many similar characteristics that I know my Dark Father has blessed me with a second chance.

Ethan Green used to be mine, but he's gone.

Ethan Green belongs to another, but I will make him mine.

My *new* Ethan doesn't remember me...he doesn't remember *us,* but in time I'll help him recall just how happy we used to be. I'll help him remember our daughter, and once I get rid of Destiny, I'll do whatever it takes to keep him happy.

I swear I won't mess it up this time.

I walk to my altar, place the torn picture of Destiny face down, and grab a pen. In a neat and ornate cursive, I write her name on the back of the photo and hope that using a personal item taken from her house will finally do the trick. After setting the picture aside, I light an incense stick and swirl it through the air for a moment before placing it onto its silver holder.

Time is of the essence. The moon is still high in the sky, but it won't be for much longer, so I hurry to the bathroom and take a quick shower. Once done, I grab a comb and run it through my long, dark hair as I make my way back to my sanctuary. I don one of my many black robes, and after securing the buttons, I place five black candles on each point of the pentagram. I position a sixth candle on my altar while staring at Destiny's image. Her beautiful blue eyes mock me.

He belongs with me, you bitch.

Resolute in my hatred for her, I light each of the candles then turn off the overhead light and lift my athame in my right hand. I ring the bell then turn to my left, pointing the athame toward the east to call upon Satan. Continuing counterclockwise, I turn toward the north and call upon Beelzebub. Then I face west, calling upon Astaroth, and finally, I return to the south and call upon Azazel.

"In the name of Satan, the Ruler of the Earth, the King of the world, I command the forces of Darkness to bestow their Infernal power upon me! Open wide the gates of Hell and come forth from the abyss to greet me as your sister and friend! Grant me the indulgences of which I speak! I have taken thy name as a part of myself! I live as the beasts of the field, rejoicing in the fleshly life! I favor the just and curse the rotten! By all the Gods of the Pit, I command that these things of which I speak shall come to pass! Come forth and answer to your names by manifesting my desires!"

I lay the athame on the altar and drink from my chalice. When the cup is empty, I stare down at Destiny's image and recite the *Invocation Employed Towards the Conjuration of Destruction*.

Once done, I add a personal prayer. "To the Dark Power of light, I summon thee to call upon the great reaper to win the life fight." I raise my hands skyward, tilt my head back, and close my eyes. "I summon thee, oh Dark Father, to call upon your soldiers of death so that they may win the life fight against Destiny O'Rourke."

I lift Destiny's picture and hold it above the flame, shifting it so each corner curls and warps before I finally drop it into my silver bowl. As the picture bubbles and distorts, I drop onto my knees and ask my Dark Father to answer my prayer while I focus on the mental image I have of Destiny. When my energy diminishes, I stand and end with, "Hail Satan!"

My hair blows around me wildly and wind presses against my cheeks. I'm still focusing on my hatred for Destiny, but I can't help but smile when another sudden gust of wind causes the candles to flicker. Satisfied that Satan has finally heard my prayer, I grab the bell and ring it while turning clockwise, a sense of peace consuming my soul as I conclude my ritual.

Two Months Later

Chapter 2

Rebecca

I can't believe I'm actually here! I shift closer to the limousine window and stare at the Hollywood sign until it's completely out of view, then I take in the sights on Melrose Avenue. There are tons of people walking along the busy street, the tourists easy enough to pick out of the crowd because their awestruck expressions aren't much different from mine. And the traffic, even at this early morning hour, is just as congested as the sidewalks. Thankfully, the studio was kind enough to provide a driver for the month I'm here so I don't have to worry about getting around. I have enough trouble with the traffic in Denver, so the daily commute from the bungalow to the movie studio would have completely overwhelmed me.

When we arrive at Paramount Pictures' grand entrance, I shift to admire the high arc. Wow, I'm *really* here. I thought my dreams had come true when I landed a literary agent, but that wasn't nearly as exciting as my book selling to a publishing house and instantly skyrocketing to success days after its release. I wasn't prepared to make the New York Times bestsellers list or to have the rights optioned to make my book into a movie. I feel so lucky to be one of the few people living this dream that I press my forehead against the window the same way my four-year-old son does and continue looking outside in awe.

As we near a large building, the driver says, "This is your lot, Mrs. Carter."

A thousand butterflies erupt in my empty stomach.

Benny steps out of the car and walks around to open the door for me. "Just call the personal cell phone number on my business card if you need to leave early. If not, I'll be here at five to drive you back to the bungalow."

I take the hand he offers and step out. "Thanks, Benny."

"Anna is waiting for you. Just take the first left you come to and you'll see her office about halfway down the hallway."

My hand slips out of his as I stare at the imposing building. I know I should be ecstatic that there's an elegant sign hanging above the door that reads *Bridesmaid for Hire,* but I'm not.

I'm petrified.

Benny must sense my hesitation because he steps closer and smiles. "Would you like me to walk you inside, Mrs. Carter?"

I nod. "Yeah, I'd really appreciate it, Benny."

As we walk toward the building, he explains that Anna usually accompanies him to pick up the consultants, or in my case, a "consulting writer," on the first day of shooting. I couldn't get here last week though, so filming has been going on for a few days without me. What's worse is that I'm an hour late. Everyone is usually on set by seven a.m., but Benny assures me that the writers don't have to keep those hours. In fact, most times they aren't even on set. Despite that, I feel I should. It is *my* book after all.

Once inside the studio, I look at the different sets in wonder. Benny is still talking, but I'm not listening. In fact, I stop altogether when we "arrive" at Cassie's apartment.

Wow—it's exactly how I had envisioned it!

"We didn't do too badly, huh?" Anna says from behind.

I turn to face her with a smile. Anna is one of the executive producers, and we've communicated via email and phone for a couple of weeks now, but her young and glamorous appearance surprises me. *Isn't she like fifty?* I shake off the rude thought and embrace her. "It's amazing, Anna," I say as I step back and smile, "and it's so nice to finally meet you."

"Ditto," she says. After saying our goodbyes to Benny, Anna wraps her arm around mine and guides me along. "I'm sorry I couldn't meet you at the house, we've just been swamped with issues since day one—"

"Oh, no!"

Anna laughs. "Honey, it's a film set so we're always swamped the first week. It's like with any new thing. You just have to work out the kinks. Come on. I'll show you around."

While we stroll along, I take in the finer details. They really have done an amazing job of capturing every detail. My Cassie is here—not just in my head as some fictional character—and not just published in thousands of books around the world—she's here, come to life. I just can't get over it.

When we stop to meet some of the crew, I pull my head out of the clouds and focus on remembering names. I'm bad at it so I'm glad everyone is wearing a badge. Then we meet Katie Dawn, the Hollywood superstar who is playing my Cassie!

Unfortunately, my elation is short lived. I had envisioned us sitting over lattes while she asked my thoughts on how she could best embody Cassie's personality, but after a quick handshake, Katie hurries past me because she's intent on killing one of the makeup artists. Thankfully, the rest of the cast and crew are pleasant, and while I didn't receive a warm welcome from Katie, several of the actors thank me for writing such a fun book.

The remainder of the morning is a blur. I watch as the cast does their read-throughs and then watch the stage crew run around preparing for the upcoming scene. It's exciting and a bit chaotic, but when the set crew runs into technical issues, everything seems to come to a screeching halt. The director lets everyone break for an early lunch while the workers frenzy to repair the problem.

Anna invites me to join her at Spago, her favorite restaurant, so we head to the limousine and make idle chitchat during the short ride to Beverly Hills. On the way, I learn that it isn't normal for the average person to leave set for lunch. Everything, apparently, is catered, and they don't like people leaving until filming is done for the day, but Anna is one of the executive producers, so she gets to bend the rules a bit.

Once we're seated at the restaurant though, she begins to explain how screenplays really work. Like how one screenwriter could be hired initially, but how that person could be fired or quits, so another person has to take over, or like other times, when a screenwriter finishes the project but then the director hates it.

That, Anna assured me, happens all the time, and so it's no big deal when the studio hires another screenwriter to come in and "tidy it up."

Howard, the director of my movie, apparently didn't *hate* the original film adaptation, but he didn't like it either, so he and Anna had reached out to my agent, wondering if I'd like to be a "guest writing consultant," since I don't have any experience writing screenplays, but I obviously know the storyline. I was honored, of course, especially because it was made very clear that the offer isn't extended often. It was also mentioned that I should be on my best behavior. Hollywood doesn't like authors who are rigid and demanding. Accepting criticism and offering suggestions for changes are pluses, so when Anna begins to broach the subject about making some changes to the current script, I nod agreeably and aptly listen to her suggestions.

"Howard and I *love* the book, Rebecca," she says, sounding sincere. "And we want to keep it as true to your story as we can. I mean, why ruin a good thing, right?" Anna says as she reaches over and pats my hand.

"Thank you," I say, my cheeks blazing as they always do when people speak so highly of my work.

"There are a few things we may have to *tweak* though," she

says as she reaches for her wine spritzer. "You know, those really internal scenes that may not translate well onto the big screen." After a tiny sip, she continues. "For instance, last night I reread the book again. Well, not the entire book," she chuckles, "just the chapter where Cassie discovers that the job she took as the maid of honor for the stockbroker is actually her ex-boyfriend's wedding."

"Yeah, that was pretty hard for me to get down. My editor kicked it back several times before everyone was happy with it."

"It's wonderful, darling, really, unfortunately, it's all internal musing, so we'll have to think of a way to show that on screen. I have some ideas, but I wanted to get your feedback before putting anything into stone."

When she looks at me pointedly, I cringe a bit. "Well..." I sigh. My agent complained about my word count before and after signing me on as her client, always quick to remind me that she wouldn't be able to justify selling a book with over a hundred thousand words to a publishing house. Romances are supposed to be short and sweet, she consistently reminded me, even if the storyline is complex. Keeping that in mind, I finally say, "Maybe she can call Randy to talk about it?"

Anna crinkles her nose and shakes her head. "That's so...ah, it's too easy and Howard doesn't like that. He wants the audience to feel her conflict with her, so just listening to a conversation won't do that. Nor does he care for the fact that she's having all of these thoughts while she's driving up to Connecticut. It works for a book, but not so much for a movie."

A waiter comes to take our orders.

Once he leaves, Anna sits back. "Tell me about Cassie. From the book, we know that she's doing this bridesmaid-for-hire gig to make enough money to open a romantic B&B far away from New York City, but I want more, Rebecca. Tell me everything *you* know about her—all the little details that never made it into the book but that helped shape her into the health conscience, green, yoga guru we meet at the beginning of the book."

I crack up at that. "She wasn't always like that, but you know how it goes, you meet a guy and you start changing for him. At first you don't notice because they're little things, like hiking more or wearing your hair a certain way for him, and Cassie was oblivious to how much she had changed until he dumped her." I fish my journal out of my purse. "And since they worked together, she was more than willing to jump on the bridesmaid-for-hire gig to put distance between them."

Anna nods as she reaches for her purse. "This is great. Give me more." She puts her tablet on the table and lends me a pen when I realize I had forgotten mine.

She, of course, teases me about it as many have before, but as much as I know it's a dying art, I'll always prefer writing to typing.

"Isn't there a scene in the beginning of the book where Cassie mentions one of her favorite professors taught the business class she and John met in?" Anna asks as she types away. "How would you feel about making his character a bigger deal in the film?"

"That's an awesome idea!"

After uncapping the fancy-looking fountain pen, I pull my journal closer. I'm beyond excited that we might be able to include several scenes that my editor insisted I cut out, so Anna and I begin storyboarding and we work through lunch.

When we arrive back at the studio, the set is ready to go. Unfortunately, we quickly learn that Katie is throwing a fit over the argument she and the makeup artist got into, and worse yet, she's insisting that the woman be terminated immediately. Anna mutters something about hating prima donnas before telling me to make myself comfortable in her office. Then she hurries off.

I take the opportunity to slip outside for a not-so-fresh-air break. I light a cigarette and take a long drag, enjoying the beautiful day and quiet respite. Just as I take another drag, a crewmember pushes open a nearby door and steps right into my smoke. He coughs then tells me that Katie and Anna are looking for me. After pointing me in the right direction, he rushes off.

Jeez, people sure do move fast around here.

I consider following suit, but after looking at my cigarette, I shake my head. Katie and her tantrum can wait until I finish my date with the Marlboro Man. I lean against the building and flip through my journal pages, my mind wandering over everything to make sure it keeps true to the book as much as possible.

After dropping my butt into an ashtray, I wander along and read the names on the trailers that I pass. I've met most of these actors, but when I get to Cory Hudson's trailer, I stop. He's a Hollywood heartthrob who has an insanely popular sitcom and several big-budget films under his belt—none of which I've gotten around to watching—but my family and students were beyond excited that he agreed to play the leading male role in *Bridesmaid for Hire.* My mom even made me promise to send her a picture of the two of us together since she's a huge *Copper Creek* fan.

Who knew Mom would get into a cheesy teen drama?

As I continue along, I try to remember if Cory is going to be in any of the scenes that are being filmed today, but then I suddenly recall that Anna mentioned he wouldn't be joining us for a few days. Mom will not be pleased about that, so I double back to Cory's trailer, step beside his nameplate, and take a few selfies. When I shift to look at the images, Anna's fancy-looking pen slips out of my journal and rolls beneath the trailer. *Dammit.* That thing looks like it's worth a hundred bucks.

I put the phone in my back pocket then drop my journal onto the ground and kneel on it. The pen rolled farther away than I expected, so I have to scoot closer and then resort to crawling halfway under the trailer to reach it. Frustrated, I snatch it off the ground, shift back, and stand. Unfortunately, I once again misjudge the distance again, so my head bangs against the under-side of the trailer. A sharp pain radiates along my skull and I have to just be for a moment until the throbbing subsides. When

I'm sure I can stand without falling back over or puking, I get onto my feet.

A little dazed by the blow, I touch my aching scalp then look at my bloody fingertips. Great. Just when I thought I had left my clumsiness in Denver, here's proof positive that I hadn't. I begin to head toward the studio, but when I notice how wobbly and off-kilter I feel, I stop and take a few deep breaths. I definitely think I hit my head harder than I'd realized. I gingerly touch the tender spot on my head again and wince, and then I look at my fingers. They're still bloody as ever. I sigh as I look at Cory's trailer door. Maybe there are hand towels or a first-aid kit in there, or at the very least some paper towels or toilet paper to hold me over until I find a first-aid station. I pull open the door and slowly take a step up, then another, my attention so focused on getting up the stairs without falling that it takes me too long of a moment to realize I'm not alone...

Cory Hudson is sitting on a nearby recliner. He's wearing headphones—which would explain why he didn't hear me—and there's a script opened on his lap, but I only see that in passing because I'm too busy staring at the tourniquet around his left arm and the syringe in his right hand. *Oh, crap.* I gingerly step down one of the stairs, hoping that he's so intent on searching for a vein that I continue to go unnoticed. I start lowering my other foot to the ground when he spots me.

Oh, crap, oh, crap, oh, crap!

Cory drops the syringe and yanks the headphones off.

Like a deer in headlights, I just stand there when he rushes toward me.

"Who the hell are you?" he shouts.

"I'm so sorry, I didn't—"

He grabs my arm and yanks me so forcefully that my feet drag along the two steps. I hang in the air for second before my feet touch the floor again.

Cory slams me against the wall. "You didn't see anything, you understand?"

I nod frantically. "Of course, I won't—"

"And take whatever the hell you brought and shove it up your ass!"

He pushes me toward the stairs and my clumsy feet lose their footing. I fall forward, somehow managing to maneuver the first two stairs, but as gravity pulls me along, I topple and trip over the last step, my palms skidding along the asphalt to brace myself as I crumble onto the ground. Sharp pains shoot up my arms and my knees as they catch the brunt of the fall. Yet, despite the agonizing sensations, I somehow manage to scramble onto my feet and back away. Cory steps out of the trailer and stops to pick up a phone that looks exactly like mine. I instinctively touch my back pocket, ignoring the pain that radiates along my palm as my inspection turns up the obvious. It's *my* phone. Unfortunately, I don't have an opportunity to tell Cory that before he throws it into his trailer and then moves closer and points his finger in my face.

"Give me your other cameras."

I shake my head. "I don't—"

"You better not. Now get the hell out of here before I call security."

I nod, but I'm too scared to move. When he steps closer still, though, I finally break into a run. I don't know where I'm going and it isn't until I'm far enough away that I realize I'm crying. I stop and lean against a trailer, painful sobs ripping through me as I struggle to catch my breath.

"Oh, there you are—" Katie gasps and then rushes over to me. "OMG, Rebecca, honey! What happened?"

"I..." I sob and reach for my aching head. "I hit my head."

"Jesus, girl! You're bleeding." She gently grabs onto my arm and guides me into her trailer. "Just sit right there while I call the medics."

I drop onto a chair, my knees wobbling so badly that I'm not sure how I had managed to run.

"Here, hold this against your head," Katie says as she places a damp towel in my hand and then reaches for tissue to wipe my face. "What happened?"

I press the towel against my head. "I just...oh, crap; I lost my journal and Anna's pen."

"Don't worry about that right now. Just relax. The medic will be here soon."

In shock over the crazy turn of events, I just nod and blow my nose.

Was I really just thinking that this was a dream come true? Amazed that the thought feels like it flitted through my mind a million years ago, I remind myself that I've only been in L.A. for two days and that it was just a crazy, unfortunate incident. I tell myself that it's no reason to overreact. It was just a series of unfortunate events. Yet, no matter how many times I tell myself that, I still find myself desperately wanting to get on the first plane back to Denver.

Chapter 3

Cory

I am sick of obsessive fans and deranged stalkers. I'm tired of getting flowers and teddy bears and panties, and this one! This bitch had the nerve to break into the studio and sneak into my trailer even though I'm not even supposed to be here today.

I wonder if she's the same chick who broke onto my show's set a few months ago? Or worse yet, maybe she was the one who broke in and trashed Destiny's house a couple of months before that. The thought crosses my mind to call the cops, but I immediately blow it off since I know that the LAPD employs the most incompetent fuckers on the planet, so calling them would just be a huge waste of my time. Besides, I definitely don't need the media attention that will ensue if someone leaks the story to the press, so I lock the door, pick up the woman's phone, and toss it into the trash.

Fuck it. I don't give a shit who she is—just as long as she's gone.

Pushing aside my frustration, I go back to my chair, put my headphones on, and retrieve my syringe. After tapping my forearm, I insert the needle into my vein. As I depress the plunger, a warm, euphoric haze flows through me. Suddenly relaxed and able to forget about reality, I turn my music louder and allow all of the intrusive thoughts of my crazy girlfriend and deranged fans to slip away. As I float along the warm and fuzzy heroin-induced tides, I wonder how it took me so long to discover this heavenly drug. I used to think smoking weed was the best shit ever, but marijuana doesn't hold a candle to heroin.

Riding my high, I turn my seventies soft rock and R&B playlist louder and zone out. I just need a few minutes to unwind after my interruption. I'll start reading the script in a few, or that's the plan, but time is a funny thing when you're high. What only feels like a few minutes is actually a little over an hour. I toss the headphones aside and get up long enough to take a leak and to grab my gaming controller. The script can wait a little longer. Right now, it's time for *Commando's Creed*.

Now this is the life.

If I could get high and play videogames all day instead of acting, I'd be as happy as a pig in shit. Maybe I should give up on my career, downgrade to weed again, and go back to tending bar. I actually miss that simple, low-key life—

Someone knocks on the door.

Dammit. I grab my stash, making sure to place the used needle in my kit to dispose of later, and then I walk down the three steps to the door. There's a small, circular window that's covered with a frilly curtain that I pull back. *Fuck*—it's my agent. Or, more like my dictator. The moment I unlock the door, Brad practically rips it off its hinges and slams a tabloid against my chest.

"What part of quit fucking up your squeaky-clean reputation don't you get, Cory?"

I roll my eyes when he pushes past me and makes himself at home. "Good morning to you too," I say.

"It's afternoon—late afternoon, in fact. Are you off your high enough to go and meet the cast and crew?"

"What? I'm not scheduled to start for two days—"

"Well, tough shit. We need to do some major cleanup after your little soiree last night."

I drop back into my recliner. "That wasn't my idea."

He turns to face me. "Do you think that matters, Cory? If you want to date some sleazy singer who lacks any fiber of self-restraint then you suffer the consequences with her."

"She isn't always like that," I mutter.

"Yeah, just on days ending in Y." Brad starts straightening up. "Go take a shower and think of what you're going to say to the press about this." He shoots me a disapproving glare. "What the hell were you thinking throwing an orgy?"

I toss the tabloid aside and shrug. "I didn't stay."

"Is that what I'm supposed to say? That a healthy, young, rich, and famous guy turned down the chance to participate in an orgy with his superstar girlfriend. Yeah, they'll eat that shit up."

I shrug again then get up and head to the bathroom. "Look, man, if God wanted me to fuck four chicks at once, he would have given me four dicks."

"That's real fucking squeaky clean, Cory," he shouts loud enough so I can hear him through the bathroom door. "By the time you're done washing your ass, I want an innocent sounding statement just like it came straight from Ethan Green's mouth!"

Annoyed, I turn the water on and step into the shower before it's even warmed up.

The jolt of cold sobers me up. After adjusting the temperature to a more bearable level, I purposely take my time, even more pissed now that I have to make it through this stupid fucking meet-and-greet without any heroin or scotch coursing through my veins. Fuck Brad. Fuck Destiny. Fuck *Copper Creek*. And fuck my fans. Everyone wants me to be Ethan Green in real life, but that won't ever happen because that guy's a punk —I'm not.

Why can't people keep reality separate from fiction?

When I step out of the bathroom, Brad is sitting in my chair playing my game. Without a word, he points to the bedroom. I walk over to find a suit laid out for me. As much as Brad gets under my skin, he's probably the closest thing I've ever had to a real father and I know he's always looking out for my best interests, so I obediently get dressed. By the time I'm done, Brad has already gotten a makeup artist. I dutifully sit and chug down the two bottles of water Brad hands me.

Then we're off to make rounds. I plaster a smile on my face and make small talk as we make our way through the crowd. I've worked with a few of the cast members in the past because many of them have guest starred on *Copper Creek*. Then Katie Dawn enters the room in her usual grandiose way. She hurries over with her arms outstretched—her fake smile molded onto her plastic face. I return her embrace and pretend I'm just fucking ecstatic to see her. I can't stand the bitch, and it still amazes me that after our last movie together all the critics and fans just loved our chemistry. I don't see or feel any chemistry. Most times, I want to strangle her. She's so damn phony, pretentious, and just plain bitchy. The girl thinks she's god's gift to the universe and that she has the right to treat the staff members and the up-and-coming actors like shit.

She begins her usual small talk—which basically equals asking questions that lead the conversation back to just how fucking perfect she is—so I give a curt nod and turn, looking for an out. Unfortunately, my only way to avoid a conversation with her is if I turn to greet Howard, the director. That isn't much of an improvement, but anything is better than small talk with Katie. With my thousand-watt smile in place, I extend my hand. Howard shakes it firmly while giving me a few nudge, nudge, wink, winks for my party last night. I'd like to tell him that I have no interest in orgies and for him to quit vicariously living through me, but I keep my mouth shut about that and about the fact that his wife is nothing but a gold-digging hoe. Ten-to-one says she's down to have a group of guys run a train on her, but that isn't my style. As much as the press likes to pin me as a playboy, I'm a one-guy-one-girl kind of dude.

"Cory, darling," Anna shouts from across set. "You're early!"

God is fucking good.

I instantly relax as I meet her halfway and when we embrace, it's genuine. Anna is actually one of the few people in this town who hasn't completely lost touch with the real world.

She leans back to look me over. "You're looking fabulous as always, Mr. Hudson. Would you mind terribly if I borrow you to introduce you to Rebecca Carter? I promise to get you back to Brad in no time flat." She winks, to which I laugh and offer my arm.

Anna knows how much I hate the intro walkthrough, so with Brad and Howard in the midst of deciding my life for me, we hurry toward her office. I ask about her husband and kids, who live normal lives in northern California because Anna thinks this town is just as nuts as I do, so she keeps her kids away from the evil influences that lurk around Tinseltown. I don't blame her, and I've always admired her insistence on leading a normal life far away from here.

"Now don't mind Rebecca's appearance," Anna says as we walk along, "she had a freak accident with a trailer earlier today, but she's a trooper, so she hung around to help with edits."

"Edits? You aren't cutting my part, are you?"

"God, no!" she slaps my arm playfully, "if it were up to me, you'd be in every scene. Maybe you can work some of that charm on Rebecca and see if you can make that happen."

I chuckle because women do tend to melt when I turn on my charm. Anna pushes her office door open and steps inside. I follow behind, my million-dollar smile in place. When I see her though, I stop short and my smile falters.

She looks up from a journal and the blood drains from her face.

Fuck me sideways. It would be just my fucking luck that I manhandled the author.

"Rebecca, here's our little star." Anna turns to look at me. "Cory, this is...oh, have you two already met?"

"No!" Rebecca blurts out. A blush ignites along her cheeks as she clears her throat. "No," she continues in a more level tone, "I just wasn't...I just didn't realize he was...so tall."

Huh? Whoa. Wait a second. Is she seriously covering for me? I meet her menacing gaze and actually flinch when she extends her hand toward me.

"Ah..." I reach for her hand. "I get that a lot," I say, still confused as to why she's covering for me instead of rightfully kicking me in the nuts. "It's nice to meet you, Rebecca."

Just before our hands connect, though, Rebecca jerks hers back and then holds it up for me to see the damage from her fall out of my trailer. "You'll have to excuse me," she says, her tone pleasant sounding even though there's venom in her eyes, "I had a little accident earlier, so I can't shake your hand."

I take a step back and drop my arm to my side. *Okay,* she might be covering for me, but she's definitely still pissed—with reason, of course.

"Yeah, Anna mentioned that..." As I stare at her raw palms, I pull the knot of my tie loose. *Way to fucking go, Cory.* I swallow over the lump in my throat before adding, "I hope it isn't too bad and that they heal quickly."

Rebecca glares for a moment longer, then nods. "I'll be fine."

I clear my throat and shift uncomfortably. *Jesus.* Is it just me or is it like a billion degrees in here all of a sudden? "That's good to hear. If you'll excuse me, ladies, I suddenly remembered that I left something in my trailer."

I turn on my heels and beeline straight for the exit, suddenly in a rush to make it back to my trailer to get that phone out of the trash. I walk at a brisk pace, hoping beyond hope that someone hadn't emptied my trash yet. I pull my trailer door open and start up the stairs.

"Hey, baby!" Destiny rushes over and wraps her arms around my waist. "I missed you at the party last night." She stands on her toes and kisses my cheek. "Are you still mad at me? I swear I didn't do anything with anyone."

I pry her off me and head toward the garbage can. "Not now, Destiny. As usual, I have to do damage control for your fuck up." I lift the phone out of the garbage can and tap the screen. Thankfully, it turns on.

Destiny rips the phone out of my hand and tosses it onto the counter. She pouts and holds up a bag of cocaine. "I bought something I knew would cheer you up."

"You know I'm not big into coke." The shit makes me way to hyper for way too long. Yet, I continue to stare at the bag intently.

"Well, I actually brought two things..." she adds as she pulls the strap from around her neck, her skimpy dress pooling around her feet.

Good god.

The woman is slightly deranged and she can definitely get under my skin, but hot damn, with a body like that, those are forgivable offenses.

Rebecca's phone vibrates, rattling noisily on the counter. I stare at it and note several missed calls and texts messages. I know I should get the phone back to her and make sure she keeps her lips zipped, but instead, I snatch the bag of coke out of Destiny's hand and head to my chair. It's been one hell of a day, so drug preferences aside, I can definitely use another trip into la-la land.

"Lock the door," I order as I pull my blazer off.

Destiny claps excitedly and skips over to the door. I drop into my chair, promising myself that I'll give the author her phone in an hour—two at the max. Right now, though, I need a minute to relax and regroup.

Chapter 4

Rebecca

I stub out another cigarette, then go back inside and start pacing. I promised my husband and kids that I would quit, but this *so* isn't the time or place to give up my only vice.

What freaking nerve of Cory to rush off without even attempting to apologize.

What a stupid jerk.

I pull the sliding glass door open to go back outside for another cigarette, but I stop short when the house phone rings. I rush over and pick up the cordless.

"Hey, babe," Rob says. "I just got out of a meeting and got your messages. What happened? Whose number is this?"

I drop onto the couch and sigh since his "meetings" usually consist of taking potential football players to high-class strip clubs. "I figured as much. How'd it go?"

"Good, I think this kid is about to accept our offer, but never mind that. How was your first big day? And how'd you lose your phone?"

"You'll never believe it," I say a bit dramatically, and then I give him a play-by-play of this afternoon's events. I end my recap with, "And even after I covered for him, he didn't even bother to apologize!"

"That's the damn problem, Beck. You're too nice—always out to give people second chances even when they don't deserve it. You want me to fly out there and kick this guy's ass?"

I roll my eyes, never one to resort to violence. "I did ask Anna a few leading questions after he stormed out and she told me he's had some major issues with stalkers. Maybe he thought I was some deranged groupie looking for an autograph?"

"I don't give a shit what he thought, Beck. After you covered for him, he should have been bowing down to you and then he should have brought you your damn phone!"

I shrug. "I don't know. Maybe I left before he got back. My head really was killing me."

He grunts. "Are you sure you're okay?"

"Yeah, the medic said it was just a scratch." I gingerly touch the bump. "Did you get to talk to the kids today? When I called, they were eating dinner, so I only got to say brief hellos."

"Robbie called me earlier to tell me about his day. I'll give them a call when I get to the hotel."

The doorbell rings. Curious, since I'm not expecting anyone, I lean off the couch a bit to try and get a look through the windows on either side of the door. The doorbell chimes again, so I stand. "Hang on, babe." I walk over and look out the peephole. My heart rate accelerates so quickly that I get a little light-headed. "Oh my God! It's him!"

"Who? Cory?" Rob asks, not sounding the least bit alarmed. "Good, maybe he's dropping off your phone."

"Yeah, maybe." Or maybe he wants to toss me around again. "Let me call you back," I whisper, suddenly petrified of opening the door without a phone available to dial 911.

The doorbell rings again.

"All right," Rob says, "I'll call you after I shower and say goodnight to the kids."

"Yeah, sounds good." I end the call and pull the door open a crack.

"Hey," Cory says. He holds up a bouquet of flowers and a bottle of wine. "Can I come in?"

I eye the flowers and wine, then look up at him. After a moment of gazing into his eyes to determine his level of sobriety, I finally pull the door open. He appears to be sober, or at least civil enough to come in and not beat me up again.

"Thanks." He steps inside and looks around. "Nice place."

After closing the door, I turn to look at him while still clutching the cordless. "I guess the studio has it for consultants and stuff."

He offers me the flowers. "I owe you an apology."

I take the them and watch as he reaches into his pocket.

"Actually," he says as he pulls my cell phone out and hands it to me, "I owe you two since I cracked your screen, but I'll take you to the store first thing tomorrow and buy you a new one."

After taking the phone and staring down at it for a moment, I look up at him and shake my head. "No, you didn't. My son dropped it the night before I left..." I shrug. "It still works though."

"Well, let me take you to buy a new one, anyway. It'll be my treat—as a peace offering."

We stand there, an awkward silence hanging in the air as we stare at each other.

Cory finally clears his throat and extends the bottle of wine. "I asked Anna if you had a drink of choice and she said you like chardonnays."

I just stare at the bottle.

When he finally notices that my hands are full, Cory reaches for the flowers but falters. "I can...ah...why don't I open this for you and serve you a glass while you put those in water?"

"Um...okay..." I nod. "Sure."

I follow him into the kitchen and set both phones and the flowers on the counter. He starts searching for wine glasses while I pull open the bottom cabinet doors, looking for a vase.

"Anna mentioned you had students," he says as he sets two wine glasses on the center island. "Are you a teacher?"

"I used to be. Now I'm a guidance counselor. Aha!" I pull a vase from the center island. "I guess these people plan for everything."

I lift the flowers off the counter and eye the second wine glass. *Well, talk about making yourself at home.*

"The studio will treat you well." He slides a glass toward me. "Just be careful with the cleaning crew. I've heard some horror stories about jewelry and electronics going missing after they show up."

I pull the cellophane from around the flowers and reach for the scissors in the knife block so I can trim the ends. I'm tempted to tell Cory that I've lived through stuff going missing before—except it wasn't a cleaning crew. It was my older brother. He would steal my parents' money, jewelry, and electronics to support his drug habit.

I mull that over for a second, my inner counselor wanting to reach out to Cory about today's incident, but I decide against it. After living with a meth addict and having many-a-student addicted to one thing or another, I know delivering upfront and direct tidbits like that usually don't work on someone with a drug problem. The books may say that tough love is an appropriate response to dealing with people like Cory, but I've learned the hard way that tough love can backfire.

Sometimes subtlety is the way to go, so I snip a few more ends and say, "The flowers are beautiful."

"It's the least I could do, and I'm sorry about earlier. I really thought you were just another stalker."

I set the flowers in the vase and reach for my wine glass. "Does that happen often?"

He snorts. "It happens a lot more than you'd probably believe. Stalkers can be a little...fanatical."

I look him over and admire his nice sweater and slacks. The outfit definitely accentuates his athletic build and is a far cry from the disheveled look he was rocking earlier, though even then I couldn't deny that he's incredibly attractive. His turquoise eyes really are amazing, and his dark brows and light brown hair color somehow brings out the golden flecks sprinkled amid the blue. My heart actually does a little bit of a pitter-patter when he smiles.

Slightly disturbed by my wandering thoughts, I nod and force myself to gaze into the wine glass. "I can believe it. After my book made the bestseller's list, people would wait at the school's parking lot for me to autograph a copy or they would come up to me while I was grocery shopping. Someone even broke into my house and stole my computer. I guess they were hoping to get their hands on my next project."

He chuckles and holds up his glass. "Here's to fans who take their passion a step too far."

I laugh. "Cheers."

After tapping our glasses together, I take a sip of my wine while he drains his.

"Well, I guess I'll let you get some rest. Thanks for being so..." he clears his throat, "forgiving and...you know, nice enough not to run to the press."

I lean against the counter and take another sip of wine, eyeing him over the rim. I finally set the glass aside and nod. "It's no biggie. Though don't be surprised if I make you open all the doors for me until my hands heal up." I hold them up so he can see the scratches. "I considered suing you, but I figured black-mailing you to be my doorman would be more amusing."

He laughs. "I will dutifully serve as your doorman until you deem it time to release me of my sentence."

"Right on." I smile. "Thanks for bringing my phone over."

"I'm still buying you a new one."

I shake my head. "That isn't necessary, Cory—"

"I know, but I insist." He turns and sets his glass in the sink and then looks toward the table. He points toward the pack of cigarettes. "Ah, a woman after my own heart...may I?"

"That'll just extend your services, you know. Those damn cigarettes are ridiculously priced in your state."

"Fair enough." He walks over and lifts the cigarettes and lighter. "But it isn't my state. I'm from a small town clear on the other side of the country." He extends the pack toward me.

I pull a cigarette free, then slap his hand when he flicks the lighter. "Outside, mister. I may be a smoker, but I don't smoke inside."

"Yes, ma'am," he motions to the door, "after you."

I chuckle when he hurries ahead to pull the door open for me. As I pass, he bows dramatically. I'm still giggling when he lights my cigarette, then his. We sit in a comfortable silence for a moment, but then his mood suddenly downshifts and fills the air with tension. I watch as he drops onto one of the patio chairs and stares up at the night sky.

"You're..." He looks over at me. "You're cool. Thanks for being so down-to-earth even though I was a complete asshole earlier."

I shrug. "Holding a grudge really wouldn't do us any good considering we're stuck with each other for a month."

He looks off into the distance and nods. "How old is your boy?"

Glad for the change of subject, I pull up a chair and sit. "He's four. My daughter is six."

"You didn't bring them?"

"Nah, my husband and I didn't want to pull them from school and bring them down here when I'm going to be gone all day at work and Rob has to fly around for business. The studio offered to set me up with a sitter, but we thought they'd be better off with their grandparents."

"That makes sense." He takes a drag of the cigarette. "What's the hubby do for a living?"

"He's a defensive coordinator for the Denver Broncos."

"Sweet," Cory says with a level of enthusiasm that only

males seem to possess. He winks, then flicks the butt into the yard. "Thanks for the cigarette."

"Yeah," I shrug, "it's no problem."

"I'll see you in the morning then." He waits until I walk over to pull the sliding door open. "Let's do lunch tomorrow? It'll be my treat, and then we'll swing by the store to get you a new phone."

"Cory, that isn't—"

"Yeah, I know it isn't, but I want to."

I take a sip of wine, wondering just how far I can push my luck. "Can we go to Rodeo Drive?"

"We can go wherever you want." He walks to the sink and lifts his glass. After rinsing it out, he serves himself more wine. "Do you have a particular destination in mind?"

"I can only tell you if you promise not to laugh."

He holds up his hand. "I swear I won't laugh."

I bite my lower lip, then snort and shake my head. "*Pretty Woman* is one of my favorite movies."

He takes a sip of wine, then leans his elbows onto the counter, eyeing me with obvious curiosity. "And that's funny, why?"

My brows arch and I chuckle. "Haven't you ever seen it?"

He shakes his head. "I'm more into gangster, mafia, horror, thrillers..." He shrugs. "Can I tell you a secret?"

I nod.

"I hate being known as the king of romantic comedies because I hate watching them." He takes a long sip of his drink. "So, in answer to your question: no, I've never seen it."

I laugh. "That's...wow. Sorry. That just totally caught me off guard."

His eyes narrow. "Have you seen any of my movies?"

My laughter dies in my throat, and I blush. "Ah...well, with my family, job, and writing, I don't have much time to sit and watch anything but little kid movies. I did see the previews for the last movie you and Katie did together and I wanted to see it, but..." I chuckle. "I can watch it while I'm here."

"Do you watch *Copper Creek?*"

I shake my head.

He laughs. "Well, aren't we a pair?" He swallows down the contents of his glass and sets it on the counter. "Okay, so aside from being your faithful doorman for the duration of your stay, I'll also be your tour guide."

"Why, thank you, kind sir," I say with a British flare and a curtsey.

He cracks up and playfully taps the tip of my nose. "Stick to writing, Rebecca, 'cause your British accent sucks." When I pretend to be offended, he laughs. "Oh, don't give me that look. You know it's awful."

"Fair enough," I say with a nod. "I know my British accent sucks, so maybe you can give me coaching lessons on top of everything else you're doing."

"Man, toss a girl out of your trailer and break her phone and you end up with a month of indentured servitude." He chuckles, then smiles. "It's a deal."

I follow him to the front door, but before I can pull it open, he scoots me out of the way and does it himself. I crack up as I step outside, but stop short when I catch sight of his yellow Lamborghini. After whistling, I walk over and run my finger along the hood. "This is a very nice ride, Mr. Hudson."

"Do you want to take her out for a spin?" He pulls the key fob out of his pocket and holds it toward me.

"Ah, pssst..." I stammer while backing away. "There's no way I could afford to fix that thing if I get a scratch on it."

"It's just a car, Rebecca—totally replaceable."

I stare at the Lamborghini while shaking my head. "I've already had a drink tonight, so maybe some other night."

He chuckles. "Okay...though I seriously doubt half a glass of wine constitutes drinking, but I'll hold you to it." He extends his hand. "Have a good night."

I reach for it, but jerk mine away just before he can grab it.

"Oh..." He clears his throat and drops his arm to his side. "Right..." He sighs, then steps closer, almost as if he's either going to hug or kiss me, but then he backs away. "Ah..." He playfully taps my nose again then says, "Night, shorty-rock."

I chuckle since it's an adequate but odd endearment. "Good night, Cory."

He drops into the driver's seat, pulls the door closed, and opens the window. "Are you sure you don't want to take her out for a quick ride?"

"Yeah, I'm sure."

He nods. "Okay, I'll see you tomorrow."

I stand there and watch him drive away, amazed by how nice he can be when he isn't strung-out or thinks I'm a deranged stalker.

Chapter 5

Penelope

When the blonde-haired woman closes the door, I start the car and speed along the quiet neighborhood. *Who is she and why did Ethan come here?* Frustrated that my spell to rid us of Destiny hasn't worked yet, and further annoyed that there's now some new woman in the picture, I romp on the accelerator while searching for his car.

Where are you off to now, Ethan?

Once I spot the Lamborghini, I slow down to keep a safe distance between us. After a few miles, I recognize the familiar route to his house, so I relax a bit because the drive is somewhat comforting. After all, it will be my home just as soon as I can get that bitch Destiny out of the picture. Ethan will seek me out then, no longer able to resist me.

Soon...very soon, he'll be mine.

I pull into my usual spot when we get onto his street and I watch as his car pulls through the gate. Once he's safely inside, I drive back to the freeway because I know he's home alone. I knew after that impromptu orgy last night, Brad would insist that he and Destiny remain apart until the fallout clears. That's why I called my paparazzi contact to cover the story in the first place.

I'll have to remember to thank him for getting it splashed on the front page of all the tabloids.

After exiting the freeway, I stop at a convenience store and pick up a protein shake and a package of fresh fruit. With my dinner in a bag on my passenger seat, I drive back to that woman's house and park across the street. She's pacing the living room while talking on the phone. I eat as she chats away. Finally, after an hour, she hangs up, pours wine into a glass, and grabs a cigarette before heading to the front porch.

Even from a distance, I can see that the woman is striking. When she steps directly beneath the light, her long blonde hair appears almost white. I reach for my camera, relieved that my high-powered telescopic lens is already on. The woman is petite, probably weighing no more than one-hundred-fifteen pounds. She doesn't have big boobs or a big booty, which is easy enough to assess as she paces back and forth while looking up at the stars.

Aside from her natural beauty, though, she has nothing on me. Except, of course, that Cory prefers blondes—but don't all gentlemen? I snicker at the thought as I take several pictures of the woman. When she returns inside, I lower the camera and watch as she flips lights off as she disappears down a hallway to where I'm assuming the bedrooms are.

Once she's out of sight, I examine the pictures, zooming in to get a better look at her face. The woman is pretty, but more girl next door than movie star. I set the camera on the passenger seat and wait. When I'm certain the lady is sleeping, I drive around the block and park a few houses down from her bungalow.

Cloaked by darkness and shrubbery, I hurry to the backyard gate. Relieved that it isn't padlocked like mine, I pull a can of WD-40 from my cargo pocket and spray the hinges. After pocketing the can, I open the gate slowly and close it behind me. The small backyard is pretty, but it lacks much to hide behind if the need arises, so I step closer to the house and slide along the wall to peer around to the patio.

Dammit. The bitch left the patio light on. I stand very still and study the house behind hers. The lights are all off, so it's either empty or the occupants are asleep, which works in my favor. I hate nosy neighbors, so the stillness means I have one less thing to worry about. I wait a moment longer to be sure, then I inch around the corner and peer into the first window I encounter. The blinds are closed, so I continue toward the next. It's the kitchen, the light above the stove turned on so I see that her wine glass is on the counter along with the flowers. I had foolishly hoped those were for me, so I'm not at all pleased to see them there.

I step closer and try the sliding glass door. It opens. *Yes.* I close the door and continue along the back patio. There are two other windows, but both sets of blinds are drawn. I make my way back to the door, then pull the gun from my waistband and disengage the safety. Thankfully, the door doesn't make a sound as it glides open. I slip inside and close it behind me. The house is still, save for the faint flickering light of a television playing down the hallway. That's actually a relief, since I'm sure that even if she's still awake, it's unlikely she'll hear me, especially since I have no intention of going into her room, not when I see what I came for sitting right on the table.

Her purse is open, so I creep over and retrieve her wallet. There are several pictures of a little boy and a little girl, and there are a few of a handsome man. The last picture is a family portrait, which reveals that this is the blonde lady's family. I slip the photo from the sleeve, place it in my pocket, and then look at her driver's license. I instantly recognize her name, and I'm amazed that I hadn't put it together sooner. Rebecca Ann Carter is the author of *Bridesmaid for Hire.*

Relieved to know that this was probably nothing more than a social visit to discuss the film, I replace the family portrait and wallet. As I leave, I pull a lily from the bouquet and let myself out. When I make it back to my truck, I debate on going home. The night before, I had lost sight of Ethan's car in traffic after he left Destiny's house. I had assumed he would go to his house, but he hadn't. He had gone to the studio, which left me frantically searching for him for hours.

He *is* home now, though, and since that whore Destiny isn't over, I decide to go home. It isn't as if he'll invite her over anyway because, for some reason, Ethan rarely allows Destiny or any woman over to his place. He prefers theirs. I'm sure it's because somewhere in his mind he realizes that his house will be our future home together, so he doesn't want it to harbor any woman's filth or skankiness.

Calmed by that thought, I take fleeting glimpses of the full moon as I hum along to one of the songs on Ethan's favorite seventies playlist. It'll be nice when we're finally together, listening to these songs as a couple. That thought inspires me to drive faster, because tonight is a great night to perform my love spell and, since I know he's home, probably thinking about me, the spell will hopefully work this time.

My exuberance reaches new heights when I push my bedroom door open and I'm greeted by hundreds of Ethan's pictures adorning the walls. A smile instantly curls on my lips as I meet his gaze. I walk to my favorite picture of him and gently caress it before kissing his image. After admiring his face for a moment longer, I place the flower on my pillow and retrieve five candles from the closet. Once the candles are placed on each point of the pentagram that surrounds the mattress, I strip out of my clothes. And since I've recently adopted a fond habit of performing my love ritual while wearing something that belongs to Ethan—which is why I've stolen his clothes from his various sets and from his hotel rooms when he travels—I make my way to my closet and pull on the varsity jacket he wears in *Copper Creek*. It still has remnants of his cologne.

Intoxicated by the alluring aroma, I eagerly reach for the wooden box that's on the top shelf. It contains all the items I need for my love ritual. After setting it on my bed, I light the candles in a counter-clockwise fashion and call upon my Dark Father to hear my prayers. "With this act, I beg of thee to grant my greatest wish to reunite Ethan and I for eternity," I whisper as I press the flame to the last candle. For a long moment, I stand within the center of the pentagram, mentally repeating my plea, then I make my way back to my bed, more than ready now to begin my ritual.

Chapter 6

Chelsea

After following Cory Hudson around for five years, I've officially been inducted as an elite member of the paparazzi. Of course, that title was only bestowed upon me because I pay attention—because I know a few things about Cory Hudson with utmost certainty. The first is that when Cory is on set, he never goes out for lunch. The man is fanatical about his workouts. The other thing is that he only hangs out with his long list of girlfriends or with Brad and Anna, or at least that's always been the case until today.

Stunned to see that he's *actually* out, I sit in the news van and watch as he, Anna, and another woman leave the Apple Store and get back into their limousine. I have no idea who the blonde-haired woman is, but they left the studio together, which is beyond odd.

Where's his beloved Lamborghini?

Jay and I follow behind the limo as it makes its way through traffic. When the car finally stops, I sit back to watch the three of them step onto Rodeo Drive. They start strolling along like college besties.

"Who is that chick?" Jay asks while snapping pictures of the three of them.

"I have no idea. Maybe she's one of Anna's friends?"

I lift the binoculars to get a better look. Perhaps the woman is his new housekeeper. Cory is a *super* private person, so he always has his housekeeper do all of his shopping. Heaven forbid he tries to wander the streets like an average human. The moment he's out in public, people pounce on him. It's no wonder the media so easily adopted my title of naming him the world's sexiest recluse.

And almost as if on cue, a group of star-struck tourists approach Cory. The man avoids the press and his fans like the plague, so I actually chuckle when he steps back and looks around for the quickest escape route. The blonde-haired woman grips Cory's arm and pulls him against her as she chats away with the mesmerized crowd.

Cory seems reluctant for a second, but then he drapes his arms over Anna and the blonde-haired woman's shoulders and poses for a picture. After several shots, Cory signs autographs and then moves to stand between the four tourists and takes a picture with them.

My jaw drops.

Oh. My. God. Who is this little blonde bombshell and how has she magically gotten Mr. Hudson to break all of his own rules?

After exchanging a few more words with the tourists, Cory, Anna, and the mystery woman disappear into a boutique. I lower the binoculars and tap my chin. It's normal for Cory to go on hiatus with his current flavor of the week when he gets bad press. Brad is one of the best agents in town and he and Cory have developed quite the father-son relationship, so when Cory messes up, which has been often since he started dating Destiny O'Rourke, Brad puts his foot down. Hanging out with Anna and company is probably keeping him out of trouble, which is all fine and dandy, but who's the blonde?

I pull my phone out of my purse and call my boss. Walt is the biggest pain in the ass, but he's the best tabloid editor in California and he knows everyone. When I get him on the line and describe the female, he requests a picture. I send one via text and a second later, he tells me that she's Rebecca Ann Carter—the author of *Bridesmaid for Hire*.

Well, it's nice to know *who* she is, but that still doesn't explain why Cory is with her or why he's acting so strangely. Jay and I sit patiently and wait for them to emerge from the store. Several minutes tick by before they reappear, but it's only so they can enter several other shops.

Jay tears open a Snickers wrapper and glances at me. "So, you think the infamous *Cortiny* will call it quits now?"

I giggle at that, loving that my little pet name for Cory and Destiny took like wildfire. "After that orgy escapade and all the bad press Cory got, I'm sure he'll release a statement soon saying something along the lines of 'we've broken up, but it was amicable and we're still the best of friends.'"

Jay chuckles. "Carson and I have a bet going that they'll lay low for a few days and then they'll go back to being Hollywood's wild and crazy couple. No way am I losing this one. Cory won't walk away from Destiny."

I glance over at Jay for a second, then lift the binoculars to watch as Cory and company leave the shop and walk along the street. My cameraman makes a valid point. This thing with Destiny has been Cory's longest relationship, which still blows my mind. He and Destiny hang out maybe once or twice a week to party—which is always shrouded in drama—but as much as Destiny will go on and on about him, Cory has never even mentioned her name during an interview.

The man should consider a political career with the way he can strategically avoid questions!

When Cory suddenly moves around Anna so he's walking between the women, I note how he playfully bumps against Rebecca's arm as if they just shared a funny story. *Hmm...that's interesting.* I drop the binoculars onto my lap and look over at Jay. For a man, he's remarkably insightful.

"Don't you think it's weird he skipped his workout, and he isn't driving his car?"

Jay snorts. "No. The guy is in hot water so he's hanging out with two old chicks until shit cools down. My money says Brad put his foot down big time and this is Cory's punishment."

I look toward the trio and snicker. "He does act like the obedient son, doesn't he?"

"Yup, but that isn't surprising considering that most foster kids tend to latch on to parental figures the same way girls with daddy issues latch onto a pole."

"Eww, Jay," I chuckle. "You've been hanging around Carson too long."

"The Big C Man is definitely an awesome photojournalist, but he also falls into the sleazy perv category, and I'm no perv, my dear—I'm just trying to keep it real."

I nod my agreement because Jay definitely isn't a perv, but *The Big C Man* definitely *is* a perv, and as much as Carson may hate it, I changed that 'C' in his cheesy nickname to cancer—like a bad case of melanoma, because my skin actually crawls when he's around, which is saying a lot since I grew up hanging out at my father's law firm. Some of the criminals he's defended were downright scary. Carson is harmless in comparison, but I still get the heebie-jeebies when he gets too close.

I'm just glad my boss noticed my disdain for him and started assigning Jay as my camera operator. Jay is good people, so even though paparazzi duty sucks, it isn't nearly as bad as when I'm stuck at this crappy job with a creepy partner like Carson.

When Cory, Anna, and Rebecca make their way to the limo, Jay hands me the camera so I can take over picture taking. Once we're following behind the limo again, I set the camera on the center console and reach for my tablet to do some research. As it turns out, Rebecca Carter is pretty darn boring. She's a guidance counselor at a high school even though her book is doing stellar. She's also married with two kids and amazingly; I can't find one shred of dirt on her, which gets me to thinking. Maybe she's just another mother-like figure to Cory. That would make sense, because it's unlikely that Cory is actually attracted to her. The man has an acute tendency to date women who walk on the wild side. Rebecca Carter looks like she's the type who doesn't even know what that means.

The limo stops by the entrance of Spago Beverly Hills. The trio gets out and Cory once again stops to sign autographs and take a few pictures. His behavior is so curious that I tap my chin as I watch Rebecca. She and Anna are leaning close to talk amongst themselves. The two women look like the best of pals, but so do Rebecca and Cory, so whose friend is she? It's hard to tell since she seems chummy with both of them.

Jay chuckles. "If you keep tapping your chin like that, you're going to end up with a bruise."

I drop my hand onto my lap. "Is Carson still following Destiny?"

"Last I heard he was."

Hmm...I wonder what she's doing. She and Cory have been inseparable for two months but after the orgy, there's been zero contact.

"Okay, I'm bored to tears," I say as I reach for my phone to call Carson. "Let's head back to the office so I can write something up that might make them release those press statements sooner rather than later."

"Are you fixing to stir the pot?'

"You know it, baby."

We both get a good chuckle out of that. When my laughter subsides, I send Carson a text message telling him to meet us at the office. Then I begin going through the pictures Jay took, my writer's brain formulating a story about how wonderful Cory is doing after finally getting Destiny out of his life. That'll definitely piss her off—her volatile personality bound to lash out—and once she does, I'll get today's top headline.

Chapter 7

Cory

The dream was...*weird.* Yeah, that's a good word for it. That's much better than calling it sexy, or hot, or erotic. I shake my head and try to quit thinking about it, but it's no use. The more I tell myself to stop, the more I keep replaying it.

It was just a dream, Cory, I remind myself. Granted, it was a *really* vivid one, and one so out of left field that I can't stop thinking about it. Not that it matters though, because it was probably just a residual effect from watching Julia Roberts' movies all night while killing off a fifth of my favorite scotch. And it isn't as if I had chosen to watch all of those movies *because* of Rebecca. I was just trying to avoid Destiny and the paparazzi after that ridiculous article about me being happier now that I was single again started trending online.

I shake my head again and focus. I skipped my workout yesterday to make my peace with Rebecca, so it's time to get my head back in the game today and pull double duty. With renewed determination, I turn my music louder and do another set of pull-ups. When I'm done, I move away from the pull-up bar and do fifty sit-ups. After another rep of pull-ups, I walk over to the treadmill. I start at a moderate speed but quickly increase it when the mediocre pace allows my mind too much opportunity to wander. The faster the run, the less my brain can focus on anything other than my breathing, and since I really don't want to think about Rebecca, or that dream, or my psychotic girlfriend, I break into an all-out sprint.

It's good, just what I need. No room for intrusive, inappropriate thoughts. It's just me and the treadmill, until the gym door swings open. For an instant, I'm annoyed. Normally, I have the gym all to myself this time of day. But then I figure some extra company may not be a bad thing. I could use the distraction, and a spotter for weight—

Rebecca pokes her head inside, her long, blonde hair spilling over her shoulders in a way that blocks the rest of her body from view, making her look like a beautiful, radiant Ichabod. *Really, Cory?* Ichabod? It's such a stupid thought that I misstep and nearly fly off the treadmill, but I manage to right my footing just as Rebecca spots me and steps inside. My eyes instantly sweep over her body, and I'm suddenly inundated with images from the dream. Her naked. Her riding me. Her moan. It's so surreal and erotic and disturbing that I'm not surprised when my foot lands on that dreaded place between the belt and rail. I trip and stumble, my hands instinctively reaching out to brace myself. The problem, of course, is that I'm going too fast, so I don't even have a chance to fall forward before the momentum of the belt yanks me backward.

"Cory!" Rebecca screams as I literally catch air.

It's only for a second though, because I slam into the wall behind me and crumble onto the floor.

"Oh, my God!" Rebecca runs over and helps me sit up straighter.

I moan.

"Oh, my God!" she repeats as she rips my earbuds out. "Are you okay?"

I shake my head for a second but then I manage to lift myself onto my elbows. "Yeah..." And amazingly, somehow I am. I mean, I'm definitely going to feel that in the morning, but my body isn't nearly as damaged as my pride. "I think I'm good," I say as I maneuver to rest my back against the wall.

"Are you sure?" She scoots closer and brushes hair off my brow. "Should I call a doctor?"

Her touch, even in this very embarrassing, painful moment, sends a jolt through me. I spring onto my feet, which causes her to gasp. Then she scrambles up beside me.

"Cory—"

I dodge a second touch and then sidestep away from her. "I'm good," I assure her as I limp toward the mirror because there's a dull, throbbing pain radiating along my right hip. "I think my pride is more hurt than anything else." I look at my reflection and study my rosy cheek. I'm pretty sure it had slammed against the belt for a painful instant when I first landed. *Damn.* I really hope that doesn't bruise.

"Well, *you* might be okay," she says as she points to the floor, "but your phone has definitely seen better days." Rebecca scoops it up, since it had somehow fallen out of my armband, and she shows me the shattered screen. "It looks like you're going to have to make another trip to the Apple Store." She hands me the phone and winks. "I bet you planned this just so you'd have an excuse to go back and flirt with that girl who helped us yesterday."

"Right..." I say as I take the phone, a little amused by her imagination. "Because I figured that the only way to go back and visit her was to crash and burn on the treadmill."

Rebecca smiles, real mischievous like—which is damn sexy.

"It's a genius plan," she says with an innocent shrug—which is also damn sexy.

I grunt at myself as I take a seat on one of the workout benches and force myself to quit staring at her. It works for less than a second. "Were you coming to work out?" I ask, my brain still trying to connect so many dots even though it's still swimming.

"No." She searches around the room and shakes her head. "I didn't even know this was here until a few minutes ago. I hadn't seen you all morning and they're just about to wrap up filming, so Anna and I wondered if you wanted to go to lunch again."

"I usually skip lunch to work out." Though it feels like I'm saying that more for myself than for her sake since lunch sounds really good about now.

"So yesterday was a fluke?" she asks as she walks over to the treadmill to turn it off.

I lean over a bit to check her out. She's been invisible the past two days, but after last night's dream, my curiosity is piqued. The first thing I really notice is how tiny she is. I've been calling her shorty-rock the past couple of days, but she's seriously so petite that she has to stand on her toes to reach the controls to stop the belt from running, which just so happens to give me a good view. She has a nice ass, but there's not much going on up top. I doubt she's even a B-cup. So, overall, she doesn't have a *bad* body, but she's no Destiny—though, if I want to keep it real, there isn't much on Destiny that hasn't been nipped, snipped, tucked, or enlarged, and I seriously doubt Becca has had any work done.

Whoa...did I just call her Becca? I scratch my head, wondering why I'm suddenly giving her a pet name and why I'm so preoccupied with a married chick who's four years older than me.

Becca kneels beside me and rests her hand on my knee. "Are you sure you're okay?"

The memory of that dream suddenly resurfaces with a vengeance. Mortified that my junk rises to the occasion, I quickly move her hand and cross my legs. When I meet her concerned gaze, my heart skips a few more beats. Her eyes are...*I don't know*. The grayish-green color is beautiful, but it isn't the color really...it's more the way she looks at me, and even though she may not have a body type I'm normally attracted to, she's pretty. No. She's *very* pretty.

How'd it take me so long to realize that?

"Cory?"

"Yeah," I chuckle, trying to sound normal despite the weird feelings. "I'm good. And yes, yesterday was a fluke because I promised you lunch and a new phone, so I skipped my work out."

She sits beside me. "Well, I've got to say that I'm not too comfortable leaving you here unsupervised, and..." she taps my phone, "now you need a new phone, so come on. Go shower up and meet us in the office." She stands and extends her hand toward me. "I'm kind of in the mood for Chinese. Are there any good places nearby?"

"Of course..." I take her hand, but only to bring it closer so I can examine the scratches on her palms. I run my finger gently over the scabs. "Maybe the treadmill was karma biting me in the ass."

"Or maybe I just needed a good laugh, because, let me tell you, if I wasn't so worried about making sure you were okay, I would have cracked up at that."

I force a scoff and shove her hand away. "That's cold, lady."

She giggles. "I wouldn't have been laughing *at* you. I would have been laughing *with* you."

We both chuckle as we head for the exit. I hold the door open for her, then I catch up to her and playfully bump my arm against hers. "You know, if the shoe were on the other foot, I wouldn't have found it funny."

"Oh, bull. That was comical and you know it."

I laugh while rubbing my aching chest. "Yeah, it was. So, since I'm on the injured reserve, I'll do lunch again today, making sure to stop and flirt with the girl at the Apple Store while I buy a new phone, but then I'm back to my regular schedule tomorrow."

She salutes. "Aye, aye, Captain."

I snort at that, amazed at how cool and down-to-earth she is even after having such a horrible first encounter with me. We part ways when we reach my trailer, but I stop before stepping inside so I can check her out again as she walks off. When I start to sprout another chubby, I go into the trailer and shake my head.

Jesus, what the fuck is this? I shift my junk while I make my way to the bathroom, suddenly in desperate need of a cold shower.

I turn the car off and lean closer to the rearview mirror to make sure my hair looks okay. I shift a few strands then roll my eyes and mess it up. *This isn't a date, Cory.* And it isn't an excuse to see Becca. *It isn't.* I am genuinely upset with the script revisions they handed out at the end of the day, and there's no way Becca is okay with it either. The changes are so different from the way she wrote the book that she has to be upset.

After grabbing the script and the bottle of chardonnay from the passenger seat, I walk to the front door. Maybe the wine is too much. It may seem appropriate, given that she invited me to dinner, but that was only after I called to ask if she had a few minutes to talk about the script. She said she didn't mind if I stopped by, and when she inquired if I had eaten and I told her that I hadn't, she insisted I stay for dinner while we discussed it. Yet, does that justify me stopping to pick up a bottle of wine? It could, or maybe it'll inadvertently give away that I don't give a shit about the revisions and just used that as an excuse to see her.

Becca suddenly pulls the door open and looks up at me, that mischievous grin etched on her face. "Why are you just standing here, silly? Is the doorbell broken?"

Before I can go with that as my excuse, she reaches over and presses the button, which is working just fine. Mortified, I walk past her and hope to make light of it. "Should I add you to my stalker list?"

"Nope. I was just walking by and saw you standing there looking like you were a million miles away." She closes the door and walks past me, heading toward the kitchen. "Though, I could probably be a stalker, but only if I could do it without sending trinkets or gifts."

"No stalker kit would be complete without the trinkets, so I think you're S.O.L." We both get a good laugh out of that as I follow her to the center island.

As I retrieve the corkscrew and extract the cork from the bottle, it suddenly dawns on me that I laugh a lot when I'm around her. It's yet another thing I like about her, which is quickly becoming a point of contention, since my things-I-love-about-Becca list keeps growing exponentially.

I inwardly groan and remind myself that I'm supposed to be getting my head back in the fucking game, but in the past few days, all I've done is fallen deeper and deeper down the forbidden rabbit hole.

Becca chuckles. "Earth to Cory."

I look over my shoulder and try to play it cool, but I have no idea what we were talking about. *Oh, yeah! Stalkers.* "Take my word on it," I say, remarkably casual considering my inner turmoil, "the job description requires that you send trinkets or gifts. My life really wouldn't be complete without the chick who sends panties—"

"Hopefully clean ones," she interjects.

"One would hope," I chuckle. "Not that it matters since I toss all that fan mail and shit out the second it comes in."

"Not the second it comes in," she teases. "I'm still having flashbacks of you slapping that piece of pineapple out of my hand yesterday."

I actually blush because I had practically tackled her when she came into my trailer and helped herself to the daily fruit basket I receive from one of "my biggest fans." I don't fuck around with anything my fans send my way and when I saw Becca moving that fruit toward her mouth, a really weird protective instinct kicked in. "Sorry about that. I just hadn't gotten the chance to toss the platter before you came into the trailer."

"Well, I absolutely promise to steer clear of all unapproved food from here on in."

"Good—oh, and steer clear of those purple flowers too."

"What, the saffron arrangement? Why? They're so pretty."

I shrug. "I dunno what they're called; they just give me the creeps. It's probably because no matter where I am, there they are, and no one ever has any idea how they get into my trailers or hotel rooms."

"Oh..." she giggles again. "Beware the creepy purple people eater."

"Ha, ha," I say as I lean against the counter and watch her lift the lid off a pan to stir something I can't see but that smells good. Curious, I walk over and peer over her shoulder. "What are you making?"

"Sautéed baby reds, chops, green beans, and a salad." She shrugs. "It's funny, but I used to complain about making dinner until I didn't have to anymore." She looks at me, a sad glimmer in her beautiful eyes. "I guess I'm just starting to get really homesick."

I nod even though I have no idea what that feels like. "Maybe you should fly home this weekend."

She snorts at that then goes back to stirring the potatoes. "Rob and the kids were supposed to come here this weekend so we could go to Disney, but he got a last-minute call about some kid in Missouri, so he's off to do some scouting." That's clearly upsetting to her, but she forces a smile. "Anyway, we were trying to decide what kind of stalker I'm going to be."

"Right..." I shift and lean against the counter so I have a better view of her. "I think you should send me a home-cooked meal every night. You can get black pants, a black turtleneck, and a black ski mask and then scurry across my lawn every night just to set a tray by the door. I'll even be nice and give you the gate code so you don't have to scale the fence with your hands full."

"So instead of ding-dong-ditch with a brown paper bag filled with poop, I'm leaving a meal I slaved over and then packed up and drove across town?"

"Now that would be the coolest super-stalker power ever."

She shakes her head and chuckles. "You are a goofball." She lifts a plate off the counter and serves a decent amount of everything onto it. After fixing up a second plate, she lifts both and then motions toward her wine glass. "Mind grabbing my drink?"

I pick up her wine glass and follow her to the table.

"Please tell me you can eat this stuff," she says as she sets the plates across from each other.

"Of course I can. Why would you think I couldn't?"

"Hmm, let's see. The first day we went out to lunch, I had a double bacon cheeseburger and you had a chef's salad. Second day, you had sushi while I ate a huge plate of General Tso Chicken and fried rice, and yesterday, you had another salad." She reaches for her wine glass. "Today, I actually ordered that salad instead of some pizza because I was starting to feel like a pig."

"It's definitely not by choice. Brad always reminds me that as an actor, my body is my instrument, and I make a hell of a lot more money when this instrument is finely tuned, so I don't mind cutting down on my meals so I can drive a Lamborghini instead of a Pinto."

We both laugh at that then sit in a comfortable silence while we dig in; everything smells good, and it tastes even better, so I decide to invite myself over more often.

"Can I ask you a personal question?" she says without looking up from her plate.

For the briefest second, I stop cutting through my pork chop to look at her. The instant our eyes meet, my stomach sinks and I remember why I prefer dating chicks like Destiny. They're too in love with themselves to bother asking questions about me. "Yeah, shoot," I try to say casually.

A lengthy silence ensues, except this time it isn't comfortable.

"You don't talk about yourself much," she finally says.

That stumps me, so I set my fork aside and reach for my wine glass. "That isn't really a question, you know. It's more of a statement."

She leans back and pulls a potato off the fork in the cutest way. After chewing, she takes a sip of her wine and shrugs. "That wasn't my question, but when I got blasted by that Artic blast of pent-up tension, I decided to forego asking anything."

A second of silence falls between us before I burst out laughing. "Was it that obvious?"

"You're pretty easy to read."

"Am I?" I set my wine down. "All right then, impress me. Tell me all about my life."

She ponders that then starts cutting her pork chop. Without looking at me she says, "You're an only child and for some reason you like that, probably because it's easier to be alone. Which is why you surround yourself with shallow, self-absorbed people who only like you for the things you can buy them."

Not bad. I lift my fork and knife again. "That's pretty basic and easy enough for any Psych 101 student to figure out. You've gotta do better than that if you want to impress me."

"Okay." She takes a sip of wine. "You run away from real relationships because there's something in your past you don't want to share. When someone gets close, you push him or her away, because, to you, it's better to keep pretending that whatever happened doesn't bother you even though it does. And when it gets bad, you rely on alcohol and drugs to pull farther away from reality, praying it'll erase it, but it doesn't."

How the...? I shake my head, suddenly not excited to be here anymore.

"Look, Cory, I don't want to pry, and I hate overstepping my bounds, but you're a great guy and I just...I don't want to see something bad happen to you when there are people who care about you and who want to help."

"You don't even know me," I say more sharply than I intended.

"I do, and even after a few days, I truly do care about you." She reaches for my hand and squeezes it. "You're funny, and sweet, and considerate, and you're unbelievably talented. I've sat back for the past few days watching you on set and I'm so impressed with how great you are." She leans closer. "And

61

between you and me, I've spent the past two nights catching up on your show just to see you in action, but don't you dare tell anyone that I'm sitting around at night watching a cheesy teen drama—my students would never let me live it down."

I don't want to, but her expression is so comical that I laugh.

She squeezes my hand again then goes back to eating. I follow suit, but after a few bites, I realize I've lost my appetite. I get up and refill our glasses, wondering if I should spill my guts or just let it go and hope she doesn't bring it up again. I'm opting for plan B since I happen to like keeping all of my skeletons in the closet, which just so happens to be a hell of a lot easier than dealing with them. Yet, as true as that may be, I take a seat and sigh. I may like keeping my past in the past, but for some reason, I *want* to tell her.

Jesus, what is it about little Miss Becca that has me doing all kinds of strange shit?

After draining my glass, I prop my elbows on the table. "My father was..." *An asshole, a monster, a disgrace to the human race?* I settle on, "He wasn't a nice guy. He drank a lot, but even when he wasn't shitfaced or whoring around town, he used me and my mom as punching bags."

Rebecca doesn't have the reaction I expect. There are no tears or gasps. She doesn't cover her mouth with her hand or allow pity to well in her eyes. Instead, she finishes chewing her food and then looks at me—a warm kindness oozing off her that's comforting and for some reason tugs on my heartstrings. "I'm sorry, Cory. That had to be a horrible way to grow up."

I snort at that since it's like the understatement of the century. "You'd think that would be the worst thing, but compared to some of the foster homes afterward, there were times where being at that house was a breeze..."

As my mind wanders to the deepest recesses, trying to find one of those rare happy times, it's like a floodgate suddenly opens, allowing memories that I've kept tucked away for years to resurface. Without planning on it, I tell Becca about my young life on the apple orchard in upstate New York that my father inherited. I tell her how, when I was younger and naïve, I loved it there. My mother and I would pick apples all day or I'd help her preserve or prepare different things like cider, jam, and applesauce. And I used to believe her back then—I used to think the bruises were because she was clumsy. I never attributed the beatings that I received from my father to her injuries, not until I was older, and by then, my dad had gotten worse. And man was he a mean drunk.

At one point, Mom finally had enough, and I remember the night we snuck away. We drove awhile and ended up in Middletown. It was a huge city compared to New Salem, but my father somehow found us—and then he beat my mother to within an inch of her life.

In the process, he broke my arm and two ribs when I tried to defend her.

But when we arrived at the hospital, Mom lied for him. She lied to protect him—even after they told her she was HIV positive. Even after he got us back home and kept beating us. I never got the lie—I never understood her insistence to protect him. Was that what love was? Staying with someone when they hurt you—when they basically signed your death warrant with a fucking disease that literally ate her from the inside out. Even as a ten-year-old kid, it disgusted me, but I still tried to make the last part of her life as comfortable as possible.

"When she was so frail that she was basically bedridden, we would watch movies all day and all night," I say with a sad chuckle. "My father rigged it up so we were stealing the neighbor's cable, which was probably the only nice thing he ever really did for us, so that was our thing—me and mom, we'd recite our favorite movies and she'd get a kick out of my impressions."

Becca reaches across the table again and takes my hands into hers. "Cory, that's so..." she looks away, but I catch the pity, "I'm so sorry you had to go through that all on your own. I just...wasn't there family or—"

"No, and it's fine." I snatch my hand from under hers and grab my plate. "Mom's family was dirt poor and scattered around the state, and once people caught wind that she was HIV positive, no one wanted to help." I walk over to the garbage can and scrape my uneaten food into the trash. "And when I finally got pulled into the foster-care system after she died, they tested me once a month, scared I was going to infect all the other kids."

"People were ignorant back then, Cory," she says, still avoiding eye contact.

Her sadness infuriates me and I quickly recall why I never tell anyone any of this. I head toward the fridge, rip open the door, and grab the bottle of wine. "It's whatever, I shouldn't have mentioned it—"

When I whip around, she's right there. I have no idea how she made it over so quickly and stealthily, and so I crash into her. She seemed prepared for it though, because she pulls me into a tight embrace, holding me steady, and then she presses her face against my chest.

In response, I just stand there. In the past few days, I've envisioned having her arms wrapped around me, but this definitely isn't how I wanted it.

"I know how hard it was to share that with me, so thank you." She leans back to look up at me. "And I'm truly sorry you had to live through all of that."

My anger and discomfort instantly melts away as I stare into her eyes, so I set the bottle on the counter and then shift a strand of hair away from her face. She smiles and gives me another good squeeze. I'm not sure why her reaction tugs on my heartstrings again, but it does, and before I even realize what I'm doing, I kiss her.

For a second, it's like time stands still, her soft lips pressed against mine. Then her posture stiffens so suddenly that I actually feel it, and her reaction reminds me that she's a married woman who doesn't feel the same way I feel about her. Granted,

I don't exactly know what I feel, but I do know that I just crossed a line.

I take a step backward and crash into the fridge.

She just stands there, looking up at me with those wide, beautiful eyes.

"I'm sorry," I say, followed by a very long exhale. "I don't know...I was just..."

"No, it was my fault. I shouldn't have hugged you, or you know..." She sighs and runs a hand through her hair. When she looks back at me, there's a forced smile plastered on her lips. "How's about we just forget it ever happened, okay?"

I nod, but a part of me has no intention of forgetting just how soft her lips are or how nice it was to kiss her in that split second before she basically locked up on me.

"How's about," she says nonchalantly, "I start cleaning up in here while you get us a few drinks and find some music."

"I could definitely go for a drink." *Or four.*

So, I make my way to the bar and extract two mini-bottles of scotch. After tossing a fifty into the provided slot to cover the damage I plan on accomplishing tonight, I grab two shot glasses, fill them to the top, and carry them into the kitchen.

Becca has just turned on the faucet when I make it over to her. "Nope, let the maid get that in the morning. Here," I hand her the shot glass, "bottoms up."

When she eyes the amber liquid suspiciously, I chuckle. She sniffs it and then clinks her glass against mine. "Cheers."

She swallows the entire contents of the glass, her eyes tearing up after she downs the huge gulp. Her expression is sort of comical, so I laugh before I shoot down what I'm suddenly sure is going to be one of many attempts to erase all of the unwanted memories that are still lingering around in the forefront of my mind.

Chapter 8

Rebecca

I drop into a chair beside Anna's desk and pull off my sunglasses. When the bright light of day causes my already aching head to pound mercilessly, I quickly set them back onto the bridge of my nose. *Jesus.* What was I thinking? I haven't done shots since just before I found out I was pregnant with Rebel.

"Rough night?" Anna asks.

I squeeze my eyes shut for a moment and nod. "Yeah, remind me to never mix scotch and wine again."

She laughs. "It isn't usually the type of alcohol—it's the amount."

"Well, I've always been a lightweight so two glasses of wine and two shots of scotch equals a massive hangover."

Anna fills a glass with water and brings it over. "Drink up. Trust me, after a few of these and some aspirin, you'll feel better." She starts rummaging through her purse. "So, what was the occasion?"

"No occasion. Cory just stopped by last night."

"Oh...did he?"

Her sudden change of expression cracks me up. "Not like

that. He wanted to talk about the revisions, so I invited him over for dinner."

"Oh, really? How interesting," she says with a smile.

"You're just as much of a goofball as he is." I gladly take the aspirin she offers and swallow it down. "I told you, I think he's comfortable befriending me because he knows I'm leaving. That's his M.O., which makes sense now that I know what happened to him."

Anna gasps. "He told you?"

I nod and have to hold tears at bay. It's ironic that after six years of college, two years of internships, four years of teaching, and two years as a guidance counselor, I still lose it when I hear a truly wretched backstory. I tried to keep it together for Cory's sake but damn my unhardened heart. That hug definitely wasn't the way a counselor should have reacted to bad news, and I know it made Cory so uncomfortable that his knee-jerk reaction was to do something that would shock me enough to get off topic.

"So. what is it?" Anna asks. "Was he molested? I've always thought—"

"It isn't my story to tell, Anna." I set my glasses on her desk and squint. "You should ask him one day. He really cares about you."

She chuckles at that then takes a sip of her coffee. "I know, but that man can be pretty closed off." After another sip, she shrugs. "I guess I never want to push it since we all have skeletons in our closets that we desperately try to keep locked away."

I don't—not really anyway.

"So, what was his deal with the script?" she asks.

"Oh, he just doesn't think we should have put him in the wedding scene."

"Why not? Does he think he won't be ready today?"

"That's what he said, but when we were driving in this morning, I tried—"

Anna coughs mid-sip. I jerk away so the mist of coffee doesn't splatter me. "Are you okay?" I ask once I'm sure I'm out of the splash zone. When our eyes meet, I instantly understand her reaction. "Oh, don't give me that look, Anna. You've told me yourself that he's gone over to your place—"

"But he's never stayed the night," she says as she wipes her face with a tissue.

"Well shame on you for letting him drive drunk. He practically drank two bottles of wine and half a bottle of scotch, so there was no way I was letting him drive home."

"Oh..." she tosses the tissue into the trash, "so he didn't sleep *with* you."

"No, he didn't sleep *with* me." I hold up my left hand and point to my wedding band. "I'm married, remember?"

Though, for just a second last night, while I was riding high on my buzz and wrestling Cory's car keys away from him, there was a flicker—a naughty, naughty glint that when he yanked me against him, threatening to retrieve the key fob I had put in my bra, that we were going to kiss...again. The first one, I know, had been an intentional ploy on his part, a defense mechanism that he knew would coerce me into silence, but that second time, *I* wanted to kiss him.

I shake the thought away, ashamed by how much I would have loved it if he had kissed me again. I *am* married, albeit, not as happily as it appears to the world. "How'd he get into acting anyway?" I ask as a distraction. "With how his life went, I can't figure out how he ended up here."

"Oh, well that part of the story I can fill in for you." Anna refills her cup then pours coffee into a second mug. "Brad was on vacation in South Beach. He likes going places incognito, you know, to scout, and he discovered Cory tending bar. The way Brad tells it, it was basically love at first sight. He knew he could hit the jackpot with Cory, so he kept hanging around the bar. Anyway, on one particularly dead night, *Scarface* was on and Cory and Brad started reciting the lines, and if you've ever heard Cory do Al Pacino, you'd know how the rest is history. Brad signed him the next day." She takes a sip of coffee then sets it aside and pours creamer into the other mug. "Cory moved to Hollywood a few weeks later and it's been *mostly* good."

I sit back and nod. That's definitely a Cinderella story, and one that can potentially have a happy ending if Cory can shake his bad habits and come to terms with his past.

One of the interns pokes his head into the office. "Ladies, everyone is heading over to set three."

"Thanks, Greg," Anna says as she hands me the second mug of coffee. "The caffeine will help with the headache."

"Thanks." I follow her to the set with the cup held firmly in my grip even though I have no desire to drink it.

"What are we eating for lunch today?" she asks.

"Oof." My stomach churns at the thought of food. "Ask me later or you pick."

She chuckles and takes a seat in her chair. I sit beside her and admire the set, still amazed by all of this even though I've been here for days now.

Katie walks onto the soundstage and waves. Then several other crewmembers and extras stroll in. The set comes to life when the director arrives. Camera operators quickly get behind their equipment, while interns scurry back and forth in haste doing stuff I still haven't quite figured out.

Then Cory arrives. I watch him, feeling slightly envious that after all of his drinking and minimal sleep, he looks perfect. He's reading his script so he accidentally bumps into an intern. After a sidelong apology, he takes a few more steps but stops short. He lifts the script closer to his face then shakes his head and looks around. The moment he spots us, he walks over.

"Morning, Cory," Anna says.

He kisses her cheek then points at the script. "Are you seriously okay with this?"

Anna reads over the scene and nods. "I am." She looks at me. "Are you, Becca?"

I shrug, to which Cory frowns. Unable to contain a chuckle

at his sour expression, I look around to make sure no one is close enough to overhear. "I know you'd prefer not having to do anymore scenes where you have to kiss Katie, but the fans have spoken."

"What?" he scoffs. "No, I don't have—"

I raise my brow and tilt my head to the side.

He rolls his eyes. "Oh, don't give me that look. I don't have a problem kissing Katie. It just isn't the way you wrote the book."

A bemused smile replaces my smirk. "You don't like her." I wink. "It's okay. Anna and I have already figured that out. Don't worry, though. Your secret is safe with us."

His eyes narrow when he looks at Anna. "I'm hoping that now that you're aware, there won't be a third movie with us as the leads."

Anna winks. "Of course not! You know I've got your back."

"*Way* back," I add, and then Anna and I high-five at our newest running joke.

He rolls his eyes again and groans. "Jesus, you two are fast becoming the fucking Bobbsey Twins." He leans closer to me. "I'll do the scene, but I'm telling you it takes away from the book."

When he glares, I laugh. He tries to maintain his scowl, but finally chortles and walks off.

Once he's back on the soundstage, Anna shifts over. "You do realize I had no idea he didn't like her until you pointed it out the other day."

"But they really do have great onstage chemistry, which is funny, because she doesn't like him either."

She pats my hand and smiles. "I think I'm going to keep you around as the resident shrink for all of my movies."

We both get a good laugh out of that then fall silent when the director calls "action!"

Cory is a phenomenal actor and he's especially good when any scene involves Katie. I still haven't gotten him to admit it, but the man definitely goes out of his way to do a single take when she's involved, which is how I figured out he doesn't like her. With everyone else, either he or one of the other actors will do something that will crack everyone up so there are always a few retakes. That's never the case with Katie, so once Howard is satisfied with the first take, Cory disappears. I'm not sure where he goes in such a rush, but I can bet that he's doing something as silly as brushing his teeth or, at the very least, rinsing his mouth out. The man definitely does *not* care for Katie Dawn.

Anna and I remain seated to watch the next sequence then head back to her office to grab our purses to go out for lunch. To my surprise—and utter relief—Cory is sitting on Anna's couch with a script on his lap.

I'm a little *too* relieved to see him, but I remind myself that it isn't because I like hanging out with him. I was just scared that my overly sympathetic response last night might have pushed him farther away, which would have been bad since he needs people like Anna, Brad, and me around to help with his demons.

That thought gets me to thinking, so I call an impromptu pow-wow session with Anna and Brad later that afternoon. They're definitely receptive to my idea, so when Cory returns to the soundstage to film the last scene of the night, Anna innocently invites everyone to her place for dinner. The following evening, Brad asks us to come over to his place for dinner and a movie. My logic is sound and proves to be working. Cory isn't the kind of person who can handle a direct intervention, so we've all agreed to go with subtlety. It's hard to get high or drink yourself into oblivion around the people you care about most, especially when they're the people you're subconsciously striving to please. Cory will never admit it, and I don't think Brad and Anna realize just how much of a parental role they've been thrust into, but Cory remains clean and sober each evening, so I just enjoy our time together—glad that the group as a whole has embraced me and have included me in their little circle—not to mention that I get a kick out of watching the dynamics between the three of them. They remind me of *The Three Stooges*.

Unfortunately, the more I hang out with them, the more homesick I become. A part of me doesn't want to place the blame on my husband, but it really is his fault. Coming out here was a once-in-a-lifetime opportunity I didn't want to miss. All I asked was that Rob and the kids come out on the weekends since I've never been away from them, but Rob's job has always been his priority. Even when I made it onto the bestseller list and the studio bought the rights to make the movie, Rob refused to consider quitting.

The memory of that argument replays as Cory drives me back to the bungalow after dinner at Brad's place, and the resentment I've been holding at bay all week suddenly surfaces and is impossible to shake off no matter how much I try. But it's with reason. If Rob wasn't working, or if he would at least take some time off, they could be here even if that meant pulling the kids out of school for a few days. But no. Rob is completely opposed to that idea and never hesitates to tell me that the NFL Draft is only weeks away. That the team needs him.

Well, screw the team. I need him. Isn't that more important?

When Cory reaches over the Lamborghini's console and squeezes my hand, my fury practically bursts like a bubble.

He chuckles. "Have you heard anything I've said?"

"No...I'm sorry, I was just..." I sigh. "Never mind, what's up?"

"I asked if I could treat you to lunch tomorrow."

"Oh, yeah...wait. Isn't Destiny leaving this weekend to go on tour?"

"Not for a few weeks, so I'm open for lunch. Wanna be my date?"

That's yet another worry of mine. Destiny O'Rourke is a disaster waiting to happen and worse yet, she's an awful influence. In fact, she's the idiot who introduced Cory to heroin, so

I'm leery of them spending the weekend together. Yet, who am I to tell him that he can't hang out with his girlfriend?

Cory laughs. "Is it such a horrible invitation that you need to consider it for so long?"

"No, not at all...I was just—"

"Getting lost in all those thoughts pinging around up there again?" He glances over at me. "I have to tell you, I'm used to being the center of everyone's attention, so when you zone out like that, it's a crushing blow to my ego."

"You're a goofball, and, for the record, I'd love to have lunch tomorrow." *Maybe a long, late one so I can figure out a way to keep him from hanging out with his girlfriend.* "Have you been to the Griffith Observatory?"

"I have not." He parks in my driveway and takes off his seat-belt. "I can take you there another night since I already have everything set up for tomorrow."

"Oh, how truly conceited of you to make plans before I even accepted your invitation." That gets me a heartfelt chortle. "Okay, so where are we going?"

"It's a surprise." He gets out of the car, walks around to open my door, and offers a hand. "Did you pack something dressy? I can take you shopping if you want."

"No, I brought a few dresses." I fish the keys out of my purse. "Is that okay? Or should I go get something else?"

"That'll work. I'll be here at noon."

I unlock the door and step inside. "Okay..." When he backs away, I frown. He always comes in for a drink. "You're not staying?"

"I have something I have to take care of, but I'll see you tomorrow."

I lean against the doorframe and watch him leave. "What are you up to, Mr. Hudson?"

"You'll see." He pulls the driver's door open. "Night, Becca."

He backs out of the driveway in his usual crazy manner and honks. I wave then head inside and call my in-law's house as I wander to my bedroom. Rebel answers and immediately starts telling me about her day while I peruse my wardrobe. I did pack a few simple dresses, but I don't have anything that's appropriate for a fancy restaurant, so after a lengthy conversation with my kids, I fish Benny's business card out of my purse. It's high time I started pampering myself a little bit.

Chapter 9

Cory

Saturday morning traffic is surprisingly light—or maybe not. I mean, I'm not usually out this early, or sober. As I make my way toward Becca's place, I wonder about my sobriety, and then, as always, my thoughts drift to Becca. I wonder what it feels like to be homesick. The thought is so foreign to me that after a few more minutes of mulling it over, I give up. I do miss my mom, so maybe if she were alive and was still living in that godforsaken town, I would miss it there.

Yeah, right. I was glad to be gone and I've never looked back.

Becca is a different story. She truly misses her children and she can go on and on about them and about her family. With every passing day, I can see it in her eyes even when she tries to pretend that she's fine. She isn't, and for some unknown reason, that's killing me. I hate seeing her sad, and I really hate it when she gets so lost in thought that she's a thousand miles away.

How ironic is that? Most chicks would kill to spend a night with me. Not Becca, though. She doesn't ever really *look* at me, which is maddening. Maybe it's because she's classy, and she's sweet, and she's—*God! Fuck me sideways.* I'm so sick of *always* thinking about her.

The moment I pull into her driveway, I get out of my car and slam the door. This is what I want. *No.* This is want I need so I can't watch her for hours on end while she thinks we're just having some girlie night out on the town. Because, in her eyes, I'm like her new best friend. Her *gay* best friend. I don't know how or when she casted me into that role, but by god, I'm not her best friend, and I sure as hell am not gay. When she touches me casually, my heart races. When she leans close to whisper something in my ear, every hair on my body stands on end. Her apple-scented shampoo is hypnotic, and the sight of her somehow makes me...short-circuit. It's the most bizarre, mysterious reaction I've ever had toward a woman, because she's not my type. She's married. She's built like a twelve-year-old girl. She has zero sexual interest in me, yet I'm hooked on her as if she were a drug. The strongest, most powerful concoction I've ever indulged in— so I need to sever the tie. I need to cut off my supply so I can get her out of my system.

Right. I just need to focus on how much I don't like this feeling and quit obsessing over her. So, with a newfound determination to get her out of my head and as far away from me as possible, I ring the doorbell. After a second, Becca pulls the door open. There's a radiant smile plastered on her lips, but I only see it for a brief moment because my eyes trail along her body. The rose-colored strapless sundress is pretty and almost...*innocent looking*, which is hilarious because I'm *so* not thinking innocent thoughts as my eyes return to admire her cleavage.

"How do I look?" She twirls slowly. "Is this okay for where we're going?"

"Ah..." *Christ—it's the perfect dress to rip off her body.* "Yeah, that should be okay."

"Thank goodness!" She motions for me to come in and hurries down the hallway.

I head to the liquor cabinet, never happier that I requested the studio start stocking a large bottle of my favorite scotch.

"After you left last night, I asked Benny to take me shopping," she shouts from the bedroom. "I bought two other dresses, but I think this one is the best." After a second of silence, she pokes her head around the corner and eyes the tumbler I just filled. "Seriously?"

"Tone it down, Mom. I'll only have one."

She rolls her eyes then holds up two pairs of shoes. "Which do you like best?"

I swallow down some scotch while paying attention to her hair. It looks nice, the barrel curls somehow making her even prettier than her usual pin-straight style. I finally glance at the shoes and point to the blingy pair.

"Are you sure this dress is okay? Do you want to see the other ones?"

Yeah, right. I'm running out of self-control so wandering to her bedroom definitely isn't a good idea. "You look fine."

She debates that for a second then nods and walks over. After turning her back to me, she pulls her hair over her shoulder. "I swear I'll never understand why designers put zippers back there. Why don't they ever stop and think, wait, what if this girl is single and doesn't have someone available to zip her up."

Beads of sweat suddenly erupt on my forehead. I stare at her bra strap and bare back for a lingering moment before I down the entire contents of the glass.

Jesus. With just one yank, I can pull the damn dress off her. I pull my tie loose then set the tumbler on the wet bar firmly, which startles her. "Sorry," I manage to say before I begrudgingly reach for the zipper and pull it up.

"Okay, give me two more minutes and I'll be ready to go." She disappears down the hallway again.

I reach for the scotch and tumbler. *Oh, fuck etiquette.* I take a long swig straight from the bottle. When I hear the familiar sounds of high heels heading down the hallway, I quickly screw the cap back on and put the bottle back into the liquor cabinet.

Becca steps into the living room with an equally blingy clutch held in her hand. "Okay, I'm ready."

My breath catches in my throat when I see the complete package. "You look amazing."

"Aw, thanks!" she says as she turns to a mirror to adjust a curl.

Oh, that was real smooth, Hudson. Why don't you just get on all fours and let your tongue dangle out of your mouth while you wag your damn tail back and forth. I clear my throat and motion toward the door. "Come on. There's a ton of traffic so it's bound to take us an hour to get twenty miles down the road."

She snakes her arm through mine. "Okay, Mr. Surprise Man, lead the way."

I stand there for a second, considering lifting her into my arms and taking her back down that hallway. When she looks up at me with her brows furrowed, I force a smile and finally get moving.

After she locks the door, she loops her arm around mine again. "Are you at least going to give me a hint?"

"Nope, but I promise to get you there as fast as traffic will permit."

"You know, one day I want to drive this baby."

I dangle the key fob and look at her chest, the memory from the other night constantly replaying in my mind. My level of self-control had tanked that night, so I still have no idea how I didn't kiss her again, or how I had actually managed to keep my hands off her knowing that there was only one thin wall separating us while I laid awake half of the night in the guest room.

When she continues to stare at the key fob, I smile. "You know, it'll even start if it's in your bra, though I'd imagine that would be uncomfortable."

Becca's cheeks turn a bright crimson as she hurries around the car and pulls the passenger door open. "One, I can't drive this thing in heels, and two, I only did that the other night because I didn't want you getting yourself killed."

I get a good chuckle from her reaction. "Don't worry. I figured out that you aren't a second-base-on-the-first-date kind of girl a long time ago." When her red cheeks get brighter still and she quickly gets into the car, I laugh. After dropping into the driver's seat, I reach over and tap her thigh. "Quit blushing before you melt your makeup off. I know why you did it, so relax."

She looks over at me, her eyes narrowed down to slits.

I crack up and tap her leg again. "You can take your shoes off and drive."

"No, thanks...I don't want to drive in traffic, but before I leave, you'll have to take me out to an abandoned parking lot or out to the sticks somewhere."

After backing out of her driveway, I drop my elbow onto the center console and rub my chin. *Before she leaves*...that's something I'm simultaneously looking forward to and dreading.

"Cory?"

"Huh? Oh, right, woods...yeah, I'm sure there's someplace around here, probably not close, but I'll take you." I reach over and tap her leg again. I'm not sure why I keep doing it, but she doesn't seem to mind, so I won't stop until she says something. In fact, I'm curious as to just how far I can push this. After another pat, I rest my hand on her thigh. "So are you a Broncos fan or do you secretly root for some other team when Rob isn't looking?"

A dark cloud passes over her exquisite features. "I like them. My dad and brothers—" She looks out the window and clears her throat. "My family loves the Giants, so I'll root for them too."

I glance over at her because that isn't the first time she's done that. At first, she used to correct herself, but now she just lets the plural form of "brothers" stand, almost as if that will somehow bring him back.

I suddenly wish I hadn't brought it up, but since I have, I let my curiosity get the best of me. "What happened to him?"

She's silent for a long while and even though I'm curious as all get-out, I stay remarkably quiet.

Without looking away from the window, she says, "Meth happened to him...he overdosed."

My hand slips off her leg as a thousand bells start going off in my head.

"You remind me of him, you know, and when you started calling me Becca..." she sighs. "After Jeb died, no one but Dad calls me that." She reaches for my hand and gives it a good squeeze. "It's been really nice hearing it again."

As much as it crushes my heart to realize that this entire time she's seen me as nothing but a fill-in for her dead older brother, I still bring her hand closer and kiss the back of it. I don't really know what to say because what happened to her brother sucks— though it doesn't suck nearly as much as figuring out why she's been so nice to me.

"You should really use your fame to help kids like him, Cory. I get why you're so private after seeing how the press hounds you, but you can use your fame for good."

I snort at that. "I'm no philanthropist."

"Everyone has the potential to be an advocate for something. I'll even volunteer my services and drop the doorman servitude to become your personal beck-and-call girl."

I chuckle at that. "I think I'm going to change your super-stalker power to being able to change the flow of a conversation."

"I like that my super-stalker power is ding-dong ditch."

*Yeah, I do too...*Annoyed, I pull my hand out of hers. "It is a good one, but you really do have a knack for making people totally uncomfortable and then turning the conversation around so they don't go running off to the hills."

She laughs. "If you went running off to the hills, I would chase you."

I'd like to see if she means that, but I don't say as much. Instead, I make sure we avoid any other sensitive topics of conversation, but the entire drive, I only half-listen to her. I'm thinking that I'm just a fill-in for her dead brother. That I'm probably just an attempt for her to save someone because she couldn't save him. It pisses me off, but it's also a relief. I've hung out with Becca long enough to see this entire situation through her rose-colored-Psych-101 glasses. I'm totally attracted to her because *she* doesn't want me. That makes perfect sense, and now that I know why I'm so into her, I'm totally over it. Totally.

Becca points at a sign. "Are we having lunch at an airport?"

Glad for the distraction and the reminder that I'm not an event planner—since I never stopped to consider that the signs might give away the surprise before I got her there—I nod. "Will it make a difference if it's a private airport with a five-star restaurant?"

She giggles. "Ah...I guess...but it's kind of weird to dress up and drive half-an-hour to eat here."

"I've really gotten to know the woman who runs the cafeteria. She's funny and she's a great cook, so trust me, it's worth it."

"Ah, so what you're *really* saying is that on top of the pretty salesgirl at the Apple Store, you also have a crush on the cafeteria lady?"

I snort at that but then look at her and nod. "God, Becca, I'm *so* transparent to you."

That gets me a playful slap on the back of my hand. I pull into a parking spot then I quickly get out and check my phone. The single-word text message from Benny lets me know that everything is in place. Beyond grateful that this is almost over, I hurry around the car and open her door. "You don't mind eating on a tray, do you?"

She smiles. "You do realize I work at a school, right?"

"Hey, I'm just making sure, but I asked Bertha to pull out the good silver trays."

"I promise that even if it's awful, I'll tell her it's delicious."

I pull the hangar door open. "That's what I love about you..." I say as Rebecca steps inside.

For some reason, though, that line replays in my mind. That's what I love about you... I mentally repeat the line again and then my heart sinks as I narrow it all down to one word. Love.

Stunned, I just stand there.

Did I seriously just use *that* word? I did...*and I do*. In that instant, it's as if the avalanche of lies I've told myself over the past few days finally gives way and crushes me.

"Earth to Cory." Becca chuckles. "I was halfway inside before I realized you were still standing here." She takes my hand and pulls me into the hangar. "Did you just see a ghost or something?" A flash of excitement passes over her features as she steps closer and stands on her toes. "Oh, my God! Is this one of those haunted places we were talking about at Brad's place the other night?"

She's practically jumping out of her skin by the time I shake my head and look into those beautiful greenish-gray eyes.

"No." *God.* I'm an ass. What the fuck was I thinking. I grab her hand and pull her back to the door, trying to keep her to myself for just a moment longer.

Becca's expression morphs from playful to concerned. "Cory?" She jerks us to a halt and takes my hands. "What is it?" She looks up at me with those big, beautiful eyes. "Are you okay?"

"No." I shake my head. Jesus. What the fuck was I thinking. I look over her head, toward the terminal. There's no one there yet so I may be able to get her outside and...*and then what, Cory?*

"Cory?" she repeats with a good squeeze to my hands.

I see her daughter a split second before the little girl spots us. Her tiny face, so much like her mother's, lights up as she starts running toward us.

"Mommy!" Rebel shouts, her voice echoing through the hanger.

Becca's expression once again flashes with surprise as she gasps and then whips around to stare in awe at her daughter.

"Mommy, mommy!" Robbie squeals as he rounds the corner and runs toward Becca at full speed.

Robbie easily outruns his older sister and jumps into Becca's outstretched arms. Surprised that her tiny frame withstands the blow, I watch on with even more amazement when Rebel practically tackles her but Becca holds her ground and scoops her up too. She showers the kids' faces with kisses.

"There's my Hollywood girl," Rob calls as he walks over.

"Rob!" Becca's voice cracks. "How did you—"

She can't finish because he kisses her.

Well, isn't that just fucking sweet? *Way to go, Cory.* Disgusted and more heartbroken than I care to admit, I stare at the man I've spoken to more times than I can count to arrange this absurd plan. I've seen pictures of him, but Becca's tiny family portrait doesn't really do the guy justice. He's easily six-foot-three—maybe six-foot-four, since he's slightly taller than I am. And the fucker is built like a brick shithouse.

Rebel runs over and hugs me. "Thanks for bringing us to see our mom, Mr. Hudson."

Robbie follows suit, though he's shorter, so he wraps his arms around my leg. "Thank you, Mr. Hudson!"

Unsure of how to respond, I just stand there and look down at their little, angelic faces. *Jesus.* They both look so much like Becca that an annoying breathlessness catches in my throat.

Rebel stares up at me with her grayish-green jewels. "Can we take a picture so I can take it to school on Monday?"

I'm really not in the mood for a photo session, but is there anyone on the planet who could say no to *that* face? By the time I kneel between her and Robbie, Becca has pulled herself out of Rob's grip and is fishing her phone out of her purse.

As she snaps pictures, she asks, "How did you guys pull this off?"

"Cory's agent contacted me," Rob says, "and it all just took off from there. Did you know this guy owns his own plane?" He makes a cheesy snapping, finger-pointing motion toward me. "I couldn't refuse that offer, so I scheduled my appointment for eight o'clock this morning and was at the airport by ten."

"Then Daddy flew in to pick us up," Robbie hollers.

With the impromptu photo session over, I get up and back away from the kids. "I'm glad it all worked out," I say, though I'm not at all happy about it. "I have some place I have to be and traffic was a—"

"Bad," Becca interjects before I drop a B-bomb. "Traffic was horrible, worse than I've ever seen in Denver." She walks over and hugs me. "I'll never be able to repay you for this."

Oh, I can think of a way or two that she can. I shake the thought off and back away from her. "Sure you can. Have fun and quit moping around. It's dragging the entire cast and crew down—especially Anna."

"I promise to come to work on Monday minus my moping."

"All right, you guys have fun." I ruffle Robbie's hair. "Benny is waiting outside to take you wherever you want to go."

Becca picks up Robbie. "Do you guys want to take a ride in a limo?"

"Yeah," Rebel and Robbie shout.

As angry and depressed as I suddenly am, I can't help but smile. "I'll see you Monday, Becca. It was nice to meet you all."

After Rebel gives me another hug, I finally make my escape and hurry to my car. I get in and punch the steering wheel. *Fuck.* What was I thinking bringing her family here? Better yet, what the hell was I thinking when I let myself fall in love with her?

Way to go, Hudson. Of all the people you could be with, you've fallen for a happily married woman who sees you as a fill-in for her dead brother. Well, that only leaves me with one option. I haven't carried around my leather case in days, but I'm suddenly in desperate need of my I'll-help-you-forget-whatever's-ailing-you buddy. I back out of the parking spot, fishtailing as I spin out, then I head home—hellbent on reconnecting with my favorite friend just so I can forget about my new one.

Chapter 10

Amanda

I'm towel drying my hair when the front door opens then slams shut. My roommate walks past the bathroom, carrying several bags of groceries. When she spots me, though, she stops abruptly. "Why are you getting ready so early?" Melody asks.

"Ang called and gave me a new job." I hang the towel and walk over to grab a few bags.

"You don't sound so enthused," Melody observes. After we get the bags on the counter, she looks at me with a raised brow. "So who's taking your place tonight?"

I shrug then wander over to the couch and plop down. "I dunno. Ang was so excited about this client dropping ten grand that all I really caught was that someone was heading over with a dress and that I had to make sure to look especially *chaste*."

"Ten grand...!" Mel forgets all about the groceries and hurries over. "Holy shit, girlie, that's some mighty fine pocket change."

"Don't get too excited, Mel. The dude is a perv."

Her smile fades away and a haunted look flashes in her eyes for just a second before she drops next to me. "And which happy fetish are you in store for tonight?"

"Pedophilia..." My stomach churns. I've had clients with

85

fetishes before, but I've never been with someone who specifically asked for a small breasted, petite blonde-haired woman in an innocent-looking dress.

Melody taps my leg and forces a smile. "Those guys mostly just want the whole school girl thing, Mandy."

"Well, this guy was specific." I point to the garment bag hanging on my bedroom door. "I have to curl my hair and wear minimal makeup." I sigh. "But whoever he is, he's important, because I had to sign two of those stupid you-talk-and-you'll-be-sued-and-imprisoned disclosures."

Melody giggles. "Woo hoo, girlie, you might just be fucking The President of These Here United States."

Mel and I have been roomies for two years now, so I know she's putting on the theatrics to try to cheer me up. Unfortunately, it isn't working. "That's a disturbing thought, Mel."

"Try to think positively, Mandy. That's five freaking big ones for one night of pretending to be a little girl. I'd fuck him with a lollipop and a smile for half that!" She winks. "And it beats screwing grandpa after three hours of trying to free Willy."

I roll my eyes and stand. George isn't too bad. Besides, most nights the old guy is so tired after his lengthy charity events that I normally only have to give him some head and wait until he falls asleep, which is never long. Besides, I'd take three hours of saving whales over a pedophile any day.

Disgusted, I go back to the bathroom and blow-dry my hair then wrap it in hot curlers. After applying just enough makeup so I still look pretty in an innocent-looking way, I pull the strapless sundress from the garment bag and admire it. The dress *is* beautiful, and it isn't as childlike as I thought it would be. After slipping on some heels so I don't feel so objectified, I step into the living room.

Melody whistles. "You sure do look pretty, little girl."

I giggle at her southern drawl. "You're an asshole."

Melody laughs then walks over and hands me a coat. "You

might want to wear this. It's supposed to rain and you wouldn't want to attract every pedophile in a hundred-mile radius."

I take the coat and kiss her cheek. "I love you. Be careful tonight."

"Not as careful as you need to be," she says sincerely. "Call me if anything, okay?"

"I will."

After a quick hug, I stroll toward the elevator. The job is for the entire evening, but I'm hoping that whatever this perv has in store for me is quick. I would really love it if I could sneak out *way* before sunrise. As I drive along, I think about my big move to New York to help my spirits. I haven't had any luck in Hollywood, but one of Ang's clients hooked me up with a small part in an off-Broadway production, so I'm hoping this will be one of my last "assignments."

When I finally arrive at the gate, I admire the mansion. I shouldn't be surprised—the guy *did* drop ten grand for my services, so I wasn't expecting a trailer park. Yet this is...*wow*. Ang has a long list of wealthy clients, but this guy will be my first super-high roller. *It's just too bad he's a perv*. I reluctantly press the call button on the intercom.

"What?" a guy says, his voice oddly familiar.

"Hey, Ang sent me," I say jovially even though the guy's attitude definitely isn't helping my spirits.

He doesn't respond, but a second later, the gate begins to open. I follow along the curvy driveway and park by the front door. After a quick check of my makeup and hair, I take a deep breath and get out of the car. *This is five grand, Mandy*. That's five big ones to put toward my move to New York, so I can do this. I climb the stairs and ring the doorbell.

Cory Hudson pulls the door open and looks me over. "You're too tall." He turns and walks away, but he leaves the front door open.

Oh. My. God. That was Cory Hudson. Cory Hudson! *Copper Creek* is like one of my all-time favorite shows and Cory's portrayal of Ethan Green is just wow! He's amazing...he's...*wait a second*. Eww. Cory Hudson is a pedophile.

I'm suddenly not a fan anymore.

As my shock wears off, I step out of my three-inch heels, silently reprimanding myself for blatantly defying a client's request. I'm just hoping I haven't blown my chance. I take a deep breath and step inside. The grand foyer is exquisite, the marble and gold trim majestic. Cory isn't anywhere in sight, so I lock the door and then walk along slowly.

The first room I pass to my left is a formal living room, but the door to my right is closed. After knocking, I push it open and turn on the light. It's an elegantly furnished English Tea Room. I close the door and continue along. There's a library to my left. The bookcases are empty but there's a beautiful desk in front of a massive bay window and there's fancy-looking leather furniture in the center of the room. Across the hallway from the library is a state-of-the-art gym.

The kitchen is directly ahead but it's empty, so I look at the hallways on either side. *Left, right, left, right...*oh, hell, I go left, but the billiard room and bathroom are vacant. I walk back to the foyer and pass the kitchen and dining room to try the other hallway.

Cory is sitting on a couch in another, more informal living room, his feet propped on the coffee table. I lean against the massive doorframe and look at the ginormous television. He's playing a video game.

"Would you like me to call Ang and see if there's another girl she can send over?"

He doesn't even look my way. "No."

I stand there for a moment, unsure of what to do. After five minutes of awkward silence, I pull off my coat and walk behind the couch so I don't interrupt his game. I place my coat on the baby grand piano then sit on the opposite end of the couch. The house is beautifully furnished and it's immaculate, but as I look around, I realize that there aren't any personal effects.

It definitely isn't how I pictured a pedophile to live, and it isn't how I imagined Cory Hudson's house. You would think pool tables, pinball machines, and posters nailed to the wall. He has a game room, but it looks as if he's never used it, which is so unlike the character he plays on his show...so maybe this is a true reflection of his personality. It's pretty on the outside, but kind of cold and sterile on the inside.

The music coming from the television abruptly changes, so I look over and see he paused the game so he can reach for his tumbler. After swallowing down the contents, he gets up and walks across the hallway, disappearing into the kitchen. When he returns, he sets his refilled tumbler on the table and hands me a glass of wine. I take the drink without question.

I've been with married guys who are like this. I think their guilt causes the initial hesitancy, so I've learned that if I just sit quietly, they'll eventually loosen up. If Cory doesn't, I'd be glad, and then I'd happily collect my five grand and be on my way.

His cell phone rings, but he reaches for the controller and resumes his game. When his phone rings again, he doesn't even budge to look at it. Curious about...well, everything, I just tuck my feet under me and sip on my wine. I'm pretty sure he'll start talking any minute now. Any minute now . . .

Except he doesn't—nearly half an hour passes before he even looks at me. "Do you want more wine?"

"I'd love some."

He disappears across the hallway, so I peek at his phone. He's missed nine calls, several of which are from Destiny O'Rourke, and there are tons of voice and text messages, but he hasn't even bothered to look at them.

When I hear him returning, I sit back and look at the television. He hands me the wine glass then pulls a pack of cigarettes out of his pocket. He drops them onto the coffee table, along with a lighter, but then he disappears into the kitchen again. He returns with his refilled tumbler and an ashtray.

After plopping back onto the couch, he lights two cigarettes and hands one to me. His phone rings again and this time he actually looks down at it, but he still doesn't answer it. With his tumbler and cigarette in hand, he leans back and takes a long drag. I don't usually smoke, but some things are part of the job. You do whatever makes the client happy, and apparently Cory Hudson is happy when his 'little girl' drinks and smokes.

Now that's a weird combination.

I scoot closer so the ashtray is within reach and then I decide to make an attempt at some conversation. "Which game are you playing?" I ask. I'm not a gamer, but I'm familiar with the popular ones. The game he's playing doesn't ring any bells though.

"*Allamanda.*"

That information isn't helpful, so I try again. "Seems creepy..." I glance at the television. He had paused it during a scene where the main character is running away from her captor. At the moment, the girl is in the woods, following along a trail of golden trumpets. From what I've gathered, the game is bound to get scarier, and probably gorier; two things I dislike, but I decide to maintain a curious façade. "Mind if I try?"

That clearly surprises him, but after a moment of searching my face, he drops his head onto the couch and shrugs. "Go for it."

After snubbing out my cigarette, I reach for the controller. I'm hoping he'll chime in to help out, especially since he seems to be loosening up, but he doesn't. He just sits there, smoking cigarette after cigarette and sipping on his drink. His phone rings several times, all of which he ignores.

"All right, I'm done," I say, forcing a chuckle. "I'm never going to get the hang of this."

He snubs out his cigarette and sets his empty tumbler on the coffee table. I hold the controller toward him, which he reaches for, but when his phone chimes—this time in a different tone than all the others—he jerks away from me and stands.

Okay? That's a weird reaction—even for him. I shift a bit so I can read the screen. The text message is from someone named

Becca. Cory lifts the phone and stares at it. He drops back onto the couch and holds the phone for a moment longer before he finally swipes his finger across the screen. He ignores the other messages and taps on hers.

The image within the text field is small, so he enlarges it. It's a woman and what looks like her two kids, the faired-haired boy and girl sharing enough traits that I'm sure they're hers. Cory swipes his fingers to enlarge the picture further, my stomach churning as I watch, certain that he's going to zoom in on the little girl.

When he centers the image on the woman though, I actually breathe a sigh of relief. She's definitely petite, but she has to be at least thirty—maybe a little older—and...*hold the phone!* With the picture enlarged, it's easy enough to note the barrel curls and... my heart skips a beat when I *really* look at the dress she's wearing.

Aha! Cory Hudson is no pedophile!

It feels as if a thousand pounds fall off my shoulders now that I finally understand—

Cory suddenly throws the phone across the room. It crashes against the wall and shatters, parts of it littering the floor all the way into the hallway. Then he snatches the tumbler off the table, the sudden movement accidentally knocking the ashtray to the floor. Not seeming to care, he storms out of the room and disappears across the hall.

Stunned, I sit there for a moment before I finally set the controller on the table and start picking up the butts. Once the room is tidy, I go into the kitchen and grab some paper towels to clean the ashes off the table and floor. When I'm done, I consider looking for a broom and dustpan to sweep up the broken phone, but decide against it. Instead, I grab my purse and head to the bathroom. After tossing the dirty paper towels into the trash and washing my hands, I purposely leave the water running and call Melody to explain the situation, minus telling her that I'm with Cory Hudson.

Mel is quiet for a moment then finally says, "Okay, here's the deal. He and this woman are probably having an affair and he's probably pissed that she's off with the family."

I ponder that for a second then shake my head. "I don't know...why would she send a picture just to rub it in his face then? Besides, the part of the message I was able to read was thanking him for something. So what should I do?"

"I say play the part. If what he wants is this lady then I say *you* be her." Melody laughs. "Or you can just pray he's so pissed off now that he'll give you the money and you can head home five grand richer without the sore pussy."

I chuckle. "You're disgusting. You know that right?"

"Yeah, but you love me. Okay, I have to go. Send me a text to let me know what happens."

"I will." I end the call and turn off the water, wondering how best to portray a woman with kids. My mom worked her butt off because she was a single parent, but she always managed to come to all of my high school plays and she kept the house in decent shape and . . .

That's it!

I pull open the door and look around. The house, save for the video game music, is still. I stroll along and peek into the living room. Cory is back on the couch with a controller in hand.

"I'm starved. Do you mind if I raid your pantry?"

He just shrugs, so I head to the kitchen. All right, it's time to play the role of June Cleaver. I pull the refrigerator door open and study the contents, grateful there are plenty of options. Despite that though, I don't know how to cook—I'm like the microwave queen—so I lean back and think. That's when I spot the breadbox. Can I screw up grilled cheese? That's always been one of my favorites and it's technically cooking, right?

I grab the necessary ingredients then search for a pan. With everything set, I prepare four sandwiches and place them on the skillet. After adjusting the heat so I don't burn them, I search for another wine glass since mine is in the living room and Becca is obviously a wine drinker.

"What are you doing?" he asks.

Startled, I turn and feign innocence. "I was just...I didn't think you'd mind."

He stands there and scowls. I try not to fidget as he scrutinizes. When he finally walks over and sets his tumbler on the counter, I relax...just a little bit.

"You know what would be awesome," I say casually, "if you had some tomato soup."

"There might be some in the pantry." He pours more scotch into his glass. "The housekeeper usually keeps it pretty stocked."

I walk toward a door that I'm assuming is the pantry. "Do you want a sandwich? I made enough for both of us." Before he can answer, I poke my head into the pantry. There isn't any soup, so I turn and shrug. "Guess that idea won't work, but the sandwiches should be plenty." I wander over to the stove and flip each of them. "I can run out and get you something else if you want." When he doesn't respond, I look over my shoulder. "Can you grab me a plate?"

To my surprise, he opens a cabinet and puts two plates on the counter. I slide two sandwiches onto each dish and set the skillet aside. "When I was little, my mom always made these on rainy days." I tear a piece of sandwich off and pop it into my mouth. It actually isn't bad, so I rip another piece off. "We'd sit in front of the television, dipping our sandwiches in our soup while we watched corny musicals all night." I shove the piece of sandwich into my mouth and smile. Good ole' Mom, even with a tight budget and more stress than I could imagine, she still made time for my movies even though she hated them.

Cory's stoic resolves softens just a bit, then he walks right up to me and pulls off my headband. After tossing it aside, he pulls my bangs forward and leans back to study his handiwork. "What's your name?" he finally asks.

I consider saying Becca or throwing out my usual, "it's whatever you want it to be, baby," but instead, I say, "Amanda."

He extends his hand toward me. "Tonight you're Becca."

I place my hand in his and smile. "Whatever you want, baby."

Chapter 11

Penelope

From my inconspicuous position across the street, it's easy to see Destiny's Porsche zipping down the street, hell-bent on getting to Ethan's house. *Good grief!* It's about damn time! What was that little tramp doing that took her so long?

I snatch the binoculars off the passenger seat and watch her press the intercom button several times. She leans out her window and speaks—though I'm sure if I opened my window, I would hear her screaming. Ethan must finally respond, because she stops talking for a second, but his reply clearly doesn't go over well because Destiny gets out of the car, kicks the callbox several times, and taps the call button repeatedly. When she grips the intercom with both hands and practically presses her mouth against the speaker, I chuckle.

The gate opens. Destiny gets back into her car and spins the tires in her haste to drive toward Ethan's house. As the car fishtails ahead, I catch sight of *her*. The whore who Cory had rented for the night. The blonde-haired tramp creeps along the side of the house and waits until Destiny storms inside before she runs to her car.

I watch her intently; still amazed that Ethan hired a hooker.

If he needed companionship, why didn't he call me?

When the prostitute gets into her car, I toss the binoculars aside and drive forward, pulling close enough to Chad's gate to activate the opening mechanism. He's one of Cory's nearest neighbors, and while it's always been convenient to have the use of his driveway, the gate is proving to be problematic. I strum my fingers against the steering wheel while I wait, making a mental note to tell that little dipshit to leave it open for me from now on. If he refuses, I'll just remind him that I still have those pictures of him getting it up the ass from his accountant. I'm sure his wife and the media would love to know that one of their most adored stars is in the closet.

Chad's gate finally opens, so I wait until Amanda exits Ethan's driveway and is about halfway down the street before I follow along at a safe distance. I'm not in any particular kind of hurry because I know where Amanda lives. I have a few cops on the payroll for intel like this, so I know that the hooker lives in Koreatown. At this time of night, her neighborhood is usually quiet. Tonight, I'm hoping it's desolate. That would definitely make it easier for me to get her out of the picture.

Amanda veers onto the highway and after several miles, exits South on Vermont Avenue. Still staying two car lengths behind, I use the opportunity the stoplights afford to screw the silencer onto the gun and load a round into the chamber. When she makes a left onto 8th Street, traffic dwindles. After driving along several blocks, we're the only two vehicles on the road.

Amanda's right directional comes on as she nears her apartment building.

I accelerate but then slow down just enough so my grille guard taps her bumper.

Her Honda comes to a jarring halt, but I quickly back into a spot near the curb. I shove the gun into my coat pocket and open the door. "I'm so sorry!" I call out.

Amanda, who hasn't moved her car from the accident sight, walks around and examines her bumper.

"Omigod!" I say in my best Valley Girl accent. "Are you okay?" I grab the keys out of the ignition and rush over. "I promise I'll pay for all of it. I dropped my phone and was trying to pick it up." I reach out and grab her arm gently. "I really am sorry, lady. Are you okay?"

Amanda sighs. "Yeah, I'm fine." She shakes my hand off and steps closer to the car. "It doesn't look too bad."

"No...but we should take some pictures for your insurance company." I point to the trunk and frown. "And you should check to see if your trunk still opens. It's pretty bent, so it might not."

"God," Amanda moans as she pulls open the driver's side door and retrieves her phone. "This is a great ending to an already horrible night." Before she leans completely out, she pops the trunk.

I'm beyond relieved when it visibly unlocks but doesn't completely pop open. "You should take some pictures before you try to open it," I suggest as I slip my hand into my pocket and grasp the handgrip. "I'm sure the insurance company will need them."

Amanda takes a few pictures. "Are you okay?" she asks.

"I'm fine..." *or at least I will be if this all works out.*

When Amanda takes a step closer, I quickly scan the street to make sure we're still alone. We are, so I release the safety.

Amanda lifts the trunk and leans closer to look inside. "It seems okay."

I pull the gun from my pocket and empty the clip into the back of her skull. She doesn't even scream as her body falls forward and collapses into the trunk. I quickly pocket the gun and ignore the searing pain on my leg from the heated silencer. I toss Amanda's legs over the bumper then slam the trunk closed and stomp on her discarded phone. Satisfied to see that it's shattered into quite a few pieces, I pocket the larger chunks of debris then hit the button on my key remote to lock my Range Rover.

After moving her seat back so my knees aren't pressing

against the belly of the dashboard, I make a U-turn and head back to South Vermont Avenue. At this time of night, I should be able to get to my cabin in Topanga in about twenty-five minutes. I hadn't planned to go out there tonight, but that's going to be the best place to get rid of her body and the car. Then I can come back and focus all of my attention on Rebecca. It hadn't escaped my notice that Amanda looks just like her, so as much as I've been a loyal and faithful servant, I've clearly done something that has angered my Dark Father because he's punishing me. I'm not sure what I did to upset him so much that he's sent yet another distraction into Ethan's life, but whatever the reason, I'll make it up to him, and then I'll finally get what is rightly mine.

Chapter 12

Chelsea

I'm parked almost half a block away from Cory's house, but even from my vantage point, I can clearly see when Destiny O'Rourke arrives. She had stormed inside and then a few minutes later, she had exited—except now she was carrying a butcher knife and she was clearly hunting for someone, no doubt the blonde-haired woman who had snuck away only moments before. Thankfully, the woman had left in time to avoid the musician's wrath. Cory, unfortunately, wasn't so lucky. He came outside, probably trying to talk sense into Destiny, but she punched him so hard that he actually fell on his ass. Then he followed her inside and slammed the door.

"Are you getting all of this?" I whisper to Jay as my gaze shifts from doors to windows, hoping to catch sight of any movement inside.

"Every horrifying moment," Jay assures me. "This will definitely get a million hits by tomorrow."

I nod as if he can see me in the darkness, though any response on my part is unnecessary because Jay doesn't need to see me to know what I'm thinking. We've worked together long enough to be in sync, and so we both sit silently, hoping to catch a bit more footage before we upload the file to the network.

The night is eerily still for a few more minutes, then a lamp flies out of a second-floor window and I catch a glimpse of Destiny and Cory fighting before they disappear from view again. I'm not sure what transpires for the ten minutes between the broken window and Destiny storming outside again, but this time, Cory is nowhere in sight, and without him there to stop her, Destiny takes the opportunity to wreak havoc in his garage.

As Jay and I sit in stunned silence, we record her destroying Cory's beloved Lamborghini. Her rage is so relentless—so brutal —that I actually say a silent prayer that the blonde-haired woman had gotten away. God only knows what Destiny would have done to her if she had caught her inside. I mean, look at the damage she's doing to the property...which begs another, more pertinent question. Where's Cory? What had she done to him that has him so incapacitated that he's not there defending his home and beloved vehicle?

With one final kick to his fender, Destiny finally tires herself enough to stumble back to her Porsche. She gets in and then speeds away. When her taillights disappear into the night, Jay and I exchange a concerned glance, but I think we're both too shocked to do anything more than look back at the house. The garage and front door remain open, and even though another minute ticks by, the gates remain wide open.

That's very unlike Cory.

"Maybe we should go and see if he's alive," Jay suggests.

I shake my head, knowing that entering his home would leave us wide open for a lawsuit. It is a tempting suggestion, though. "Maybe we should call the cops?" I say halfheartedly.

After disconnecting the camera from the dashboard, Jay throws his door open. "I say we go and take a peek to make sure the cops are really necessary."

"He could have us arrested, Jay." Lord knows that would give my father and brothers yet another reason to hate my job.

"Now why would he do that?" Jay says as he gets out of the

van and looks over at me. "We're just doing our civic duty as concerned citizens to make sure he survived Destiny's rampage."

He walks around the front of the van and pulls my door open.

"I don't know, Jay...I really don't think this is a good idea—"

"How often have you seen him leave his house wide open, Chels? The guy has a state-of-the-art security system that he uses religiously."

I grunt and strain to look at the front door, hoping that it's closed now. It's not. I peer into the garage and shudder when I survey all the damage. The Lamborghini was Destiny's first victim. She slashed the interior and smashed all the windows. When she was done with that one, she had unleashed her fury on his Corvette, and then on his Audi.

"Okay," I lament. "*Maybe* we should go and check on him, but once we know he's safe, we leave."

I hop out and Jay locks up the van, then we head toward Cory's house. We both intuitively stop at the gate and look at each other. This is it. If we cross this gate, regardless that it's open, we can potentially get into a lot of trouble. Jay takes the plunge first and then looks back at me. I sigh but then take the hand he offers and hurry toward the house.

When we get to the front door, we stop just outside the threshold. Of course Jay has been recording every step of the way, but now he lifts the camera so he's getting the entire bird's eye view.

"Mr. Hudson?" he shouts. "This is Jay Rogan with *Entertainment Nightly*."

A few seconds pass before I try. "Mr. Hudson, this is Chelsea Matthews..." I want to say, *you remember me, right?* I mean, after all these years of reporting on him and interviewing him, I would like to think we're on a first-name basis. But to save face just in case he doesn't, and also to save our asses in the event of a lawsuit, I call out, "We've only come onto your property to ensure that you're safe..." I wait another moment then add, "We're coming inside the house now."

Jay once again leads the way. He steps inside and looks around. "Jesus. His foyer is bigger than my house."

It *is* impressive, and it doesn't appear as if anything has been disturbed in the immediate area. Jay steps farther inside and calls Cory again. We wait for a moment, but when there still isn't a response, I walk past Jay and peek into the rooms as I pass. They all seem undisturbed, so I walk toward the grand archway that leads into the kitchen.

As I near the room, the hairs on the back of my neck suddenly stand on end. Apprehensive, I continue ahead slowly. Then the smell hits me. My stomach churns as the coppery scent of blood mixed with vomit fills my senses. "Mr. Hudson?" I call as I take a few more steps into the large room.

There are knives all over the counter and floor, and some-thing had broken—probably dishes—because there are shards of porcelain everywhere. I stop to stare at a grilled cheese sandwich for a second, because it seems so surreally out of place amidst the disaster.

"He's over here," Jay whispers as he steps closer to the center island.

My stomach sinks as I hurry after him.

"I think he's just unconscious," he announces as he leans out of sight.

He thinks? I make it the rest of the way over and then stare down, horrified, as I take in Cory Hudson's battered body. Blood is covering his face and he had fallen in a puddle of vomit.

Jay hands me the camera. "Keep getting this while I check for a pulse."

My hands are shaking badly, but the reporter in me somehow manages to keep Jay and Cory in the frame.

"Well?" I ask as Jay's fingers move around Cory's neck.

"He's alive," he finally says. "Though I don't know how..." he motions toward a nearby skillet, "I think she whacked the hell out of him with that."

Cory moans and rolls onto his back. Jay moves away quickly despite his hefty size.

"Mr. Hudson?" I say, stepping closer. "My name is Chelsea Matthews. I'm a reporter with *Entertainment Nightly*. We apologize for entering your premises, but we were genuinely concerned for your well-being."

Cory grips his head and groans. As he attempts to pull himself into a seated position, his abs contract oh-so-nicely. I know it isn't an appropriate time to admire his physique, but it's hard not to since he's only wearing boxers.

When he falls onto his back, I kneel beside him, making sure to avoid bile and blood. "Would you like us to call an ambulance?"

"No!" He moans again then rolls onto his side. "Jesus, turn off that fucking light."

I motion for Jay to do that while I shift a little closer to him. "Mr. Hudson, you really do look like you're in need of medical attention."

He grunts and rolls onto his back again. One of his eyes is swollen shut, but he finally opens the other and looks at me. "Get the fuck out of my house."

Suddenly sad for him, I don't move except to nod. "Okay, we'll leave. We just wanted to make sure you were okay, and we wanted to let you know that Destiny did some major damage to your cars and left the garage and gate open. Can you get up to close everything behind us?"

He grumbles something then punches the floor. His eye closes and he takes a few deep breaths before he sits up. I shift back a little then get onto my feet when he tries to stand. He stumbles, so I instinctively reach out to steady him. Cory shrugs my hand off and grabs onto the counter for support.

Startled when he pukes, I jump back and look away. Unfortunately, that doesn't protect my nose from the putrid smell reaching my overly sensitive gag reflex. I retch as I move farther away.

Cory wipes his mouth with his arm and looks at us. "I'm giving you five minutes to leave before I call the cops."

I consider staying for six minutes, just so he does call them. The poor guy really needs to report this and get to the hospital. Cory walks toward me, so I quickly hurry to stand behind Jay, but he doesn't seem interested in us at all. He staggers across the hall and sits on the edge of the coffee table. After lighting a cigarette, he touches his left ear.

I step into the hallway. "We're leaving now, Mr. Hudson."

He nods and waves dismissively before moving his fingers to examine his swollen eye.

Jay moves closer to me. "You should probably ask him if we can close the gate ourselves. I'm pretty sure he's not even going to remember that we were here, so there's no way he'll remember to close everything up."

"I got the gate, asshole," Cory snaps. "Destiny might have knocked the shit out of me, but I'm not stupid or deaf, so get the fuck out of my house."

I actually chuckle at his unexpected response. When Cory looks at me though, my laughter dies abruptly, and then I squirm under his scrutinizing gaze. It takes him a moment, but I can tell when he finally recognizes me. Despite his menacing glare though, I still manage to find it flattering that he does know who I am.

"Get out of here, Chels," Cory orders in a no non-sense way, and then he goes back to his self-examination.

"We hope you feel better, Mr. Hudson," I say in response, and then shove Jay toward the foyer.

He thankfully doesn't need any more coaxing than that, so we hurry ahead. When we get to the door, I stop and look over my shoulder. "Maybe we should call the cops anyway. He looks like he's in pretty desperate need of medical assistance."

Jay shakes his head. "I say we just got off easy, so let's not push our luck. I've got some great shots and footage, and we didn't get arrested, so let's get the hell out of here."

I pull the front door closed behind me and hurry to meet Jay at the bottom of the stairs. A mechanical sound catches my attention and I look over to see that the garage door is closing. My heart races as I look toward the front gate. Crap, what happens if he closes it before we get out?

Jay must have the same thought because he grabs my arm and pulls me along as he jogs down the driveway. The moment we step on the other side of the gate, it closes. Jay and I stand there for a moment, watching it swing completely closed.

"I really think we should call an ambulance. There might be permanent damage to his eye..." Jeez, not to mention that his earflap looked torn in half.

"Are you nuts? We'll be lucky if he doesn't sober up in the morning and report us for trespassing. Come on. Let's get back to the office; I want to get these pics to Walt."

I instinctively grab his arm. "Delete the ones you took inside the house."

"What?" Jay shakes his head. "No fucking way."

"Yes, way," I snap. "We can use the video footage of Destiny trashing the house, but using the pictures you took inside will definitely get us a lawsuit." And it isn't just that. My heart is suddenly going out to Cory Hudson in a way I've never experienced with another celebrity. "He at least deserves that amount of privacy and I'm sure he won't press charges if we don't air those shots."

Jay snorts. "Listen, Chels, we all know you have a soft spot for this guy—"

"I do not," I lie, since everyone knows I do. Still, I cross my arms over my chest and try a different approach. "Can you afford to lose your job? Because I can't?"

Jay debates that then sighs and walks back to the van. I follow along, getting into the passenger seat without another word. Hopefully, I've said enough already.

I pull my tablet out of my purse and start writing about this latest battle between *Cortiny*. I'll definitely mention that there was another woman at Cory's house, but I'll exclude that the woman looked a lot like Rebecca Carter. I don't think Cory and Rebecca are having an affair because I've spent a few days researching her and she really must be striving to win a sainthood merit. The woman definitely doesn't seem to be the cheating kind. Regardless, my story isn't about her, so I'll leave that out until I have definitive evidence to the contrary. Right now, my headline is about the fight between Cory and Destiny.

There's clearly another woman in the shadows though and lots of trouble in paradise, but I'm suddenly not so gung-ho to drag Cory Hudson through the mud. Maybe Jay is right. Maybe I am getting a soft spot for him, so I intend to make sure that Cory Hudson appears like the victim in all of this. I'll gladly let Destiny O'Rourke take the blame for driving Cory into the arms of another woman because of her crazy partying and insane temperament.

Chapter 13

Rebecca

The kids have only been gone for fifteen minutes and I already miss them. I swipe through pictures on my phone and can't help but smile as I stare at Robbie and Rebel's little faces. When I get to the pictures of Cory and the kids at the airport, my smile falters and I sigh. *I miss him.* Annoyed by the troublesome thought, I turn the phone off and drop it on the seat. It isn't just *missing* him that's bothering me. If I had innocently wondered how he was doing all weekend, I would be okay with that, but I hadn't just been harmlessly missing him. That false pretense fell apart at the seams when that Wilson Phillips's song came on the radio yesterday. As the trio sang about being impulsive and getting lost in his kiss, I wasn't thinking about my husband. I was thinking about Cory.

I drop my head against the seat and wonder if I'm having all of these misplaced feelings because Cory actually listens to me and seems to care about what I feel and think. He makes me feel beautiful and appreciated and, whenever he's around, I laugh...a lot. Once upon a time, Rob listened and cared...or maybe that's just wishful thinking.

After nearly a decade of marriage, things have progressively gone downhill, so these weird feelings toward Cory are probably stemming from my insecurities with Rob—especially since he's acting funny again. The telltale signs are apparent even though he promised he would never cheat again, so I think Cory might just be a distraction from yet another load of denial I've been feeding myself. Granted, he's a *very* nice-looking distraction and when he's around, it's easy for me not to care what Rob's doing when he's supposedly "scouting" for the team.

"Have you heard from Mr. Hudson today, Mrs. Carter?" Benny asks.

Suddenly worried that my thoughts were so obvious that Benny noticed, I blush and shake my head. "Please, Benny, call me Becca. And no, I haven't heard from him..." *Though it isn't from a lack of trying.* "Have you?"

Benny glances in the rearview mirror and I read the unease in his eyes. My heart sinks as my concern about him relapsing returns with a vengeance. He's been doing so well, but what if he had a little *too* much fun last night. Worried, I call him again, but it goes straight to voicemail.

"Do you know where Cory lives, Benny?"

"Of course. Would you like me to take you there?"

Showing up unannounced is rude, but what choice do I have? The kids made Cory homemade cards to thank him for lending them his private jet and bringing them to California, so I'll use that as my excuse for just showing up. It's cheesy, but it's better than nothing. "If you don't mind," I finally say. "But only if you don't already have plans."

"It's no problem, Mrs. Carter. I don't mind."

After correcting him about my name again, I stare out the window for a few minutes before I try to call Cory again. I leave a message letting him know I'm on my way, but by the time we get to his house, he still hasn't returned my call. Benny opens his window and presses a button on the intercom.

"What?" Cory barks.

Benny actually flinches. "Good evening, Mr. Hudson—"

"Benny? What the—wait, is Becca okay?"

"Yes, sir, she's fine. I just dropped her family off at the airport and—"

"That's great, Benny," Cory interjects. "Do you need something?"

I gasp and hurry to the front bench to stop Benny from telling Cory I'm here.

"Mrs. Carter is here, sir. She'd like to see you."

Dammit.

"What...I..." The speaker crackles obnoxiously. "Come on in," he finally says.

The gate opens, which inadvertently releases a thousand butterflies in my stomach. Benny drives along and parks behind a black Dodge Challenger. Before I can tell him that I've changed my mind, he gets out and walks around to open my door. I scoot along the seat and get out, but I just stand there and look up at the beautiful house.

"Would you like me to walk you to the door, Mrs. Carter?"

"It's Becca," I say absently as I look around and admire the gorgeous landscaping. "And no, I'm okay, but thanks."

He nods and walks back toward the driver's door. As I watch him, I consider retracting that because, for some reason, I'm suddenly apprehensive. I shake the feeling away, climb the steps, and press the doorbell. It takes a minute, but Cory finally opens the door.

I instinctively gasp at the sight of him. "Oh, my God! What happened?"

With my attention acutely focused on Cory's battered face, I don't see that he has company until a striking-looking man steps beside him and hands him a business card. "Call me if she contacts you or if you think of anything that can help," the man says.

My instincts scream that this guy definitely isn't here on a social call, so I stand quietly and watch as Cory inspects the card and nods. "Yeah, I will," he says as he slips the card into the pocket of his shorts.

The man looks me over intently as he steps outside. I squirm a bit, wondering who he is and why he's examining me as if I'm an unidentified species.

He finally turns to Cory. "You should probably have a doctor take a look at that ear."

"Yeah, I will."

The man gives a curt nod and heads toward the Challenger.

Relieved that he's gone, I step closer to Cory and examine his torn earflap. "What happened?"

He rolls his good eye, since the other one is bruised and swollen shut. Without an explanation, he turns and walks down the hall. I close the door and follow him to the kitchen. The room is in shambles. There are sandwiches and glass littering the floor, but what alarms me most is the dried blood on the counter and the stench of vomit. Yet, despite all of that, perhaps the most disturbing aspect of the disarray is that Cory walks over the mess and serves himself a scotch as if there's nothing amiss, and then, without asking, serves me a large amount of chardonnay.

My mommy-mode instincts kick into overdrive. I pull a stool out and tap it. "Sit down."

After setting my wine on the counter, he obediently drops onto the stool, probably because my voice leaves no room for debate, and he downs the scotch. I gently tilt his head back and scrutinize the scab that has formed along a jagged line spanning from the corner of his eye to his ear. The gash is most prominent on the middle of his earflap, the cut still oozing blood through a crusty, brownish-red scab.

"That could probably use some stitches," I finally say.

He pulls his chin out of my grip. "I'm not going to the hospital." He pushes me back and stands. "What the hell are you doing here anyway?"

His anger startles me and for a second, I actually consider leaving. That won't do him any good though, so I walk over the mess and start going through drawers. "I was worried about you. I tried calling last night and then this afternoon, so when you didn't answer or return my calls or text messages, I asked Benny to bring me over." As I pull a large Ziploc bag out of the box, I realize that I had totally forgotten the reason I came. "The kids made you cards because they were so excited about flying in your plane."

Cory refills his glass then walks toward the hallway. "That's nice. Just leave them on the counter and let yourself out."

I watch him stagger toward the staircase, amazed that he manages to climb up without tumbling back down. About halfway up, I lose sight of him and consider going to make sure he made it. I shake the idea off and continue adding ice to the bag. I'll know if he falls, so I'll let him cool his heels for minute. I set the makeshift icepack into the sink and hurry outside. The passenger-side window is open, so I lean against the door. "Hey, Benny, I hate to ask, but would you mind going to the drug store and grabbing some first-aid stuff and liquid stitches?"

He sets the newspaper aside and nods. "Okay. Anything else?"

"I..." Apparently this isn't as surprising to Benny as it is to me. "I think he needs to go to the hospital, but he seems pissed at me for some reason..." I stare at Benny, wondering if I can use their little friendship to my advantage. "Do you think you can convince him to go?"

Benny starts to say something but falters. After a moment of returning my gaze, he finally says, "The funny thing about hospitals is that they tend to asks questions. Maybe do a little blood test if they suspect the person is...ah, potentially under the influence of certain things."

I lean back, suddenly understanding Cory's determination to be alone.

"I'll run to the drug store," Benny offers. "Do you need anything other than the basics?"

"No, that should be enough. Oh, and maybe an icepack."

"I'm on it."

"Thanks, Benny. Can you just give me a second to grab something from the back?"

He nods, so I quickly retrieve the cards. I watch him drive off then I go back inside. After stopping to grab the icepack and a dishtowel, I head upstairs, the second-floor landing leaving me right in the middle of a long hallway. I look right then left, unsure of which way to go. I take a right and poke my head into all the rooms I pass. The four bedrooms are beautifully furnished but vacant, as are the two bathrooms.

I turn around and head back the way I came. The first door past the stairs in the opposite direction is partially open. I push it open and nearly drop the bag of ice as I absorb the disaster within. The nightstand nearest the door is knocked over. The lamp is broken and there are hundreds of unopened condoms lying atop some clothes. Most of the garments are male apparel, but the lacey bra and panties are definitely female. The comforter and sheets are strung along the floor heading toward a door on the other end of the room, and the mattress is hanging off the box spring precariously. When the torn drapes suddenly flutter on a breeze, I note that the window is shattered as well.

Jeez. What happened in here? And where is Cory? This must be his bedroom, but he isn't anywhere in sight. I peek into the adjoining bathroom but it's empty too, so I go back into the hallway and continue my search. The two fully furnished bedrooms I pass are vacant, their appearances pristine and untouched, so I make my way to the end of the hallway. The door to the right opens to an office—it's sparsely furnished with very manly looking dark leather furniture, but it's empty. The door across from it is partially open, so I knock lightly and poke my head inside. Cory is lying face-down on a huge four-poster bed. I walk over, set the kid's cards on the night table, and sit beside him.

He shifts to look at me. "Why are you still here?"

Even though he only has one good eye, a chill sweeps over me as I register the coldness within it. I shake off the uncomfortable feeling and force a smile. "I've never been one to follow orders well." I reach over and brush hair off his forehead. "Besides, when I was in the classroom, I always stayed after class with the smelly kids."

He rolls onto his side and glares. "Are you implying that I'm the smelly kid?"

I smile despite his harsh tone. "Just a little bit, but I still love you."

Cory rolls his eye and pulls a pillow over his face. "Get out."

His muffled words remind me of my daily struggle to get Robbie out of bed in the mornings. "What if I promise to leave once you've taken a shower and I've patched you up?"

He lifts the pillow overhead. "And then you'll leave?"

I hold up my hand and nod. "Scout's honor."

After tossing the pillow aside, he scoots to the edge of the bed and looks at me. "You were never a scout, so shove that hand up your ass."

That stings, but I know he's trying to push me away, and I know he wants to be alone so he can drink or dope himself into oblivion, but I refuse to give in. After a calming breath, I force another smile and place my hand over his. "All right, then how's about I swear to God, hope to die, stick a needle in my eye?"

Cory stares at me for a second then mutters something as he staggers toward the bathroom. I follow behind, reaching out to steady him when he nearly falls. He shoves my hands off and reaches for the faucet. Once the water is going, he leans back but sways, so I help him again.

He whips around and slaps my hands away. "Would you get the fuck out of here already? I'm a big boy and I can shower on my own!"

I flinch and instinctively step back because his even harsher tone petrifies me. It's the first time since our initial encounter that I'm actually scared of him.

"Becca..." His stone-cold expression melts away. "I didn't

mean to..." he takes a step closer, "I would never—" He trips on the bathroom rug.

I catch him, but he's over a foot taller and a hundred pounds heavier, so we crash against the wall. Air rushes out of my lungs and I struggle to get a breath in with all of his weight pinning me there. Thankfully, Cory quickly plants a hand on the wall so he isn't crushing me anymore. I take a deep breath then gasp when Cory brushes his nose against mine. My already frenzied heart rate quadruples, and when Cory presses himself against me, this time pinning me against the wall in a really nice, erotic way, a thousand goose bumps erupt all over my body.

When he gently cups my cheek with his hand and rubs his nose against mine again, it feels as if times stops. Then he kisses me. Repulsed and aroused all at once, I shove him away. He stumbles a bit but manages to stay on his feet, so I back away, still breathless and suddenly *very* warm. He doesn't give chase, so we stand there and face off. I'm panting like a rabid dog while he stands there with this cocky, crooked, and oh-so-damn-sexy smile.

"I'll just..." I back up a bit more, suddenly in desperate need of space—*lots* of space. "I'll be outside if you need anything."

"Do you wanna join me?"

Do I? That random thought surprises me so much I forcibly shake my head. "No, thanks."

Cory shrugs and adds, "It's your loss, lady."

Oh, I bet it is.

When he pulls his tee shirt over his head and exposes his fabulous physique, I'm suddenly sure of it. Good grief, those dedicated workouts really do pay off. When he hooks his thumbs onto his boxers, I finally snap out of my musing and turn to leave. My hand is sweaty and shaking so badly that my grip slips when I grab the knob.

I've just gotten some traction when Cory's arms suddenly appears, his hand resting against the door to bar my exit. When he presses his body against mine, I squeeze my eyes closed and sigh. "Cory—"

"Are you sure you don't wanna join?" He kisses the back of my head. "I mean, this boner does have your name written all—"

"Cory!" I scoot up just enough so that our bodies aren't touching anymore. "Let me out!" I yank on the doorknob and he steps away so suddenly that the momentum causes me to stumble backward. When he reaches out to steady me, he has the audacity to laugh.

That does it.

I whip around, suddenly enraged. Thankfully, he's still wearing his boxers. "You pull something like that again and I will leave," I growl through clenched teeth.

We stand off, both our eyes narrowing as a thick tension seems to grow out of the steam accumulating in the room. I finally turn and let myself out. I reach for the knob to pull the door closed but stop short when Cory calls me.

I don't look at him. "Cory, just take a shower. I'll be out here if you need me."

"Becca?" he repeats, this time softly.

I sigh. "What?"

"I need you."

My heart skips a beat, and I finally give in to the temptation and look over my shoulder. "I know, Cory. I'll be right here waiting."

"You promise?"

"I swear."

We face off again, but after a few seconds, he nods and closes the door. My knees are wobbly, so I make it to the bed and plop onto the mattress. After a moment to catch my breath, I stare at the bathroom door and wonder if I can rehabilitate a heroin addict? Maybe the better question is can I help him even though I'm insanely attracted to him, and also, on some very twisted, unhealthy level, a little bit scared of him. I don't know the answers to either of those questions, yet despite that, I still get him fresh clothes and plan to stay even though I know I shouldn't.

After Benny, Brad, and Anna have come and gone, I call Rob to make sure he and the kids made it home safely. After a quick chat with Rebel and Robbie, I tell Rob everything that happened after they left—well, *most* everything, since he doesn't need to know about the shower incident. Rob understands, knowing how much I regret not being more of a help in Jeb's rehabilitation, but he doesn't think I should stay here alone. Neither do I, and for a ton of reasons I won't share with him, but I assure him I'm fine even though I'm not. Yet, what choice do I have? Cory is finally sleeping soundly and, if he's anything like my brother, he won't remember anything about today. Nor do I want him to wake up and give in to the temptation of using heroin again or even drinking for that matter. Anna said she'd go into work tomorrow and rearrange the schedule so Cory can have the next few days off, but he'll have to be back to work by week's end. Brad, who has nursed Cory back to health often, offered his services, but I know how draining it can be, so I volunteered to stay this time.

Besides, Brad has a more important mission. He needs to find out why this mysterious Detective Morris was here. We ran through scenarios when I discovered his business card, but as much as Anna and Brad believe that it's Destiny related, I'm hesitate to agree. The way Detective Morris eyed me when he was here, and with the small portion of conversation I overheard, his visit doesn't add up to Destiny.

After a final walkthrough downstairs to make sure I didn't miss any messes, I engage the high-tech security system and head upstairs. I stop by the door of the room that Anna and I had dubbed the sex room. I still can't get over the fact that Cory has a room dedicated for bringing women home, but Brad confirmed that it's exactly what he uses it for—apparently Mr. Hudson likes to keep his sex life in a different area from his sleep life.

That's sort of bizarre to me, and as I look around the room, which is still a wreck even though Brad, Anna, and I had straightened up the furniture, I wonder what other idiosyncratic behaviors Cory has amassed over his lifetime. Clearly, he's very conscientious of STDs, the tons of unopened condoms littering the floor a testament to that. I head into the room and pull open the top drawer of the nightstand. The piece of furniture had been knocked over earlier so I know it's where he keeps his stash, along with lubes, dental dams, flavored condoms, and a few pairs of edible panties.

As I bend to pick up the unopened condoms off the floor, I think of the contents of the other drawers. Cory has invested in some toys—lots of the same ones, almost as if he uses one and then tosses it. Though that would make sense given his compulsion to remain germ free. But there isn't anything truly out of the ordinary. No whips, chains, clamps, or gear that speaks of some pathological need to demoralize or demean women. That's a good sign, at least.

After adding the condoms to the drawer, I walk to the window and pull the curtains firmly together in hopes of keeping the bugs out for the night. I'll call someone in the morning to fix the window. Right now, I need to find pajamas, and since I know there are no clothes in here, I tiptoe into Cory's room in search of anything I can throw on after I take a much-needed shower. My clothes are filthy from hours of cleaning, so there's no way I'm sleeping in them, but his dresser only turns up socks, underwear, and ties. I move to the bureau and retrieve the first tee shirt I come across.

As I turn to leave, a glimmer catches my attention. I step closer to the entertainment stand and examine the trophy and awards that are neatly lining the top shelf. Then I notice artwork and pictures of Cory with various celebrities scattered about the room—several of which include either Brad or Anna. On the nightstand that I've sat by all evening, I finally notice a small, framed picture. I walk over and lift it, certain that it's of him as a young boy with his mother.

I run my finger along the glass and tears blur my vision as the memory of one of my former students suddenly resurfaces. His story wasn't nearly as heart wrenching as Cory's, yet I remember how he spoke about how he would set up his room if he were ever lucky enough to get adopted. He eventually did, but Cory wasn't so lucky. He remained in the foster system until he was eighteen, forever ostracized—treated like a leper. So, this is *his* room now, all his really special, personal items nearby.

Beyond saddened for him, I set the picture down, pull the covers snugly around his shoulder, and walk over to the bathroom. I always leave the light on for Rebel and Robbie just in case they wake up in the middle of the night, so I do the same for Cory. On my way out, I turn the lamp on his bedside table off then I head down the hallway, my mind a million miles away as I try to picture his life before Brad found him tending bar in South Beach. The man definitely got the short end of the stick, but he's been given an excellent opportunity now—a chance that most people would kill for. Despite that, here he is, throwing it all away.

Well, not if I can help it. Suddenly more comfortable with my decision to stay and help him, I head toward the guest room's bathroom and decide to make myself at home.

Chapter 14

Penelope

It feels a little *too* easy, which suddenly makes me *extremely* uneasy. I pull into a parking spot right by the back door of Destiny's house and peer out of the windshield. How odd that I felt safer breaking into her house than compared to now. Walking right up to the door under the guise of delivery girl is brave...and maybe a little imprudent. Granted, the wig, sunglasses, makeup, Whole Foods uniform, and stolen car are bound to keep my identity safe, but I'm still nervous.

I don't really have a choice though. Once *Entertainment Weekly* released the footage of Destiny destroying Ethan's garage and cars, she became a recluse, so my only option was to come to her. As the future Mrs. Hudson/Green, I feel it's my place to make her pay for what she did—not so much for the property damage, since I have the money to replace all of it and then some, but for what she did to Ethan's beautiful face.

With renewed determination, I take a long, steady breath then grab the container of tilapia off the passenger seat and walk to the back door. The housekeeper pulls the door open with a smile that instantly falls away when she sees me. Her eyebrows arch and she plants her hands square on her hips. "Where's Jose?"

"He had some car trouble." *Like four slashed tires worth.* I extend the Styrofoam cooler toward her. "He told me to tell you he'll be back tomorrow."

The housekeeper takes the box and heads inside, motioning for me to follow. "Sorry about snapping like that, I just figured that when you spoke into the intercom, Jose was training someone again. Shame to hear about his car, I always enjoy our daily chats." She chuckles, her plump frame jiggling disgustingly.

"No worries," I say with a forced smile. "He said I should wait until you check to make sure the fish is up to Ms. O'Rourke's satisfaction."

"Yeah, that's the way of it, but between you and me, I think it's a bit hypocritical of Ms. O'Rourke to be so particular about her pescatarian diet when she spends all night and all weekend boozing and drugging up that body of hers."

The housekeeper and I chuckle, and I'm suddenly glad I went with the plan to only distract her long enough to put the arsenic into Destiny's stash of chai tea. Her sense of humor and spot-on observations are characteristics worthy of the living—not the dead.

When she pulls the lid off the cooler, I step beside her and watch as she shovels ice chips aside to expose the tilapias. I was worried the oleander sap would be obvious, but there was clearly no need to be anxious. *I* can't even tell each of the fish has a healthy amount of sap glazed over it.

"How's it look?" I ask.

"These look great," she says as she lifts one of the fish out of the container. "Eww...this one is kind of slimy though..." She drops it back into the container and walks to the sink.

"I think they're trying something new to make sure it stays fresh during the commute."

"It's a twenty-minute drive," she scoffs as she turns on the water and starts scrubbing her hands. "How bad can it get with all that ice?"

I walk over and look at her hands. "Beats me, I'm just the

delivery girl." I lean closer. "Hey, your hands look pretty red... maybe you're allergic to that stuff."

The housekeeper begins to scrub her hands vigorously. A tiny squeak of angst slips through her parted lips as she adjusts the water temperature so it's hotter. "It's...ah," she puts her hands before her and examines them, "they're going numb."

"Uh, oh," I say with a level of sincerity I don't possess. "Do you have a first-aid kit around? Maybe we can use some alcohol?"

She puts her hands under the steaming water again and nods. "Yeah, it's in the pantry."

I wait until I turn around to smile. As I mosey toward the pantry, I pull latex gloves from my cargo pocket. The pantry is full to the gills, but I instantly spot the glass container that's labeled chai tea. It's one of Destiny's favorites and since she's ramping up to go on tour, she'll be drinking this stuff by the gallons. I unclasped the top and reach into my pocket for the bag of arsenic.

"Gloria!" Destiny shouts, her voice way off in the distance. "Gloria!" Destiny calls again, this time a little closer. A moment later, she stomps into the kitchen. There's a tall man on her heels.

My heart leaps into overdrive the moment I recognize Detective Morris. I quickly pocket the arsenic, pull the gloves off and push them in the other pocket, and then I grab the first-aid kit.

"Will you tell this moron that I came straight home right after I got done at Cory's place on Saturday night?"

Gloria doesn't bother to pull her hands from beneath the stream of water. Instead, she looks over her shoulder. "Yes, she was here." Her eyes focus on me. "Can you hurry it up?"

I rush over, set the first-aid kit on the counter, and open it.

"What's wrong?" the detective asks the housekeeper.

Oh, this is just fucking great.

"Nothing, I think I'm just having an allergic reaction to the fish." She takes the hand towel I offer, dries her hands, and reaches for an alcohol pad.

I take the opportunity to walk over and put the lid on the

Styrofoam container. "I'll call the store right away and let them know to send over some more fish. And we won't charge you for these." I lift the cooler off the counter and take a few steps toward the door.

"That's never happened before," Destiny says as she examines Gloria's hands. "Maybe I should call an ambulance."

"I'm fine," Gloria insists as she scrubs away with an alcohol pad.

While Destiny and the detective fuss over the housekeeper, I slink closer to the door. "I'll call the store the second I get to the car."

Grateful no one seems to care that I'm leaving, I pull the door open and slip outside. The car feels a million miles away even though it's just a few feet. When I finally get there, I open the passenger door, drop the container on the seat, and slam the door shut.

"You there," the detective calls as he walks toward me.

Dammit. I force a smile and turn to face him. "Yes, sir?"

"What's in the container?"

"Tilapia...Ms. O'Rourke has us deliver them daily." Thank goodness for stalking, otherwise I wouldn't have gotten so close to accomplishing my mission.

"Is this your regular stop?" Detective Morris asks.

"Nope. I'm just filling in for the usual guy." I shrug. "My boss said he had some kind of car trouble."

He pulls a notepad from his inner jacket pocket. "What's the usual guy's name and do you guys deliver on the weekend?"

"Ah...his name is Jose. I think he only comes during the week. You want me to call my boss and ask?"

"Which Whole Foods is it?"

"It's the one on Santa Monica Boulevard." I lean against the car. "Is Cory Hudson pressing charges for all the crap Ms. O'Rourke did to his cars?"

Detective Morris stops writing and eyes me for a moment, his emerald-colored eyes scrutinizing me so thoroughly that I have to keep from squirming. Instead, I smile and curl a strand of the blonde wig. Luckily, he goes back to writing.

"What's your name?" he asks.

"Amber Watts." The lie rolls off my tongue easily. "Listen, I have two other deliveries so can I go?"

"Yeah, I'll be in touch if I need anything else."

"Well then I hope you need something else." I twirl another strand of fake hair and smile demurely. The flirtation is just a cover, but I can't say I mind having to look at him.

"Good day, Ms. Watts," he says stiffly before disappearing back inside.

The moment the door closes behind him, I get in my car and rethink my plan. Poisoning Destiny to finally get her out of the way was a brilliant idea, but maybe my Dark Father sent me here for a reason. Maybe poisoning Destiny was never his ultimate plan. Maybe He wants me to frame her for Amanda's murder instead, which is an even better idea since she's clearly being investigated, so...I get the car in motion and start considering all the logistics necessary to frame Destiny for Amanda's disappearance. With the detective already questioning Destiny's whereabouts on Saturday, it should be easy enough to flame those fires, and my life would be all the better if that little bitch is behind bars. Besides, there's no way I can let anyone think that Ethan did something to Amanda. That could ruin our future together and I won't let that happen.

So after passing safely through Destiny's security gate, I pull the blonde wig off and toss it aside. When I get to my cabin, I'll dump this car then go through Amanda's car and grab some stuff that I can plant in Destiny's house. That should take care of that bitch, which is great, because from here on in, I need to focus on getting Rebecca Carter out of Ethan's house, and out of his life, for good.

Chapter 15

Cory

Where has Amanda gone? I've been avoiding the question, but after five days, I can't pretend it isn't bothering me. Where is she? And more importantly, would she be missing if I hadn't asked her to come to my house on Saturday? The reoccurring questions are like an itch I can't scratch.

Speaking of which...I rub the inner part of my elbow because the healing needle-tracks are aching for some heroin. After almost a week of being clean, I'm still craving a hit. My daily dose of Buprenorphine helps, but there are still times when a craving will pop up out of the blue...like right now. Becca and my doctor have given me lengthy, researched lectures assuring me that the worst is over and I'm doing great, but I'm not buying it. I may have gotten over the worst of the withdrawals, but there are moments when I'm willing to sell my soul for just one more blissful, euphoric high of my liquid amnesia.

Becca thinks it will help if I start seeing a therapist so I can get to the root of my addiction. Every time she mentions it though, my kneejerk response is, "you're out of your fucking mind." She always giggles and says she'll keep trying to convince me. I laugh too...but only on the outside. There's no fucking way

I'm lying on a couch to tell some stranger about my childhood. Besides, if I did that then I wouldn't have an excuse to keep Becca by my side. She may think I'm a fill-in for her dead older brother, but I'm no longer under any false illusions. I love her, and if this is the only way I can have her, then I'm okay with that.

Well, for the most part anyway.

Sometimes it really burns my ass that of all the women I could have fallen for, I chose a married one. I chose a chick who isn't even attracted to me! But as much as it *does* burn my ass, a bigger part of me loves that she's comfortable enough to stay with me, which has really helped "our friendship" blossom. It's like we're fast becoming Forrest Gump and Jenny Curran.

I mentioned that to her the other night and Becca totally agreed that we've become "like peas and carrots," and now she keeps asking me to do my Forrest Gump impersonations. I still get a chuckle by the reaction she had when I changed one of his infamous lines to, "I'm not a very smart man, but I have a huge cock." Becca nearly peed her pants.

Becca shakes my arm. "Earth to Cory."

"Huh?" I look up from my plate of uneaten food. "What's up?"

She and Anna stare at me for a long moment then Becca squeezes my arm gently. "They'll find her, Cory."

I pull away from her and pick up my fork. "Yeah, they will. I wasn't even thinking about that."

Becca gives me a look; the one that says she knows I'm full of shit. After spending every waking hour with me in her saintly attempt to keep me clean, she probably knows me better anyone. Thankfully, before she can remind me of that, her cell phone rings.

She scoops it up while dabbing her mouth with a napkin. "Excuse me for a second." She stands and turns toward the door. Just before she steps out of my trailer, I hear her say, "Hi, babe."

I drop my fork again, the clanking reverberating through the tiny space.

Anna shifts into Becca's vacant seat. "I need your help."

I sigh and push the plate away. "What's up?"

She chuckles. "Don't sound too enthused."

"Oh, Anna, how may I be of service? Is that enthusiastic enough?"

"Okay, smartass, that works." She smiles and leans closer. "I need you to help me convince Becca to add a sex scene."

I drop against the chair and sigh. This is just great. As if the kissing scenes with Katie weren't enough, now I have to screw her. That's just fucking lovely. "You're the producer, so that's your call." I pull my napkin off my lap and toss it over my plate.

"I know, but Becca has been such a great help and I like her, so I'm trying to keep it as true to the book as possible."

I shift my attention to the window. Becca is very animated as she talks, so I watch her for a second and allow myself a moment to enjoy the fact that she and Rob are arguing again. It isn't the first time. After spending five days together, I think I know her just about as well as she knows me, so when she says she's happily married, I know *she's* full of shit. I've thus far managed to contain the constant urge to seduce her, or slip into her room in the middle of the night and—

"Cory?"

"What...oh, right. She won't go for it," I finally say. "The first people she thinks of when she's writing steamy scenes are her kids, then her parents, and then her students."

Anna sighs. "I know." She walks over to her purse, pulls out a script, and hands it to me. "I finished this up last night. Let me know what you think her reaction will be."

I flip to a page and skim over the first few lines. My jaw drops. "This is between Cassie and John."

Anna laughs. "Oh, don't act like you're disappointed now that you know you aren't the one who has to pretend-screw Katie."

After looking up to glare, I laugh dryly and flip through the pages. "Becca isn't going to like it. She had enough problems writing a scene where Cassie kisses John, so screwing him at the church on his wedding day is like doubly sacrilegious."

"What about at the hotel right before he leaves?"

I shake my head. "It isn't about the lo—"

When Becca stomps back inside, I quickly close the script and shift over to set it under my thigh. Anna and I sit silently while Becca storms over to her purse, fishes out her cigarettes and lighter, then slides the window open so violently the trailer rocks. She lights her cigarette, takes a long drag, and leans against the counter before slowly exhaling a plume of smoke.

After I make sure the script stays on the chair, I walk over and light a cigarette. "Is there trouble in paradise?"

Becca leers at me.

I chuckle. "What did he do now?"

She takes another drag then shakes her head. "Nothing. I don't want to talk about it."

"In that case," Anna starts, but when I shoot her a dirty look, she gets the hint and doesn't mention the sex scene. Instead, she continues with, "Cory and I were just talking about his upcoming charity event."

Oh, fuck me. I'm sure Anna thought that was a safer subject than the sex scene, but it really isn't. I quickly think of a change of subject, but before I can get the conversation away from my plans, Becca looks my way.

"Oh, yeah...I forgot about that. Do you want some company?"

"Ah..." *Dammit.* "You know, the funny thing about this charity event is that it isn't close by, so with Rob and the kids coming, you—"

"They aren't coming."

Hold on. This just might work in my favor, but with Anna listening intently, I decide to play it safe. "Listen, Becca," I finally say. "You know I'm always on your side, but with the draft just around the corner—"

Becca actually growls.

Anna chuckles. "You might want to shut up, Cory. Not unless you want to get dinged in the head with another frying pan."

Becca chuckles at that, which instantly lightens the mood. "Okay, so where's this not-so-close-by charity event that I've invited myself to," she asks.

I shift a bit; suddenly uncomfortable even though she and Anna will eventually find out since I'm sure the goddamned media will post it all over the internet before I even get back to L.A. "It's up in Denver."

Becca's jaw drops.

Anna steps in front of me. "As in Denver, Colorado?"

"No, as in Denver, Minnesota," I snap. After stubbing out my cigarette, I look at them. "There's a non-profit child placement organization up there I think I can really help." When they just keep gawking, I roll my eyes and look at Becca. "It was your idea for me to use my fame to help foster kids."

She blinks several times then snaps her mouth shut. "Yeah...I mean, yeah. That's awesome, Cory. I guess I just assumed you'd do stuff around here."

"Well, it's Destiny's last weekend home before she goes on tour, so I just wanted to be far away to avoid any other confrontations." I light another cigarette. "If you want to tag along, you can spend the weekend at home with the kids while I do my thing. Then we can fly back together."

Becca's eyes brighten and she smiles. "That's an awesome plan!" She punches my arm playfully then grabs her phone and hurries back outside.

Anna starts clearing the table. "So, Denver, huh?"

Here we go. "It's a quick flight, but far enough away that I don't have to deal with Destiny." When Anna looks over her shoulder and eyes me for a second, I add, "Nor do I know anyone there, so I won't be tempted to go out and party or have access to my dealer."

"Uh-huh," Anna says without looking at me.

I roll my eyes. "Jesus, just fucking say it already."

Anna walks over, sets the dishes in the sink, then turns and leans against the counter. "Say what? I think it's great that you're embracing sobriety and using your fame to help foster kids." She reaches for my free hand and squeezes it. "Just remember that no matter how much they may argue, and as miserable as she can appear, she loves her family."

I consider yanking my hand away to pretend that I don't know what she's talking about, but I'm starting to realize I'm a lot more transparent than I've let myself believe. "I know." I sigh. "That's why I have no intention of overstepping my bounds."

Anna chuckles and taps my hand. "Oh, I didn't say you shouldn't tell her. I'll be the first person to admit I don't approve of adultery, but you two...you have something special." She turns and looks out the window. "And as much as Becca likes to tell me that you're like an adorable little brother, I see the way she looks at you when she doesn't think anyone's watching, so I say tell her and let her know the option is there."

Now that's a completely different tune than the lecture Brad had given me a couple of days ago when he figured out how I truly felt about Becca.

Anna turns and looks at me. "Do you love her?"

Every muscle in my body suddenly becomes tense, but when I seriously consider the question, I relax. "I do."

Anna taps my cheek affectionately then walks over to collect her stuff. "On my way out, I'll let Becca know she can take tomorrow off too. I wouldn't want that to be the issue that keeps her from tagging along. And FYI, maybe suggest stopping by the school to surprise her students, and then make sure you do something with her kiddos." She leans up and kisses my cheek. "I know it isn't right, but I'm actually rooting for you two."

I'm stunned into silence, so all I can do is watch as she leaves. When Becca comes back inside a few minutes later, I still haven't moved from my spot.

"Okay, it's all set up," Becca announces. "My in-laws will

bring the kids over to the house after school so I can surprise them."

I finally snap out of my stupor and nod. "That sounds good." I light another cigarette. "Hey, now that you have the day off, why don't we leave earlier and stop by your school and surprise your students with an impromptu autograph session?"

"Really? They would just die if they met you!"

"Hopefully not *die*." I chuckle. "Then after you surprise Rebel and Robbie, we can all go out for dinner."

Becca smiles and stands on her toes to kiss my cheek. "You're the best, Cory."

I take a drag off the cigarette and watch as she makes her way to the bathroom. Suddenly apprehensive, I smash the cigarette into the ashtray and start on the dishes, all the while wondering if I should listen to Brad and stay the hell away from Becca, or if I should follow my heart and listen to Anna.

Chapter 16

Chelsea

As Jay films and photographs Cory and Rebecca at the airport, I reflect over this most bizarre week. Painting Cory Hudson as the victim of Destiny's insane jealousy was easier than I thought, especially since he's taken the entire week to do everything right. On Monday morning, he released a press statement apologizing to Destiny for his infidelity and stated that he forgave her for what he considered a severe but understandable reaction to his behavior. Then, out of the clear blue, on Tuesday morning, his press secretary announced he would begin charity work to help the public gain a better perspective on foster homes and adopting older children.

Later that same day, I received a bouquet of flowers from him, thanking me for not posting the pictures Jay had taken in his house. Jay received a thank you card and two courtside tickets to a Laker's game. And for the remainder of the week, Cory Hudson has been on his absolute best behavior. He went to the studio on Wednesday and Thursday afternoon, but even then, I got word from one of my inside sources that he only shot a few scenes and then spent the rest of his time at the gym or in his trailer. Apparently, the studio wanted to take advantage of his battered appearance since they filmed the scenes that take place after Cory's character gets into a fight.

And today he's off from work, en route to do a charity event in Denver while Rebecca visits her family. He's like a new person, and the world is starting to think that it's all thanks to Mrs. Rebecca Carter. I'm inclined to agree, and even though other sources are claiming adultery, I'm still not sold on that idea. I'm about ninety-nine percent certain that Cory Hudson is in love with Rebecca Carter—but I'm not sure if the feeling is mutual.

Once Rebecca and Cory have disappeared onto the plane, I look at the dashboard clock and tell Jay we have to go. One of my buddies at the police station told me Detective Morris frequents a particular bar every Friday night and I need to talk to him about Amanda's missing-person case. He refuses to take my calls, though, but that's okay. I have other ways of milking information out of cops.

I look over at Jay. "Is Carson all set for tonight?" I inquire.

Jay laughs. "Are you kidding! You asked him to show up at a bar with one of his sleazy chicks and told me you'd pick up the tab, so what do you think?"

"Yeah, but I need him to remember that this isn't a social visit. I need him to act like a belligerent moron who spills beer on me and Detective Morris so I'll have an excuse to invite myself over to his place."

"He's got it, Chels. Trust me," Jay chuckles.

"Okay, I'll finish this up at home and email it to Walt. Do you mind running the footage in so I can go and get ready for tonight?"

"Nope, don't mind at all," he shakes his head, "just remember not to give Detective Morris the footage of that night until he gives you some good intel on what he thinks happened to Amanda."

"I know."

"And be careful, Chels. Just because he's a cop doesn't mean you should trust him."

I smile and pat Jay's hand affectionately. He tries not to be too paternal, but as a father of three girls, I'm often bombarded with endearments, which I don't mind at all. "I will be very careful, and I'll call you if anything even feels off."

"Good girl," he says as he pulls onto the road. "We'll all get to the bar at different times and sit way in the back. I'll be watching and I'll keep the phone close just in case."

I chuckle, knowing I should probably be offended or creeped out, but I'm not. I love Jay, and I'm glad he dishes fatherly affection my way. It's so different from my real dad that I would miss it if he suddenly stopped doing it.

As we head back to the office, I reach into my purse and grab my tablet, figuring that I might as well get started on the story about Cory leaving town for the weekend. Should I include that it appears as if he chose Denver just to be closer to Rebecca? That's too much of a coincidence to dismiss when you consider that there are plenty of foster home organizations in California, but I'm still not sure if they're having an affair, and I'm once again not worried about it. If they are, I'll eventually find out. For now, I just want to get the footage of last Saturday's events to Detective Morris so he knows that Amanda Hancock left Cory's house that night. That should help get Cory off the prime suspect list, which is a bonus, because currently, he's the only one on it.

Chapter 17

Penelope

What did I do to deserve a weekend getaway? I sit, consumed by self-loathing and rage, and watch Ethan and Rebecca board his private jet. My Dark Father is very angry with me. I don't know what I've done to deserve his wrath, but he's punishing me for something.

Perhaps He is displeased because I killed the prostitute when it wasn't the proper time for sacrifice. Well, I won't make that mistake again. Today is the vernal equinox, a night for orgies and animal and human sacrifices. I hadn't planned to participate in this most important night of nights, but I know it will please Him, so I pray he forgives me and accepts my efforts as penance.

After Ethan and Rebecca board the plane, I drive toward the interstate, my thoughts absorbed on the task-at-hand. My cabin in Topanga is scant prepared compared to my house in L.A., so I stop there first to grab supplies. Once I've gotten everything I need, including the overnight, priority package I had ordered the day before, I drive to Topanga.

I quickly unload my luggage then cut open the box. The Apple of Sodom is stored in a clear container, blanketed in bubble-wrap. The Foxglove is also lying within a transparent box, the cluster of beautiful purple flutes deceptive, as these particular blossoms are highly poisonous. I hurry over to my purse and retrieve latex gloves, suddenly in a hurry to begin my evening. I don two pair of gloves and return to the goodies. I've put considerable thought into the best way to deliver the flower and apple to my victims. And since I won't be able to taste how the ingredients would fare in baked goods, I think it's best to chop both finely, allow them to dry, and then sprinkle them into beer.

Convincing the drunken men to come home with me shouldn't prove difficult, but attempting to get them to eat a slice of cake or munch on a loaf could be a lot harder. Suggesting that we each have another beer when we get here will be easier. I just hope the Foxglove and Apple of Sodom don't disturb the taste too much. I've purchased a twelve pack of apple-flavored hard cider that I'm hoping will mask any peculiar flavors. The lucky men will be a lot easier to kill if they're suffering from the effects of the toxic ingredients. Of course, the timing may be difficult, considering that I will partake in the orgy beforehand, but I must complete all three rituals despite my hesitancy. That is the only way my Dark Father will forgive me.

Once satisfied with the minced flower petals and apple, I spread the mix onto wax paper to speed up the drying process. Satisfied with my handiwork, I pull the gloves off, dispose of them, and then head down the hallway toward my old bedroom. The night before, I had snatched up my neighbor's annoying little Chihuahua to use him as my guinea pig. The yapping dog is in a kennel and he'll be the perfect animal to sacrifice since the ritual is always more powerful when you sacrifice something you truly despise.

I push the door open and the little shit starts barking up a storm, but there isn't anyone around for miles to come to his rescue. I set the kennel on the kitchen table, retrieve a can of dog food from my purse, and grab a small plate. After mixing the food and toxins together, I open the kennel and place the dish just inside.

"I hope you're hungry, little man," I say sweetly so as not to spook him. The pup stops barking and sniffs the plate. After a moment, he starts eating. "That's a good boy," I say as I close the door. "You eat that up while I shower."

I head to the bathroom and start getting ready. It takes the hot water heater a bit to warm up when I haven't used it in a long time, so I take my time placing fresh toiletries in the shower and undressing. I unravel my thick bun and massage my scalp. It's been awhile since I've spent more than five minutes on my long, dark hair. I stare at my reflection and consider how to style it. I should definitely leave it down...maybe add a few curls. After testing the water with my hand, I step under the steaming spray and consider changing my hair color. Ethan clearly prefers blondes, but I don't think my olive complexion would do blonde hair justice.

Maybe I should get my skin bleached. If Michael Jackson did it and looked somewhat okay, I can definitely pull it off, and blonde hair wouldn't look so bad if I were a shade or two lighter. It's definitely worth a try, so after today, I'll do some research. Money isn't a problem, and I'm willing to do whatever it takes to speed up our union. I've waited for him for too long.

After showering, I towel dry my hair and run a comb through it. I think it would look better down, but the thought of it reeking of cigarette smoke gives me pause. It's such a disgusting habit, and one that Ethan will have to give up, but for tonight, and for as long as it takes Ethan to quit; I'll endure the smell. The moment I'm done with the ritual and disposing of the bodies, I'll thoroughly wash it again.

I wipe the condensation off the mirror and admire my naked body. The thought of other men touching me makes my skin crawl, but I remind myself that it's necessary. The Reaper spell clearly isn't strong enough without a sacrificial gift, and I *need* Rebecca out of the picture. Destiny, though a mild inconvenience, has never threatened me the way this woman does.

Suddenly consumed with rage, I pull my robe on, open the

door, and walk to the kitchen. It's quiet, the dog either sick or hopefully dead. I peer into the kennel but instantly jerk away as the stench of urine, feces, and vomit assaults my senses. My stomach churns, but with my curiosity outweighing my reserve, I unlock the door and lean closer. The dog is dead.

As I poke it to be sure, a smile curls onto my lips. How wonderful.

Calmer now, I lock the door and start whistling as I carry the kennel outside. As bad of a day this has been, the dead dog is like a silver lining in the midst of my darkness. I set aside my uncertainties and go to the bathroom to dry my hair. For the briefest moment, I had considered skipping out of the vernal equinox festivities because I truly loathe defiling my body. It's bad enough I endure that puny, repulsive security guard to gain access into Ethan's trailer for his daily flower and fruit arrangements. Yet, what if my avoidance of sexual participation is the cause of my Dark Father's dissatisfaction?

I must go through with this, especially now that the animal sacrifice has set the wheels in motion. I push aside my doubts and discomfort and then take a moment to shake off the sadness of losing yet another weekend of seeing our daughter. I only wish that instead of the ritual, I could spend the weekend figuring out the best way to frame Destiny while I made the drive out to Modesto to see how little Eve is doing. I haven't been there in months and I need to make the trip, but my visit will once again have to wait.

It won't be much longer now, Eve. Daddy and I will be out there to get you soon.

Tonight, I'll complete all the sacrificial offerings and perform the Reaper spell for Rebecca. Tomorrow, I'll get what I need so Detective Morris's attention shifts from Ethan to Destiny. Next weekend, I'll drive to see Eve.

Soon, baby girl, very soon, we'll be a family again. Mommy promises.

Chapter 18

Chelsea

As I follow Detective Morris into his lovely home, I still can't believe my plan worked so well. Who knew that all you needed to do to get invited to a cop's house was to set up a few well-placed lies, perform a ton of heavy flirting, and then have someone spill beer all over you?

"Nice place," I say as I follow him into the living room.

"Thanks. And make yourself at home. I'll grab something for you to put on so I can get your clothes in the washer."

Grateful that he leaves his briefcase on a nearby chair, I hurry over, pull Amanda's file out, and slip it into my oversized purse. With my heart racing, I peer down the hallway. "Hey, Detective Morris, do you mind if I use the little girl's room?"

"It's Darryl," he shouts from a distance. A second later, he emerges from the farthest doorway and points to another door. "Sure. Help yourself." He meets me halfway and hands me a pair of sweatpants and a tee shirt. "Do you want a beer?"

"Sure." I smile. "That would be great. And thanks again for being so awesome about letting me come over to clean up. It would have sucked to drive all the way to Inglewood soaked in beer."

"What can I say, I guess I'm just a sucker for damsels in distress."

"That must be an occupational hazard," I tease.

He smiles. "Yeah. There are plenty of towels in the linen closet, so help yourself.. I'll have a beer waiting in the kitchen for you."

"Okay." I slip into the bathroom and lock the door. Time is of the essence, so I quickly slip out of my clothes, pull his on, and then proceed to take a picture of each of the pages and photos within the folder. Once done, I tuck the folder back into my purse and grab my soiled clothes.

He's standing in his kitchen, his back to me as he leans over to grab a couple of beers. It's a nice view. The man is definitely fit for duty with his exquisite height and build. It's too bad I don't mix business with pleasure because with his dark hair, sparkling green eyes, and square jawline, I *so* wouldn't mind spending more time with him.

He turns and greets me with a breathtaking smile. "Just in time." He pops open a beer and hands it to me. "I'll take those," he says as he motions toward my clothes.

"Oh, I can do it. Where's the washer?"

"Don't worry about it; I'll take them. Why don't you make yourself at home?"

"Are you sure?"

"Yeah, I'm sure. I'll be right there."

I wait a beat after he disappears into the laundry room to make my way back to his briefcase. Before retrieving the file from my purse, I peek in his direction. He's nowhere in sight, so I slip the folder back into his briefcase then hurry over to a nearby couch. I've just gotten comfy when Darryl walks back into the room. He takes a seat on a couch opposite mine.

He gulps a swig of beer then asks, "Comfy?"

I nod. "Yeah, this is a really nice place."

"I like it. The house is in a good location and the neighborhood is quiet, but you knew that already, didn't you?"

I cock my head to the side. "How would I know that?"

He chuckles and sits back. "Well, we are practically neighbors. You only live a few miles away."

Shit. Despite the sinking feeling in my gut, I shake my head. "I live in Inglewood, remember?"

"Do you?" He points to my purse. "Mind if I take a peek at your driver's license then?"

"Excuse me?" I pull my purse closer. "No, you may not."

"It's okay. I think I've got it." He takes a long swig of beer and eyes me over the rim, a mischievous glow sparkling within those emerald jewels. "Your name is Chelsea Matthews. You work for *Entertainment Nightly* and you're covering Cory Hudson's career." He leans forward and plants his elbows on his knees. "You usually wear glasses and keep that pretty black hair up in a ponytail and, if memory serves, you were the one who coined the adorable yet annoying term Cortiny."

I sigh, since I had hoped to keep up the ruse a little while longer. At least for the rest of the evening. Maybe even for a couple of days. "How long have you known?"

He chuckles. "You aren't the only one following Cory Hudson around, so I've seen you before. I wasn't a hundred percent certain until Carson showed up, but once I saw him, I knew. I've had the misfortune of bumping into him in the past."

"Yeah, me too." I sigh again. "So why didn't you say anything sooner?"

He shrugs. "It was a slow day and I needed a good laugh." He takes another sip of beer then nods his head toward me. "So, what's so important that you felt the need to put on such an elaborate show?"

"I've tried calling you all week, you know." He shrugs that off, so I continue. "The night that Amanda went to Cory's house, my cameraman and I were there and recorded her leaving his house around ten p.m."

"So?"

"So? That means Cory Hudson shouldn't be on your suspect list."

He snorts at that. "Listen, lady, just because you witnessed Amanda leaving doesn't mean Cory couldn't have followed her after you and your cameraman departed."

I grunt and set the beer down firmly. After pulling my purse open, I retrieve the pictures Jay and I had taken of Cory right after Destiny left. "Look at these pictures, Detective. There's no way he could have gotten up after that and followed her." I hold up my data stick. "This is the entire footage of that night. Can you just take a minute to watch it?"

Detective Morris ignores the data stick, but he does take the pictures and starts flipping through them. "Why didn't you air these?"

"Because it didn't seem right."

He glances my way. "So you're paparazzi with a conscience?"

"Yes." When he just continues to scrutinize me, I cross my arms over my chest and glare just as intently. "Look, I realize that this job is nothing more than being a paid stalker, Detective, but after following Cory Hudson and a bunch of other celebrities around, I feel bad for them. They're like caged animals, not even able to scratch their asses without some sleazy tabloid plastering it on the front page. So I guess..." I shrug, "I guess if I can actually do some good with the stuff that I capture on camera then it isn't so bad."

He holds my gaze for another moment before he goes back to looking at the pictures. "Do you mind if I keep these?"

"Yes."

"What if we do a trade? I'll let you keep the file you already snagged and—"

"I didn't touch your file."

He rolls his eyes and reaches for his beer. "Let's skip the dramatics and make the deal. You keep what you copied, and I'll keep the pictures and the data stick. Wasn't that the game plan?"

Hang on. This suddenly seems too easy. "Seriously?"

"Yeah, seriously. Maybe if we get some press on it, we'll get some leads, because right now, we've got nothing. That girl left Cory Hudson's house and then fell off the face of the planet."

I nod. "I interviewed her roommate and mother and it does seem that way..." I take a sip of beer than meet his gaze. "You know, both mentioned she was planning on moving to New York, so maybe something happened to her en route? That seems a lot more plausible than thinking Cory hurt her."

Darryl takes a sip of beer and chuckles. "What are you, his paid advocate or something?"

"No. I just want to do the right thing. Something isn't adding up here, but whatever weirdness is going on with Amanda has nothing to do with Cory Hudson."

"Is your journalistic nose sniffing something out?"

I just sit back and glare, not particularly caring for his tone or statement.

"Okay, truce." He chuckles. "Do you need another beer?"

I shake my head and watch him walk to the kitchen. He puts his bottle in the sink, grabs another beer, then stops long enough to grab the file out of his briefcase. A moment later, he hands me Amanda's file. I flip it open and go through all of his reports. He interviewed Amanda's roommate and mother, but since I personally interviewed them too, I bypass those reports and read about a woman named Ang. She's a madam and was the person who reported Amanda missing. According to her statement, Ang always keeps a close eye on her girls, and she feared the worst when Melody called to let her know Amanda never made it home that night.

Ang went on to say that she provides all her girls cell phones that have a tracking application running at all times, so she knows for certain that Amanda made it back to her apartment—or pretty damn close before the signal stopped. The rest of the report is routine police stuff, so I move on.

There are several notes concerning Destiny's activity that

evening. One piece of information that peaks my curiosity is that she states that Cory's neighbor was the one to call to let her know that he had another woman over. *How interesting.* And it's equally interesting to see that he's collected a list of all the people who were at her place that night, the guest list is pretty star studded.

It's obvious that Darryl is suspicious of her story and alibis, but as far as I can tell, Darryl hasn't accumulated enough evidence against her just yet. The girl *is* nuts, but as my father loves to say, if craziness were the only thing a judge needed to sign off on a warrant, everyone in California would be in jail.

After reading over Amanda's roommate and mother's reports, I flip through several photos of an apartment building and adjoining parking lot. When I encounter a picture with numbered markers placed at particular places on the street, I hold it toward Darryl. "What are these?"

"That's about twenty-five feet from the parking lot of Amanda's building. There was blood, parts of a broken cell phone, and part of a Honda decal. The decal and cell phone match Amanda's, but without the car or the SIM card, it's just another dead end."

"What about the blood? Is it a match?"

"The lab couldn't get a good enough sample to DNA match it."

I sigh then go back to reading. After going through the entire file, I sit back and tap my chin. Detective Morris has done a stellar job of interviewing Amanda's friends, ex-boyfriends, and fellow employees, but none of it has panned out. She's just gone.

The only good thing about going through the entire file is that Amanda's roommate, Melody, gave Detective Morris more information than she did me. It seems that "the john" who hired Amanda was looking for a "fill-in" for his mistress. She didn't know who the client was, but said that the john became upset after receiving a photo from his mistress with her two children.

Well, well, well...that sure as hell matches someone's description pretty well.

When Darryl suddenly sits on the arm of the recliner, I startle. "Jeez, announce yourself next time."

"You get pretty engrossed when you're reading. It's kind of cute." He motions to the kitchen. "Your clothes are in the dryer, so we have time to kill. Tell me what you think."

"You..." I shake my head. "You seriously washed them?"

"I said I would, so shoot, what do you think after reading everything?"

"Okay..." I close the file and place it on the coffee table. "Well, for starters, I think you are *very* good at your job." After taking a sip of my beer, I rest my head against the cushions. "And after reading your file, I get why you think Cory's a suspect, but I know he isn't involved. Something definitely happened to Amanda, and my gut keeps telling me it's something weird, but I can't put my finger on it."

"Me too," he says as he props his feet on the table and crosses them at the ankles. "Unfortunately, without anything else to go on, this will probably become a cold case."

That sucks. I take another sip then look at him. "Why did you jump on this case so fast anyway? She's a call girl, so it's kind of weird—"

"That I'm going out of my way to find a prostitute? You could look at it that way, or you can think of it as a nice business arrangement. Ang, she has some important clients and she and her girls give us a lot of information, so we turn a blind eye to some things..." He shifts closer. "I've learned that it's good to have connections because you never know when someone who would normally be deemed the enemy can help you out in a pinch."

"Oh, is that why you're being so nice to me...so you have a paparazzi connection?"

He smiles. "I'm okay with connecting with you."

"In that case," I say as a hundred butterflies suddenly flutter in my stomach, "maybe next time you can take my call and save me the trouble of ruining a perfectly good outfit."

"Normally, I would say yes." His voice drops down a notch and he reaches for a strand of my hair. "But I have to say, I kind of like all the effort you've put into this."

When the dryer chimes, I flinch and hop onto my feet. *Whew!* Saved by the bell. A second longer and I would have happily remained under the hypnotic draw of his gaze. "I'll grab my clothes and get out of your hair." I hurry to the laundry room, suddenly anxious to leave.

After I grab my clothes, I head to the bathroom and change. When I emerge moments later, Darryl is setting the beer bottles into the recycling bin. With him distracted, I beeline for my purse but stop short when I spot a manila folder on top of it.

"I made you a copy of Amanda's file," he says from just behind.

Startled, I whip around. The man is quite stealthy and too damn close again. "Thanks...I appreciate it."

"No problem." He steps closer and holds up his keys. "Are you ready to go?"

I know the polite thing to do is offer to take a cab since I've imposed on the poor guy enough tonight, but when I look into those mesmerizing eyes, that thought leaves my mind as quickly as it enters it. Getting a cab out here on a Friday night will take a while—well, maybe not *too* long—but I'm sure it'll take longer than my libido can hold off.

"Yup, all set." I quickly lift the file and sling my purse over my shoulder.

A sexy smile suddenly curls on his lips. I squirm a bit, suddenly not a fan of being around an intuitive detective.

"Do you want me to drive you to your place?" he asks as we walk toward the door.

"Nah, I have to get back to the bar. The gang will wait there until I get back."

"Is that some kind of journalistic pact?"

"Yeah; it's kind of cool that we all look out for each other." I slip into the passenger seat of his very nice Challenger and wait until he starts the car before I add, "Thanks again for the file."

"No problem."

That sexual tension is still hanging in the air, so I make idle chitchat about celebrity gossip, hoping it alleviates the stupid butterflies that continue to dance around in my belly. When he double parks in front of the bar, I breathe a sigh of relief and take my seat belt off. "Thanks for the ride, and for everything..." I hold up the papers. "It was nice meeting you."

He just nods. "It was...amusing...and nice." After shifting the transmission into park and turning on his hazards, he looks at me. "Do you have the weekend off since Cory is in Denver?"

"Not really..." I chuckle. "There are tons of other celebrities I can stalk, and now I have some research to keep me busy..." I strum my fingers on the file. "Speaking of which, did you ever get a chance to interview Cory's neighbor about the reason he called to tell Destiny that Amanda was visiting?"

"Actually, I haven't. The man is playing hard to get for some reason. Why don't you swing by tomorrow morning? We can do some digging."

"Ah..." I look at the bar. "What time does this place open?"

He shrugs. "I don't know. I meant swing by my place. I'll make you brunch."

Those butterflies take flight again. "Ah..." *Don't mix business with pleasure, Chels; don't make an exception.* "Okay, what time?" *Dammit.*

"How does eleven sound?"

"Sounds good, do you need me to bring anything?"

He chuckles. "Just you—I'll take care of the rest."

I actually blush, which isn't something I do often or easily. After exchanging phone numbers, I open the door. "I'll see you in the morning."

"Can't wait."

My cheeks ignite again so I get out of the car and give a lame wave, totally mesmerized and off-kilter from the entire night.

"Night, Chels."

"Night, Darryl." I wave again, and then stand there and watch him drive off, my cheeks still warm from my blush way after his taillights disappear.

Chapter 19

Rebecca

Cory is staring at me expectantly, but I continue to look out the window and pretend to watch our ascent. He knows something is bugging me because he's gotten scary good at reading me, but I'll be damned if I'm going to tell him that I'm...I'm...dammit it all to hell! I'm jealous!

In reality, I *should* be pissed at my husband for showing up unexpectedly yesterday to accuse me of being unfaithful. I should be livid that the stupid tabloids have blown Cory and mine's friendship out of proportion, and I *should* be glad that Rob wasn't the least bit worried that Cory and I were having an affair. Unfortunately, I'm not any of those things. What I am is pissed that Rob was so easily pacified because, when he didn't find me home, he stormed over to Cory's hotel and discovered a "fine-looking, half-naked brunette" in his room. I *shouldn't* be upset about that. I shouldn't even care! Yet here I am, seething.

When the pilot announces that it's safe to remove our seat-belts, Cory heads to the bar. He chuckles as he pours scotch into two glasses. "So...are we going to talk about the elephant in the room or should we wait until its weight causes the plane to go down?"

Oh, I don't know; that all depends on you, jackass. I take the drink he offers and resort to super-extreme snooping tactics. "Thanks again for keeping the kids overnight on Saturday. I hope it wasn't too much of an inconvenience."

Cory sits beside me. "It was actually pretty cool. Well, aside from the fact that Rebel forced me and Robbie to watch *The Princess Bride* twice in a row." He stretches his arm across the top of the couch and leans closer. "Thankfully Robbie beat Rebel on a dare when we were down at the pool, so we didn't have to watch it again when we finally got back upstairs."

Curious and a little surprised, I eye him over the rim of my tumbler. "Robbie beat Rebel on a dare?"

"Well...technically, I beat her on a dare." He shrugs. "But my dare against Rebel was Robbie's idea, so I'm giving him all of the credit."

I chuckle. "What did you do to my daughter, Mr. Hudson?"

"It's Uncle Cory, and Robbie suggested that Rebel and I reenact a little scene. The rules where whoever forgets a line, loses."

I playfully slap his arm. "That seems a little unfair. Did you at least pick something she had a fighting chance of winning?"

He scoffs. "Can you give me some credit here?" He winks. "After a little convincing on my part, Robbie picked *The Princess Bride,* and we even let Rebel pick the scene. She chose the part where Wesley catches up to Buttercup and Vizzini?"

"Okay, seems fair. So, how'd it go?"

He cracks up and shakes his head. "After a bit of a fight—since she's about as hardheaded as her mother—she took Wesley's part because it's easier, and she started out pretty strong. I was impressed, but sadly, she couldn't finish, so I won."

I ignore the playful jab about being hardheaded and shift a bit so I can look directly into his eyes. "And you could recite all of Vizzini's line after only seeing the movie twice?"

"Of course." He pulls his arm off the back of the couch and squeezes my hand gently. "I don't get paid crazy amounts of money for nothing, you know. And..." he adds dramatically, "it really is amazing how easy it is for me to remember lines when I'm sober. Who knew, huh?"

"Well, I'm glad you guys had fun..." I sip my scotch, wondering how to divert the conversation back to his hotel room, and the fine-ass brunette.

Cory gives my hand another gentle squeeze. "Did *you* have fun this weekend? I was hoping that since I volunteered my babysitting services, you and Rob would have had a great time alone."

"Well, the funny thing about being married is that after your spouse shows up just to accuse you of sleeping with your friend, a night without the kids tends to be a little tense since it's tough to let go of the reason he's there in the first place." I down the rest of my drink. "I'm only sorry you and your girlfriend had to cut your day short so—"

Cory laughs. "Okay, one, she isn't my girlfriend, and two, I can totally understand your position, but in Rob's defense, I have to say that if I showed up to confront my wife about a supposed affair and she wasn't home, well, I wouldn't instantly think she was at the gym with her BFF and the kids either."

"Well, I was! Tara and I have met with the kids for years now and he knows that! Regardless, that still didn't give him the right to interrupt you and your little friend." I manage to get that last part out through my clamped jaw. "So, for that, I apologize."

"It's all good. I'm just glad I could reassure him it was just the media blowing shit out of proportion." He takes my empty tumbler and goes back to the bar.

I stare at his back and sigh. Okay, it's official. I suck at prying, and that's a good thing. What Cory does on his own time isn't any of my business. I'm married, and as much as I can admit that I have a bit of a crush on Cory Hudson, I really do have bigger problems.

"For what it's worth," he says without looking my way, "I can tell that something is bothering you, and it seems grossly unfair that you're always lending me an ear and helping me through my problems but I can never return the favor." He walks back over, sits beside me, and hands me the refilled tumbler. "I'm here for you, Becca. I hope you know that."

I stare into his eyes for a moment then look out the window. I have two options here. I can either tell him the truth about how I'm feeling—though I don't fully understand it myself—or I can stick to what I know.

Plan B sounds better. "I think Rob is having an affair."

Cory chokes on his scotch and splatters my arm.

Amused and annoyed all at once, I roll my eyes and take the handkerchief he offers. "You should really consider seeing a doctor about that."

He laughs as he pulls his tie loose. "I really should, but I only seem to do it around you, so maybe you should quit randomly dropping bombs on me when my mouth is full."

"Oh, so now it's my fault?" I hand him the handkerchief.

"You're clearly the culprit." He chuckles again as he dabs his shirt clean. After tossing the handkerchief on the end table, his humorous grin dissipates as he sits forward and rests his elbows on his knees. "So, what's making you think Rob is being unfaithful?"

"It's just a feeling. I know that sounds lame, but...I guess I just haven't worked up the courage to do more than stew on the dread of it."

"Ah..." He looks at me thoughtfully for a second. "Maybe he's just distracted. You know the draft is coming up, which is big business, so his mind is probably all about players and stats right now." He sighs. "Dudes are weird like that. Trust me."

"So, when you're getting ready to start production, you're distracted?"

His mouth opens then shuts. He exhales loudly then nods. "Yes. Yes I am." He gets up and heads to the bar, and before I can ask him why he suddenly sounded so strange, he turns to me. "How'd you two meet, anyway?"

I watch him pour more scotch into his tumbler and wonder

why he seems so anxious all of a sudden. "We met in college. I was his tutor."

He turns and leans against the bar, that thousand-watt smile plastered on his perfect lips. "I can *so* see you as a tutor." When I shoot him a dirty look, he laughs. "That isn't an insult," he emphasizes. "Anyway, what were you teaching him?"

"It started out for math, but then I helped him with English." I shrug. "He was a football player, so they don't really stress schoolwork during the season."

There's a beat of silence then Cory chuckles. "You do realize that people write books and movies about the geeky girl winning the super-hot jock, right?"

I look at him and glare. "Forgive me for not agreeing, but my life doesn't feel like a romantic comedy at the moment."

He cracks up at that. "Okay, I'm sure it doesn't, but if it makes you feel better, I don't think you should worry about him cheating."

"Oh, yeah? Why's that?"

"Well, he isn't playing football anymore so I'm assuming he got injured, which means that he's probably vicariously living through his players or—"

My heart skips a beat when I note the brief yet distinguishable flash of apprehension that flickers over his exquisite features. "Or what?"

He clears his throat and smiles. "Or nothing, Becca. Look, I'm sure he's as into his team as I am with acting. He can't play, so he coaches. I didn't have a normal life, so I act."

My jaw drops, but I quickly snap it shut. "Cory, that doesn't make any sense."

"Sure, it does. Do you think I had a carefree high school career and dated the most popular girl in school, or that I went to my prom? Nope. I got my GED when I turned sixteen and started working, so for a little bit of time every few months, I get to be that kid on *Copper Creek*. It's the same thing with Rob."

I stare at him for a long moment then take a sip of scotch. I guess that makes sense, but Cory doesn't know our history. He doesn't know that Rob has cheated on me in the past. Granted, it was when we were in college, but...I don't know. The signs are all there again. Moreover, this weekend was...well, it was downright weird. Rob was so convinced I was cheating on him with Cory, but once he found the little "fine-looking, half-naked brunette" in Cory's room, he was all about apologies. He was sorry that he doubted me, and he assured me that if I ever did cheat, it would probably be with good reason, so he'd probably forgive me. Why traumatize the kids with divorce when forgiveness is a simpler and better option, he said at one point? *Why indeed*. Between my idiot husband and Cory, I'm bound to develop an ulcer.

Cory walks over to the liquor cabinet, pulls open a drawer, and retrieves a script. "Okay, since you've obviously had a bad weekend, let me make it worse. Anna asked me to give this to you on Thursday, but I decided to wait until now so it wouldn't ruin your weekend." He drops the script on my lap.

I read the first few lines and gasp. "She wants Cassie and John to have a sex scene?"

Cory nods. "Unfortunately, yes."

I scan a few more lines then slap my hand over my mouth. When the shock wears off, I clench my hands into fists and glare at Cory. "She wants them to have sex *in* the church *on* his wedding day!"

He nods again. "I know."

I toss the vile script aside and start pacing. "Is she serious? She can't...but I specifically left stuff like that out because I would be mortified to go to work, or look at my parents, or—" I turn to look at Cory. "Can you imagine how humiliating that would be for poor Rebel?"

Cory nods. "I know—"

"No, you don't!" I shake my head. "Kids can be mean, Cory—like really mean. I see it every day at work."

"You don't think I know that?"

He says it softly and without malice, but I instantly regret taking my temper out on him. "Cory, I'm so sorry, I didn't—"

"Don't worry about it." He sets his glass down and takes my hands into his. "Let's just fix it. We have until tomorrow morning, so change the scene so that, at least, on some level, you're okay with it."

"But I won't ever be okay with it." I pull my hands free and run my fingers through my hair. "It's supposed to be funny and cute, not steamy and immoral!" I drop onto the couch and sigh. "This is exactly why I've always wanted to write middle-grade books."

He stands there for a second then heads over and picks up the script. After dipping into his inner jacket pocket, he hands me the script and a pen. "Fix it."

I snatch both out of his hand and open the script to the first page. Cory refills both of our glasses then walks over and sits silently as I read the entire scene. Once I'm done, I take the scotch and apologize for my outburst. It isn't as if he asked me to add the sex scene, but since we apparently need one, I mull it over for a few minutes.

I know one thing with utmost certainty—the whole church thing has to go. Who has sex with their ex-fiancée on their wedding day—in the freaking church! Jeez, that's in bad taste, so I consider doing it the day before, but that still seems wrong. Perhaps setting it during John's bachelor party is best, but he isn't even in town for that because his friends take him to Las Vegas.

I'm nowhere near figuring it out by the time we land, so after we greet Benny and are on our way to Cory's house, I keep picking my brain. The problem is that I never wanted Cassie to sleep with John. Did I want her to realize that she still harbored feelings toward John? Yes, of course, but she ultimately belongs with Randy—her sort-of assistant who's played the role of friend even though he's loved her all along. That's who she belongs with —not John.

That's it! Maybe I can ask Anna if we can do the steamy scene with Cassie and Randy instead—

But...*dammit*. That won't work either because even if Anna agrees to that, then poor Cory would have to have a sex scene with Katie. I know he doesn't want to do that...not unless I beg and plead, in which case, I'm sure he'd do it. I chew on my lower lip for a few minutes and mull it over. It seems grossly unfair of me to ask him, especially since I've made it a point to tell him I've known all along that he doesn't like Katie. How cruel would it be to ask him to pretend-sleep with a girl he hates?

"Oh, Jesus!" Cory exclaims. "I can't watch this anymore."

Shocked, I look over at him. "Watch what?"

"Anna bet me that within thirty minutes you'd beg me to do the scene with Katie so you wouldn't have to write a sex scene between Cassie and John. I said you'd take less than fifteen minutes, but damn, Becca, it's been almost an hour and steam is practically coming out of your ears!"

"Cory, as much as I'd love that, I just..." I sigh.

"Rewrite the script so the sex scene goes to Cassie and Randy. I seriously don't mind."

"Are you sure?"

He nods. "Yeah, I'm sure. And thanks for giving it so much consideration. Most times people can't read me the way you do, and even if they did, they wouldn't give a damn if I wanted to do the scene or not."

I shift over and hug him. "Thank you."

"Yeah, I'm just a regular fucking prince."

I kiss his cheek. "You are."

Excited, I shift so I'm leaning against his arm. After tucking my feet under me, I get to work. There isn't a steamy scene in the book, but now I have endless opportunities to place one somewhere in the story. Initially, I consider the scene after John and Randy get into their fight—which happens when Randy walks in on Cassie and John kissing—but that moment is filled with anger and a heated argument that nearly ends their friendship—not to mention that Randy is all beat up from the fight—so that won't work.

Before I realize it, we're at Cory's house. He ushers me inside, claiming that he has a feeling we're going to be burning the midnight oil, so I head into the living room while he disappears to order take out. When he returns, I use him as my sounding board. Should I make it during one of the weddings or on a night they're just chilling and having dinner? Yet, the question I throw out most often is why do we need a sex scene at all, to which Cory reminds me that sex sells and the gods-that-be want one, so I need to stop asking.

Yeah, I guess I do, but the idea of it still makes me squirm.

When dinner arrives and we're sitting at the smaller kitchenette table, Cory intentionally steers the conversation to recount his time spent with the foster home organization. I know he's trying to calm my nerves, but he's actually doing the complete opposite. I'm still hurt that right after he left the kids and me on Friday night, he probably ran off to pick up that sleazy "fine-ass looking half-naked brunette." Moreover, I'm hurt that he hasn't confided in me about it. Yes. It would kill me to sit and pretend as if I'm the best BFF in the world as I listen to him recount his tawdry tale, but damn it, I would do it.

"Becca?"

My head snaps up. "Huh?"

"I said that you should probably keep using me as a sounding board instead of getting lost in your head like that."

"Yeah, of course." I push the Styrofoam container aside. "I was just thinking about..." I sigh. "Truthfully, I've got nothing."

He shakes his head and laughs. "Okay, can I give you some advice?"

"Of course."

"I think it should happen while they're arguing." I start to object, but he holds up his hand. "Hear me out. As it stands right now, Randy admits that he loves Cassie, but she tells him she doesn't reciprocate, so Randy storms off. Let's scratch him leaving and replace it with their argument escalating and then they have sex. If you write it that way then the next morning Cassie can tell him that it was a mistake and kicks him out. Randy leaves and heads back to California. Cassie still goes through with John's wedding and comes to the realization that she does love Randy." He leans back and winks. "Then we can have two sex scenes if you're good with Cassie screwing John on his wedding day."

I crumple my napkin and throw it at him. "It's bad enough they kiss again."

"Ah, but it's not true love's kiss, so she runs after Randy. See, that wasn't so hard."

"Yeah, but it's easier said than done. We already filmed the fight scene between you and Katie, *and* I'll have to rewrite the dialogue."

Cory rolls his eyes. "What dialogue, Becca? We'll start off with the same lines then wham-bang-thank-you-Katie."

I giggle and push the script toward him. "Okay, Mr. Director, if it's so easy, then *you* rewrite the scene while *I* wash the dishes."

"What dishes? That's the joy of take out." He reaches for the pen and starts writing in the margin of the script. "Cassie unzips Randy's jeans and sighs. Oh, Randy, what a huge cock you have. I don't—"

I gasp and snatch the pen away. "That's so wrong on so many levels!" I crack up for a second. "But when your show is canceled, you can get a job writing cheesy porn."

"What? You said it was easy." He stands and reaches for the empty food containers. "You write. I'll clean up." He stacks boxes one on top of the other and shakes his head. "Jesus, I have to do everything around here," he mutters just before bumping my chair playfully.

I giggle and watch him for a second before I get to work. I try out a few lines then push the script away. In the scene that Cory suggested, Cassie and Randy are in the midst of a huge argument. Maybe it's just me, but I don't usually feel too sexy when

I'm in the middle of a shouting match with Rob. Could I hit him over the head with a frying pan? Absolutely. But would I stop midsentence to make love—probably not. After thirty minutes of staring at a blank page, I sigh and throw in the towel. I have the foundation, so Anna can take it from there.

Cory has since disappeared, so I walk over to the living room and sit on the arm of the couch to watch as he plays some creepy video game.

He pauses the game and sits back. "Are you all done?"

I nod. "I never started, but I'm all done." I slide off the arm and drop beside him. "I just wasn't made for writing sexy stuff."

Cory considers that as he lights two cigarettes. After he hands one to me, he leans back and blows smoke rings. "You just need to get into Cassie's head again. She's your character—your invention—so if anyone is going to do it justice, it'll be you, not Anna." He stubs out the cigarette, takes my hand, and pulls me onto my feet. "Let's act it out."

"What?" I chuckle. "Cory, you of all people know that my acting skills are about as bad as my sex-scene writing skills."

"Bullshit. Everyone can act."

I stub out my cigarette and sigh. "All right, but at least remember you were forewarned."

I follow him into the kitchen to look over the old script. After a moment of going over it, Cory begins, but when it's my turn, I burst out laughing. Actually acting out a scene rather than just saying the lines is a lot harder than I would have ever imagined. I can't do it, especially if it means slapping Cory across the face, which is part of the scene.

After several other hilarious attempts—all of which Cory ends with a loud "CUT!" I seriously attempt to try, but fail miserably.

Cory takes my hands. "Get mad, Becca. Find a moment in your life that pissed you off more than anything you can remember and channel that into Cassie."

Find a moment that I was pissed... That's easy enough to do.

Hadn't I channeled my betrayed emotions when I wrote about John cheating on Cassie? Yes, and it had been easy because I had lived it, so when Cory asks if I'm ready, I am.

As the scene progresses, Cory—playing the part of an enraged Randy—steps closer and points his finger in my face. "What the hell were you thinking, Cassie? He cheated on you before, so now what? You're just going to return the favor—"

Cory should finish that line, and Cassie has several others as well, but I'm so caught up in the moment that I slap him—hard. It feels like the right thing to do, but my own brutality shocks me. I step back to apologize, but Cory yanks me against him and kisses me.

That's definitely off script. The argument is supposed to escalate until Randy finally storms off, but the intensity of Cory's kiss is perfect and just...*wow*. After another second, Cory no longer has to keep gripping my arms so I stay close. Instead, I wrap my arms around his neck and press myself against him.

It's the kind of kiss I write about in my books. The one where there are sparks, butterflies, and lightheadedness. But there's more too. Something I had never known because I've never experienced it before. Hunger. A deep, throbbing ache in the pit of my stomach that churns and spasms the longer we kiss. It's like I've been starved for weeks and I've gotten my first nibble—the forbidden bite that destroys the last of my resistance. I'm in love with Cory Hudson, and I want him in a way I've never wanted anything or anyone before. I rip his shirt open and send buttons flying everywhere, my sudden ravenous appetite needing more.

Cory matches and then exceeds my passion. As he lifts and then slides me onto the table, I suck in huge gulps of air between long, ardent kisses that send goosebumps all over my body. When we fall backward onto the marble tabletop, the jolt of cold adds more goosebumps and I shiver even though I'm not cold. I'm actually burning up, so it's a relief when Cory rips my blouse open. I still gasp though; the brute force of him destroying the garment unexpected but amazingly exhilarating. He pulls the shirt completely off then shifts farther away to kiss and lick my stomach.

I grip a handful of his hair and pull him up for another kiss. I'm not sure how he manages to unsnap my bra while kissing me so passionately, but he does, and then he proceeds to suck on each of my nipples. My back instinctively arches, but the abrupt exposure provides just enough shock to give me clarity.

I bolt into a seated position and push against his shoulders. He leans back a bit, but before I can do or say anything, he kisses me. It takes extraordinary effort, but I finally manage to shift my face away. Regrettably, Cory's response to that is to graze my shoulder with his teeth before kissing my neck.

Damn, why does that have to feel so good?

"Cory—" I moan when he sucks on my earlobe. I summon willpower from some unknown source and shift away from him. When he tries to kiss me again, I press my hands against his chest and hold him at bay. "I'm not Cassie." I breathe in a huge gulp of air. "And you aren't Randy."

He plants both hands on either side of my thighs and stares at me. My labored breathing catches as I recognize the serious-ness captured within his eyes.

"I know." He shifts hair off my face and smiles. "It's kind of funny that you can read everyone so well, yet you can't see what's right in front of you even though it's blaringly obvious."

My frenzied heart rate races faster, the truth in those words so ironic because I've always known that our attraction was mutual—I've just chosen to pretend that it wasn't.

Unsure of what to say or do, I just squeeze my eyes closed when Cory gently kisses my temple.

He exhales loudly. "You've got about five seconds to grab the keys to one of my cars before I force you to stay."

My eyes pop open and I nod, but I don't attempt to stand. Instead, I just stare into his eyes while I search for the right thing to say. Should I apologize? Should I try to explain? I don't know. It isn't as if I have experience in situations like these. Yet, as a thousand thoughts flood my mind and then leave just as quickly; I realize I'm not moving because I don't want to move—not to leave anyway.

Suddenly reconciled in my decision to make the blatantly wrong choice, I still hesitate. Rebecca Carter always plays by the rules. That gives me pause...for a second anyway, but in the end, the lyrics of that Wilson Phillips song pushes me over the edge.

I grab Cory's arm and pull him closer. Oddly enough, he's the one who resists, his posture suddenly so stiff that I have to scoot to the edge of the table so I can press my lips against his. For the briefest moment, it's like I'm kissing a statue, but when Cory's stoic resolves gives, that near-savage intensity returns with a vengeance, and any thoughts of leaving cease to exist—at least for a short while.

Hours later though, with Cory sleeping soundly with his arm draped over my waist, those nagging thoughts return to the forefront of my mind. As exhausted as I am, I take a moment to absorb what just happened because it seems weird that there isn't any regret. *Is that normal?*

Cory stirs and nuzzles his face against the back of my neck. "You okay?" he whispers, a chill shooting down my spine as his breath caresses my skin.

I roll over to face him.

He nuzzles my nose with his, then he cups my face within his hand. "I love you."

And in that instant, I understand why I'm not upset; why there's no guilt or regret. "I love you too." I kiss him softly then roll back over and scoot against him, loving the feel of his body contouring mine. He drapes his arm over my waist and tugs me closer. And as I happily settle into the nook of his body—on the exquisite comfort of the California king bed in *his* bedroom—I allow my eyelids to close slowly, my mind suddenly clear enough to drift off to sleep.

Chapter 20

Chelsea

My grandmother couldn't have picked a worse time to have a heart attack. I know that sounds awful, but flying to Phoenix in the midst of Amanda still missing, Destiny still being nuts, Cory and Rebecca seeming even more chummy than usual, and me and Darryl desperately trying to find time to spend together with our crazy schedules, couldn't have come at a worse time. Despite all that, I went—dropped everything and got on the first flight to be with her, and she's fine now—totally, so I'm beyond ready to get back to my life.

When the airplane door opens, I grab my carry-on and sling it over my shoulder. As I move down the aisle, I send Darryl a text message letting him know I landed safely. Then I check my email. There's one from my Nana thanking me for the visit. It's sweet of her but I remind myself that she still has some venom in her bite, her recovery and my visit slightly marred when I told her I was "talking to" a detective. I shouldn't be surprised though, when you come from a family of criminal defense lawyers, it isn't surprising to hear that they don't like cops.

I send a short email letting her know I made it home then I make my way to the luggage claim. I'm sure my father would send a car if I call him, but it's just easier to take a cab home and let him pay for it. I don't often take advantage of his wealth, but just this once, I'm okay with it. Of course, Mom always tells me that it's silly that I pay them rent and that it isn't necessary, but it's the principal of it, which she doesn't get.

"Chelsea!" Carson shouts from across the terminal.

Oh, no. I shake my head, hoping that I'm just having a waking nightmare.

"Chelsea!" Carson waves ecstatically as he hurries over.

Dammit. Can this night get any worse?

"Hey," he shouts from several feet away. "How's Grandma?"

My cheeks blaze when everyone looks between us. *Jesus, why can't this guy take the hint?* When he finally makes it through the crowd, I wave. "Hey, Carson...Grandma's doing better." I sigh. "What are you doing here?"

He scoffs at that. "I came to give my favorite girl a ride home so I can catch you up on everything you've missed while you were gone."

I sigh again because I know what's going on. It's not like there isn't internet access in Arizona, so I know that all of the tabloids have blown Cory and Rebecca's relationship completely out of proportion...or maybe they haven't, but it doesn't favor Cory and it doesn't help his case regarding Amanda's disappearance.

"I've been keeping up on the stories, Carson. And you didn't have to come and pick me up. I'll just take a cab home."

"No way, the van is parked in short-term parking, so let's grab your bags and go. Are you hungry? We can stop to grab whatever you want."

"Ah..." I clear my throat. "I grabbed some dinner at the airport beforehand so..." I force a smile. "That's sweet, but I just want to go home and...you know...unwind."

"Yeah, for sure," he says. "I totally understand."

Grateful that the conveyor belt starts moving, and lucky enough that my bag is one of the first on there; I grab it and signal Carson to walk ahead. A brief struggle ensues when he insists that he'll take my bags, but the thought of him carrying my luggage seems too kind for my taste. Thankfully, he takes the hint and leads me outside.

"We aren't far from here," he assures me. "If you want, when we get to your place, you can just go in and start getting comfy while I bring the bags inside."

I cringe at the thought. "This stuff is so light, Carson...it's really no problem for me to just take them in with me so you can go home." As we step outside, I decide to switch tactics. "How's your girlfriend doing?"

"Who? Oh, the chick from the bar...it didn't work out—"

He startles when a police siren goes off. Equally startled, I search around to find the source. The flashing lights part like the Red Sea so a black Dodge Challenger can drive through the traffic. Those butterflies erupt out of their cage as I stare at Darryl's car in awe. *Wow. Talk about a grand entrance.*

The Challenger skids to a halt right in front of me. Darryl throws the driver's door open and walks around the front of the car. I'm so stunned to see him, and I'm beyond mortified when the other cops start honking their horns, that all I can do is stare into those beautiful green eyes as he approaches.

There's no hello; no how was your flight—none of that would be his style. Instead, he kisses me. The crowd erupts in applause, which I only hear briefly before I let myself get swept up in the moment. His kisses are always so passionate and intense that I'm actually lightheaded when he leans away.

"I missed you," he says, seeming just as uncomfortably happy about that as I am.

I smile. "I only really thought of you occasionally..." I shrug. "Pretty much whenever you sent me a message."

He laughs that sexy, deep rumble of his, then he kisses me again.

"I can use a beer," I say when he shifts so our foreheads are pressing together.

"All right." He kisses me briefly then picks my luggage off the ground. "Let's get out of here, and I promise, absolutely no interruptions tonight."

I smile and happily let him guide me to the passenger door. It isn't until I'm sitting in the car and Darryl is setting my luggage in the trunk that I finally remember Carson was in tow. "Oh!" I lower the window and stare at Carson, not at all sure what to say to him.

Darryl drops into the driver's seat and leans over the console. "Hey, Carson...I've got it, man. Thanks for the effort though."

I nudge Darryl's arm with my elbow and give him a cross look. He chuckles, so I look back at Carson. "Thanks for the offer, Carson," I say sincerely. I feel bad for the poor guy, but I hope he gets the hint now.

Darryl lowers his window and reaches upward. "All right, let's go get some drinks."

"Wait!" I completely disregard Carson and point toward the car's roof. "Do you really have to take that down?" I inquire of the police light. "I was kind of hoping you still had some beers in your fridge..."

He brings his arm back into the car and looks at me. "I do."

I smile. "Well, since you've got all of this traffic held up, and you already have that flashing light up there, maybe it won't hurt if you leave it on so we can make it to your place quicker."

"Your wish is my command." He chuckles and pulls onto the road. "Is your grandmother feeling okay?"

"Yeah, she's good." When he extends his arm over the cup holder, I place my hand into his. "How's your murder investigation going?"

He shakes his head. "We're at a stalemate."

That's a point of frustration for him, our late-night conversations sometimes focusing on the fact that all of his open murder investigations are floundering—and nothing has changed in Amanda's case—a point of contention for both of us.

After kissing the back of my hand, he sets our joined hands in my lap and squeezes it. "It's whatever. Eric's finishing up the interrogation."

After days of getting to know each other, I know that Darryl and Eric aren't just partners—they're best friends. "Without his trusted sidekick," I tease.

Darryl snorts at that. "I'm not the sidekick."

When we get onto the freeway, Darryl hits Mach Three. I gasp and grip the door handle. *Are we going to make it to his place in one piece,* I wonder, but as usual, Mr. Darryl Morris impresses me, his driving skills, along with his sweet text messages and stellar arrival at the airport pushing me over the edge. I'm totally in love with him—giddy as a damn schoolgirl.

"Are you sure you're up for drinks?" he asks as we near the exit for my house. "I don't mind if you want to just go home and relax after such an impromptu trip."

"I'm good," I assure him. "Unless you want to head back to the station to make sure everything is okay."

He snorts at that. "I'm good."

Then he punches the accelerator. As we blow past my exit, my head presses against the seat rest and I say another little prayer for our safety. "Do cops always use their sirens like this?" I manage to ask even though it was my suggestion in the first place.

He laughs. "Truthfully...and with full disclosure?"

"Absolutely. You know I'll always protect my source."

He glances over at me then looks out the windshield and shakes his head. "Most times, it's important—not that wanting to get some serious alone time with my girl because she's been gone for days isn't important—but for the most part, it's an emergency."

I grin over the reference, especially because I'm suddenly sure I'm not the only one who has taken the chemistry between us to another level. "You are the sweetest man I've ever met."

He brings my hand to his lips and kisses the back of it again before accelerating to even faster speeds. Terrified, I grip the door handle with both hands. Thankfully, he veers toward his exit, but damn if he only slows down marginally as we tear through the residential neighborhood. Darryl switches off the siren a block away from his place and finally slows down. The world is spinning a bit, so I breathe in a huge gulp of air and thank God we made it. Jesus. That was petrifying and thrilling all rolled into one.

Darryl pulls into his garage, turns the car off, and hits the garage remote to close the door behind us. "Are you okay?" he asks, chuckling a bit.

I shake my head and look at him. His beautiful smile falters as he reaches to stroke my cheek. I press my head against his for a second then lean over the console and kiss him. For just a second, it's a gentle kiss, but when his passion intensifies, causing those butterflies to go crazy again, I climb over the console and straddle him. It's a tight fit, but we're both oblivious.

I'm not sure how he manages to open the door and get us out of the car, but he carries me along until we crash against the door to get inside. I pull one arm from around his neck and I find the doorknob. When it swings open, he stumbles forward and nearly drops me. Clinging to him for dear life, I take a second to thank my lucky stars that he rights his footing to keep us from crashing onto the floor. Then I go right back to kissing him.

We make it as far as the living room, Darryl dropping onto the couch so I'm straddling him again. He pulls my shirt overhead, tosses it aside, and then wraps his arms around my waist and kisses my stomach. I moan and have just moved to kiss him when he visibly jerks and then groans and squeezes his eyes closed. I lean away quickly, scared that I somehow just hurt him. "What's wrong?" I ask breathlessly.

He shifts over with me still on his lap and pulls his cell phone from his back pocket.

You've got to be shitting me. This is what happened on our brunch date, but there's no way I'm letting him leave again—not after that picture-perfect reception at the airport and this awesome welcome-home reunion.

Before I can stop myself, I grab his phone and toss it onto the recliner a few feet away. "Five minutes, tops." I kiss him. "No interruptions."

He laughs and lays one of those passionate kisses on me. I lean back, practically rip his shirt overhead, and have just pressed my lips against his when, as if on cue, my phone starts to ring.

Dammit.

Darryl must feel it because he shifts me over and rams his hand into my cargo pocket. "Five minutes." He throws the phone over his shoulder. "Maybe ten," he adds before kissing me again.

I laugh between kisses, suddenly sure that I've met my perfect match.

Chapter 21

Cory

Since Becca and I have taken our relationship to the next level, I've started compiling a list of things I truly dislike about being with a married woman. The first—obviously—is that she's married. The sneaking around, the lying, and the walking away so I'm not subjected to listening to the woman I love talking to her husband as if I don't exist are just a few of the things that top my list. It all pretty much sucks, but I knew what I was getting myself into. Even so, here's what I can't deal with: not knowing if she's going to leave her husband to stay with me. I've spent all week not pushing the subject. I've been patient, and I get that this is probably harder for her than it is for me, so I'm biding my time even though I hate not knowing.

Of course, my little list seems trivial now compared to this newest complication. When Rob showed up on my doorstep this morning to hang out because Becca and Anna went shopping to prepare for tonight's party, I added being BFFs with my girl's husband to the very top of my list. Frankly, it probably wouldn't be so bad if Rob weren't a complete asshole. It's one thing to keep my mouth shut about me and Becca so she has enough time to figure out what—or rather who—she wants; it's quite another when I suddenly understand why Becca thinks that Rob is cheating on her. He isn't a subtle man, by any means, so I'm having a hard time keeping myself from kicking his ass. I get the irony in that sentiment since I've spent a lifetime womanizing, but I'm not married, and with the exception of Becca, I've at least had the decency to respect the sanctity of marriage.

Rob slaps my shoulder as we follow the hostess to our table. "Dude, I thought we got five-star treatment in Denver, but this shit you guys have out here...well, this is just wow."

Brad, who we picked up along the way so I wouldn't have to deal with Rob alone, catches up and falls into step with Rob. "Cory tells me you're the defensive coordinator for the Denver Broncos."

Rob proudly delves into his job description while I proceed to ignore them as I take a seat. Brad gives me one of his "fuck you" glances as he drops into the seat across from mine. I just smile and order a scotch. Yes, I pried his hung-over ass out of bed so I wouldn't have to deal with Rob by myself. That probably wasn't cool, but too fucking bad. The guy owes me because I've singlehandedly made him a millionaire twice over.

As Rob and Brad talk sports, I excuse myself to the restroom. There are perks to being a celebrity, so I flag a different waitress over and ask for a private area to make a call. She excitedly guides me to the general manager's office in exchange for a picture of us together and an autograph on one of the linen napkins. Once she's gone, I lock the door and call Becca. She had no idea that Rob would show up at my place and she apologizes profusely. I tell her not to worry about it, that I only called because I hadn't taken any of her calls this morning and I probably won't until he's gone. I'm all for blowing her cover, but as much as I want that, what I want more is for her to make up her mind without any outside pressure.

Thankfully, lunch commences without a hitch and the conversation focuses primarily on the upcoming NFL Draft. Surprisingly, as much as I think Rob is a douche, and as much as his wandering eye incrementally increases my blood pressure as lunch progresses, the man knows and loves his job. I'm actually actively involved in the conversation until he asks if there's some place we can go to grab some "adult" beverages *and* entertainment.

Naturally, Brad knows every strip club in a fifty-mile radius, so we pile into the limo and head to one of his favorite "classier" joints. I'm not big on strip clubs and I definitely don't appreciate that when we arrive, the paparazzi comes a-flocking to take a billion pictures of the three of us entering the building. In Brad's defense though, the place isn't some sleazy dump with unsavory buck-toothed women milling around. It's nice, and the private room we're directed to is ornate. I grab the seat that's facing a huge, mounted television and ask for a bottle of scotch.

Rob takes the seat next to mine and slaps my shoulder. "What's your poison, man?"

I rotate my shoulder a bit, not appreciating his brute force for a number of reasons. "I got a bottle of scotch."

He laughs. "I wasn't talking alcohol, bro." He motions toward the door. "Destiny is oh-la-la, and that fine-ass looking brunette you were keeping company with in Denver was pretty enticing too, but I was wondering what you planned on ordering off the menu today."

Disgusted, I still manage to force a smile and motion toward Brad. "That's the man who knows all about the menu. I always trust him to do all the picking since this is his spot."

Thankfully, Brad chimes in just as my scotch arrives. As I fill the glass to the rim, I think about that "fine-ass looking brunette," who, sadly enough, was the director of the foster home I visited in Denver. It was amazingly fortuitous for my sake that she just so happened to be there planning the day's events with me so everything went smoothly considering the media circus. I had planned to drop an easy ten-grand donation, but when the front desk called to forewarn me that Rob was on his way up, I asked her to help me out. If she did, I'd hand her a blank check to fill in as she pleased. It took her all of five seconds to make up her mind. She stripped out of her clothes in record time and played the part very well. Her performance was definitely worth the twenty-five grand I ended up paying. It even had Becca fuming, though I didn't hear about that until a couple of days ago.

"Okay, gentlemen," Brad announces, "I ordered food, booze, and ladies. This should hold us until we get to Howard's party."

Oh, joy. It's the director's sixtieth-birthday bash, which I can't miss because I'm Anna's date. Her hubby's off on business, so I get to play the part of fill-in, which I'm not looking forward to. It's one thing to babysit Rob all day; it'll be quite another to endure watching him and Becca at the party tonight.

"You going to the big shindig too?" Rob asks Brad as he pours my scotch into his glass.

"Hell, yes. Howard's parties are infamous. Remember last year, Cory?"

I chuckle. "Oh, yeah."

"Good shit, it should be..." Rob starts but falters as a troop of ladies enters the room.

The scantily clad women definitely deserve his full attention. Being madly in love for the first time in my life aside, I'm still man enough to sit back and eye the women appreciatively for a moment. Brad did a fine job of picking the variety mix. After another moment of admiration, my attention shifts to Rob. He grabs one of the women and pulls her onto his lap. The spell of the beautiful, half-naked women dissipates as I reach for the scotch and refill my tumbler, wondering why I'm so pissed when I really shouldn't be. This is great. Rob is an asshole, which means that aside from fathering Becca's children, I really don't have any competition. So why am I so pissed all of a sudden? And why do I want to snap Rob's neck?

Brad drops in the seat to my left and leans close. "You remember when I said to just have fun while it lasted and to let her handle her own business?"

I look at him and nod.

He pats my cheek a few times and stands. "Forget I said that."

I chuckle, since I never planned to take his advice, but now that I have his stamp of approval, I feel a little more confident about just spending a small fortune on an engagement ring.

Chapter 22

Rebecca

As Rob and Brad go on and on about football, I lower the limo's rear window and pull a cigarette out of the pack. Without notice, and still mid-sentence, Rob grabs the cigarette from between my fingers and tosses it outside. I gasp and then turn to glare at him. He matches my scowl, and we continue to eye each other as I fish another cigarette out of the pack.

Rob drops back and crosses his arms over his chest. "It's a disgusting habit, Beck."

My eyes narrow into fine slits as I light the cigarette. I take a long, hard drag and then exhale the smoke into his face. "So is fucking whores, but that doesn't seem to stop you."

He flinches at my blatant use of profanity. It's a rarity—so is speaking my mind.

After a quick glance toward Brad, Rob clears his throat and shifts closer to me. "If you want to be pissed about the strip club then at least have the decency to bitch about it when we're alone."

I snort. "I'm sure Brad has heard worse." I look to the opposite end of the limo and smile. "Haven't you, Brad?"

He holds his hands up in surrender. "I make it a habit to never get in the middle of marital bliss." He refills his tumbler and winks at me. "You need a refill?"

God, yes. Before I can move to hand him my glass, Rob snatches it out of my hand and shifts closer to the bar. He apologizes to Brad for the awkward marital moment and after handing me my refilled tumbler, goes right back to talking about football. Brad, ever the neutralist, doesn't skip a beat and falls right into the conversation as if nothing happened.

I take a long drink of scotch then lean my head against the cushion and enjoy my cigarette. My thoughts, as they often do lately, wander to Cory. I usually enjoy thinking about him, but at the moment, I'm pissed, seething with a combination of jealousy and carnal rage.

It doesn't surprise me that Brad and Rob went to a strip club, but Cory! Seriously? I mean, hiring a call girl aside, I never pictured him as the kind of guy who frequented such a place— even if it was some high-class joint. Besides, Cory had long ago confessed that Amanda was a fluke. His intent was for her to be nothing more than my replacement, and he admitted that he was glad Destiny had interrupted them before they could sleep together, so why would he agree to let some stripper give him a lap dance? I get that he was just trying to play everything off for Rob's benefit, but that doesn't help my temper.

Talk about hypocrisy.

I could care less that my husband went. I stopped caring about that a long time ago—my complaints always being ignored —but Cory! I actually growl as I light another cigarette. I try to calm myself down, but then I start to realize these befuddled emotions are a good thing. They remind me that I need to figure out what I'm going to do about this huge mess. I'm in love with Cory Hudson. That's a fact I cannot refute, and the only comforting aspect is that I'm not having some random affair *just because*—as Rob once claimed happened long ago. I love Cory, probably more than I've ever loved any man, but that doesn't make it right, and it doesn't make it easier. Am I really going to pack my stuff up next weekend and never come back? Just the thought of it crushes my heart, but I'm a mother and a wife, and a daughter-in-law. Rob's parents are a very big part of our lives. So, despite the difficulties Rob and I have lived through, he *is* my husband and he *is* the father of my children. Not to mention that my in-laws have always been wonderful to me and they would be heartbroken if I move the kids here.

Nor does it help that I was raised to believe that when you get married, you stay married. My mother-in-law has reminded me of that often enough, always quick to pull me aside to reiterate that Rob is a chip off the old block; that he'll eventually realize what a gem he has and he'll finally settle down. That sounds fine and dandy, but how much longer will that take?

Regardless, two wrongs don't make a right, so I can't justify my relationship with Cory based on Rob's continued misgivings. Yet, despite that, after my first night with Cory, I started doing some research. I went through Rob's phone records, then his bank and credit card statements, so I know he's calling a particular phone number on a regular basis, and when he flies to Texas, he spends a lot more money than he usually does on business trips.

Is it another cheerleader? A Dallas Cowgirl? God knows he has a weakness for them.

I sigh, actually not caring this time. Everything I discovered made my relationship with Cory blossom, so does it matter who she is? No. Nor do I really care about Rob and his infidelity. My thoughts are always on Cory. Is he okay? How can I make him laugh? When will I see him again and, most importantly—should I stay?

It's the first time I've ever seriously considered getting divorced, but what if it's for nothing? What if this amazingly, hot relationship fizzles and I walk away from my marriage—permanently scarring my children—for nothing?

I don't believe that—can't let myself consider it, and I know that Cory loves Rebel and Robbie. He sends them tons of gifts and he video chats with them daily—even when I'm not around. Rob ignores Rebel most of the time and he only spends time with Robbie when he's willing to play a sport. Still, would Cory be a good father? I shake off the thought, not wanting to think about *that* right now because that's yet another source of stress I don't need tonight.

I sit back and stare at the passing scenery, so lost in my assessment of my marriage and my relationship with Cory that Rob has to shake my arm to get my attention. He shifts closer and wraps his arm over my shoulders.

"I'm sorry. I know how much you hate me going to strip clubs, but it's a guy thing, babe. We just had a few drinks and a couple of laughs." He kisses my cheek. "You forgive me, right?"

I look at him, studying his face for the first time in what feels like a lifetime. It's funny how marriage can almost make your spouse invisible, but in this moment, I see his handsome face clearly. Then I suddenly remember the first time he walked into the tutoring lab. I remember the way my heart had raced and my cheeks had flushed, and how I giggled when he winked at me and took a seat at my desk. It was love at first sight.

The thought makes me smile, but as I continue to look into Rob's eyes, one particular thought keeps recurring. *He isn't Cory.* He doesn't make me laugh the way Cory does, he doesn't sing and dance with me, or makes me feel as beautiful or desired. And most importantly, he doesn't listen to me the way Cory does. After almost ten years of marriage, I'm pretty sure Rob still doesn't remember my favorite author, actor, or musical group. He can recite the roster of the Super Bowl's winning team from twenty years ago, but he can't remember our anniversary, and most times, he forgets my birthday. I know Cory knows all of that stuff and then some.

Rob kisses my cheek. "Babe, you forgive me, right?"

I sigh. "Yeah, Rob. I forgive you."

He smiles and kisses my cheek again. "That's my girl." He scoots even closer. "How's about we let Brad take our gift in so we can go back to the bungalow?" He runs his finger over my knee and up my thigh. "You really do look pretty tonight."

The thought of us being together makes me feel somewhat ill, which makes me wonder how Rob does it. How does he casually bed women and then come home to me without the least bit of remorse?

He chuckles and squeezes my thigh gently. "What's gotten into you tonight? It's like you're a million miles away or something."

I shrug. "I'm fine. How's about we go in, make an appearance, and then leave."

That seems to satisfy him, so he goes back to his sports conversation. I just stare out the window and sip my drink. When we finally arrive at Howard Knight's house, I take a moment to admire its grand splendor.

"Now this is an impressive house," Rob says as he helps me out of the limo. "We can probably afford something like this now."

I snicker at that. "Maybe, but it's a bit much, don't you think?"

Rob shrugs then wraps his arm around my waist. "Who cares? Let's just go say your hellos and then our goodbyes."

I stop and look up at him, amazed that I used to long for these random nights where I was suddenly the center of his attention. Now all I want is for him to go away because my emotional state is so jumbled that I don't want to be around anyone.

Brad takes the lead and heads inside, leaving the door open for us. The sound of a piano drifts through the air and pleasant aromas assault my senses. Rob pulls me along, once again commenting on my strapless, mid-thigh cocktail dress. He loves it and continues to remind me that he can't wait to get me out of it. I walk along in silence, a forced smile plastered on my lips all the while.

Just as we step inside, Howard rounds the corner and stops to greet us. I introduce him to Rob and after pleasant small talk, Howard guides us to the grand ballroom where most of the guests are dancing or talking amongst groups. My behavior becomes repetitive. I smile and give a hug or shake a hand, introducing Rob and myself, then we move on to the next group of guests. It isn't until I spot Anna that I suddenly perk up. I search the room, looking for Cory, but he isn't anywhere in sight.

"Can you excuse us?" Rob says to Katie Dawn as he pulls me snuggly against him.

"Of course," Katie says before flitting off toward Howard.

Rob guides me through the room.

"Where are we going?" I ask as I follow him down a hallway.

"The bathroom..." He looks at me and winks.

"What for?"

He laughs as he pulls me inside and locks the door. "Because you think it's rude to just leave, so..." He kisses me then guides me backward until my butt bumps against the vanity. I gasp when he grabs my waist and lifts me onto the countertop, the cold porcelain jolting through me. I shove against his chest, but he pushes my hands aside and kisses my neck.

"Stop." I push him again. "I can't do this."

"Ssh. Just go with it." He kisses me roughly, and then forcefully separates my legs so he can squeeze between my thighs.

I shift my face away when he tries to kiss me again, then I place my hands against his chest and push, this time harder. "Stop." I avoid another kiss. "Dammit, Rob!"

He grunts, planting his hands on either side of me. "Jesus, Beck, can't you just loosen up this once and have fun? I'm sure everybody out there has fucked in the bathroom before."

That cuts like a knife. I push him away and get off the counter. "I want a divorce." I don't shout it, or even say it harshly —it comes out more as a saddened whisper.

"What?" He reaches for my hand but I move away. "Beck, where the hell did that just come from?"

"What do you care?" Tears suddenly blur my vision. "I'm just boring and I don't know how to have fun because I don't want to screw you in a bathroom!"

"I didn't mean it like—"

"Oh, yes you did! Because those are the kinds of girls you like to be with!"

"If those were the kinds of girls I wanted to be with, I wouldn't have married you."

I snort at that. "You married me because you knew you could still have all of those girls while I sat around not saying anything because I was just so lucky to have landed a guy like you. Well, guess what. I'm not your Mom, Rob. I'm not going to keep sitting around turning a blind eye while you do whatever the hell you want!"

He grabs my hand. "Okay, I swear I'll never go to another strip club—"

"That's not what I'm talking about and you know it!" I snatch my hand out of his.

Rob runs his hands through his hair then rubs his face roughly. "It's not—I haven't—"

"Just stop. I'm so tired of your lies, Rob." When he reaches for me, I slap his hand away and walk to the door. "You can go back to the bungalow tonight. I'll go to a hotel, and when you get back to Denver, get as much of your stuff out of the house before I get home next week."

"Beck, can you—" He presses a hand against the door and grips my arm. "Can you just wait a sec—"

I ram my elbow into his stomach and yank the door open, making sure to keep my tear-streaked face cast downward as I hurry downstairs and cut through the kitchen to avoid any questions. By the time I get outside, Rob is right on my heels again.

"Please, Beck, can we just talk about this? I'm sorry."

I quicken my step, the limo only a few more feet away. "It's over, Rob."

"Is everything okay, Mrs. Carter?" Benny asks while walking toward us.

"Can you get me out here fast, Benny?"

He quickly backtracks and pulls the passenger-side door open. "Yes, of course."

Rob follows along, begging me to stay, but when I get into the limo and Benny closes the door, Benny and Rob go back and forth a bit. Thankfully, Rob isn't one to make too much of a scene in public, so when Anna calls to him from the front door, Rob turns to reply to her. Benny takes advantage of the distraction and hurries around the limo to get us on the road.

Once we're through the gates, Benny offers me his handkerchief. I take it, intent to blow my nose, but when his phone rings, I startle. "Please don't answer that," I beg.

"I'm sorry, Mrs. Carter, but I have to take it." He pulls his phone out of his pocket and looks at the screen. "It's Mr. Hudson."

I shake my head. "I just..." I wipe my nose. "I don't want to see anyone, Benny. Can you just take me to the Beverly Wilshire?"

He nods and answers the phone. Sitting so close to him, I can hear Cory's concerned voice, which makes me feel worse. I shift closer to the door, open the window, and rest my head against the side panel, glad that the wind muffles Benny's conversation. When he ends the call, I remain in place, wondering if Rob was with Cory during that entire conversation.

Where else would he be though? I had left him stranded at a stranger's house, in a strange city. I just left.

Who am I lately?

In the course of a month, my entire world has turned upside down, and my behavior is so erratic that it even shocks me. I just asked for a divorce. I've been having an affair, and I just called Rob out on his wandering ways, never once divulging that I'm no better than he is. Disgusted with myself, and angry, sad, and confused, I shift so my head is hanging farther out the window in hopes that the wind will quiet the turmoil in my head.

When we arrive at the hotel, Benny insists on walking me inside so he knows there's a room available for me. It is Saturday night, after all, so the hotel could already be at maximum occupancy. Thankfully, there are several rooms available, so Benny escorts me upstairs. The moment we're inside the lavish room, I drop onto one of the couches. Benny serves me a drink and sets it on the table, along with the keycard. We exchange our goodbyes and I promise that I'll call if I need anything. I watch him leave and manage to wait until the door closes before I finally allow myself to cry. Several painful sobs rip through me as I bawl, and it takes a few minutes before I calm down enough to take some calming breaths.

Annoyed by life in general, I snatch my purse off the table, grab my scotch, and make my way to the balcony. It's a smoke-free hotel, but I don't give a damn. I sit on one of the lounge chairs and light a cigarette. There's a chill in the air that at first feels pleasant, but after dropping my butt into the partially empty cup, I shiver. I go inside, grab another drink and a blanket that I wrap snuggly around my shoulders, then head back outside. I'm not sure how long I sit there contemplating the crazy turn my life has taken, but I'm not surprised when someone knocks on the patio door. In fact, the only thing that *does* surprise me is that it took him so long to get here.

Without turning around, I reach for my glass. "I'm going to kick Benny's butt for telling you that he dropped me off here."

Cory walks around the chair and sits beside me. "He actually didn't tell me, and when I figured it out and told him to bring me here and he refused, I fired him."

I jerk at that, some of the scotch slushing out of the cup. "Cory!"

"He just let me have my say." He shrugs. "We both know I don't have the authority to fire him. I was just pissed he didn't make it easier for me to find you."

"Did it ever occur to you I didn't want to be found?" I sigh. "And how did you find me? You got some tracking device on my phone or something?"

"No." He reaches for my hand. "I just stopped and asked myself where you would go on a whim." He kisses the back of my hand then looks up at the night sky and shrugs again. "That was pretty easy to consider given that there's only one hotel in *Pretty Woman*."

I roll my eyes and snatch my hand out of his.

He chuckles. "Scoot over."

I watch him pull his blazer off, but I don't move from my spot because I'm working up the strength to tell him to leave. It's sweet that he came, and sweeter still that he knows me well enough to know that I would pick this hotel above all others, but I want to be alone.

Yet, after he tosses the blazer over the back of another chair, I shift so he can settle against the cushions. Once he's comfortable, I cuddle beside him and rest my head against his chest. It's strange that despite everything that's happened, we can sit in such a comfortable silence. And even when I start crying again, Cory just kisses the top of my head and pulls me more snuggly against him, never saying a word.

I'm not sure how much time elapses before I shift to look at him. "Are you okay?"

He wipes my cheeks and nods. I search his eyes, knowing that he isn't, but I don't say as much. I'm sure all of this is more than he was ever prepared to handle. Don't people like having an affair because it typically means not having to deal with all the drama of a real relationship?

He tucks hair behind my ear. "I love you."

"I love you, too." I kiss him gently then stand and hold my hands out to him.

When he gets onto his feet and reaches for my hands, I'm still unsure of which direction I'm taking him. I know I should be alone to sort through my mixed emotions. I know I should walk him to the door and bid him goodnight, but when we get inside, I glance at the front door for only the briefest second before I continue to the bedroom. I've never acted rationally where Cory is concerned, so there's absolutely no point starting now.

Chapter 23

Penelope

I will enjoy killing this bitch with every fiber of my being. Not only because I've violated the sanctity of my body by participating in an orgy, and not only because Cory has desecrated his body by being with her, but because I've run out of patience with my Grim Reaper spell. I'm ready for a good ole fashion sacrifice now, so with Beltane fast approaching, I've decided that this most important holiday is the best and most enjoyable way to get rid of Rebecca Carter. After extensive research, I know I need to capture her days before Beltane to prepare her and myself for the ritual. My only major problem is figuring out how to abduct her when she's rarely alone.

My best bet would be when she's still in the midst of her day. I've considered the studio, but even though I have an informant there, I don't think that will go smoothly. No. My best bet is to grab her when she's out, and since she, Ethan, and Anna frequent the same restaurant for lunch, I think that would be the best place to grab her. Of course, I'll have to make sure I have enough time to get her alone, but I've thought of an excellent idea to make sure that happens.

So, after another hour of staring at the staff entrance of the Beverly Wilshire, I start my truck. Ethan has been inside for three hours now, having left Howard Knight's party with Rob in Anna's car after getting into an argument with the limo driver. Ethan dropped Rob off at the bungalow then drove straight here. He must have called ahead, because the general manager discreetly met him at the delivery entrance at the back of the hotel, taking Anna's car to park it after Ethan disappeared into the building.

I can't wait until I get to use some of that celebrity star power to come and go at every establishment in this city on a whim—and I will—because once I'm Mrs. Hudson, I won't have to hide in the shadows anymore.

Upset but slightly relieved to know that Ethan probably won't leave tonight, I drive to my house to grab a couple hours of sleep since I'm utterly exhausted after following them around all week. They've been busy, so I haven't yet been able to begin my preparations. I'll sleep in L.A. tonight but I'll have to drive out to my cabin first thing in the morning. There's much to prepare for, so I push my anger aside. It will only distract me from everything I have to do.

I get to the house and pull into the garage. Having only been here to shower the past few days, I walk down the driveway and get the mail. None of my actual mail comes to this address, but I still end up with a bunch of junk mail regardless. Of course, the walk to the mailbox isn't bad anymore—not since I got rid of that obnoxious dog.

As I head back up the driveway, I look at my neighbor's front yard and smile. The living room curtain shifts suddenly, so I stop and look at the window intently. The old bitch pulls the curtain back again, but when she sees I'm still staring, she quickly lets them fall closed. That's right, bitch; mind your damn business and make sure you don't get another little yapper. I'll happily kill that one too—just for the sake of keeping the world a quieter place.

With a bit of a spring in my step, I head into the house.

Chapter 24

Cory

I shift my salad plate aside so the waitress can put my lunch on the table. I absently thank her while keeping my attention on Becca. She's distracted again, which is making me antsy.

"Would you like some fresh-ground pepper, Mr. Hudson?" the waitress asks.

I shake my head. "I'm good. Thanks."

"Would you care for some, Mrs. Carter?" the waitress asks.

"Oh, no thank you." Becca pushes her chair back and stands. "Can you excuse me for a second?"

Reflexively, I scramble to stand. Becca smiles at me before hurrying off. I continue to stand there and watch her. When the waitress shifts to put pepper onto Anna's grilled-chicken dish, I drop back into my seat and take a huge sip of water.

The moment the waitress leaves, Anna casually says, "You know, she's leaving next week..." She takes a sip of iced tea, eyeing me over the rim of the glass all the while, then she goes back to cutting up the chicken breast. "I'm starting to wonder what Brad said that's making you diligently refuse to take my advice."

I chuckle at her attempt to get me to divulge information.

187

She's been at it for days now, but keeping our relationship a secret was Becca's idea, and since I won't betray that trust, especially when I'm feeling positive that she isn't going to leave, I focus on my lunch even though I'm not even remotely hungry.

Startled when Anna slaps my arm, I drop the fork. It clanks against the plate then falls to the floor.

"You son of a bitch!" she whispers vehemently. "Did something happen between you two?"

"What? No?" I shake my head, utterly confused. "Nothing happened."

"You are so full of shit, Cory Hudson. Jesus. How did I not see it before?"

"See what? There's nothing to see."

She slaps my arm again, this time with brutal force. Then her eyes narrow and she leans closer. "On Robbie and Rebel's lives, Hudson."

Ah! Not that...she knows how superstitious I am with shit like that! I look toward the bathroom to make sure Becca isn't on her way back then I meet her scrutinizing gaze. "You *cannot* say anything, Anna. Not a damn peep."

She smiles and pats my arm. "I won't. So when and where? Give me details."

I roll my eyes. "No. I took your advice and now we're..." I lean back and sigh.

"Oh, no..." Anna squeezes my hand. "Did she totally shoot you down?"

I shake my head. "No."

"So? What's the plan? Is she leaving Rob?"

"We haven't really talked about it, but after this weekend...I don't know." I sigh. Shit. I don't know myself—not really—it's more like wishful thinking at this point. "I don't want to push her into anything, so I'm trying to find the right time to ask her to stay."

Anna leans back in her seat, clearly disgusted. "What?"

"She's married, Anna. It's not like she's unattached and she can just pick up and move."

"But you can."

I laugh. "What would you have me do? Move next door and come over to occasionally borrow sugar and be the man on the side?"

"Is that what you want?"

"No, that's not what I want." I look her right in the eyes. "I want it all, Anna. I've even got the ring to prove it."

Anna squeals and squeezes my hand again. "Oh, Cory...I'm so..." She smiles. "She'd be a fool to walk away from you."

The waitress steps next to the table and examines the plates. "Is everything okay with the food, Mr. Hudson?"

"What? Oh...yeah, it's fine. We're just waiting on Mrs. Carter."

She reaches for Becca's plates and mine. "Then I'll just keep these warm for you—"

I shake my head. "No. It's fine. She should be right out." I glance at my watch then look over at the bathroom.

"Would you like me to go check on her?" the waitress offers.

"No..." *Or maybe she should.* We've been here thirty minutes and this is the second time Becca has gone to the bathroom. I look at the waitress. "No, thanks. I'm sure she'll be right out."

After the waitress is gone, Anna reaches for her iced tea and smiles. "If I didn't know that you were the king of prophylactics, I'd guess she's pregnant and that's why you rushed out and bought a ring."

I chuckle at the reference, but then I suddenly begin to feel uncomfortably warm. I *am* the king of prophylactics, but I haven't been using any as of late. It's not because...I mean she surely must be on some form of birth control...*isn't she?* It isn't a question I usually have to ask because my dedicated use of condoms probably keeps Magnum in business. The problem, of course, is that I haven't been so dedicated lately.

"Oh, my God, Cory! Is she pregnant?"

"What?" I shake my head. "No. I..." I look at her, my jaw unhinged. I grab the napkin off my lap and wipe my suddenly sweaty brow. "Why would you even think that?" I finally manage.

"Seriously? The woman has used the bathroom like twenty times today."

"Well..." The room suddenly spins on its axis. "She could be sick."

When Anna's brows arch and she crosses her arms over her chest, my stomach experiences a queasy roll. *Holy shit.* Could I be a dad? Me? How can I be a father when I have absolutely no basis of comparison? Better yet, how is this even a thought in my mind when I've spent my entire life trying not to have kids?

Anna chuckles. "Oh, this just might be what the doctor ordered to get you to finally pull your head out of your ass and work up the courage to give her that ring."

I want that, but I'm not sure this is *how* I want it.

"I'll go check on her." Anna gives my shoulder a reassuring tap before she walks off.

Stunned, I sit back in my seat and run my fingers through my hair. A dad? I'm only twenty-nine years old, which seems young considering, but Jesus, I'd be nearly fifty when the kid left for college. Well, unless it wanted to go into show business. If that were the case, I'd make sure she went to college...wait—what if it's a boy. Nah, I'd want a little girl. I could picture her now, with Becca's blonde hair, and my eyes, but with Becca's smile and laugh.

Wait a minute! What the hell am I thinking about this for? There's no way she's pregnant. She has to be on birth control— though, if she weren't, would that be such a bad thing?

"She isn't in there," Anna says, startling me from my reverie.

"What?"

"Cory," Anna leans on the back of Becca's chair, "she isn't in there. The closed-for-service sign is up, but I still went into the ladies' and then into the men's bathroom and Becca isn't in either."

"What? That isn't possible." I flag the waitress over. "Excuse me. Is there another bathroom our friend could be using?"

The waitress looks at me curiously. "Ah, no, and I saw her go into the ladies' room on my way back to the kitchen. Would you like me to go check on her?"

"I just did," Anna says. "She's not in the ladies' or men's room."

"Maybe she stepped outside to take a call?" the waitress suggests.

I grab Becca's cell phone and hold it up. "Not possible. Is there a staff bathroom? Anna said the closed-for-service sign is up so maybe she's somewhere else?"

The waitress nods. "I'll go check."

After the waitress hurries off, I pull my phone from my pocket and call Benny. Becca isn't in the limo, but Benny could have sworn he saw her drive off with someone. I end the call, more confused than ever since there's no way Becca would just leave in the middle of lunch.

"Well, what did he say?" Anna asks.

"He said he thought he saw her in a Range Rover, but he blew the idea off because he didn't recognize the chick who was driving."

The waitress beelines around some tables and kneels beside me. "She isn't back there, Mr. Hudson. Would you like me to check outside for you?"

"Yeah, I'll go out back with you. Anna, can you and Benny check out front?"

Anna heads to the front of the restaurant while I follow the waitress through the kitchen and out the back door. There's a small parking lot and a single-lane alley that disappears around the building. Becca is nowhere in sight.

"There's really no way she could have gotten back here

without the staff stopping to ask what she was doing, Mr. Hudson."

I loosen my tie because a sudden, inexplicable fear starts racing through my veins. *Where the hell is she?* I take a deep breath to force myself to think rationally, which doesn't help. I can't explain it, but I know something's wrong. With trembling hands, I reach into my pocket for my phone, hoping Anna or Benny have found her, but my hand freezes in place when I spot the purple blossom on the ground. *That flower*...I hurry over and pick it up. It's from a saffron plant, the purple petals and distinctive yellow stigmas a familiar sight because this particular plant has mysteriously been delivered to my trailer every morning for years now.

"That's pretty," the waitress says.

I grab her arm and yank her closer, clearly scaring the shit out of her. "Go inside and call the police. Don't let anyone leave."

As she struggles to pry her arm loose, she looks at me with wide eyes. "What?"

I shove her toward the door. "Now, dammit! Go inside and call the police! Tell them there's been a kidnapping."

Thankfully, the waitress hurries inside, though I doubt it's to go and do what I asked. I jam my hand into my pocket and nearly drop my cell phone after I finally manage to get it out. I dial the Los Angeles Police Department number from memory. The moment an officer answers, I cut him off. "I need to speak to Detective Morris immediately. Tell him it's Cory Hudson and it's an emergency."

Anna and Benny burst through the back door. "Did you find her?" Anna asks.

I hold up the flower. Benny stares at it curiously. Anna gasps.

"Ah, Mr. Hudson," Detective Morris answers offhandedly, "I was just starting to miss—"

"I need you to come down to Spago Beverly Hills. I think my girlfriend has been kidnapped."

"What?" His condensing tone disappears and is replaced with an innate curiosity. "Isn't Destiny on tour? Where—"

"Not her," I snap. "Rebecca Carter is missing. She disappeared after going to use the bathroom and I found a flower—"

"Hang on, Mr. Hudson. I need you to take a deep breath and start from the beginning."

The waitress pokes her head around the door. "The police are on their way, Mr. Hudson."

I nod. "I'll explain when you get here," I tell Detective Morris, then I end the call.

"What's going on, boss man?" Benny asks.

I hold up the flower. "I get this plant delivered every day. It was the same flower they found the night Destiny's house was broken in to, and it's the same flower they found at the studio when my wardrobe was stolen." I stare at the flower, my heart racing and my head spinning from shock. "So I don't think Becca suddenly going missing is a coincidence..." In fact, the longer I stare at the flower, the more I'm certain of it. Becca hasn't just wandered off. She's been kidnapped.

Chapter 25

Darryl

I'm not often stunned into silence, but after Cory ends the call, I stand there and stare at my phone for a long moment before I finally pocket it.

My partner clears his throat to get my attention. "What's going on?" Eric asks. "Did he hear from Amanda?"

I stand and pull my blazer off the back of my chair. "No...or... I don't know, but I intend to find out."

Eric pulls his blazer on as he follows me to the exit. "I'm intrigued. Care to recap?"

"He didn't mention Amanda. He just told me to get to Spago's because he thinks his girlfriend was just kidnapped."

"I thought she was on tour?"

I chuckle as I grab the keys to our squad car from my pocket. "Not Destiny—Rebecca Carter."

"Really?" He drops into the passenger seat and pulls on his seatbelt. "That's not surprising, though. Your girlfriend's tabloid released that story a few days ago."

"She isn't my girlfriend." I start the car and back out of our reserved spot, ignoring Eric's snort of derision.

A few agonizing minutes pass before Eric finally caves. "You know, D, this would be a hell of a lot easier on everyone if you'd just admit that you're crazy about her." He looks over at me. "Falling in love isn't a bad thing."

I avoid glancing his way, and I almost convince myself not to play into his Dr. Phil routine, but he's been at it for days now and I figure it's time to shut him up. "I'm sure falling in love isn't a bad thing when you end up with a beautiful wife and an awesome kid."

Another excruciating beat of silence ensues before he finally says, "You need therapy, man. I'm only saying that because I love you."

I roll my eyes, but I keep my lip zipped. There's no way I'm walking into that conversation. Instead, I look at the dashboard clock and try to estimate if I can make my lunch date with Chelsea. It's a possibility, but I might be pushing it close to the wire.

"I like her," Eric says casually.

Inwardly, I cringe. Outwardly, I'm as cool as a damn cucumber. I knew his relentless attempt to talk about Chelsea would hit peak velocity today. It was only a matter of time since he unexpectedly showed up at my place this morning and met her. Though after nearly four years of being partners, I damn well know he didn't just show up because he was concerned that I hadn't answered my phone. The guy is nosy, and I love him for it, but this whole thing with Chels has me on edge, so Eric needs to back off until I can figure it out.

I glance his way. "Think you can keep your estrogen in check and let it go?"

He chuckles. "Yeah, I can let it go. Can you? Because most guys don't call in assistance to get to LAX for a booty call and then spend days falling off the grid for no particular reason."

"You damn well know I had no intention of getting laid that night, and, just for the record, I'm not falling off the grid. Is there a law that says you can't turn your phone off so you can sleep?"

"Nah, no law broken there, bro. I'm just saying though, it's been a while since you have."

Annoyed that Eric has become more feminine the longer he's been married, I resist the temptation to continue this conversation and move onto more pressing matters. "I'm thinking it isn't much of a coincidence that Amanda disappeared a couple of weeks ago and now we have Rebecca Carter missing too."

"True," Eric says, "but Amanda disappeared after only one night of hanging out with Cory. Rebecca's been hanging with him for weeks with no problems, so what's changed?"

"I don't know, but Chelsea never believed they were having an affair until fairly recently. She said she's pretty sure something has changed since he and Rebecca have suddenly gone from hanging out openly to now keeping shit on the down-low."

"Oh, did Chelsea say that? So instead of pillow talk, you're talking cases?"

I roll my eyes and continue. "Haven't you wondered why Cory all of a sudden stopped calling every day to ask if we've found Amanda?"

"Not really, dude. The man is a famous movie star, so he's probably busy or—and I'm just putting it out there—he doesn't give a shit. We both know he doesn't have anything to do with Amanda's disappearance."

"He might be innocent, but he's the only real lead we have, and the fact that he quit calling got me to thinking that something happened. That's when Chels told me about Rebecca sneaking over and staying the night at his place."

"Chels? Cute pet name."

Grateful for the red light, I take a moment to glare. "Will you shut the fuck up about it if I say I like her?"

Eric shrugs. "I don't know. Try it."

"You're an asshole."

He shrugs again. "Yeah, but you still love me."

I roll my eyes. "Fine, I like her, and I have a lunch date with her in fifty minutes, so can you quit the Dear Abby bullshit and focus for me? Why would a guy who has a sexy musician as a girlfriend—who at the time was still be in town—call Ang?"

Eric shrugs. "Why do happily married guys call Ang? People do it all the time. They usually just want a piece of ass without the attachment."

I shake my head. "It's the similarities, man. Cory was real specific with Ang—like down to details on how to do her makeup and what she had to wear. We've been thinking that he just has a thing for blondes, but what if he was *that* specific for a reason?"

I give Eric a second to mull that over since I didn't make the connection until Chels—whose brain is always on overdrive—brought up that point last night after I mentioned I loved her hair color. I don't normally say cheesy shit like that, but I've always been into blondes myself, so her raven locks are a source of intrigue for me lately. And while I wasn't thinking about the case at all, the second I mentioned it, something clicked in her mind because she scrambled out of bed before I could stop her.

I found her, as I usually do, sitting at the dining-room table pecking away at her laptop. I waited patiently while she pulled up two pictures from her archive. One was of Amanda arriving at Cory's house that fateful Saturday night and the other was of Rebecca and Cory leaving her bungalow earlier that day. Both women were wearing very similar sundresses and their long, blonde hair was similarly styled.

Eric snorts—the obnoxious sound letting me know that it didn't take him nearly as long as me to figure it out. "So, you and Chelsea are thinking Amanda was filling in for Rebecca."

I nod. "Yeah, but that still begs the question, why would Amanda go missing after one night, but Rebecca wasn't threatened until today. And why today? Chels said Cory and Rebecca have been inseparable for days now."

"Maybe whoever is behind the kidnappings doesn't mind if Cory has friends. It only becomes an issue if he's bedding them."

"That could be, but what about Destiny then? Why hasn't she been hurt?"

Eric glances my way. "Maybe because *she's* the one behind the disappearances. Think about it, bro. We blew her off the suspect list because so many people corroborated her alibi, but what if it's been her all along?" He fishes his cell phone out of his pocket to call the station while I flip the siren on and maneuver through traffic. When we arrive at Spago's, there's a squad car in front of the restaurant, so I park behind it. We step inside and the hostess, who's clearly frazzled, greets us.

"I'm so sorry, gentlemen, but we—"

Eric and I hold up our badges.

"We're looking for Cory Hudson," I say.

Her mouth hangs open as she stares at the badges. "He's insisting that we don't let anyone leave, but some of the patrons—"

"Can wait," I say. "Has anyone left the building?"

She shakes her head. "No, Mr. Hudson was adamant and even posted his chauffeur outside."

"That guy right outside," Eric asks while pointing.

The hostess nods and Eric heads to the door.

I turn to the hostess again. "Where's Mr. Hudson?"

"The general manager took him to his office because—"

"Thanks," I say before she can work herself into hysterics. I head into the dining area and look toward a uniformed officer who's kneeling by a table, probably getting the couple's information. Another uniformed cop is standing just outside a door at the back of the restaurant, which I'm assuming is the GM's office. I head back outside because, at this rate, the customers will be here another hour before we can question everyone and get their information.

I signal Eric over and ask him to call for back up, then head into the dining room and hold up my badge. "Good afternoon, ladies and gentlemen. A woman has gone missing from this establishment and we need to question everyone. We're asking for your patience while we work through this. Please remain at your tables; a uniformed officer will come around shortly."

I ignore the angry rants and moans that ensue upon my request, and instead of answering any of the irate questions thrown my way, I head toward the back of the restaurant. I don't know the cop who's diligently taking notes, so I introduce myself and ask him to help his buddy out so I can take over with Cory. Once the officer is out of the way, I note that the stressed-out manager is standing behind his desk. There's an equally distressed woman sitting in a chair opposite the GM who I recognize as Anna, one of the executive producers. Ignoring them, I set my sights on Cory. His face has cleared up pretty good since the last time I saw him.

I look at the GM. "I need you to make sure that all of your staff is present and accounted for." The fat man just stands there, a wild look in his eyes. "You speak English, hombre?"

That clearly offends the man. He squares his shoulders and huffs. "We are right in the middle of our lunch rush, monsieur," he says in a thick French accent.

"Listen, man, I don't really give a shit how I'm inconveniencing you. A woman is missing, so round up your staff and get them into the dining room for questioning." I look at Cory. "Unless she's back."

"No. She's been gone for about forty-five minutes now." He holds up a flower. "And I found this in the alleyway behind the restaurant."

I eye the purple flower. "Does that mean something to you?"

He nods. "Yeah, we found a flower just like this one at Destiny's house after it was broken into, and I found a bouquet in my hotel room once."

"So, someone broke into your hotel room to leave flowers?" I pull out my notepad. "When and where?"

"When I was in Vancouver—"

"I thought I told you not to leave the country—"

"I didn't. It was over a year ago when I was on location. I never reported it because nothing was missing, but I don't think it's a coincidence that these flowers are delivered to my trailer every day and I keep finding them whenever there's trouble."

"Put that way, I'm inclined to agree." I lean against the desk. "Okay, start from the beginning."

Cory is barely comprehensible, clearly upset over the loss of the author, so Anna chimes in often to help with recounting the day's events. I stand there, listening without interruption. When they finish, I rub my hand over my stubble. "And you're sure the closed-for-service sign was up when you went to check on her?"

Anna nods.

"And your chauffeur is positive he saw Rebecca leaving in a Range Rover?"

Cory shakes his head. "He wasn't sure...he thought it was her, but he didn't recognize the driver, and he knew Becca wouldn't leave without us."

I think all that over for a moment. "Okay, I need you two to stay in here while I question the patrons and staff."

Just as I reach for the doorknob, Cory blurts out, "Detective Morris! Did you find Amanda?"

I don't even bother stopping, I just shout a "no" over my shoulder, then close the door behind me. Several uniformed officers are milling around now, while some are kneeling beside or sitting at tables speaking to the patrons. Eric has since made his way inside, and he's questioning the staff. I look at each of them, but I stop short when I notice a Hispanic man who is sweating profusely and is folding a napkin into tiny squares.

Cory suddenly steps beside me. "Shouldn't you call an Amber Alert or something?"

I look over at him. "Didn't I tell you to stay in the office?"

He matches my stare.

I finally roll my eyes. "Just stay the hell out of my way, Hollywood." I step closer to the suspicious-looking man. "You speak English, hombre?"

The young man looks up at me. His eyes widen and his jaw drops as his attention shifts from me to Cory. "*Si, un poco.*"

I look over at Cory. "You got a picture of Rebecca?"

He pulls his cell phone out of his pocket and swipes through several screens before he holds the phone toward me. I take it, look at the image for a second, and then I look the man over again. I've met guys like him before. He's probably trying to support a family of ten on his meager busboy salary and he probably doesn't want trouble. Or at least I hope not.

I finally face the screen toward him. "Do you recognize this woman?"

The busboy stares at the screen, a bead of sweat rolling down his cheek when he shakes his head. "No."

Oh, this is just fucking great. Starting with a lie is definitely going to make me miss my date. "Listen, man—"

"He's lying," Cory interjects.

Incredulous, I look over at him. "Do you mind?"

"He's lying," Cory shouts.

Before I can tell him to fuck off, Cory grabs a handful of the busboy's white tee shirt, lifts him out of the chair, and slams the man onto the table. Then, to make matters worse—or more interesting depending on how you look at it—Cory grabs a nearby steak knife and presses it against the busboy's neck. "Where is she?"

The distant chatter that filled the restaurant a moment ago abruptly stops. I take a quick glance around before stepping closer to Cory, not at all surprised that every eye is now on us. I gently place my hand on Cory's arm and apply just enough pressure so he gets the hint to get the knife off the man's neck. He doesn't let up, though, which doesn't surprise me. Family members are notorious for overreacting, so I keep my hand on Cory's arm and step closer still.

I look into the petrified busboy's eyes. "You might want to tell the man what he wants to hear because I might not be quick enough to pull this knife away before he does some serious damage."

"*Si...si...*I talk."

Cory backs off, but not by much. The busboy rubs his neck a few times then jams his hands into his apron pocket.

Instinctively, I shove Cory back and pull my weapon from my holster. "Pull your hands out nice and slow."

The man slowly pulls his hands out of the pocket, a wad of rubber-banded cash clutched in his right hand. "The lady give me money." He starts crying. "She give me money and tell me put sign when *rubia* go to the bathroom."

His accent is so thick it's hard to understand him, but after years of working with Hispanics, I pick up enough of what he says, and I get the sense that this part of the story is true. I put my gun back into my holster and take a step back. "Tell us what we want to know and we'll back off."

The man doesn't move other than to nod. "She here early. She show photo and say put sign." He starts to reach for his apron again.

I pull my gun out of the holster again and release the safety.

"It money." The man says, holding the wad of cash toward me and then pointing to the apron. "She say she no get hurt. She say...ah, *un autographo*."

I holster my gun, take the wad of cash from the busboy's hand, and then I reach into his apron to grab another wad. I unravel and count it, then hand the two grand to Eric.

"Describe the woman who gave you the money," I order.

"Ah...eyes dark..." He looks at a fellow busboy and he begins speaking Spanish too quickly for me to catch much of any of it.

The other busboy nods and looks at me. "He said she was tall, about his height, and she was thin and well-dressed, and very pretty." The busboy rattles something off to the man who looks at me in turn. "He said she was very friendly and that she had the lady's book. She told him that she just wanted an autograph."

I look at the busboy. "Did she come here before they got to the restaurant?"

"*Si*. She come early...ah, *diez y media*."

"He said she was here around ten thirty," I say to Cory and Anna since, at some point, she made her way over. "Who would know you guys were coming here for lunch today?"

"I don't..." Cory looks at Anna. "We come here all the time."

"Right, but did you plan to come here today? Did you mention that to anyone other than between the three of you and the limo driver?"

"I told my assistant," Anna offers. "I asked her to call in our reservation, but Claire always makes the reservation."

I signal the nearest uniformed officer over. "Can you get a sketch artist over here so the busboy can give us a description of the woman?" I turn and look at the GM. "Do you have security footage of the alley out back?"

He nods. "But it only shows the back door and part of the entryway."

"It'll be a place to start. Eric, can you head over to the studio and have it locked down?"

"I'm on it. What's the first and last name of your assistant, ma'am?" he asks Anna.

"Claire Woods."

"We'll meet you there," I tell Eric, tossing him the keys. "Mr. Hudson—"

A phone rings, startling Cory. He pats himself down before reaching into his trouser pocket. He stares at the phone, clearly shocked, or maybe scared. I can't tell which. After another moment of staring, he finally answers the phone.

"Rob, have you—" He runs his hand through his hair. "It's Cory. Have you heard from Becca?" He looks off into the distance while he listens to the response, then he shakes his head. "I...listen, I don't know how to say this, but Becca's missing—" He flinches and exhales sharply. "It's been over an hour now..."

He turns his back to us then steps farther away, making it impossible for me to hear what he's saying. I look at Anna. "Is that her husband?" I ask to clarify.

"Yes," Anna confirms.

And the plot thickens. "Where is he now?"

"Denver, or maybe somewhere else...I don't know; he travels a lot."

"Does he know...?" I motion to Cory.

Anna gasps and pulls me farther away from Cory. "Rob doesn't know about them, and it needs to stay that way. Nor is Rob a suspect—"

"I never said that, lady."

"Well, you didn't have to. Isn't there some security footage you should be watching, or shouldn't you be putting out an APB on every Range Rover in this city?"

I roll my eyes, always amazed that people think I can make everything happen all at once while *they're* the ones taking up my time. I turn to the GM. "You wanna show me that footage?"

"Of course," he says. "Can we allow the guests to leave now?"

"Not until we've questioned everyone and we've gotten their contact information." I look at Anna. "Where's your limo driver?"

A short, Caucasian man steps closer and raises his hand. "I'm here. Benny Banks."

"Come with me," I say as I motion to the GM so he gets moving.

The surveillance cameras are located in the GM's adjoining office. It's a small space, but there's enough room for Benny and me to sit. The GM, who's a large man, moves closer to help with the equipment, but after his gut brushes against my back one time too many, I tell him I can manage. Thankfully, he takes the hint and disappears.

While I rewind the footage, Benny explains he believes he saw Rebecca leaving with an unknown woman in a Range Rover. I half listen as I stop the tape at exactly ten thirty and allow it to play. True to the busboy's word, he steps outside with a cigarette and a mug of something—probably coffee—in hand. He takes a few steps away from the door, but I can still see a pretty good portion of him as he leans against the railing, smoking and sipping his drink leisurely.

When the busboy suddenly shifts, I stop the tape. Benny,

who's clearly just as intrigued, obscures my view when he leans closer to examine the monitor. I clear my throat. He drops back into his seat, apologizing while I scoot my chair closer to the desk. After a quick rewind, I play it again, this time carefully watching the busboy when he abruptly turns west because something gets his attention. I rewind and replay the tape in slow motion, monitoring every part of the available screen for clues. Unfortunately, no additional information is forthcoming other than the busboy dropping the cigarette, stepping on it, and then walking westbound until he's no longer in view.

After rewinding the tape to earlier in morning, I fast forward through hours of footage in hopes of catching sight of whoever signaled the busboy over to the dumpster. Unfortunately, whoever was hiding behind the dumpster was smart enough to stay off camera. Frustrated, I leave the office to go look around. Benny follows behind, so I consider telling him to wait inside— especially since I suddenly feel like I've been thrust into an episode of Scooby-Doo and the gang—but I keep quiet since I need his statement. After I get it, I'll be completely done with Benny Banks and all of Cory Hudson's would-be sidekicks.

I push the back door open and step onto the small loading dock.

Benny stops beside me. "She must have been waiting behind the dumpster."

I look over with narrowed eyes. Benny takes the hint and apologizes again.

After a thorough inspection of the alleyway, I walk over to a pair of muddy tire tracks that are a stark contrast against the cracked, gray cement. "What color was that Range Rover?" I ask Benny.

"It was white with chrome trim."

I kneel beside the tracks, wondering why that vehicle description nags at me. Annoyed that I can't put my finger on it, I decide to walk over to the dumpsters because I know that if I quit thinking about it, it'll eventually come to me. "Where did you say you were parked?"

Benny walks over and points down the alleyway. "If you drive around here, you'll come out on the street. I was parked on the other side."

I signal him to follow, and he thankfully doesn't run his trap as we walk along, smart enough to notice I'm not too chatty-like in the first place. Once we round the corner and we have a clear view down the alleyway, he says, "You should ask Mr. Hudson where he found the flower. That might help."

I'm usually amused when people think they can solve a case because their favorite show is *C.S.I.* Today, though, it's just annoying me further, so I stop and glare. "Yeah, I'll get right on that." I point to the limo across the street. "Is that yours?"

"Yes, sir," Benny says.

"And that's where you were parked when you saw Rebecca?"

He nods. "I looked out the window and I thought I saw Mrs. Carter in the passenger seat, but the lady made a right just as my window was coming down, so I couldn't tell for certain."

I continue along, heading toward the street. "Does the driver match the busboy's description?"

"Yes."

"Did you happen to catch any part of the license plate number?"

He shakes his head.

Damn, that would have made this a hell of a lot easier considering there are probably a billion white Range Rovers registered in the Los Angeles area. I walk toward the street, intent to see if the restaurant has any cameras pointed in such a way that it might have caught the SUV on film, but I abruptly forget about my search when I see the media frenzy in front of the restaurant. *Dammit.* As if hanging with Scooby and the gang isn't bad enough, now I have the media to contend with too.

Double dammit! The crowd gathering around the restaurant suddenly reminds me of my date. I look at my watch and sigh.

Great, another date down the drain. It's no wonder my marriage only lasted fifteen months.

A nearby horn honks and snaps me out of my reverie. I turn and see Chels getting out of the passenger side of an *Entertainment Nightly* news van.

"Fancy meeting you here, Detective," she says innocently.

When she flashes that sexy smile of hers, I grab her arm and pull her along as I hurry us back down the alleyway. "What are you doing here?"

"Um, I'm working, silly. I'm Cory's paid stalker on duty, remember?"

Damn she looks good. I shake the thought off while letting my hand trail along her arm to grab her hand. "I'm gonna have to skip our lunch date. Can we do dinner instead?"

She smiles again and pulls her hand free so she can rummage through the purse that's hanging crosswise along her torso. "I kind of figured we'd have to skip lunch, so here," she pulls a small, brown paper bag out of her purse, "a dozen Krispy Kreme donut holes and a chocolate-flavored Muscle Milk." She kisses my cheek. "Go find the damsel in distress. I'll see you whenever you can squeeze me in."

When she starts to walk away, I grab her arm and pull her back. After a quick kiss, I shift her bangs away from her eyes. "Where have you been all my life?"

She giggles then kisses me again, this time a little bit longer. "Oh, I don't know. Dealing with my own shit, I guess." That sparkling smile fades and reveals a level of concern that she quickly attempts to cover with another smile—except this one isn't genuine. "But I'm here now, so can you be extra careful for me?"

I nod, suddenly reminded that this thing between us is moving way too fast and neither one of us is comfortable with that. "Can you call me if you find anything out on your end?"

"Will do, and likewise, mister." She pokes my stomach then

turns and heads toward the street. "I'll see you tonight," she calls over her shoulder, "even if it's just for five minutes."

"Ten at most!"

Her laughter reaches my ears and I get a chuckle from what's become our running joke. Five-to-ten minutes the night before had lasted all night and damn near all morning, which is why Eric showed up at my place to see why I wasn't answering my phone.

Benny suddenly steps into view and clears his throat.

Before he can open his trap, I walk past him. "Shut up. I know it's hard for some people to believe, but cops do have lives outside of work."

He chuckles. "I didn't say anything."

"Good. Let's keep it that way."

We walk to the front of the restaurant in blissful silence, and when Benny enters the building, I stop long enough to look toward the news van. Chelsea waves and blows a kiss. I give a slight nod in response and head inside, a little bit concerned that I can't entirely focus on the case because I'm way too busy thinking about her.

Chapter 26

Penelope

I yank Rebecca's limp body toward me so she falls out of the Range Rover. I attempt to break her fall, but her body is so limber that she slips through my arms and lands on the ground, her left foot awkwardly catching on the running board.

Damn, who knew pistol-whipping someone was so effective?

The bitch is out cold, and I'm sure the jarring fall hasn't helped, so I kneel and grab handfuls of her shirt, expecting her to be light enough to drag to the porch, but it's like pulling a bag of bricks. *Jeez.* They really do make this look a lot easier on TV.

I release her shirt and loop my arms through hers, pulling her back against my chest and hoisting her up a bit. With extraordinary effort, I finally manage to drag her inside the cabin. Once her feet are over the threshold, I drop her. She crashes onto the hardwood floor, an audible and quite amusing thud reverberating through the room. I chuckle as I wipe sweat off my brow. After stretching to alleviate the burning sensation in my lower back, I head toward the kitchen. Water is definitely in order before I drag her to the back room. I go to the refrigerator, open a bottle, and take a long swig while I stare at Rebecca.

As resentment and anger replace my exhaustion, I slam the

water bottle onto the table and walk over to her. I kick her, and I become angrier when she doesn't respond. I kick her again, but I get the same non-response, which further infuriates me. With rage coursing through my veins, I grab a handful of her hair and tug her down the hallway, dropping her only long enough to open my old bedroom door, then I grab her again and drag her inside.

I prepared the room earlier this week, hoping to bring her here days before, but the bitch was impossible to get because she was either at the studio or with Ethan. Before now, I wondered how I would get her atop the inverted cross I prepared for her, but with a fiery rage coursing through my veins, I have no such doubts that I can lift her. The section of cross where the two thick pieces of wood intersect is wide—Rebecca's tiny frame fitting onto it perfectly. I press my hand against her chest to keep her from sliding off then I reach for the leather strap with the other hand and drape it across her breast. After securing that strap, I fasten her knees, ankles, and wrists in the same manner.

Rebecca's cheek rests against the wood. I shift her face so I have a clear view of her bloody, matted hair. I run my finger along the blood, forcing away the temptation to shed more of it— to just kill her now and be with done with it—but I can't. Not until Sunday, so this will have to do for the moment. I suck the blood off my finger then place the final strap across her forehead. She probably won't wake up for a while, but I put a piece of tape over her mouth so I don't have to listen to her when she finally does come around.

Glad that this part of my job is over, I step back and admire my handiwork. A chill suddenly creeps up my spine as I stare at duct tape, the memory of my mother always saying that "silence is golden but duct tape is silver," just before she taped my mouth shut resounds through my mind for a brief instant before I force the annoying memory aside. Rebecca Carter deserves to be bound and gagged. I never did.

More annoyed than ever, I hurry out of the room and slam the door behind me. There is much to prepare for, so even though I have to wait until Sunday to sacrifice her, I intend to make sure that she knows just how much I hate her before that day comes.

Chapter 27

Cory

Getting to the limo is a nightmare, the media frenzying so much that I'm groped and tugged at; a member of the press actually ripping my watch off in his desperate attempt to ask me questions. Detective Morris and several uniformed cops finally clear the path enough for Anna and me to get into the car. Detective Morris sits in the back while a uniformed cop gets up front with Benny.

My cell phone has been ringing off the hook, so I pull it out my pocket. My hope soars to drastic heights because I'm praying it's the kidnapper calling for a ransom, but the caller ID dashes them. It's just Brad. I ignore another incoming call from him and fish Becca's phone out, setting each on my knees.

"They're going to find her," Anna says. She takes my shaking hands into hers and squeezes them. "They'll find her."

I stare at her, but I can't respond. I feel sick—like really sick. I rip my hand out of hers and lower the window, my stomach so torn up that I think I'm going to puke.

This seriously can't be happening.

I have to be having the worst nightmare I've ever had—even worse than the beatings I used to get as a kid—even worse than watching my mother wither away to skin and bones as the virus slowly destroyed her.

This is worse. So much worse.

Detective Morris scoots to the other end of the limo and starts whispering into his phone while scribbling on his notepad. My stomach settles down as I watch him, for some reason reassured that this man—who has been nothing but a pain in my ass the past few weeks—is going to find Becca. I'm not sure where my faith comes from, but it gives me enough hope to lift the cell phones off my knees and move closer to him.

My cell phone rings again. It's Brad, so I press the ignore key and slide toward the detective. "Shouldn't they have called to ask for a ransom by now?"

He holds up a finger, scribbles something down, and ends the call. He looks me over while he sits back. After placing the notepad and pen back into his inner jacket pocket, he rubs the screen of his phone against his slacks. "How long have you had this stalker of yours?"

I shrug. "I don't know...maybe a while, I try not to pay attention."

Detective Morris sits forward and places his elbows on his knees. "The funny thing is Mr. Hudson; I need you to think about it long and hard, because if this man or woman has been after you for a long time, there might not be a ransom call."

"Why not? I'll give them whatever they want—"

"But what they want is *you*—not your money, not your house, or not anything you possess, so focus for me. How long have you had this stalker?"

Anna scoots closer. "She was sending you those flowers and edible arrangements on our first film, so it had to be before then."

I sit back and try to remember when I started receiving the saffron plant. In an odd moment of clarity, I snap my fingers. "It was right after I did a mandatory charity event for *Copper Creek*. I've only ever done a few, but it was right after those wildfires. The producers asked us to show our support because we had just started filming our first season and he wanted the press coverage to help with our ratings."

"Okay, good start. Can you give me specifics?" Detective Morris asks.

"Um...not really. The studio planned it all and they bused the entire cast to all the places we went." I try to recall all the places I went that day, but it was so long ago that I'm only pulling up the vaguest memories. "I'm pretty sure I started getting those flowers right after I started filming the second season," I finally offer, though I can't be certain of that.

Detective Morris pulls the notepad out of his pocket again. "Where were these charity events?"

I snort. "Are you serious? I don't remember!"

"I'll find out," Anna interjects. She scoots over, reaches for her cell phone, and places a call.

"Is there anything else you can think of?" Detective Morris asks. "Anything, Cory? Even the smallest detail might help us find Rebecca."

Suddenly overwhelmed with sickness again, I drop back onto the seat and pull my hair. After a lifetime of habitual drug and alcohol use, my memory is shot.

Anna scoots closer, her tablet in hand. "They did two appearances with the American Red Cross, one with the Salvation Army, and one with The Humane Society."

"Did you meet with fans or did you just do appearances?" Detective Morris asks.

"Both. I sat for hours signing autographs and taking pictures."

He writes something in his notepad. "It's not much, since I'm sure you signed hundreds of autographs, but it gives us someplace to start. Were all of these appearances in California?"

I nod, grateful that I at least remember that much. Detective Morris receives a phone call, so he holds up a finger and answers. Anna slides closer to me and hands me a tumbler filled with scotch. I consider pushing it away, but after a second, I down it.

Benny announces that we're at the studio, so I look out the window, disgusted by the large crowd of reporters surrounding the gates. It takes a bit for us to get inside the studio, my cell phone ringing four times while we wait. All the calls are from Brad, and I consider answering each, but I don't want to tie up the line in case the kidnapper does call to ask for a ransom—something that I would pay without hesitation—even if that meant exchanging places with Becca.

When we get to our lot, Detective Morris steps out first. The studio already increased security since Rebecca's disappearance, so the second he hits pavement, he turns to leave.

I grab his arm before he can rush off. "Where are we going?"

He shakes my hand off. "I'm going to question the cast and crew. You can go to your trailer and wait. I'll let you know what I find out."

"What?" I shout, but the detective hurries away.

Anna grabs my arm and starts dragging me in the opposite direction. "Let him do the investigating," she says as she pulls me along.

Despite my desire to pull away from her, I can't. My entire body is numb and I suddenly have a raging case of the shakes. I thought they would dissipate after shooting down a drink, but I'm still trembling badly. Nor can I stop the nagging questions that continue to resonate through my mind. Where is she? Is she safe? Have they hurt her?

The relentless questions turn my stomach. Could someone really harm her delicate skin? Images from slasher flicks ensue even though I try to push them away. *This isn't a movie, Cory—it's real life—so there's no way that stuff applies.* Yet, even as I tell myself that, the persistent notion that those movies usually have a grain of truth to them drives my stomach over the edge. I yank my arm away from Anna and puke.

Becca doesn't deserve this—not her...anyone but her. She's sweet and kind, so could someone really hurt her when she's so undeserving of harsh treatment? Would they harm her because of me? Would they make her disappear the way Amanda did?

"Come on," Anna whispers, "we're almost there."

I follow along and take the napkin Anna offers to wipe my mouth. I trip up the stairs, but Anna guides me along and pushes me onto my recliner. I plop down, a million thoughts going through my mind all at once. Anna kneels beside me and places my hand around a glass. I look at it, gawking at the amber liquid for a long moment before I throw it across the room. A bit of scotch splatters my arm as it sails out of my grasp and crashes against the wall, shattering upon impact.

"They'll find her," Anna says softly, seemingly unfazed by my tantrum.

I look her straight in the eyes. "What if they don't?"

She squeezes my hands. "They will."

The door suddenly opens so violently that the trailer rocks. A huge Guido-looking guy steps inside. An equally huge black guy follows. I get onto my feet and shove Anna behind me. "Who the fuck are you?"

Without answering, the guys shift against the wall to let Brad and my publicist walk up the stairs. "Would you answer your fucking phone?" Brad shouts. "Why the fuck do I need to find out what's going on with you through the fucking media!" He walks over to me, his displeased expression melting away to reveal genuine concern. "Are you okay? Have you heard anything?" He slaps my face a few times. "We're going to find her, my man, but first we have damage control. Dana!"

Dana hurries over and taps her tablet. "CNN, BBC, NBC, CBS, and every other network are covering the story. Social media has Cory and Rebecca trending in the top ten."

Shocked by the news, I stumble back a bit. "What?"

"You can't hold fifty people hostage at Spago Beverly Hills for an hour and not expect this! The media is frenzying," Brad shouts.

I drop into my recliner again, the room suddenly spinning so much that I squeeze my eyes closed.

"They have photos and video of Cory holding the knife to the busboy's neck," Dana says in a sterile tone. "And enough time has elapsed that they've retrieved photos of him and Rebecca together. Right now, the media is stating the source of the kidnapping is because of a lurid affair—"

"What?" I get onto my feet, my shock subsiding to allow my rage to take center stage.

"Some of the media outlets are claiming a vicious stalker while social media is pinning the abduction on her spouse."

"That's ridiculous!" I snatch the tablet out of her hand. "Rob would never hurt her." I tap on the tabs Dana has opened, the flame of my rage intensifying as I read the headlines. "This is all making Becca look like she deserved this!"

"You and Destiny broke up two weeks ago, so your fans are blaming her," Brad says evenly. "We need to release a statement to try to keep this from getting completely out of hand before it affects your reputation—"

"Fuck my reputation, Brad! Becca is missing. That's the only thing that matters—"

"What matters is keeping you as the Golden Boy in the eyes of the public, Cory. Your fans pay your salary—"

"And yours!" I shove the tablet against his chest. "But this isn't about me, or you, or the fucking media! Two innocent women are missing because of me, Brad, so I don't give a rat's ass about the press at the moment!"

Anna steps between us. "Okay, let's all count to ten and take a minute to cool down." She looks at Brad. "Get rid of the publicist and the goons."

Brad glares for a moment but then turns and dismisses everyone. Once they step outside and close the door, Anna walks over to the bar and serves three drinks. "Brad, you need to back off, and Cory, he's right. You need to make a statement."

I start to object, but she holds her hand up to silence me. "If you want the media to quit dragging Becca's name through the mud then use that star power to change their minds."

I take the drink she offers and consider that. Without taking a sip, I hand the glass back to her and nod. "Okay. Tell Dana to release a statement saying that I've been struggling with a heroin addiction for—"

"Are you out of your fucking mind?" Brad shouts. "That's not damage control, Cory, that's career suicide!"

"We do it my way or you're fired!"

Brad and I exchange murderous glares before Anna steps between us again. "Take a deep breath, fellas. I'll write the press release. Brad, go get Dana. Cory, go change your damn shirt because you smell like vomit."

Anna grabs my arm and drags me toward the bedroom. After shoving me inside and slamming the door behind her, she whips around to face me. "You need to pull it together, kiddo, and you need to take advantage of the media. They are all over this story so use them to help the police find her."

I've spent my entire time in Hollywood hating the press, but in this instance, she's right. I tug my blazer off and pull my tie and shirt off.

"Atta boy," she says then nods, "get changed and pull it together. Don't worry about Brad or the press release. I'll do those. You need to focus on Becca and getting her back."

Anna leaves, pulling the door closed behind her. More focused than I can ever remember being, I walk over to the closet and pull the door open. After putting on another button-down shirt and tie—mostly because Becca prefers me in them—I pull on another blazer, fish her cell phone and mine out of my old jacket, and step into the living room area. Anna and Dana are leaning over the table, hushed whispers passing between them as they type away on the tablet.

Brad walks over and we face off for an intense moment. As is usually the case though, Brad relents first and pulls me into an embrace. I'm still pissed, but I squeeze him tightly.

When he finally steps away, he slaps my cheek a few times and smiles. "Okay, what do you need from me?"

Glad that we're on the same page, I nod toward the bodyguards. "Can you have one of your goons find Detective Morris for me?"

Brad walks over to the Guido-looking guy, and I head to the girls. "Call a press conference," I tell Dana. Then I look at Anna. "I know what I need to say."

Dana hesitates, but when Brad nods his agreement, she disappears outside. A moment later, the door opens and Benny comes inside. We all turn to stare at him.

"Have they found anything yet?" I ask him.

Benny shakes his head.

More determined than ever to face the media and ask for help, I walk to the door, but the bodyguards bar my exit. I go to tell them to move out of my way, but I manage to bite my tongue. I've never used bodyguards before, but I suddenly understand the need for them. It takes a second to coordinate, but we eventually end up corralled between the two guys like cattle. The walk to the main gate feels as if it takes an eternity, but I force myself to slow my pace so we remain sandwiched between the behemoth bodyguards.

As we near the gate, the press becomes eerily quiet. I'm not sure why I'm so unnerved by that. I step behind the podium, making sure to grip the wood with both hands so no one can see them shaking. I've never had stage fright before, which further unnerves me, so I avoid looking at anyone in particular.

"I would like to confirm reports that earlier this afternoon Rebecca Carter was kidnapped from Spago Beverly Hills. We are asking for everyone's cooperation during the investigation."

A murmured whisper passes through the crowd.

"Regarding the less important matters that are currently being discussed, I feel it's imperative to emphasize that Rebecca Carter is an amazing mother, wife, educator, writer, and friend. She and I *have* been spending a great deal of time together the past few weeks, along with some of my closest friends," I motion toward Anna, Brad, and Benny, "because they are all helping me overcome my addiction to heroin."

There are audible gasps, and several reporters step closer and begin shouting questions. I ignore them and continue.

"Rebecca and Robert Carter have welcomed me into their family and it is with their encouragement and support that I have made the decision to enter rehab following the completion of filming *Bridesmaid for Hire*. As their friend, I'm asking everyone to pray for Rebecca's safe return and to respect her family's privacy during this difficult time."

I look over at Anna, and in her usual nurturing way, she nods. With that out of the way, and with the hope that I've ensured that Becca's reputation is untarnished, I turn and lean closer to the microphone.

"Regarding the investigation. I am offering a twenty-five-thousand-dollar reward to anyone who can provide information to the police regarding Rebecca's disappearance, and I'm offering a million dollars to the kidnapper if he or she returns Rebecca unharmed."

The reporters begin shouting questions, but I step away from the podium and signal the bodyguards to head back to the trailer. I fall into step with Anna, Brad, Benny, and Dana. Everyone is silent as we walk along, but Anna moves closer and wraps her arm around mine. Brad taps my shoulder a few times, and for once, his annoying habit is actually comforting.

When we get back into the trailer, Dana sits at the table and begins typing away on her tablet. "I'll post the press release onto your social network sites, Mr. Hudson. Is there anything else you would like to say about the matter?"

I open the refrigerator and pull out a bottle of water. "No. The only thing you need to do is maintain damage control about Becca. Anything negative being said about her needs to be addressed immediately. Do you understand?"

She looks over her shoulder and nods. "I'll personally call with a press release prepared for your approval."

I shake my head, knowing there's no way I can handle that on top of everything else. "Call Anna for approval on all press statements."

Benny, who has sort of blended into the background, steps into full view. "Anything I can do to help, Boss Man?"

"Ah..." I nod. "Call Rosie and ask her to prepare a room for Rob. Then, can you call the airport and see when his flight is landing and arrange picking him up for me."

"I'm on it," Benny says.

I look at Brad. "Can you get me a few more goons? I want someone with Becca's in-laws just in case the press is heading that way. Absolutely no one is to go near her kids. And get somebody for Rob."

"Will do." He walks toward the bodyguards.

Anna steps closer. "What do you need me to do?"

When I look over at her, a sudden and intense longing to hug her overwhelms me for some reason, but I take a deep breath and blink away tears. "Just stay close."

She nods and straightens my tie. "I'm proud of you. And I promise to stay close right after I go and grab my stuff from my office."

I nod and head toward my recliner, but just as I'm about to sit, I jerk around. "Anna, wait!"

Startled, she whips around and looks at me with wide eyes. "What's wrong?"

I look at one of the bodyguards. "Go with her," I order, suddenly petrified that whoever this nutcase is will take her next.

One of the bodyguards opens the door for her and follows her outside.

"When did you arrange for your plane to pick Rob up?" Brad asks.

"Right after I got off the phone with him at the restaurant." I look over at Benny, who still has his cell phone pressed against his ear.

"ETA is in one hour," Benny confirms before going back to his conversation.

Brad nods and retrieves his phone from his pocket. "All right, I'll have some guys head over to Van Nuys to meet up with Benny and stay with Rob."

"Money isn't an object, Brad. I want the best."

He taps my face. "Only the best for my boy," he says before walking off.

"Mr. Hudson," the Guido-looking bodyguard calls.

"What?"

"This guy is here to see you."

I walk over to the door and look at the security guard who's standing at the bottom of the stairs. I'm pretty sure he works at one of the studio gates. "Not now..." I sigh. "What's your name?"

Guido guy points to himself. "Who, me?"

The security guard points to his nametag. "Mitchell."

"Yeah, right, Mitchell." Then I point to the bodyguard to clarify. "What's *your* name?"

"Josh."

"All right, Josh, do your job and keep everyone away from this trailer." I look at Mitchell. "And don't let anyone into the studio until—"

"No, that's not why I'm here—" Mitchell starts.

"I'm not answering any questions," I snap. "Even for you— I'm sorry, but I have—"

"I think I know who kidnapped Rebecca," Mitchell blurts out.

My heart races into overdrive as I bolt down the stairs. "What? Who is it?"

Josh, who's a lot more limber and agile than his size implies, is out of the trailer and between Mitchell and me in the blink of an eye. He looks my way with a raised brow, and I get the hint. I go back inside and wait until Josh pats down the short, Hispanic man.

"What's this?" Josh asks while tapping on the guard's jacket.

"It's a thumb drive," Mitchell explains while slowly reaching into his pocket.

Josh takes it from him then escorts him up the stairs. He slams the door closed and shoves Mitchell forward a bit. "Start talking," he orders.

Mitchell looks up at the bodyguard, gulps, and finally nods his head. He looks my way and takes a deep breath. "I'm sorry, Mr. Hudson, I didn't think...I swear if I would have known—"

Suddenly apprehensive, I step very close to him. "Known what?"

He fidgets. "It's just...she's been harmless for so long, Mr. Hudson, so I didn't—"

"Who's been harmless, Mitchell?" I ask in a level tone despite my rising alarm.

"I never thought...but then this morning she disappeared for the first time and when I found her in Mrs. Wilson's office, I didn't think anything of it until the news broke."

"What the fuck are you talking about?" I shout.

"I'm talking about Penny." Mitchell points toward the thumb drive that Josh is still holding. "I recorded a piece of today's security tapes for you so you can see her."

I snatch the thumb drive out of Josh's hand. "So you think this girl is behind the kidnapping?"

"I don't know," Mitchell says, wiping his brow. "I hope not."

I hurry to the television and insert the thumb drive into my Xbox. "Then why do you think she has something to do with it?" Brad asks.

"I..." He takes a step closer. "She showed up right around the time you guys started filming the second season."

I turn and glare. "Go on."

"Can I just start by saying that I'm sorry? I swear I would have never—"

"Talk, dammit!"

He nods. "She only wanted to leave that plant in your trailer —that's all she ever asked."

"And you let her?" I stand there, incredulous.

"No!" Mitchell shakes his head back and forth violently. "No...not at first. She would bring it to the studio and I'd put it in here for her." He sighs. "She came every day for months and then..." He loosens his tie. "She wanted to see the inside of your trailer."

I run my hand through my hair, tempted to ask him if he let her, but what's the point when I already know the answer?

"She offered..." he gestures with his hand and nods his head, "you know."

My jaw drops as a raging case of disgust and anger suddenly overcomes me. To help quell the urge to bash his face in, I squeeze my eyes shut and pinch the bridge of my nose. "So, in exchange for some ass, you let some deranged, psycho bitch into my trailer?"

"I know that sounds bad—"

My eyes pop open and I drop my arm to my side, once again speechless.

"Okay, it sounds bad," Mitchell shouts, "but look at me. Do you know how hard it is to find a woman when you're as short as I am?"

My lips part and I stammer—short bursts of stunned gasps choking out instead of words. "Are you fucking kidding me?" I finally manage. "Is that supposed to justify something?"

Mitchell looks away. "No." He looks at me again. "But I swear I thought she was harmless. Other than coming in to drop off the plant, she left. She never asked for more, she never touched anything, or took pictures, or did weird shit."

I scoff. "Fucking *you* to bring *me* a plant wasn't weird enough?"

"A guy like you would never understand what—"

"You're right, I'll never understand what it's like to be short or fat or stupid!" I snatch the Xbox controller off the table and quickly scroll through my dashboard to access the thumb drive. "And you'll never know what it's like to have deranged women sending you panties and all kinds of weird shit or having your friend kidnapped to prove a point, so start. Fucking. Talking!"

Mitchell steps closer and points to the screen. "That's her. I'm not sure if she took Mrs. Carter, but this morning she asked me if I could walk her on set. It was the first time she ever asked for anything other than coming in here, so I took her—"

When I shoot him a dirty look, he backs away, clears his throat, and points to the television again.

"This is footage of me escorting her off the lot after I found her. I lost her on set. She totally slipped by me, but it was only for about ten minutes. When I found her, she was just stepping out of Mrs. Wilson's office."

"Did you see her doing anything? Was she messing with Becca's stuff?"

He shakes his head. "She said she had to use the bathroom."

I stare at him for a moment, then move closer to the television and rewind and stop the screen on the clearest shot of the woman. In comparison to Mitchell, she's tall, but Becca is probably taller than he is, so that doesn't give me a good sense of just how tall she is. The woman has long dark hair and her profile, though fuzzy and a bit out of focus, is a pretty one. The woman is well dressed too...and...well, she definitely doesn't look nuts. In fact, the closer I get to the television and the more I study her, the more I get Mitchell's point. Would I think this chick was dangerous? There's a smile on her face, almost as if she and Mitchell were right in the middle of a funny story.

"How tall are you?" I ask him.

"Around five-two—"

"How tall is she? And how much does she weigh?" Josh asks.

"Um...she's probably around five ten or so, maybe a buck-twenty. She's well-spoken and hasn't ever really..."

I look over my shoulder because his tone piques my curiosity.

"She's always been really polite, but sometimes...and today..." He shivers and touches the crucifix hanging on a gold chain. "She can come off as really creepy."

Brad snorts at that. "Just sometimes?"

"Listen..." Mitchell sighs. "I put in my resignation shortly after the news broke. I came here to give you the footage and apologize. I really don't think she's capable of this...or I guess I hope not, but other than her name being Penny and knowing she drives a Range Rover, I hate to say it, but I don't know much else about her."

"A white Range Rover?" I ask.

He nods.

"I appreciate you coming clean, man. And I get that you could have kept this shit to yourself and probably gotten away with it, so thank you." Then I punch him—more for the principal of it—but ten years of being a foster kid taught me how to make one punch count. Mitchell falls like a ton of bricks, and unfortunately catches the corner of the table on his way down. I kneel and roll him onto his back, then I become even more pissed. *Dammit.* The guy is out cold.

Josh kneels, grabs the guard, and tosses him over his shoulder as if he's as light as a feather. "I'll take out the trash, boss."

I stand there and watch him turn to leave, amazed by his fluidity despite his imposing size. I wait until he trots down the stairs before I move back to the television. Brad and Benny join me and stare at the screen.

Brad points at the television. "Are you—"

"Jesus. Fucking. Christ!" Detective Morris shouts as he stomps his way up the stairs.

Startled, I shift to see Josh climbing back up the stairs, the unconscious security guard still slung over his shoulder. Detective Morris and Anna are right on his heels.

"What the fuck is going on in here?" the detective asks while motioning toward the guard.

Anna looks at the guy, her head shifting to get a better view. "Is that Officer Mitchell?"

"Explain it to the man, Josh," Brad orders and then points at the television again. "You seeing what I'm seeing, kid?"

My brows arch as I look between him and the television. Finally, I shake my head.

"She goes by the name of Penny, she has long dark hair, and she dresses like a stable girl."

I study her image more closely and instantly notice that despite the pleasant April morning, the woman *is* wearing riding boots and a leather-riding jacket. As clarity dawns on me, the room sways a bit. *Jesus.* She's playing the part of Penny Blacksmith, my character's girlfriend on *Copper Creek*.

Detective Morris steps beside me. "You recognize her?"

I shake my head. I have no idea who she is, and I'm not sure if she's the person responsible for Becca's disappearance, but as I stare at her image, a chill creeps down my spine. What if it isn't her? What if she's the first in a series of women who are at the tip of the crazy iceberg? What if we never find Becca? The realization of that hits me like a ton of bricks. The room sways again and I only manage to stay on my feet because Detective Morris steadies me. Thankfully, his reflexes prove to be as quick as Anna's, because he darts out of the way right before my stomach erupts again.

"Get him home," Detective Morris orders, "and try to keep him calm. I'll be in touch."

I want to argue, but as Anna guides me toward the door, I just follow along. He's right. I just need to get home and give him time to do his investigating. After a shower, I'll sit and start compiling a list of everything I can remember about my stalkers, since that's going to be a hell of a lot more productive than me standing around puking all over the place.

Chapter 28

Chelsea

What a day. When I finally get into my car, I drop into the driver's seat and sit there for a few moments, still too shocked to do anything more than stare at a nearby street lamp. *Wow*. My heart has always gone out to Cory Hudson, but it's nothing compared to how badly I feel for him right now. It almost seems as if life refuses to give the poor man a break.

After another moment of reflection, I start the car and head toward Darryl's house. I'm still a little leery of heading over without him being there, but he assured me that if he doesn't beat me there, he wouldn't be far behind. He gave me the code for his garage keypad, which I'm not at all comfortable using, so I take my time, for the first time in years driving along in the slow lane with all the windows rolled down.

My hair whips around wildly, sort of in the same, tumultuous way my thoughts are bouncing around inside my head. One minute, I'm focused on the information I've gathered about Cory's stalker. The next, I'm wondering if Rebecca Carter is okay. Yet, the prominent thought I keep going back to is the fact that I have Darryl's garage code. *This thing between us is moving way too fast.* I know that with every ounce of my being, but it's like my feelings for him are a runaway snowball. I snort at the ridiculous analogy, but for some strange reason, my twisted comparison helps calm my nerves.

I roll the windows back up and take a few minutes to call my mother. I know it's cheesy, but I rent the guesthouse and it only seems right to let them know that I won't be home even though they've made it clear that it isn't necessary. I also want an update on my grandmother, so Mom and me chat for the rest of the ride, mostly about Gram, but also about Rebecca Carter and Cory Hudson. The news is everywhere, every station covering what has been dubbed the story of the century.

When I get to Darryl's house, I park my Lexus on the street and feel slightly relieved that he pulls up just as I'm getting out of my car. I wait until he pulls into the garage before I walk inside. We exchange a lingering kiss before I shift to look at the bag of food he's carrying. I'm starved and he knows it, so I follow him into the house, taking note of how clean the place is. Once we're in the living room, I drop my purse on the couch and turn a hundred-eighty degrees. The room is *too* tidy—the blankets and clothes that had littered the floor this morning are gone, and the dishes we left in the sink are clean and sitting in the dish rack.

"Do you have a housekeeper?"

He pulls two beers out of the fridge. "Yeah. Why?"

"Oh, no reason. I just remember the house being a little less clean when we left for work this morning."

He shrugs. "My grandfather and dad were in the military, and so was I for a bit, so I was raised in a very clean, dress-right-dress house." He drops the beer caps into the trash then hands one to me. "I guess it kind of stuck."

I take a swig of beer and head to the dining room table with my laptop, silently reveling in that bit of newfound knowledge. "How many years did you serve?"

"Four," he walks over, drops into the chair, and pulls me onto his lap, "it was more out of obligation because I always knew I wanted to be a cop."

I set the laptop aside and shift to give him a quick kiss. "And what a damn fine cop you make."

He stares at me for an uncomfortable moment then shifts his attention to the laptop. "So, you found some stuff on Penny?"

I hesitate but finally nod and turn back around to open my laptop. "What was that look about?" I ask as I key in my password.

"What look?"

I glance at him and narrow my eyes. "You know what look, mister."

He chuckles. "It was nothing. I'm just glad you're here."

Ah-ha. So, I'm not the only one who's uncomfortable with just how fast this is moving. I give him another quick kiss then turn my attention back to the laptop. "First things first; Walt pulled me into his office right before I left to tell me he thinks one of his anonymous informants may be Cory's stalker."

"Why's that?"

"He said he's always gotten a weird vibe from her, so he's looking into his call history."

"Is that not normal?"

"Most informants give off weird vibes." I shrug. "Most are harmless though, just devoted fans, but he said this chick comes off as creepy. He made sure to tell me to tell you that it's just a gut feeling, but he already called headquarters to have his phone records printed out. He said he'll give them to me tomorrow so you can look over them."

He kisses my cheek. "Thank you."

The gesture is innocent enough, but it takes monumental effort to refocus my attention away from my suddenly hyperactive libido. "Anyway, after Cory was basically barricaded into his house by a small band of bodyguards and a bunch of your buddies blocking us off his street, Jay and I went back to the station and I started going through all of our old footage." I turn and look at him. "I know you told me all that stuff in confidence, so I didn't mention Penny to anyone, but her truck is in our footage, Darryl—a lot. I went as far back as a year and started fast-forwarding through all the videos. To save you the agony, and probably a few gray hairs, I copied all the shots of the Range Rover and made a compilation." I go to reach for my purse, since my notes are in there, but I realize it's still on the couch. "Hang on."

When I go to stand, he pulls me back onto his lap. I look over my shoulder and laugh. "I have my notes in my purse."

"Are your glasses in there too?" he asks while brushing my bangs away from my eyes.

I remind myself to go get a haircut while I stare at him. "They are..." I shift around to look into those breathtaking emeralds. "Are my contacts somehow bothering you?"

"No, but the first day I saw you, you were wearing glasses and your hair was up in a bun. You were seriously so sexy I almost rear-ended the car ahead of me."

"Oh..." I blush. "I have no idea how I didn't notice you." *Seriously.* He's hard to miss.

I go to stand again, intent on telling him everything I discovered so I can dive into that bag of food and then spend the rest of the night getting my fill of him. But when he yanks me back onto his lap again and lays one of those mind-blowing kisses on me, I gladly forget about the case and the food, and eagerly return his kiss.

Chapter 29

Darryl

As the eerily familiar black and white landscape comes into focus, I know I'm dreaming. This has happened before, so all of my senses heighten as I pay close attention to my surroundings. It takes a few moments, but I finally recognize that I'm standing *within* the picture I had taken of the numbered markers on Amanda's street. I continue to search the colorless environment, but I still don't understand what I'm looking for.

Then, as it always happens in my dreams, I'm suddenly yanked out of the photo, the 2D image remaining sprawled on a brick wall as I sail into an endless abyss that opens and catapults me back into consciousness. I bolt into an upright position and nearly fall off the bed. The sudden movement wakes Chelsea, but I don't bother to explain. I pull on my boxers, hurry into the living room, and shuffle through the stacks of paperwork on the coffee table. When I don't find the picture I'm looking for, I turn in search of my briefcase.

"What's wrong?" Chelsea asks.

"Nothing..." I take a second to note how sexy she looks in my bathrobe then I force myself to beeline to my briefcase. I retrieve the photo and hold it up.

"Really?" she inquires. "Because it almost seems like you had an epiphany in your sleep." Chelsea steps beside me and leans her head against my arm. She runs her finger along the sheet but stops short and allows her finger to hover. "There!" She taps the edge of the picture.

I note the front end of a white Range Rover captured within the image. "Jesus." I hurry over to my desk and retrieve a magnifying glass.

"I'm no statistician," Chelsea says as she once again steps beside me, "but the likelihood of another white Range Rover parked on that street, and on that day, is probably statistically impossible."

There's a guy down at the station that's all about numbers. I'm sure he could scribble some figures onto a sheet paper and proceed to tell me the exact percentage of how likely or unlikely that could be—not that I would care. My spidey-sense is telling me that Chels is right.

"You sure are mighty sexy when you're brooding like that."

I tear my attention away from the picture and chuckle. "Am I?"

She nods and wraps her arms around my neck. "Yes, very much so."

Focus on the case. Focus on the case. *Dammit.* I wrap my arm around her waist and pull her in for a kiss.

My lips press against hers for a split second before she jerks her head back. "Wait a second! If Penny took Amanda *and* Rebecca, maybe there's a chance we can find them together and alive!"

"We?" I chuckle at her enthusiasm. "I thought I was the detective here." I kiss her forehead and head to the kitchen to turn on the coffee machine. "And, as nice as your theory sounds, my gut is telling me that Amanda, and more than likely Rebecca, aren't being held captive. I think this girl wants Cory all to herself, so she's getting rid of the competition."

"Then why hasn't she hurt Destiny?" Chelsea wonders as she taps her chin.

I can tell she isn't asking me, per se. She has a habit of talking herself through stuff, which I find a bit sexy. "I don't think it's from a lack of trying," I finally say. "Destiny's home security system is high-tech, but it's still been breached twice this year. Whoever broke in easily disabled it, and even though Destiny has bodyguards on hand when she's home, there have been a few times when they've had to chase people off her property, so maybe Penny has made several attempts but has failed."

Chelsea reaches into the fridge and grabs the creamer. "Or maybe she was just trying to scare her off since she never had any intention of hurting her because she knew Destiny would eventually leave on tour."

"Could be." I shrug. "But without the license plate info and without that security guard giving us anything worth going on, we won't know for certain until we find her."

My cell phone rings just as I'm about to fix my coffee. It's Officer Cooke letting me know a guy called the station claiming to have information on the Hudson case, but that he refused to talk to anyone but me. I head over to my notepad, jot the number down, thank Cooke, and then turn to finish fixing my coffee. I nearly collide with Chelsea, to which she giggles as she extends a mug toward me. "I guess you aren't the only stealthy one in this relationship."

"I guess not." I take the coffee. "Thank you."

"My pleasure," she says as makes her way back into the kitchen.

I just stand there and watch as she pulls food from the refrigerator. *It's too fast, Darryl.* She shouldn't be in the kitchen making breakfast while I'm trying to solve a case, especially when I still haven't decided if I can trust her or not. She could just be out to gain intel on the case in an attempt to boost her career.

I shake the thought off because my spidey-sense says she's

trustworthy. Though that isn't too comforting considering that my spidey-sense once told me to get married, and look how that ended.

As Chelsea sets eggs on the counter, she catches sight of me watching. "Are you okay?"

"Yeah, I'm fine." I pick up my cell phone.

"Do you want me to leave?"

"What?" I shake my head, wondering where the hell that just came from. Then our eyes meet and I sigh. It's like she can read my mind sometimes. "No, I don't want you to leave."

"But you're thinking that this is moving too fast." She walks over. "If it's any consolation, I do too, so I don't mind leaving."

I shift hair away from her eyes. "I don't want you to leave." I absolutely do—but I absolutely don't all at the same time. "Let me make this call then I'll help with breakfast."

She leans up, kisses me, and nods. "Okay."

Without another word, she walks past me toward the bedroom. I lean back to watch her, and then consider following. I may not like how fast this is moving, but hell, if she's here, I shouldn't let that fine ass and those lovely long legs go to waste.

When she rounds the corner and I lose sight of her, I sigh and dial the number. A man answers, his voice echoing as if he's in a small space—probably a bathroom. "Good morning, sir. This is Detective Morris with the Los—"

"Thank God," the guy whispers. "I have some information about the lady they've been showing on television."

So do a billion other people trying to get Cory's reward money. "What's your name?"

"I don't..." he sighs, "Can you promise not to release it to the public?"

"Tell me what you know and then I'll decide."

"No. I *cannot* be associated with this."

The tone of his voice is so desperate that I speak the lie easily enough. "Okay, I won't release your name, but I need to know who I'm talking to."

He hesitates and sighs again. "Chad Hightower."

It's like a slap in the face. "Chad Hightower? As in *the* Chad Hightower, who just so happens to live across the street from Cory Hudson?"

"Yes. That's me."

"You do realize I've been trying to get in touch with you, right?"

"Yeah, I know, I just..." He sighs. "Look, I don't want to be involved in any of this."

My blood pressure skyrockets, but I take a deep breath and clench my jaw for a second. *You catch more bees with honey, D.* I exhale slowly. "I understand Mr. Hightower, so why don't you tell me why you called."

He's silent for a long moment, but then he sighs again. "I've met the woman you're looking for—she...after finding a few notes from her, I met her."

His flustered and angered tone piques my curiosity. "What kind of notes?"

"She has...pictures of me. Pictures I don't want anyone to see."

I drop the pen. "So, she's blackmailing you."

"Yes, in exchange to use my driveway."

Wonderful! So, on top of kidnapping and probably murder, she also dabbles in extortion. I'm slowly starting to realize I haven't given this girl all the credit she deserves. "We've been running that picture all night, Mr. Hightower. Why'd you wait so long to call?"

"I just wanted to make sure...she comes every night when Cory is home—sometimes all night and sometimes just for a few hours, so I just wanted to see...then I thought maybe she wouldn't with all the press outside, but..."

"She never showed?"

"No."

"Do you have any additional information that can help us find her?"

"Yeah, I have her license plate number."

I snatch the pen off the table. "What is it?"

The second I'm done writing down the number Chelsea taps my arm. I shift to look at her and shrug when she mouths something I don't catch. She grabs the pen out of my hand and scribbles a question on the notepad. I read it and nod.

"Mr. Hightower, did you or your wife happen to call Destiny O'Rourke to let her know there was another woman at Cory Hudson's home a few weeks ago?"

"My wife doesn't know anything about this and it needs it to stay that way," he snaps. "I called Destiny because Penny asked me to. Why do you ask?"

"No reason. I'm just confirming Ms. O'Rourke's statement. Thanks for calling and letting me know."

"Yeah, sure. Just please, if you can, don't mention my name."

"Sure thing, Mr. Hightower." I end the call and pull Chelsea over for a kiss. "Thanks for insight."

"We make a killer team, don't we?"

"We do..." I search her eyes for a second then kiss her again. "I have to skip breakfast, but I can make up for not cooking by washing your back in the shower."

"Oh, so tempting." She kisses me. "But I have a funny feeling if we hit the shower together, it'll be a long while before you run off to rescue the damsel in distress."

I groan, but damned if the woman doesn't make a valid point.

"Go," she motions toward the bedroom, "I'll make you a bagel."

"You're the best." I kiss her again, almost tempted to carry her to the room—almost. I finally pry myself away and walk to the bathroom, definitely needing a cold shower. Before I step into the bathroom though, I call the station and request the address associated with the license plate. Once I've got it down, I ask the officer to call Eric so he can meet me there.

I shower and get dressed in record time. As I'm finishing off knotting my tie, I start down the hallway. "Hey, Chels—" when I look up and see that she's pulling her jacket on, I stop short. "Where are you going?"

She giggles. "Home, silly. I need to take a shower and get ready for work."

Right, because we've only been dating for a week and she doesn't have any of her stuff here. *Yeah, D, and it needs to stay that way.* Yet, even as I think that, I walk to the kitchen and grab a spare key from the junk drawer.

As I walk toward her, she eyes the key. "I thought we just established that this was moving too fast."

"We did." I nod. "But as much as I keep telling myself to slow down, I can't, so take the key and meet me here when you get off work tonight. Only if you want to, of course."

She hesitates, her attention acutely focused on the key. After another moment, she takes it and drops it into her purse. "Are we actually going to eat this time, or should I stop for something before I come over?"

I smile. "Eat beforehand...just in case." I kiss her. "Call me later."

"I will." She gives me another peck and hands me my travel mug.

"You really are too good to me," I say as I sling my briefcase strap onto my shoulder and reach for my bagel.

"I know," she teases, that radiant smile of hers in place.

I walk her to her car and after a very long goodbye kiss that has my elderly neighbor whistling as he runs past, I wave her off and head into the garage. I drop into my car, slam the door, and shake my head. *Jesus.* I've stuck my foot in it good this time. And of all the women I could have fallen for, I've picked the one I should be keeping at an arm's length. Cops and paparazzi shouldn't be friends, let alone lovers...*and maybe more.*

I start the car and sigh, reminding myself that there are worse things in the world than falling in love...even if it is with someone you shouldn't be loving at all.

Chapter 30

Penelope

What a lying bastard! How dare he go on national television and tell the world that Rebecca is an amazing person. How dare he offer money to bring her back safely! I don't need his money—I need him—and with her in the picture, that won't happen.

Oh, I won't let you fool me, Ethan. If I bring her back unharmed, you wouldn't leave her, and there's no way I'm sharing you with anyone!

After turning off the television, I grab a pack of cigarettes and head to the bedroom. The moment I push the door open, Rebecca stops struggling against the restraints. The little bitch has been quite the noisy and annoying guest this morning, but I intend to put a stop to that.

Rebecca tries to say something, but the tape over her mouth makes it sound like a bunch of muffled mumbo-jumbo. Satisfied to see that she's been crying, I set the cigarettes on the table and pull up a chair.

"You can huff and puff all you want, bitch, but no one is going to come and save you."

Rebecca struggles against the restraints, so I pull the lighter out of my pocket and light it. She instantly stops moving and stares at the flame.

I smile. "Oh, you are a smart one, aren't you? Too bad you weren't smart enough to keep your hands off my man!" I lean closer, holding the flame by her face. "He's mine!"

My harsh whisper causes the flame to flicker and die. I drop the lighter onto the table and lift the pack of cigarettes. "You do realize that Ethan didn't smoke as much until he met you." I lean back and pull a cigarette from the pack. "Every now and then he might have indulged in these disgusting things, but not as often as he has since you came into the picture." I study the cigarette. "It's such a nasty habit, but you know that, don't you?" I scoot my chair closer to her. "Which makes you a hypocrite because you told him not to do drugs, yet you've provided him with another one in its place—a nasty one!" I shove the cigarette up her nostril.

She struggles to shift so the cigarette isn't so far up her nose, and she coughs despite the tape being over her mouth. I pull the cigarette out and snicker as Rebecca desperately blows tobacco out of her nose while also trying to inhale, the combination causing another coughing fit.

"That isn't what you want, is it?" I say over her obnoxious sounds. I toss the broken cigarette aside and pull a fresh one from the pack. "Do you have any idea what these things do to your lungs? Do you know how ugly these make you on the inside?"

I light the cigarette and hold it up so she can see it.

Rebecca is crying, tears streaming down her face as she struggles against the straps.

"He's so perfect—so handsome." I look at the pictures stapled to the walls. "*I'll* help him beat all of his addictions." I glare at her. "And unlike you, bitch, I won't ever give him anything that would take away from his beauty—not on the inside or the outside!"

I extinguish the cigarette on her exposed thigh. She screams, the tape not enough to hold her anguished moans at bay. Disappointed that the cigarette goes out so quickly, I light another, puffing on it several times without inhaling, then I press the burning tip onto her other thigh, her snow-white skin turning crimson and the flesh beneath the cigarette's cindering head bubbling and oozing. I smile and begin to hum as I light cigarette after cigarette, my artistic nature kicking in so that I create an image of the five points of a pentagram on her right thigh.

By the time I'm done, Rebecca is unconscious.

Disappointed that she's no longer even attempting to put up a fight, I sit back and sigh.

This isn't nearly as fun as when she isn't screaming through the tape and struggling to get free.

I roll the chair toward her feet, pull one of her shoes off, and hold the lighter just beneath her heel. The smell of the panty-hose melting onto her flesh is putrid, but I finally get the response I was waiting for. She screams and frantically tries to move her foot away from the flame. I hold it there a second longer, relishing her cries, then I release the button and roll back toward her head. Her tears and snot are dripping unchecked, some tobacco leaves caught in the mucus.

"You don't know pain!" Her pathetic appearance enrages me. "You don't know what it's like to hurt or to long for someone so badly that every part of your body aches for him!" I stand and slap her. "I hate you!" I slap her again, her one eye already swollen shut from the butt of the gun so I focus my fury on her good eye.

I don't know how many times I strike her but when I finally get my fill, her face is bruised and bloody. Winded, I lean back and curse her for being unconscious again. *Dammit.* It just isn't any fun torturing her when she's not up to appreciating all of my effort. Frustrated, I stomp to the door, switch off the light, and hurry to the back door. After pulling on my work gloves, I head outside, figuring that I can use my still pent-up rage to build the ceremonial bonfire.

Chapter 31

Darryl

Several months ago, the white Range Rover received a traffic violation for running a red light. The photo-enforced camera captured a portion of the windshield, giving us just enough of a shot to see that the women driving the vehicle resembles Cory's stalker. Her name, at least according to her driver's license, is Penny B. Smith.

On *Copper Creek,* Cory's on-again-off-again fictitious girl-friend's name is Penny Blacksmith. There's no way that's a coincidence. Neither is the fact that the traffic violation was issued on the same night that Destiny's house was broken into. And if all of that weren't enough, the mansion that Penny B. Smith has listed on her driver's license looks a hell of a lot like the mansion that's used on the show.

As I pull up to the call box that's just outside of the lavishly manicured and gated lawn, Eric and I look around in awe. It's a rare day when we're both stunned into silence.

After another second of gawking, I finally recover. "Okay, I give. It's fucking weird; just plain fucking weird to spend millions of dollars to have a house built that looks exactly like one you've seen on a television show."

Eric snorts. "Agreed."

As I wait for Officer Cooke to call us back with additional information on the property, I take the time to adjust the squad car's laptop for a better view of the screen. I pull up the official *Copper Creek* website to be sure, but after the picture comes up and I look back and forth between the laptop and the house, I finally shake my head. *Wow.* This stalker, Ms. Penny B. Smith, has clearly gone so far off the damn reservation that she's in her own mental state.

When my phone vibrates in my pocket, I actually startle. I accept the call while ignoring Eric's snickering. "This is Officer Morris."

"You are not going to believe this," Officer Cooke says without preamble, "but that house was built in 1985 and the studio uses its image a lot because the owner is the late wife of Hollywood director Vincent Aramid."

"So, this *is* the house they use on his show," I say more for myself, incredulous. "How the hell was this woman able to use the address on her license then?"

"Got me there, boss," Cooke says. "I'll do some digging on my end and get back to you if I find anything."

"Thanks." I end the call and look at Eric.

He shakes his head and sighs. "And the creep factors just keep on coming," Eric says.

They sure do. I hit the call button on the intercom and a moment later, a woman answers. I introduce myself and tell her that I need to question Mrs. Aramid. There's a brief silence then the woman tells us to come in. The gate swings open. We park in front of the grand entrance and the housekeeper walks us through the mammoth foyer to the back of the house. Mrs. Aramid is sitting by a window with a pair of knitting needles and yarn in her lap, but her hands are resting atop them as she gazes outside.

"Good morning, Mrs. Aramid. I'm Detective Morris. This is my partner, Detective Gordon. We'd like to ask you some questions about a young lady by the name of Penny B. Smith." I hold a picture toward her.

Mrs. Aramid glances at the photo then goes back to looking out the window. "I had a feeling you'd be paying me a visit today. It's a shame to hear about that author."

"Do you know this woman, Mrs. Aramid?" Eric asks. "She lists this house as her address on her driver's license."

"I don't know her personally." She finally looks at us. "Unfortunately, I *do* know her." She motions toward a nearby couch. "Please, have a seat." She waits until we're seated before continuing. "A little over a year ago, that woman contacted me claiming to have some photos of my grandson." She goes back to looking out the window.

I glance at Eric then back at her. "I'm assuming she asked that, in exchange for your silence, she could use your address."

Mrs. Aramid nods. "I couldn't—" She sighs. "It seemed harmless enough...the girl, she looked so much like that girl on the show, so I didn't think it would hurt anything. I assumed she was just a devout fan."

"How long ago was this?" Eric asks.

"About a year...maybe fourteen months ago at most...I haven't heard from her since, but she occasionally sends a picture —almost as if to remind me..."

"Would you mind letting us look at the envelope?" I ask, my hope rising.

She shakes her head. "I burn everything when it comes now that I recognize her handwriting."

Well, that's just fucking great. I stand, fish a business card out of my wallet, and hand it to her. "If you hear from her or get another letter, contact me directly. I'm not interested in the pictures, Mrs. Aramid. We just need the envelope."

Mrs. Aramid takes the card and nods. "Of course."

We say our goodbyes and walk to the door. "There are all of our leads," I say on a sigh.

"Then I guess we should head over to Hudson's place while

we wait for the computer guys to work their magic and track Penny through her paper trail."

I look at my watch. Almost twenty-four hours have passed since Rebecca disappeared, so the likelihood of finding her—especially alive—is quickly dwindling. I sigh again. "Yeah, that sounds good."

I follow behind Eric, my mind wandering over everything while simultaneously being amazed that this woman is really giving us a run for our money. Irritated, I push any negative thoughts aside and focus on what I *do* know as we make the drive back to Beverly Hills. Penny B. Smith is young and unattached—there's no way she can be in a real relationship or have children with the amount of time she devotes to Cory. She's also loaded, and she literally spends every waking moment following Cory around, so she can't have a job—well, not a normal one anyway.

When we turn onto Cory's street, I snap out of my reverie and take in the media circus before me. There are so many vehicles and people milling around that three squad cars are parked outside Cory's front gate. A uniformed officer is trying to hold the media at bay while simultaneously directing traffic. It takes a few minutes to get to the driveway, all of which I use to search for Chelsea. When I finally spot her van, I ease on the brakes and wonder why she isn't in the van with Jay.

Startled when one of the officers taps the hood of my car, I look at him and nod when he signals me inside. I park by the front door and eye the guy who's standing by the front door. *Jesus.* When Brad said he was going to get some muscle to make sure Cory was safe, the man wasn't kidding. Eric and I show him our badges, which he scrutinizes before letting us pass. There's another bodyguard just inside and yet another one standing just outside the living room. When we finally gain access, I note that Cory, Rob, Anna, Brad, Benny, and his publicist are all hunkered down in front of laptops. I almost chuckle, since it looks like a makeshift command center.

"Did you find her?" Rob asks.

"No, we haven't found her yet," Eric answers. "We have some questions, Mr. Hudson."

Cory signals us to sit in the loveseat next to his chair. He offers us water and then takes a long swig from a bottle. *That's interesting.* The last time I was here, he was so stoned, drunk, and disorientated that I considered taking him to the hospital. Today, he looks worse even though his face is all cleared up from where Destiny cracked him with the frying pan, but he hasn't slept—or if he has, it wasn't for long—and the haunted look in his eyes is easy enough to read. This guy isn't in on the kidnapping—he's genuinely worried—and so is Rebecca's husband.

"Any ransom calls?" I ask.

Cory and Rob shake their heads.

"Here's the deal," Eric starts, "we had some leads, but this woman has covered her tracks pretty well. We're getting tons of tips and we're still questioning the staff and crew on the movie set and on your show's side, but we need to know if you remember anything else."

Cory gets onto his feet. "How is that possible? How can someone create an entire persona and not leave any clues?"

"She has money, and by the looks of it, lots of it." Eric says. "It's amazing how much you can accomplish when you can pay off the right people."

"So, what are you saying?" Rob snaps. "Are we just giving up?"

I shake my head and look at Cory. "Can you remember anything else that might help us?"

Cory runs his hands through his hair. "I've been up all night trying, and we've all been pouring through the footage for the charity events, but most of that stuff has the camera on the cast, not on the audience, and I must have signed a thousand autographs." He drops back onto the chair. "I called Destiny and the hotel in Vancouver. Neither of them has the tapes of that night anymore. Not that it would help, because we already know what Penny looks like."

"Listen, Cory, I can't even begin to imagine—" My phone vibrates. I pull it out and hit the talk key. "Detective Morris."

"Hey, it's Baltimore."

I glance at Eric, who nods and takes over while I pull my notepad from my inner jacket pocket. "What's up, Captain?"

"A call came in on the tips-line from a woman in Glendale claiming to know Penny. The lady's name is Pamela Reich. She says she's pretty sure Penny is her neighbor."

"Pretty sure?"

"Yeah, we checked into it because Pamela says the girl is always in and out so she can't positively identify her, but she drives a white Range Rover and she matches Penny's description. On top of that, we looked into the house's owner information and discovered that it belongs to a Patrick Fitzgerald. One of the uniforms did some digging and it turns out that this Patrick Fitzgerald is dead, but he has a stepdaughter by the name of Penelope. That's pretty close to Penny and, the icing on the cake is that her stepfather was a wealthy banker who died in a car accident four years ago. The wife was with him, so Penelope was the sole beneficiary."

Meaning that she's loaded, which is perfect. "What's the address?" I ask as I move closer to the door because Rob is hovering like an annoying gnat. After writing it down, I shove the notepad and phone into my pocket then look at Cory. "Call us if you hear or remember anything. We'll be in touch."

"Wait!" Rob grabs my arm. "Did someone see Beck?"

I shake his hand off. "No, but if this pans out with any decent information, I'll be in touch."

"I want to go with you," Rob says.

What the fuck is up with these people? "It's best if you wait here and contact me if Penny calls for a ransom."

"I can't just keep sitting here doing nothing while my wife is missing!"

"If you want to do something, then help jog Cory's memory.

The more leads we can follow, the more likely we'll be able to get your wife home safely."

I turn and walk toward the door, but both men follow behind asking questions. I ignore them even though I'm somewhat sympathetic to their plight, but I'm not in the mood to waste any time trying to console them. They follow Eric and me to the squad car, but we get in and drive off, leaving the two men and their bodyguards standing outside.

As we wait to get out of the driveway, I bring Eric up to speed and we bat around ideas as we make the drive to Glendale. Unfortunately, with traffic, and of course with having to stop to accommodate Eric's raging case of Crohn's Disease, it takes nearly an hour to get to Mrs. Reich's house. When we finally round the corner, I slam on the brakes because the big Italian bodyguard is leaning against an Impala that's parked in front of Mrs. Reich's house. And even more concerning is that there's a white news van parked farther down the street.

"What the hell is he doing here?" Eric asks.

"Oh, did I forget to mention just how annoying Scooby and the gang are?"

Eric snorts. "I meant how did they know we were coming here?"

"How the hell should I know?"

I pull up behind the Impala, and before I even put the car into park, Eric gets out and says, "I have no idea how you knew we'd be here, but get back in the car and take everyone back to Mr. Hudson's house."

The big guy shrugs. "I can't."

I get out of the car and slam the door. "Why not?"

Pamela's front door opens. She waves then steps aside so Cory can stand next to her.

"I can't because they're already inside," the bodyguard says.

I shake my head, making sure to glare at the bodyguard before I look over at Eric. His expression says it all, and when I point down the street and he spots the white news van, he swears under his breath and continues along the walkway. I just stand there, and when my phone vibrates, I'm not surprised.

"Hey," Chels says. "I'm sorry I didn't call sooner. We just beat you here by a few."

"Why didn't you call me sooner?" I ask, trying to keep my tone level, but the heads-up would have been nice.

"I didn't know where they were going!" she snaps, the edge in her tone easy enough to read. "I mean, after following Cory for a year now, Jay and I have gotten hip to his tricks of ditching cars and sneaking out of back exits, but we had no idea what they were up to, especially because *you* didn't tell me there was another lead."

My jaw clenches, but I exhale a slow but steady breath. "I didn't want to say anything if it turned out to be nothing."

An awkward, tense moment of silence ensues before Eric clears his throat.

Right. I turn my back to him and lower my voice. "I'm sorry," I say, though it's mostly to keep the peace. "And I promise to keep you posted from here on in."

"Darryl..." She sighs. "I'm sorry, too. I didn't mean to snap."

Another tense moment passes before I say, "I'll see you tonight, okay? And park in the garage if you beat me home."

"Yeah. Okay, I'll see you later."

I end the call then walk over to Eric.

"Trouble in paradise?" he inquires.

"Shut up." I roll my eyes and walk past him, not in the mood to share how worried I am that my faith in Chels's motives for being with me is just because I can give her leads like these. Though, when I really give it any real thought, she obviously doesn't need much help getting to the heart of things, especially since she beat us here.

When we reach the door, Mrs. Reich ushers Eric and me into the house and practically shoves us onto the sofa across from Scooby and the gang. "What can I get you boys to drink?" the elderly woman asks with a smile.

"I'd love some water," I say.

"Me too, thanks," Eric adds.

The minute she leaves the room, I glare at Cory. "What the hell are you two doing here?"

"I can't just keep sitting around waiting for a call that isn't going to come," Rob says.

"Well, you can't be here, so go back to Cory's and I'll call—"

Mrs. Reich steps back into the room with two glasses in her hands. "Here we are. It's bottled because the tap sometimes doesn't taste quite right." She sits between Eric and me and taps our legs. "I was just telling the boys I wasn't surprised that girl didn't answer her door—"

"Whoa, wait. You guys went over there?" I snap.

"She didn't answer." Rob is clearly the spokesman. "The back fence is padlocked and we can't climb over it because the damn thing is ten-feet high—"

"That's when they came to visit me," Mrs. Reich says cheerfully. "They wanted to borrow my ladder but I told them I had a perfectly fine view into her backyard if they wanted to see. Though I told them she hasn't been home in days so they wouldn't see much."

"Mrs. Reich," Eric says, "Can you tell us about your neighbor? Do you know her name?"

"Oh, heavens no, but she's a strange one, that girl. Comes and goes, in and out all day and night. If I weren't so aware of my neighborhood, I would never even know she was there. She parks that big truck in the garage, making sure to close it the moment she gets inside."

"So what makes you think she's the lady we're looking for?" I ask.

"Well, sometimes she'll slip right past me and get into the house when I'm not sitting by the window, but she can't get past my dog most times..." Mrs. Reich pulls a tissue from the box on the coffee table and dabs her eyes. "He went missing last week, so I've been up and down the neighborhood looking for him. Two days ago, I was posting flyers and saw her loading up a few boxes in her truck. The garage door was open, so I hurried over and asked if she'd seen my dog." Mrs. Reich blows her nose. "She said that I shouldn't let him out all night if I really cared about him." She sobs.

I sit back and look at her, wondering how long it's going to take for her to regain her composure.

"She was so heartless; her eyes the coldest things I've ever seen. I tried to explain I have doggy doors and Buddy only goes out if he hears something, but she said she didn't care and that I needed to get off her property." Mrs. Reich dabs her eyes again. "She left a few minutes later and hasn't come back since."

"Could she just be getting in late at night?" Eric asks.

Mrs. Reich shakes her head. "That very day my daughter bought me a little puppy because she knew I was so upset about Buddy, so I've been outside often to take the little darling out for potty. The house has been very still." She dabs her eyes again then smiles. "Would you like to meet Blossom?"

"No, that's—" I start.

"Oh, I'll bring her in!"

Eric and I exchange our usual 'you've got to be shitting me' looks then we shift our attention to the men. "How the hell did you get this address?" I ask.

"I've spent years peeking over shoulders to glimpse play-books," Rob says. "You don't have any game, Detective. That address was in my memory before you lifted your pen off the page."

Rob and I have a bit of a stare down before I nod. "You aren't doing anybody any favors here, Mr. Carter, so go back to Cory's house. We'll handle this."

Mrs. Reich hurries back into the room, a Chihuahua puppy cupped in her hands. "Isn't she adorable?" She sits between Eric and me again. "She'll never replace Buddy, but until he comes home, it's nice to have the company."

I bet. "She is very pretty," I say, rubbing my pointer finger on the little dog's head. "Thank you for your time, Mrs. Reich. If we have any other questions, we'll be in touch." I fish a card out of my wallet and set it on the coffee table. "If you happen to see Penelope come home, can you call me, please?"

"Yes, of course."

After we all step outside, I point to the Impala. "If we find anything important, we'll call."

Rob falls into step with me. "She isn't there."

"Goodbye, Mr. Carter." I keep walking, Eric matching my hurried pace.

Penelope's lawn and hedges look decent and nothing really stands out. I pull my notepad out and scribble down a note to ask Mrs. Reich if she's noticed a regular lawn service. The residents on this street probably hate having an old, nosy neighbor, but they're a gold mine for cops.

"We looked in the windows," Rob says, still following along. "It seems quiet."

I stop and look at him. "Listen, Mr. Carter, I understand how—"

"You don't understand shit! You don't have any idea how it feels to call your wife and have someone answer the phone to tell you that she's missing! And you have no idea how hard it is to try and keep it together so you can lie to your kids, pretending that she's safe when you know she isn't, so don't stand there and try to tell me you get it or that I have to leave, because I'm not."

I grind my teeth because I sincerely feel the guy's pain.

"You don't have to go," Eric finally says, "but you *do* have to wait in your car."

Cory steps closer and grabs Rob's arm. "Come on, man. Let them do their thing. All we're doing is holding them up."

Rob resists, but then finally backs away. I ignore him and look at Cory. His eyes are teary and for some reason, his distant and stoic appearance is bugging me more than Rob's tenacity. When they finally walk away, I stand there watching.

Eric walks up the steps and rings the doorbell. "What are your thoughts on those two?"

I exhale loudly. "I'm pretty sure Cory hasn't told Rob about him and Rebecca, but something happened last night. I'm not sure if they just had a male bonding moment or if Rob is blaming Cory for Rebecca going missing, but both men are carrying heavy burdens." I knock on the door then look at Eric. "She isn't here."

"Yeah, I know." Eric sighs. "I'll call and see if we have enough to get a warrant. I only came up here hoping they'd leave."

I snort. "Ten bucks says that within five minutes after we leave, they'll break in."

"Twenty bucks says they break in before we even round the corner."

"At which point we can come in and escort them out—"

"And while we're in there, we can take a look around," Eric adds.

"Well, let's at least cover our asses. Make the call requesting the warrant while I do recon." I walk down the stairs to look into the windows.

After surveying the property, I go back to Mrs. Reich's house and knock on the door. She opens it with the puppy still cradled in her arms.

"Mrs. Reich, I hate to bother you again, but does Penelope use a lawn service?"

"Yes, they come like clockwork every Monday. Would you like me to get their card?"

"I'd really appreciate it."

She hands the dog over, so I take her, suddenly scared I'm going to crush the little thing in my hands. I'm definitely a big dog type of guy, but I can't resist the temptation to stroke the dog's head and wonder if Chelsea likes dogs.

Mrs. Reich returns to the door and we exchange the card for the puppy, but it still takes another five minutes before I can walk over to Eric. "That woman needs friends," I say on a sigh.

"Rock, paper, scissors for who tells them," Eric says.

Fuck. We turn to face the door, our fisted hands held close enough so they can't see. We count to three and I throw out a scissor. Eric chuckles and crushes my scissors with his rock. *Dammit.* We walk over to the Impala.

"Okay, here's the deal," I start. "Penelope either isn't home or she isn't answering the door, so we called in for a warrant—"

"What? Can't you just break the door down?" Rob asks.

"No, unfortunately, we have to abide by the law, but we have the best ADA working on it, so it shouldn't be long, especially with the press attention. Head back to Cory's and we'll call the second the judge signs off on it."

My cell phone vibrates. I look at the caller ID and have to keep from smirking. It's Eric. I put the phone to my ear. "Morris." I step away and turn around. "Yeah, okay. What's the address?" I pull my notepad out, being sure prying eyes can't see this time. I end the call, shove the notepad in my pocket, and tap Eric's shoulder. "Let's roll." I look at Cory and Rob. "We'll be in touch."

They don't follow, though we don't give them a lot of time to decide if they're going to stay here or follow us since Eric and I hurry to the car, get in, and drive off.

Eric chuckles. "You better have cash on you."

"Don't get too cocky," I say as I look into the rearview mirror and watch them pile into the car.

"Make the next right," he orders while shifting to get a better view in the side-view mirror.

"Dude, give me my money." I laugh. "You said around the corner, which automatically implies the first corner we come to, not the second."

He grumbles and reaches for his wallet. After pulling a twenty out and handing it over, he suddenly snatches it back. "They started moving."

I snatch the bill out of his hand and make the first right. "You said they'd break in before we even rounded the corner, champ, and they haven't broken in."

"You know I have a wife and son to support."

I roll my eyes. "Cry me a river."

We sit in silence as we drive around the block. I keep checking the rearview, hoping that they took the bait and started to follow, but there's no sign of them. When we make the final right onto Mrs. Reich's street again, and the Impala is gone.

Eric snatches the twenty back. "Looks like we were both wrong," he says.

I roll my eyes as I pull ahead and park so that my window is right beside the news van. Jay is in the driver's seat, but Chelsea leans over him and sticks her head out the driver's window. "Hey, where'd they go?"

"Hi, Chelsea," Eric shouts even though he leans over me to wave at her like a moron.

She giggles. "Hello, Eric." She points to the house and says, "They broke the garage door open and parked the Impala inside."

I shove Eric back so he quits looking at Chelsea's very nice cleavage then I yank the twenty out of his hand. "Thanks for that, bro." I lean out the window. "Can you send me a message to let me know when those yahoos finally get back to Cory's, please?"

She nods. "I will."

My stomach suddenly sinks when I catch an odd glimmer in her eyes. I try to shake it off, knowing full well I need to get Cory and Rob out of Penelope's house, but I can't help myself. "What's wrong?"

"Nothing's wrong." She shakes her head and sighs. "It was just a rough morning. I'll tell you about it later."

I study her for a second but finally relent and nod. "I'll call when I'm on my way home."

"Bye, Chelsea," Eric shouts.

She laughs and waves. "Bye, guys."

I reverse my way to the curb and throw my door open. When Eric doesn't move, I look at him.

"I'll call when I'm on my way home?" He chuckles. "Exactly whose house are we talking about?"

I get out of the car and slam the door.

Eric gets out and falls into step with me. "She's got a nice, little rack on her."

He's trying to get a rise out me, so I ignore him and yank the garage door open, stopping to look at the Impala parked in the center of the garage.

I pull my gun from the holster and move to the door. Eric's comedy routine finally dies away and he becomes deathly serious as he creeps closer with his weapon in hand. I knock on the door before opening it, unsure if the bodyguard carries a piece.

When I don't receive a response, I push the door open slowly and step into the kitchen. The bodyguard is standing by a window while the guys try to hurry out of the room.

"Hold it right there," I shout. "You do realize we can arrest you for breaking and entering."

Rob turns around. "You wouldn't have left if you didn't want us to break in, so after we search the house, you can arrest me."

This guy thinks he's Dirty Fucking Harry. I roll my eyes while putting my gun back into the holster. "Get out while we secure the premises."

I step farther into the kitchen then walk toward a large kennel in the corner of the dining room. There are two empty bowls and a seemingly clean litter pan inside. I scratch my head, wondering who keeps a cat in a kennel. Then I turn around and study the area, noting that the house is immaculate. I head back to the kitchen and pull open the refrigerator door. It's empty and looks as if it's never been used before. I open a few cabinets—all of which are empty—then I open the pantry. There are cans of cat food, an unopened bag of dry cat food, and a tub of litter.

What the hell is up with the cat stuff?

I step into the little foyer and look around. The house is

just as clean here, but something doesn't feel right. It almost seems like one of those staged homes a real estate agent sets up before putting it up for sale...*actually*...it's a lot like Cory's house. It's pretty and has all the right furnishings, but it lacks any personal touches, and there's something just *off* about the place...something I can't put my finger on but that's making me uneasy.

"Get outside and get your goddamn car out of her garage," I say to the bodyguard then I signal Eric closer.

His spidey-sense must be going off too, because we pull our guns from our holsters at the same time. He signals that he'll take the front of the house so I creep toward the hallway.

Rob falls in step with me. "What is it?"

Annoyed, I look at the bodyguard. "Get them the hell out of here." Once Rob has backed off, I take a few steps down the hall-way. "This is Detective Morris with the Los Angeles Police Department. If someone is in the house, identify yourself."

"The front of the house is clear," Eric whispers as he inches closer to me.

We stop by the first door we encounter. Eric opens it and I bring my weapon to the ready. The room appears empty, so we move inside. The white, childlike bedroom furniture looks brand new. I can even still smell the wood, almost as if someone delivered the furniture and minimally decorated the room before they closed the door and never opened it again.

After checking beneath the bed and in the empty closet, we move to the next closed door. It's a bathroom, which is set up with all the basics, and is spotless and sterile. We aren't as tense when we try the next door, but we go on high alert when we discover that this door is locked. Eric and I exchange a look then I step aside so he can kick it open.

It takes two good kicks, but the frame finally creaks then gives. I step closer and push the door open. Once I get a look inside, I nearly drop my gun.

"Holy bat shit, Robin," I say.

Eric makes the sign of the cross then pushes the door open the rest of the way. "I think we found our stalker."

I reach in and flick the light on, wanting to make sure my eyes aren't deceiving me. They're not. That's definitely a pentagram in the center of the room. I step inside, unable to focus on one thing because there are so many things to look at. There has to be a thousand pictures of Cory plastered on the walls—not one inch of wall visible with all the photos.

"A satanic stalker," I whisper as I step closer to the pentagram to look at the box spring and mattress covered in dried blood. "Jesus Christ." I look around the room again.

Eric walks over to the closet and pulls the door open. There's a mini-fridge and a microwave sitting on top of it. There are several items hanging neatly off the wooden bar—some of which look too big to be Penelope's clothes. Boots line the floor and there are jeans folded on a shelf. On another floor-to-ceiling shelving unit, there are several black candles—enough to fill two shelves. There's also a wooden box on the top shelf and a bin beneath the bottom shelf.

This is her room—probably the only room of the house she uses regularly. I walk toward the only other piece of furniture; a black dresser that's blocking the only window. I open the thick, black curtains and look into the backyard. It's just as nice as the front yard, so I shift my attention to the dresser and open the top drawer. There are a bunch of different herbs and spices, all neatly boxed and labeled. The remaining drawers contain underwear, bras, and more clothes.

Well, at least the creepy satanic stalker is meticulous.

"Holy shit," Rob exclaims as he points to the mattress. "Is that blood?"

I whip around, my attention once again shifting to Cory, his expression almost comical as he looks around the room. They both walk inside, Rob staring at the pentagram while Cory's eyes dart around to look at all the pictures. Then he points to the closet. "Those are my clothes." He steps farther into the room, his eyes finally settling on the pentagram and bloody mattress. "She's a Satanist?"

I'm not sure if that's a question or a statement. I watch him walk over to the wall and run his hand through his hair.

"There aren't any pictures of Beck," Rob observes as he looks around.

"There wouldn't be," Eric says, finally finding his voice. The guy is a pretty devout Christian so I can tell he's shaken up. "This is her room, so everything in here will be about Cory." He points to one of the pictures. "See, she'll even tear the pictures so no one else is in it."

Cory walks over to the picture Eric pointed out. "That was last week." Cory studies the picture then says, "I was leaving Becca's house."

"Is that blood?" Rob asks again, his attention back on the mattress.

"I'm pretty sure it is, but it isn't enough to..." Eric clears his throat. "I don't think she's ever brought Rebecca here."

I walk over and pull the wooden box off the shelf. I open it slowly and when I finally register its contents, my nose wrinkles and I hold the box farther away from my body, acting as if the bloodied vibrator is going to jump out and bite me.

Cory reaches for the box and snatches it out of my hand, startling me. I turn to snap at him, but stop short of saying anything when I notice that the blood has completely drained from his face. He reaches for the box, my stomach churning at the thought of him touching the vibrator, but he doesn't reach for that. Instead, he opens the box completely and removes a picture of a woman and boy from the velvet-lined lid.

I step closer to him. "Do you recognize this picture?"

"This is my mom. It's the last picture we took before she died." He looks at me. "How did she get this?"

"Was it at Destiny's house?"

He shakes his head.

"What about the hotel?" Eric asks.

"Yeah, I always take it with me when I travel, but I still have it."

"Maybe she made a copy when she broke into your hotel room?" I suggest.

He stares down at the photo and shakes his head. I don't think it's because he's disagreeing; I think it's because he's in shock. I know because I've seen the look enough to—

I hear the explosion a split second before I feel it. Then the far bedroom wall and window shatter, flinging the three of us forward. A searing pain radiates along my back as I crash against the closet door, the momentum causing my head to crack against its edge. I stagger forward then, trying to keep my footing, but I'm too dazed from the blow. I collapse onto the floor as pain consumes every part of my body, but even still, I try to focus. *Eric.* Did he make it? I moan as I shift onto my side, trying to find him despite the black spots before my eyes. I see Cory first, well, his legs anyway, since the top half of his body had landed inside the closet, obscuring my view of his face.

Then I spot Eric struggling to get onto his hands and knees. Relieved to see that he isn't dead, I press my hands against the floor and push myself up. The black spots shrouding my vision get worse, and as a tidal wave of nausea and pain consumes me, I fall onto the floor again and finally succumb to the darkness.

Chapter 32

Chelsea

After handing my tablet to Jay so he can proofread the article I intend to send Walt, I drop against the seat and suddenly wish I carried around a flask. *God.* It's bad enough I'm totally head-over-heels for Darryl and my mother and grandmother don't approve—but now my dad is giving me shit, too. I don't think he cares so much that I'm in love with a cop; it's more the fact that Darryl was the arresting officer for two of his clients. Now, my father has to turn those cases over to another attorney because the court could throw them out if they find out that Darryl and I are involved. Why should that even matter?

I swear that this is just like college all over again. Everyone in my family is opposed to my decisions. Back then, it was me choosing journalism over law. Now it's about dating a cop over some snobby attorney everyone has in mind for me. I pointed out that I had gone down that route once before and I ended up calling off the engagement. My father didn't appreciate the reminder—neither did I, especially because I was stupid enough to mention it in the first place.

Jay hands me the tablet. "It's good, but it would probably be better if you added some of the stuff you've learned from your boyfriend."

I roll my eyes and snatch the tablet away. "I'm not betraying his trust, Jay."

Jay laughs. "Well, aren't you just touchy, touchy today?"

"You have no idea."

"I was pretty sure your mood would get better after your heavy flirting session with your little beau, but something is obviously on your mind, so start talking."

I drop the tablet onto my lap and look at him. "I just..." I sigh. "Do you think I should call if off with Darryl?"

He seems to consider his words carefully. After another moment of staring out the windshield, he finally looks at me. "I think you need to follow your heart and screw whatever your parents have to say about it."

I meet his eyes and nod. "Thanks, Jay."

He reaches over and taps my hand again. "I've never seen you—"

A sudden blast rocks the van. Once the shaking and initial shock wear off, I search around, then I stare in horror at the flames and smoke that are engulfing the back half of Penelope's house. Without considering the danger, I run toward the inferno, my heart pounding and aching all at once. *He's okay,* I assure myself. He somehow managed to survive the blast. Yet even as I repeat those reassurances, tears begin to blur my vision, a fact I'm unappreciative of as I hurry into the still-open garage and step into the kitchen. "Darryl!" The smoke chokes me, but it isn't entirely blinding, so I continue ahead. "Darryl!"

With my heart racing faster than it ever has before, I hurry through the kitchen and actually scream when the big Italian-looking bodyguard comes around the corner. Blood is running down the side of his face, but despite the injury, he's dragging Cory's limp body toward me.

"Get the door!"

I don't hesitate. I turn and open the front door for them. "Where's Darryl?"

"Back there," he says as he passes.

I turn and run down the hallway, only stopping long enough to pull my shirt around my nose because the smoke is thicker here. My eyes sting, but I just squint and keep moving. I reach for the doorknob of a closed door.

"Get out of here, Chelsea!" Eric shouts.

Startled, I turn and my heart feels like it stops when I see he's dragging Darryl's limp body toward me. I hurry over; dropping low enough to grab Darryl's other arm so I can drape it over my shoulders.

"You got him?" Eric shouts.

"Yeah, come on!"

With my help, Eric moves faster. Darryl's feet drag behind as we rush to the front door; the smoke getting worse as the fire spreads. When we get outside, I use the last of my energy to get Darryl down the porch stairs without dropping him.

"Lay him on his stomach!" Eric shouts as we hurry over to Mrs. Reich's yard. "There's a shard of glass embedded in his back!"

In that moment, I somehow manage to contort enough to look at Darryl's back. There is, indeed, a shard of glass protruding from it.

"On his stomach!" Eric shouts. Again. Which leads me to believe that Eric's hearing may have been damaged in the blast. He seems okay otherwise, a little banged up, sure, but okay. Darryl, sadly, clearly hasn't fared too well, and as we set him beside Cory's body near Mrs. Reich's front door, I also fear the worse for him, too.

With Mrs. Reich and the bodyguard fussing over Cory, I go back to worrying about Darryl. The glass sticking out of his back is disturbing, to say the least, but as I start to reach for it, Eric slaps my hand away. "Don't take it out! Call 911!" And with that, he taps the bodyguard on the shoulder and then they both run back into the smoldering house.

Thankfully, I don't have to call 911 because Jay and Mrs. Reich are on their phones, and I can hear sirens approaching. When Darryl moans, my attention instantly shifts back to him. I lean close. "Hey, it's okay, help is on the way."

He rolls onto his side and looks up at me, then he searches around. As if clarity suddenly dawns on him, he gasps and struggles to sit up.

"Stay still," I order. "An ambulance will be here soon."

Blood is oozing from his nose and from a gash on his forehead, but he looks right at me as if all is well in the world. "Get the hell away from here, Chels. It isn't safe."

No shit. "Stay still," I repeat as I grip his arm to keep him from getting up.

He pushes my hand off and sits up, moaning through the entire process. "Where's Eric?"

"He went back inside." I grip his shirt when he tries to stand. "I said don't move! There is a piece of glass in your back and you are badly injured." *Why do I even have to explain this?*

In one smooth motion, which defies logic considering his condition, Darryl manages to get onto his feet. I stand and reach for him, but he shoves me away. "Go," he orders as he limps toward the house.

Jay is suddenly there, his imposing three hundred pounds barring Darryl's path.

I grip his arm and force him to look at me. "Dammit, Darryl, I am not letting you go back in there!"

He shakes my hand off, takes a step closer to Jay, but then suddenly stops. I shift closer to him, wondering if he's okay since he seems transfixed by something. I follow his line of sight and see that Eric and the bodyguard are rushing toward us; they're carrying Robert Carter's badly burned and bloody body.

The sight of him causes bile to rise in my throat and I suddenly feel faint. Then Darryl stumbles, so I tear my eyes away from Rob's charred body and pull Darryl's arm over my shoulders again. Sirens wail in the distance, so Jay and I help Darryl back onto the ground. Then we all just watch as the body-guard and Eric lie Rob onto the ground a few feet away from us. Cory is still out, but Rob is conscious—though in his condition, I don't know how.

"Hang on, man," Eric says after kneeling beside him. "Help is on the way."

Rob coughs, blood splattering Eric's face. My stomach churns.

Eric continues talking to Rob, only stopping when Cory moans and shifts a bit. I watch as he slowly opens his eyes and blinks several times. Then he looks around, sort of like Darryl did, then he jerks into a seated position. For a moment, he looks into my eyes. I wince and give the slightest shake of my head, then motion toward Rob. His eyes drift away, slowly glancing over the crowd until his attention settles on Rob. A horrified expression replaces the distant, confused look on his face in an instant. He crawls over, shoving Eric aside to get closer to Rob. He lets out an anguished moan as he cradles Rob in his arms.

Rob's eyes flutter open. He coughs, blood running out of his mouth and getting lost amid the charred flesh of his chin. "Find her..."

"We'll find her," Cory says. He shakes him again. "Dammit, Rob!"

"Tell her..." Rob moves his badly burned hand and grips Cory's shirt. "I'm sorry."

"No." Cory shakes his head, covering Rob's hand with his. "You'll tell her." Cory sobs, rocking himself and Rob. "You hang on, man. Hang on so you can tell her." He tries to rouse Rob several times, but after a moment, Cory just pulls Rob against him and keeps rocking.

With tears streaming down my face, I watch as Eric places his fingertips against Rob's neck and then shakes his head, letting us know the obvious. Robert Carter is dead.

Chapter 33

Cory

Three years—I've lived in this house for three years and I've never sat in this room before. Until yesterday, I rarely, if ever, came on this side of the second floor. Yet, for some reason, when I got home from the hospital a few hours ago—after refusing to stay overnight despite my doctor's insistence—I grabbed a bottle of scotch and locked myself in the guest room, or what I've officially dubbed "Rob's room."

The housekeeper had since made up the bed, and she had washed and then neatly folded Rob's clothes and placed them on the bureau. She assumed he would come back and would need something to wear since he hadn't bothered to pack much before he rushed to get here.

I thought he'd be here too.

I thought I would have to spend another night listening to his confessions and to his remorsefulness and guilt.

It's funny how I thought hearing all of that had been hard.

No.

Hearing him confess to several lurid affairs doesn't seem so bad now. Listening as he professed that he had selfishly begged his general manager to reach out to one of his literary agent friends so Becca could get published, thus freeing up more time for himself, was sad and troubling, but that was nothing compared to the way I feel now. Watching him cry and pace, wrought with guilt because a small part of him was glad she was missing was seriously like a walk in the park in comparison.

In hindsight, all of *that* shit was easy.

Having him die in my arms—calling his parents to tell them that their son is gone—hearing Rebel and Robbie cry in the background—*that* was hard.

It was the most difficult thing I've ever had to do.

Someone knocks on the door.

"Go away!" I shout, then take a swig straight from the bottle.

Keys jangle, then the knob turns and Anna pokes her head inside. When she spots me, she flips on the light. "Cory, Detective Morris and Detective Gordon are here to see you."

I don't move. "Did they find Becca?"

"No, but—"

"Then tell them to leave."

Detective Morris pushes the door completely open with his right hand, his left arm held against his body in a sling. "Cory, Special Agent Tegid is here to see you." Detective Gordon and another guy step into the room. "He has experience working with satanic crimes."

"Mr. Hudson," Agent Tegid nods, "I'm very sorry for your loss."

I sit back in the chair and give him a good once-over. He's older, his dark hair graying at the temples. He isn't fat, per se, but he isn't fit either. He looks like a desk jockey—some guy who's spent his entire FBI career reading case files and surfing porn.

He walks over and sits in the reading chair opposite mine. "I'm Dr. Tegid, a psychologist with the FBI. How are you feeling?" He points to the cast around my left hand and forearm. "Are you comfortable?"

I lift the scotch and take a swig. After setting it on my thigh, I motion to him. "Are you helping them find Becca?"

"Yes, and I have some information I'd like to share with you if you're willing to give me a few moments of your time." He places a manila folder on the table and waits. When I nod, he flips the file open and looks at me. "For starters, I just wanted to give you a sense of what we're dealing with here. Individuals who practice Satanism are—"

"Fucking nuts—completely off their goddamned rockers." I sit forward, my eyes narrowing. "That bitch is crazy, Doc, so save your psychobabble for someone who gives a shit. Can you, or can't you, help them find Becca?"

He stares at me, then sits back, props his ankle on his knee, and nods. "I believe I can be a valuable asset to the team."

I scoff. "Great, thanks, you're hired. Now get the fuck out and find her."

"You believe she's still alive?"

Stunned, I gawk. "Should I think otherwise?"

He shakes his head. "No. I agree with you. Are you familiar with Beltane?"

"No."

"Well, many religious groups recognize it as a holiday, but for Satanists, Beltane is very important, and it's often celebrated on the thirtieth of April, which typically lands right between the spring and summer solstices and is directly opposite Halloween."

"Okay? What does that have to do with Becca?"

"Typically, Satanists view Beltane as a holiday focused on rebirth and fertility, but it's also a day where telepathic communication with the Gods and spirit world is open, so it's an excellent time to communicate with demons."

I light a cigarette. "I still have no idea what this has to do with Becca."

He nods. "I understand, and that's probably because there's a lot to their religion—"

"That shit is *not* a religion," I snap. "They're a bunch of fucking psychopaths!"

Dr. Tegid nods again. "Many people would agree with you, as do I, but if you give me a moment to explain, I think you'll have more faith that Rebecca is still alive and that we still have time to find her."

For some reason, the sincerity in his voice sends a wave of relief over me. "Talk."

"Overall, Mr. Hudson, most Satanists don't believe in ritual sacrifice. Many covens forbid it, but some covens and individual practitioners still perform the rituals." He scoots to the edge of the chair and taps the file. "After reading Penelope's profile and interviewing her neighbor and visiting her home, I believe she thinks that sacrificing someone to Satan will appease and appeal to him so he grants her prayers."

I scoff. "Tell me again how that's supposed to make me feel better?"

"The good news is we still have until sundown on Sunday to find her. The bad news is that after visiting Penelope's home, I think she's been performing traditional rituals for well over a year and is becoming increasingly more frustrated as time goes on. Rebecca was the final straw—your relationship with her causing her to take drastic measures."

"Again—not making me feel better, Doc!"

"We still have time," he says calmly, "but I need you to lay-low. I don't want you talking to the press, making statements, or doing anything that may cause Penelope to believe that Satan is punishing her. Any little statement or behavior on your part could result in her taking extreme measures and hurting Rebecca—"

"Then I'll make a statement offering an exchange—"

"No." Dr. Tegid says firmly. "Not until we've exhausted every other possibility."

"Why wait?" I put my cigarette out and get onto my feet. "I'll do it—I'll totally give myself over in exchange for her safety."

"I agree with you, to a point." Dr. Tegid nods. "Let's just see if we can find another way before we have to resort to that option." He grabs the file and stands. "Lay low—we'll be in touch." The shrink stands and heads to the door.

"I'll be right there," Detective Morris says. Once everyone has cleared out of the room, Darryl pulls his cell phone out of his pocket and begins tapping on the screen. "Rob's father called me a little while ago."

I drop back into the chair, my confusion and anger quickly fading to re-expose my anguish. "Oh, yeah?" I gulp down some scotch, set the bottle aside, and wipe my mouth with the back of my hand. "What did he want?"

"He wanted to know if he had to come and get Rob."

It takes a second to process that, but when it finally settles in that Rob's parents would want to bury him in Colorado, I reach for the bottle again. I guess I never stopped to think about the logistics of that, but now that Detective Morris mentions it, sending Rob "home" only seems right. I'm sure his parents—and probably Becca—would want him laid to rest in his native state.

"I told him I'd see if you were willing to take him home."

"Me? Why would I—"

"You *do* own a private jet, and you do know her kids, right?"

My mouth hangs open for a second, but I snap it shut and nod. "Yes...and I know his parents. We only met briefly, but—"

He extends his phone toward me. I lean over and take it, looking down at the picture of him with a little boy. Confused, I finally look back at him.

"That's my godson." He shrugs. "I'm not a religious man, but Eric insisted we make it official with the whole church and water thing." He points to the door then adds, "You know, Detective Gordon."

Still confused, I look down at the picture again.

"In my line of work, you see a lot hurt and a lot of loss. The adults...they take it hard, especially parents and siblings, so sometimes they forget that these little guys are hurting bad—just not in the most obvious way—not like us." He walks over and takes the phone. "Take Rob home and spend time with the kids, Cory. They'll need you, and I'm sure Rebecca would rather have you looking out for her children instead of sitting here drinking your-self into oblivion."

I shake my head. "I can't."

"Why not?"

I pinch the bridge of my nose despite it being tender to the touch. "Because this is my fault—none of this would have happened if it weren't for me."

Detective Morris sits on the edge of the reading chair and sighs. "Listen, man, the first thing you need to come to terms with is that this isn't your fault. Sometimes people are just in the wrong place at the wrong time, and in this case, you just so happened to be the object of some twisted bitch's obsession. You didn't pick her out—you didn't lead her on or give her the slightest indication that you were interested in her. She's sick, man, and you just so happened to be the unlucky guy who caught her eye. That wasn't your fault, and the sooner you get that through your head, the better everybody will be."

I shake my head even though I agree with him. I didn't ask for this—but I did pull Rebecca, Rob, and her entire family into this the second I fell in love with her.

"I talked to your bodyguard," he says. "He said that going over to Penelope's house and going inside wasn't your idea."

I sigh. "I could have stopped him or..." *Fuck.* I don't know. I've gone over the entire day repeatedly, wishing more than anything that I could go back in time and tell him no, but I wanted to go too, so when he suggested it, I was totally game.

"I'm pretty sure you know you couldn't have stopped him from going. Guilt does funny things to people during shit like this—trust me, I've seen it more times than I wish to count."

I look into his eyes because the guy is a lot more insightful than I ever gave him credit.

He taps my knee, then stands. "Take him home tomorrow and help her kids through all of this. A lot of times, while you're helping them—they're helping you too." When he gets to the door, he grabs the handle but doesn't open it. "Just out of curiosity's sake...did you tell him about you and Rebecca?"

I scoff and shake my head. "The funny thing is, I kept thinking to myself that if I did, he wouldn't feel so bad." I look at Detective Morris. "And I wanted him to feel bad. I sort of took pleasure seeing him so consumed with guilt that I couldn't bring myself to tell him." I reach for the bottle. "She deserves so much more than that."

He nods. "If I hear anything, I'll call. Can you do the same?"

I nod.

"And if you decide to go, just let me know."

"I will."

He leaves, closing the door behind him. I sit against the cushions, taking long swigs of scotch while I go through the pictures on my phone. I have tons of pictures with Becca or just by herself because with her upcoming departure, even though I truly believed she was going to stay, I wanted to capture our time together.

I pull her engagement ring box from my pocket and open it. Would she have said yes? Would I have just let her go if she said no? I force myself to stop thinking about her in the past tense then close the box, set it back in my pocket, and scroll through the pictures of me with Rebel and Robbie. I lift my finger off the screen and stare at their little faces. They both took after Becca—Rebel practically a clone of her mother. I sit there, taking a few sips of scotch while staring at the image. I would love to see them, but I'm not sure if *I'm* the one who should take Rob home. Yet, what else can I do? Just keep sitting here, doing nothing? Maybe Detective Morris is right—maybe the best thing I can do is take care of Rebel and Robbie.

The kids will keep me busy...but how will Rob's parents feel about that? Would they blame me for his death? Would they tell me to leave? I have no idea how to handle complicated family matters. My knee-jerk response is to run...but I've never run away from Becca—even when I wanted to, I've faced every bad memory—every addiction and every fear—dead on. Facing Rob's parents to make sure her kids are okay is yet another thing I'm willing to take on—another uncomfortable and frightening experience that I'll face, even though a bigger part of me wants to bolt.

After another moment of looking at the picture of me and Rebel and Robbie, I get up and screw the cap on the scotch. Detective Morris is right. Becca wouldn't want me to sit here drinking or shooting up—Becca would want me to do the right thing. I'm not quite sure of the exact moment when her opinion started mattering so much, but it does, so I walk over and pack Rob's belonging into his suitcase. When I'm sure I've gotten everything, I go downstairs. Anna and Brad are sitting on the couch.

"Hey..." I lean against the doorframe and watch as they scramble onto their feet with expressions filled with concern and just a little bit of fear. I haven't been very nice to them since I've gotten back from the hospital. "I'm sorry about earlier."

Brad shrugs. "It's all good. Are you feeling better?"

I shake my head, the movement reminding me of my broken nose and the stitches along my hairline. "Did Detective Morris leave?"

"Yeah," Anna nods, "they left to go interview some of the people Penelope's father used to work with."

A part of me suddenly wants to get more information. A part of me wants to tag along to hear what they find out, but when an image of Rob suddenly resurfaces, my desire to do police work falters. Do Rebel and Robbie need all three of us dead? A better question is, can Rob's parents take care of the kids on their own? Becca's father is battling cancer and her mother suffers from diabetes and arthritis, so I know they can't. Nor can her brother and sisters—all of them struggling to care for their own families. But I can. Aside from my house, car, and plane, I've banked my cash—never one to indulge in much but my alcohol and drug use—the alcohol nowhere near the cost of my heroine, which I've thankfully quit.

"I'm going to Colorado tomorrow," I announce. "I'd like it if you guys can come."

It isn't only for moral support. My constant fear that they'll suddenly disappear or something horrible will happen to them is irrational, but I can't help it. What if that crazy bitch goes after them, too? I wouldn't be able to live with myself if more people got hurt because of me.

"I could use a trip," Brad says. "I'll call the airport and get the ball rolling."

I look at Anna.

She nods. "Of course, I'll go. Do you need me to help with anything?"

"I think I got it. It'll help keep my mind busy."

"Okay." She walks over and grips my hand. "I'll go make you something to eat."

I consider objecting because my appetite vanished the second Becca disappeared, but I nod. "Yeah, that sounds good."

Anna and I walk out of the room together. She walks toward the kitchen while I go in search of Josh. When I can't find him anywhere, I ask a new bodyguard where I can find him. He tells me Brad gave Josh the night off, so I ask for Josh's number because I like him—trust him for some reason—so even though the guy deserves a much-needed night off; I call to ask if he'll come with us to Colorado.

Josh agrees and says he has a few other guys who can come too. I tell him I'll call back to let him know where we're staying so he and the other bodyguards can secure the location. I'm fairly certain Colorado is a bit out of Penelope's psychotic reach, but I don't want to risk it. Nor is she my only super-fan, so I won't ever make the mistake of thinking they're harmless.

When I ask Josh to bring me a gun, he hesitates, then asks if I have any experience handling a weapon. I don't, but I assure him I'm a quick learner. That doesn't seem to convince him, so he offers to take me to a range first thing in the morning to show me the basics.

With that arranged, I head up to my bedroom to call Mr. Carter. Whether he's okay with it or not, I'm going, but if he's really hostile, I'll keep my distance. There's no need upsetting the man more than he already is, but the least I can do is get Rob home and hope to see the kids, even if for a few minutes.

I lock my bedroom door, sit on the edge of the bed, and lift the framed photo of Mom and me. I run my finger over the glass but then shiver and place it on the nightstand again. Disgusted that Penelope had her grubby, Satan-worshipping hands on it, I decide that it's time for a new frame. I lift it up again, flip it over, and pull off the back, intent on retrieving the photo, but when a dried saffron flower falls to the floor and lands between my feet, I stare at it. Stunned that it's been there for so long without my noticing, I slowly reach for it. How did I not know it was there? Yet, does anyone really pull a picture out of its frame on a regular basis?

After removing the picture and setting it aside, I throw the frame and flower into the garbage. Pestered with feelings of rage and utter violation, I take several calming breaths, then reach for the phone. My priorities at the moment are getting Rob home and taking care of the kids. I can't and won't let my rage toward Penny consume me right now. I'm not sure when I started to subscribe to the theory of karma, but I've decided that I'm only going to put positive vibes into the universe. Once Rob is home though, and the kids are okay—or as okay as they can be—and I have Becca back, then, and only then, will I allow myself the pleasure of thinking up ways of how to torture and then kill that psychotic, satanic-worshipping bitch.

Chapter 34

Penelope

As I watch the relentless news coverage of Rebecca's missing-person case, my blood boils. *Dammit.* No one important was even supposed to notice she was gone, and Ethan definitely wasn't supposed to care this much! I switch the television off and walk down the hallway. The only good thing that's come of all this is that Rebecca's husband is dead. That serves him right—the bastard had no right to go into my sanctuary. Ethan, it appears, was spared, but there are conflicting stories about how serious his injuries truly were.

Some say they were minor injuries, while others are reporting that he sustained some sort of traumatic brain injury. That would at least explain his sudden and utter concern for Rebecca. I mean, because otherwise, why would he care? He belongs to me, after all, and deep down, he knows that. Or...maybe all of his reactions are just for the sake of his fans? Could he just be acting? Doing what he thinks the public wants to see.

That has to be it.

I head toward Rebecca's room and push the door open. The stench of urine, blood, and singed flesh is so offensive that I walk over and open the window. "Guess what I just saw?" I say casually. "That really sexy husband of yours is dead."

Rebecca stops struggling against the restraints, her eyes becoming the size of saucers.

"I know. I was surprised too, but that's what he gets for nosing around my house." I suck my teeth and shake my head. "It's just too bad he went so quickly. I probably should have thought of something other than explosives." I step closer and pretend to strain to understand her muffled speech. "What's that you say? Oh, you think I'm lying?" I laugh. "Oh, I wouldn't lie about that." I lean closer, my smile turning to a scowl. "You're just lucky those little shit kids of yours are too far away for me to waste my time on. I would have happily skinned them right in front of you, you whore!"

I slap her, but instead of crying or cowering away, she glares at me. Her eyes are swollen, but I can still register that innate motherly instinct burning within them.

"Oh, did I touch a nerve?"

I squeeze her nostrils shut and count to five. The moment I release it, she sucks in huge gulps of air, but rage is still burning bright within her eyes. I squeeze her nose closed repeatedly; always counting to five before releasing it, yet the burning wrath in her eyes only intensifies.

One-one-thousand, two-one-thousand, three-one-thousand, four-one-thousand, five—

Rebecca jerks her face away, so I allow my hand to fall to my side to give her a second to catch her breath. Then, after several other suffocation attempts, the duct tape pulls away from her upper lip. I move to press it against her face, but I stop short when she whispers something.

A chill sweeps up my spine. "What did you just say?"

She uses her tongue to move the tape farther out of her way. "He will never forgive you."

Her words, for some reason, don't disturb me as much as that feral look in her eyes. I move to replace the tape, but she shifts away.

"He'll hate you. Will never want to touch or be touched by someone who hurt me, and if you hurt my kids, he'll hunt you down and he'll kill you."

Stunned, I step back and shake my head. "He loves *me*. All of this is just an act for his fans—"

"No one could love you, you sick, crazy bitch!"

I rush over and grip her face, squeezing her cheeks together. "You shut up!" I slam her head against the wood beam, the strap across her forehead not giving much room to lift it too high, but I do it several times—stopping only when her eyes close and her head goes limp in my hands. Shaking and breathless, I quickly release her face and step away.

Oh, no. Did I just kill her? My Dark Father would not like that at all. I place my fingers on her neck and search for a pulse. It's faint, but that doesn't mean I didn't just do some major damage. Will Satan be angry for sacrificing a brain-dead woman even though I despise her with all of my being? Worse yet, what if she's right? What if it isn't all an act and the only chance I have to be with Ethan is to give her back to him?

No. He doesn't love her.

Despite my certainty, I remove the straps from around her ankles, knees, and waist. Her legs slip off the wood, but the binds around her breasts and forehead hold her torso up, her body hanging oddly. I remove the forehead strap first, then wrap my arm around her waist to hold her up while I undo the breast strap.

After lowering her to the floor, I search around. It would be better to take her to the fallout shelter, but it's too late now so there's no way I'm venturing out in the dark. Yet, if I keep her in the house, she might try to make a run for it when she gains consciousness. Not that I'd advise that for anyone since there are tons of booby-traps and landmines out there.

Dammit. I don't need the bitch to blow herself to

smithereens, but dragging her along without the aid of a flash-light could be dangerous for both of us, so I'm stuck with keeping her here...*somewhere.*

I grab her ankles and pull her along, walking backward to the bathroom. Once inside, I release Rebecca and hurry back into the room to retrieve rope. If I were home, I'd have a pair of handcuffs handy.

How sad that I won't ever be able to return there. I liked that house.

I walk back into the bathroom, set the rope aside, and then lift Rebecca into the tub. The faucet comes up through the floor, the water line running along the basement ceiling to the hot water heater so there's no way that in her condition she'll be able to pull herself free.

After I tie her up, I step back to admire my handiwork. This will have to do for tonight. To ensure silence, I put duct tape over her mouth, then go into the living room. I turn the television back on and then pull my laptop over, searching the internet for news about Ethan.

Articles are popping up every few minutes because the story instantly became a national headline within an hour of Rebecca's disappearance. Then, after Cory made his statement, the news went international—the entire world wanting a play by play of the events and investigation.

Good grief. This is bad...like really bad. It seems as if the entire world wants my head on a platter, so at first light, I'll have to move her to the fallout shelter. No one will find us there, not unless I want them to, which I just might. Perhaps my best bet is to use Rebecca as bait instead of as my ritual sacrifice. If he does love her as much as she claims—and as much as it truly does appear, then maybe the only way of getting him here is to lure him by using her. It's worth a shot, because at this point, I'm running out of time and options.

Chapter 35

Darryl

I'm starting to see why Penelope is so nuts. After interviewing four of her stepfather's co-workers, it's pretty self-explanatory. The girl spent her entire life in captivity because her parents were doomsday preppers. Home-schooled and rarely seen by her stepfather's co-workers, Penelope Fitzpatrick was destined for an asylum.

Exhausted after so many lengthy interviews, I drop onto one of the plush leather seats in the conference room and take a sip of my cold, stale coffee. Then I reach for the file for my next interview. Father Marcus is a Catholic priest who claims Penelope and her mother were members of his congregation for a brief time several years ago. He's currently down in Brazil participating in some Catholic fellowship crap for Easter, but when he saw the news, he contacted the station.

I got the call right after I got home from the hospital and I hadn't appreciated the interruption. Chels and I had just gotten into it about her not wanting to date a cop who's crazy enough to run into a burning building when he was already injured. I tried to explain the bond between partners; tried to tell her that today wasn't an average day at work. She didn't want to hear it; said she couldn't handle it.

And that's where we left it once her family started blowing up her phone after seeing her run into Penelope's burning house, compliments of her own cameraman. Not to mention that I had interviews to conduct, even though I should be in bed, recovering from all the injuries I sustained.

That was yet another point of contention on Chels's part, which I had no argument for. The only thing I could do was ask her to meet me at my place later. She said she would.

She won't come, though. Of that, I'm certain.

It's amazing how much that thought bothers me, so I look around the room to gauge my timeframe. Eric is still on the phone with his wife, and the annoying FBI shrink we're now stuck with is reading something. Further irked that The Bureau and the ATF are trying to steal the case away from us and are riding our asses, I grab my cell phone and step into the hallway. Chels doesn't answer her phone, so I stand there debating on letting Eric and the shrink handle this last interview. That would go over like a lead balloon with Captain Baltimore, though, but I'm almost at the point of not giving a shit.

"Detective Morris?" the shrink calls from the doorway. "Father Marcus is ready to speak with us."

I nod and head back inside. While Eric finishes his conversation with Monica, I walk over and dump my coffee in exchange for a Coke. After cracking the can open and swallowing down more pain meds, I turn and look at the shrink. The guy has been fairly quiet all evening, only interjecting to ask random questions before going back to scribble in his journal. I walk over and take a seat across from him.

"So, is any of this stuff helping to get us closer to her?" I ask him.

He nods while leaning closer to finish writing something. "Oh, yes—plenty." He caps the pen, shuts his journal, and leans back in his seat and looks at me. "From what I've gathered, Satanism is something Penelope has recently started dabbling in so thankfully she's a novice, and with her preference for working alone, she hasn't joined a coven and has probably learned a lot about it from the internet."

"So, what's that mean for us?"

He twists the pen in his hand. "I'll know for certain after listening to what Father Marcus has to offer, but if this girl was raised to believe that the end was near, hence her parents' doomsday-prepping mentality, then at some point, it's more than likely that she turned to the only person she believed could help her rebel."

I scoff. "So, she turned to Satan to piss off her parents?"

He shakes his head. "Not necessarily piss off her parents— probably more as a means of escape." He props his elbows on the table. "Many people raised in dysfunctional homes eventually... embrace the crazy, for lack of a better term, but some people realize that the environment they're living in isn't normal and they want out."

"So, the alternative to being a fanatical Christian was to become a Satanist?" I roll my eyes as I take a sip of soda. "Who knew that finding normal meant seeking Satan?"

"Some people—"

"It was a rhetorical question, Doc," I say before he can continue with the psychobabble. Thankfully, just then, Eric ends his call and takes the seat next to mine. "Are we ready?" I ask him.

"Yep, hit it."

Using the large speaker centered on the table, I connect the conference call and then sit back. "Hello, Father Marcus. This is Detective Morris. Thanks for contacting us." After introducing him to everyone, I say, "What can you tell us about Penelope Fitzpatrick?"

"Unfortunately, not much...I only met her a few times. Her mother started coming to mass about six years ago. She was a nice lady, very well spoken, but reserved. She sought me out after attending for about six months, asking if I was willing to bless her house."

"But your church is in Malibu. Didn't it seem odd that she was driving all the way from L.A.?"

"Initially, it did, but then she told me she and her husband were having a cabin built near Topanga, so we arranged for a day I could come out for a visit."

"What about Penelope?" Eric asks. "Did she go to church too?"

"For the first four months, she did. At the time, the church was going through a bit of a scandal so we began a youth group that she attended separately from mass. We thought it best the younger folks could have a fun, Christian experience with an affiliate from the local YMCA and one of our youth group leaders rather than sit through our usual service."

Right, because that's so much better than being molested by the priest. I let that unfortunate reality go to focus on the more pressing one. "Father Marcus, why did Penelope only attend the youth group for four months?"

"It's hard to say because I wasn't involved in youth group activities, but I do recall the youth group leader mentioning that Penelope and one of our other members had developed a crush on one another, which definitely upset Penelope's mother." He shrugs. "After that, only Mrs. Fitzpatrick returned to mass."

I reach for a pen and pad. "What was this boy's name?"

"Ethan Green."

The moment the name slips through his lips, Eric and I glance at each other. Cory plays a character named Ethan Green on his show, and since I don't like coincidences, I pull my notepad closer and start writing.

"I hate to continue to be the harbinger of bad news, gentlemen," Father Marcus continues, "but if you'd like additional information about their relationship, you would have to reach out to his parents. Unfortunately, after their son went missing a while back, no one has really heard from them."

Eric and I exchange another mournful look, then I signal Officer Cooke over. After handing her a slip of paper with

Ethan's name on it, I quickly ask her to get all of the information she can on his case. "Father Marcus, did you ever get to the cabin in Topanga to bless it?"

"Unfortunately, no. Mrs. Fitzpatrick came to church for another two months faithfully, but then she suddenly stopped. I called her home in L.A. but she said she had decided to attend her husband's church and that my visit was no longer necessary because a minister from her husband's church had already done it."

"Do you remember the name of his church?"

"She never mentioned it. Nor did I ever meet Mr. Fitzpatrick. I'm very sorry, Detective, but there isn't really much more I can tell you. Mrs. Fitzpatrick never came to church after that and I only heard about her again when the media began posting her picture on the news."

"You've given us plenty, Father," I assure him. "Thanks for your time. If you remember anything else, call me directly." I give him my personal number, then end the call.

"So Penelope falls for a kid named Ethan Green, *who is currently missing*," Eric enunciates each word dramatically, "and then she starts stalking an actor who goes by the name of Ethan Green." He rubs his forehead, then pinches the bridge of his nose. "You can't make this shit up."

"You know," the shrink chimes in as he types something into his phone, "names aren't as uncommon as most people think..." He studies his screen for a moment then looks at Eric. "For instance, my Google search on Ethan Green just pulled up a film based on a comic strip, a photographer, a tennis player, another actor—aside from Cory, and a ton of other Ethans."

"What are you suggesting?" Eric counters. "That all of these guys are in danger too?"

For once, Dr. Tegid is tentative to respond, which gets my attention. I had been logging into the conference room computer to pull up a map of Topanga on the big screen, but I pause to glance his way.

"I think," he begins slowly, "that it would be worth checking to see if there are other missing-person cases associated with this name."

Eric sighs. "So much for getting home in time for dinner." He begrudgingly reaches for his phone and starts tapping on the screen.

I go back to logging in and pull up a map of Topanga. From there, I key in directions to Father Marcus's church in Malibu. It isn't a far drive, but without knowing the exact address of the cabin, I can't be certain.

Eric leans against the table and says, "I'm pretty sure it's no coincidence that Ethan disappeared when he did." He strokes his chin and then, using his Yoda impersonation voice, he adds, "Methinks Penelope's parents' car accident wasn't an accident either, and methinks that right after she laid them to rest, she went after Ethan."

The shrink uncaps his pen. "Valid assumptions, Detective, but I think the better question is, what happened to Ethan? I agree with you that her parents' accident has to be revisited, but if she went after Ethan *after* they were gone and then he went missing, what went wrong?"

"That's a good question, Doc," Eric says, then he looks my way. "You up for chasing after that mystery solo for a few? I just need to get home for an hour or two, calm everyone down, let them see I'm okay."

"I've got this, bro. Go home for a bit." I shift my attention to Officer Cooke as she beelines our way. "Give everyone my love."

Eric nods and shifts out of the way so Officer Cooke can drop a file on my desk. "I've got the information you requested on Ethan Green."

"Awesome." I pull the file closer.

"It's a cold case now, but Ethan Green went missing after attending one of his classes at UCLA. He was never seen again."

"No leads?" I ask while leaning closer to read the report myself.

"None...he attended his math class and was supposed to meet his friends later that evening, but he never showed. His roommate saw him the morning he went missing, said they left for their classes as usual, but when the roommate returned, he wasn't there and never returned. Nothing looked amiss, though, and a review of the security cameras on campus showed Ethan getting into his car alone at four-thirty. None of his behavior stood out as concerning."

"Did they check light cams or ATM footage around the area he was supposed to meet his friends?"

"No, but they pulled his phone records and there weren't any calls that morning, but the last ping from his GPS placed him at a mall clear on the other side of town around five. Then it went dead. They contacted the friends he was supposed to meet, but none of them were alarmed because Ethan had mentioned he might not show up the day before. It wasn't until the following Monday, when he didn't show up for any of his classes, that he was reported missing."

"Are you serious?" I pull the file closer and flip through the pages. "Jesus, it's no wonder they never found him. Can you do me a favor and get me the names of his roommate and friends he was supposed to meet? And then get me his parent's info."

She nods. "Sure. Are you going to stay in here or should I bring it to your office?"

"Oh, and after that, can you see if you can find the accident report for Penelope's parents' accident and maybe their death certificates, too?" I reach for the keyboard and pull up directions between the campus and the mall Ethan was last known to have visited.

"That might take a while, so shall I meet you back at your office?"

"Yeah, I guess." I look at my watch. "If I'm not there, just leave whatever you find on my desk."

Officer Cooke stands. "Okay...?"

I turn my attention back to the map of Topanga. "This is a

pretty big area," I say to Eric as I enlarge the image. "Do you think the tech guys can do some of that triangulating crap from Father Marcus's church to different locations to give us a better chance of finding the cabin?"

He stares at me a moment before nodding.

I roll my eyes. "Go home; I'll send in the request."

"No...I can do it." He motions his head toward Officer Cooke.

I stare at him for a second, then I look up at her. I seriously have no idea why she's still even here. "Thank you?"

Her brows furrow, then she purses her lips as if she's about to say something but then decides against it. "I'll be sure to get this stuff to your office when I find it."

"Okay...thank you," I repeat, suddenly feeling like I'm missing the punchline.

When she finally leaves, I look at the monitor again. "Shit. I should have asked her to get in touch with the Topanga unit so they can do some recon for us."

Eric chuckles. "Dude, you've got it bad."

"I've got what bad?" I pull up the number for the Topanga unit then reach for the phone.

He laughs. "You just blew six months of trying to get into Cooke's pants by practically treating her like she was invisible." He taps my shoulder. "I'm just saying, bro, you've got it bad."

Yeah, I do, and a lot of fucking good it's done me. I begrudgingly yank the phone off the hook, call the station, and then explain the situation. When I'm done, Eric is nowhere in sight—probably in our office calling the tech-genius guys about making some kind of map we can work with, so I stand to grab another Coke.

"Are you done for the night?" Special Agent Tegid asks.

Now there's someone who's been invisible. "No, I'm just going to..." I catch sight of Chels as she steps into the open bay area. She stops and talks to Officer Cooke, who in turn, points in my direction. Chels follows her line of sight and smiles when she spots me. Relieved to see her, I wave and can't help what I'm sure is a goofy smile when she holds up a brown paper bag. God love a woman who brings me donuts and chocolate-flavored shakes.

"Is that your wife?" the shrink asks.

I shake my head while retrieving my stuff. "Not yet, but I'm working on it. I'll see you in the morning." Then I head out to meet Chels halfway, suddenly very okay with letting the uniformed officers' work on compiling research while I go home with my girl for a couple of hours to get some much-needed rest.

Chapter 36

Rebecca

The pain radiating along my skull is excruciating. I blink several times, a part of me wishing I could remain unconscious. *I don't know how much more I can take.* My body aches, and the cigarette burns on my thigh throb, an uncomfortable warmth surrounding each affliction. My right heel also still feels as if it's on fire, with sharp bursts of pain occasionally shooting up my leg. Yet, despite the agonizing headache and other physical ailments, the worst is the cold. I'm freezing.

I shift and move my head slowly, hoping the blurred vision from my left eye can help estimate my surroundings. My right eye is swollen shut and is probably permanently damaged—the bitch never seeming to consider that she could walk around the table to strike my other side. Speaking of which...I'm no longer on that table—the freeness of my limbs evidence of that. *But where am I now?* I lift my head off the hard surface and focus. Sunlight is filtering in from a window above a nearby toilet.

I'm in a bathtub, a rope tied to the faucet with enough slack so my bound wrists are lying on my chest.

Well, at least that explains the cold. The porcelain tub feels like ice pressed against my skin. I test the rope to see how much slack I can get. Sadly, it isn't much, but I manage to get into a seated position. The bathroom isn't large, only big enough to fit the tub, toilet, and a small vanity. The door is closed and I'm sure the window is locked, but if I can manage it, that would be my best bet of getting out of here.

First, though, the duct tape on my mouth has to go. Grateful that I've always been limber, I bring my hands to my face and yank the tape off. After several deep breaths, I lie against the tub again, completely drained. I give myself a few moments, since Penny has done some serious damage, though the physical part of it doesn't feel nearly as suffocating as the emotional part. *Rob is dead.* That resounding thought makes me sob because, despite our issues, I loved him; he was the father of my children and he didn't deserve to die, especially by her hand.

If I survive, I'm going to come back one day and kill her. I will...but today is not that day. Right now, I need to find a way out of here.

I shift my hands back and forth, then try to pull them apart to loosen the knot. It takes extraordinary effort, but I finally manage to get enough slack. I shift my face closer, using my teeth to pull the knot free. I gently lower the rope to my side, scared to make even the slightest sound to alert her, then I sit back up and rub my sore, rope-burned wrists gently for a moment.

Will she hear me get out of the tub? Will I be able to stand or open that window or climb through it to run for help? For a moment, a billion other scenarios run through my mind, and I almost reconsider an escape attempt, but then, almost as if God himself intervenes, the memory of Penny talking about Rebel and Robbie resurfaces suddenly. That's all the motivation I need. I grab the sides of the tub and push up, making sure to place more of my weight on my left foot. I sway and fall forward. Thankfully, I catch myself before falling, but all of the effort takes a lot out of me. Exhausted, I just stand there for a moment.

I need food and water desperately. At the moment, there's no hope of me getting anything solid, but if the water is working, I can at least drink. Worst-case scenario, I can scoop water out of the toilet if the sink doesn't work.

As quietly as I can, I step out of the tub, resisting the urge to hop even though each time I place weight on the toes of my right foot, an unbearable pain shoots from my heel straight up my spine. Winded, I grip the side of the vanity and look at the mirror.

Tears instantly blur my already poor vision, but my face is so battered that I can't help the reaction. I gingerly press my finger-tips against my cheek and eye. The right side of my face is so swollen, bruised, and bloodied that I barely recognize myself. *If you survive, it'll heal,* I remind myself, and this definitely isn't the time for vanity. *Right.* Calmer, but not by much, I reach for the cold-water handle. Thankfully, the faucet doesn't squeak. Nor do sounds of screeching pipes ensue when the water begins to drip. Not wanting to push my luck, I don't turn it on beyond that, the drip enough to gather handfuls of water that I bring to my cracked and bloody lips.

The coppery taste of my own blood fills my mouth with the first few scoopfuls of water, but I don't care. Parched in a way that defies words, I bring water to my mouth for a long time, but the effort proves to be too much. I finally move my mouth to the faucet and drink, lapping water like a dog. When I've finally gotten my fill, I carefully turn the water off and reach for the medicine cabinet. It's empty. I step back and pull open the door of the vanity. There's a first-aid kit that I grab and take with me to the toilet. I close the lid and take a seat. I know I need to go, but I'm hoping there's something in here that I can wrap over my heel.

Luckily, the first-aid kit has all the essentials, so I wrap a bandage around my foot, making sure to put the bulk of it over the burn on my heel to help with the pain. Not worried about anything else at the moment, I set the box aside then climb onto the toilet seat. My balance isn't good, but I grab onto the windowsill to keep from toppling over.

Dizzy, I let the feeling pass before I unlock the window and open it slowly. I'm on the ground floor so it's probably only a five-or-six-foot drop to the ground, and I'm small enough to fit through the window. If I pull myself out, though, I'll fall face-first. I look around the bathroom, hoping there's something I can use so I can climb out backward. There isn't.

Determining that it's better to be outside than in, I pull myself through the window. After a moment, gravity takes over and I fall forward, my arms shooting forward to brace for impact. I land with a thud, my body pivoting slightly before I hit the ground like a ton of bricks, which causes my left arm to take the brunt of the fall. With no time to sit around crying over yet another bodily injury, I scramble onto my feet and press my back against the house. *Which way should I go?* I look left, then right, but neither option is appealing. I'm in the middle of the woods, no neighboring houses in sight.

Deciding that it's best to avoid windows and the front and back doors, I study the nearby tree line. If I make a run for it, I might be able to get into the woods without her spotting me. Of course, that plan will only work if she isn't in one of the rooms on this side of the house. Not wanting to risk it, I slide along the house to the corner. Maybe my best bet is to run diagonally from the corner, though that might just make me visible from the windows on both sides of the house rather than just one.

I peek around the corner. The back door and windows on this side seem more dangerous than the bathroom and two windows on this one, so I judge the distance to the woods, then take a moment to listen. I don't hear any telltale signs of company, so I make a run for it. Despite the pain, I make it past the first row of trees, then the second before I finally stop, wrapping my arms around a thick trunk. I press my cheek against it for support while I catch my breath.

The cabin is still, the vision of my good eye darting back and forth to make sure she's not following me. Certain that she's still unaware I'm missing, I turn and walk farther into the woods, hoping I'll eventually hear the familiar sounds of traffic or even a train to help guide me back toward civilization.

When someone whistles, I hurry to a nearby tree and drop behind it.

"Here, Becca, Becca, Becca," Penny calls. "I wouldn't wander off if I were you. Daddy didn't much care for company, so you best mind where you step!"

I search around the thick woods, wondering if there really are booby-traps. *Is she bluffing to scare me back to her?* I don't think so. This girl is crazy enough to rig her house with stuff, so that only leaves me with one question. Is it better to surrender or risk it?

"I've made a decision," Penny shouts, her voice closer now. "I'm going to exchange you for Cory, so I won't hurt you anymore." It's silent for a moment then she adds, "I doubt the landmines will give you such a kind offer."

Did she just say *landmines?*

I search around again. I have no idea how to tell where a landmine might be, but isn't that the purpose of them—to hide in plain sight so the unsuspecting trespasser blows to smithereens before he or she can get to the cabin.

"Come on out. The plan was to drag you to the fallout shelter, but since you're feeling spunky enough, you can walk and save me the lower back pain."

A twig snaps—the sound so close I shift around the tree in the opposite direction, then peek around it. *Dammit.* She's right there!

"Peek-a-boo, I see you." I hear the telltale sound of a round being loaded into a chamber. "I'm giving you until the count of five, and then I'm shooting. I'll try to hit a nonlethal part of your body, but I can't promise anything."

Dammit. There's no way she won't see me make a run for it. Nor am I in any shape to try and outrun her. I don't believe she won't hurt me again, but if my alternative is a gunshot, damn near at point-blank range, then giving myself up really is my only option.

"Five, four, three—"

A shot rings through the air. I instinctively duck and press myself against the tree. Penny steps around it, standing a few feet ahead of me.

"Let's go." She motions with the gun. "*You* don't try any funny business, and *I* won't shoot."

I stand, holding my hands out so she sees that I'm going willingly. She directs me toward the thicker part of the woods. We walk for at least ten minutes, the heel on my right foot throbbing and aching with each step. Nor does the dampness of the grass soaking through the bandage help. And on top of the foot pain, my head is throbbing and my stomach is cramping painfully, probably from the water, or maybe from the lack of food.

We walk for another ten or so minutes before she stops. "Go sit by that tree," she orders while pointing to a huge spruce.

I hobble over, grateful to drop onto my bottom and rest. Penny walks toward another pine tree while tucking the gun into her waistband. She kneels and pulls a patch of grass away. I'm assuming it's fake, but it looks so much like the surrounding area I can't be sure if it's real or not. Nor would I have noticed it if I were just walking by, which is a thought that sends a chill down my spine.

If I go down there, no one will find me.

I'm not sure how long I've been in that cabin, but if they haven't found me yet, then the likelihood of them finding me in the fallout shelter is nil to none.

I should run, I know that, but I can't outrun her and I have no idea where to go. The entire time we walked, I strained to listen for any signs of civilization, but none came, so we really must be in the middle of nowhere.

Penny scoots closer to a huge valve and turns it. After a moment, she pulls a metal lid up.

"Let's go," she orders, standing and pulling the gun from her waistband in one smooth motion.

I get onto my feet and walk over. The opening is dark, giving me no clue as to what heinous new place I'm going to end up in next.

"There's a ladder there," she points, "get going."

I drop onto my bottom again and scoot to the edge, my feet dangling over. With some effort, I manage to grab a hold of the ladder. After going down the first few rungs, a light turns on, which must be rigged by motion sensors. With the light on, I study the immediate area as I continue my descent. The room is large, much bigger than I would have ever imagined. To my left, there are tons of shelves, all of which have canned foods of every variety. To my right, there's a living area. Couches and chairs scattered about, and there's a long desk with old-fashioned radio equipment littering it.

"Step aside, but not far," she says as I near the bottom.

I follow her instructions, but continue my inspection. Ahead of me is a hallway that leads to a closed door. Behind me is another hallway that leads into a galley-style kitchen. The fallout shelter reminds me of a ship—some place livable despite the metal walls and cold, damp feeling hanging in the air.

Penny drops from the third step and motions toward the hallway. I walk to the door, lights popping on as we move along.

Once I'm there, Penny shoves me aside, opens it, and pushes me inside. "Keep going to the next door," she orders.

I hurry over to the second door, only taking quick glimpses of the bedroom as I pass. She opens that door, which reveals a locked gate just beyond. She pulls a keychain from around her neck and unlocks it. Then she pushes me through, pulls the gate closed, and clicks the lock back into place.

"The door to your left is a bathroom. Don't bother trying to open the other door in there because it won't give; it's sealed shut. The door to your right is your room. I'll slide your grub through this hole." She kicks the gate near the floor and I notice the small, rectangular space that a tray can slide through, and maybe an arm, but it's definitely not a means of escape. "Don't shout or try to escape. If you do either, I'll tape your mouth shut and shackle you to the wall. Behave and I won't bother you. Try my patience and I'll make this place just as unpleasant as the last."

With those haunting words, she turns and walks into the first bedroom, slamming the metal door behind her. I hear the lock engage and then there's silence. I stand there for a moment, staring at the gate and the metal door. Double protection, so there's no way to escape there. I finally turn and open the bathroom door. It's even smaller than the bathroom in the cabin, but there's a sink, toilet, and shower stall. There's also a door to my left, almost as if it connects with the first bedroom we walked through, but the steel door is welted shut; the telltale signs that someone used a blowtorch evident because the metal is raised and rough looking.

Thankfully, the water works, so I sit and use the bathroom. I'm actually offended by my own smell, though it isn't surprising given that I had urinated on myself several times, my bladder not allowing me as much lenience as my bowels. I eye the shower with longing, but first walk over and look at the other room. It's smaller than the first bedroom, but there's a twin-sized bed, dresser, nightstand, and a waist-high bookcase. There's a Bible, a few devotionals, and lots of juvenile Christian fiction. I walk over to a door and pull it open. There are clothes neatly folded on labeled shelves. Sweatshirts and sweatpants are the only option, but I'd imagine they come in handy against the damp cold. There are also flannel pajamas, towels, underwear, socks, slippers, and sneakers.

I pull a towel, fresh clothes, and slippers off the shelves. That's when I notice the writing. I lean closer, trying to make out what it says, but the closet is too dark. I turn, drop the clothes, towel, and slippers onto the bed, then lift the bedside lamp and bring it closer. After switching it on, I lean closer.

The initials E.G + P.F cover the walls. Sometimes the writing is in an elegant cursive while other times it's printed and surrounded by a heart. It's kind of juvenile—something you would see on a teenager's notebook—and I wonder what the initials stand for. Could one of those initials be hers? That thought resonates again and as I run my fingers over the writing, I shiver as the truth of it sinks in.

Good grief, I bet this used to be her room.

Had she been locked in here at some point? She must have been because the entire closet is covered in her writing. What the hell was wrong with this girl's parents? And is it really any wonder that she's as crazy as she is?

I move the sweatshirts out of the way and kneel to get a look at the wall beyond that cubby. My heart frenzies when I see another name. *Who the hell is Eve?* It matches the other cursive that's on the wall, and farther down, the name is within a heart. I pull the sweatshirts out of the cubby and look at the wooden base of the shelf. The words Eve Green are written in calligraphy, a date written just beneath the name. That was three years ago.

Startling when the door in the hallway opens, I quickly get the clothes back in place and turn off the light. Another loud thud resonates then the door slams closed. I sit there for a long moment, petrified that she's come to torment me. After several other moments of silence though, I place the lamp back on the nightstand and get onto my feet. I left the door open, so I creep toward it and peer around the corner.

The main door is closed and so is the gate, but there's a tray of food on the floor now. It's pasta in a bowl, a can of soda, and something in a bag that I can't make out. I stand there for a moment, debating on getting closer. It could be a trap, or worse yet, she might have poisoned the food. Yet, as the smell of the pasta reaches my nose, my body makes me move forward even though I don't want to. I haven't eaten in days—or at least I think it's been days. And there's something comforting about the package of fruit snacks. Maybe because it's something I've packed in Rebel and Robbie's lunches a thousand times. Starved, I lift the tray and take it into the room, closing the door behind me. I drop onto the floor, my back pressed against the door as I reach for the spoon and start shoveling food into my mouth. The bowl empties too quickly, so I tear open the fruit snacks and pour them into my mouth, chewing the large wad for only a second before I swallow. Still hungry, I pop open the can of soda and drain it.

When I'm done, I drop it and burp. Now that hit the spot. I gather everything onto the tray and stand. After sliding it through the hole, I go back into the room and grab the clothes and towels. There's only a bar of soap in the shower, but the water is warm so I scrub myself clean, including my ratty, tangled hair, all while ignoring the searing pain from all the wounds that are covering my body.

Once done, I don the sweatshirt and pants. The clothes are big on me, so the shirt and pants require several cuffs so they don't hang too long. Then I toss my clothes into the small garbage can. Regardless of what happens to me from this point on, those clothes have reached their limits.

The vanity mirror doubles as a door for a medicine cabinet. This one has a first-aid kit as well, so I swallow down four ibuprofens with tap water, then I go to work on covering all my wounds with an antibiotic ointment. There's a brush and comb, so I rinse each under the stream of water and work out the knots in my hair, braiding it afterward and using one of the hairbands to secure it.

Feeling better than I have in days, I tidy up the bathroom, more out of habit, yet it's oddly comforting. Closing the door behind me, I stop short when I notice the tray is gone. I stand there for a moment, staring at the empty space, then I walk across the hallway and close the bedroom door behind me. There isn't a lock, so I drag the bookcase over, not wanting her to be able to barge in easily.

The small bedroom is windowless, the only open fixture on

the wall an air vent that's also sealed shut—almost as if Penny had tried to escape through it long ago and her parents had put a stop to it. Had she tried all the escape routes? Will I be able to find something she hadn't? I drop onto the bed and sigh. If she couldn't get out, then there's no way I'm getting out.

Glad that she, at least, has held true to her word and not beaten or tortured me, I lie on the bed and stare up at the ceiling. The initials are written or sometimes carved onto the ceiling as well. Exhausted, frightened, and cold, I pull the covers back and get under, wondering who E.G is...

Do the initials stand for Eve Green? Maybe Penny is gay and her uber-Christian parents trapped her down here so she wouldn't commit a mortal sin. Yet, after pondering that for a moment, I dismiss it. If she were gay, why would she be so obsessed with Cory?

As my eyelids continue to grow heavier, I push aside any thoughts of her and focus on Cory, and then on Rob, and finally on Rebel and Robbie. Tears spill onto my cheeks despite my exhaustion and I curl into a fetal position, pulling the sheets up to my shoulders as I sob and then finally fall into a dreamless sleep.

Chapter 37

Cory

Transporting human remains isn't easy. Not only has it caused serious delays, but if I have to hear that stupid phrase one more time, I'm going to punch someone. Reducing Rob to a bureaucratic inconvenience is maddening and sad, and after the media caught wind of it, more frustrating than anything.

Naturally, the media pounced on the news like flies on shit, which set us back even further because the airport we had originally planned to leave from was compromised—the goddamn media swarming in like locust—so a last-minute change caused yet another delay.

"We're ready to go, Mr. Hudson," Josh says.

I push the curtain aside and look at my driveway. Trying to leave this morning so Josh and I could go to a firing range was nearly impossible. Of course, since the news of me personally getting Rob home was released, the amount of reporters, paparazzi, and news vans has tripled, so I have no idea how the hell we're getting out of here short of a miracle.

"The police are nearly here to help clear the way for us," Josh adds.

Anna gets off the couch and steps closer, her hand extended. "Come on."

I look at her, glad that she, Brad, and Benny have become my ever-faithful companions. They know me well enough to not pester me, but they've been invaluable—not only making most of the arrangements, but being supportive always when I need it— like right now. I take Anna's hand and walk to the foyer. The moment the door opens, the volume of chattering and camera flashes erupts. Josh comes to stand behind Anna and me while the other bodyguard named Will steps outside first. Brad and Benny go next, followed by Anna and me. We hurry to the limo, everyone but Benny and Will getting in the back.

A total of four bodyguards are staying at the house to make sure no one breaks in, but they're currently outside to help the cops with crowd control. Annoyed, I drop my head onto the seat and sigh. "Has anyone heard from Detective Morris?"

"I spoke to him earlier," Brad says. "He said he's confident they'll find Rebecca before sunset tomorrow."

That's not comforting, especially since he's been saying that all day. How long could it take to find a cabin? I run my hand through my hair as I pull up a mental image of a map of California. Topanga isn't a particularly large area, but when you're looking for one house in the middle of nowhere, it's apparently difficult to find...sort of like how hard it is to get out of my goddamned driveway.

It's takes fifteen minutes to finally get clear of the media and another forty-five to make it to the airport. Reporters are swarming the place, one of them even jumping onto the hood of the limo. Will opens the door and gets out, lifting the reporter and tossing her aside as if she's light as a feather. The bodyguard then continues alongside the limo as Benny drives ahead slowly. Thankfully, we make it through the gate without another reporter getting tossed, but we still pull into an empty hangar for added security.

The pilot greets us as we exit the car, explaining that we just need to walk through a connecting hallway to get to my plane.

"Is Rob already onboard?" I ask.

He nods. "Yes, Mr. Hudson, everything is taken care of."

Fearful that I'm going to have to sit on the plane with the casket right in front of me, I'm relieved when the pilot tells us that the coffin is secure in the belly of the plane. That's a huge relief. Now if Detective Morris could call and tell me he has Rebecca, this would be the best fucking night ever. We step into the other hanger, but I stop short when I see that Detective Morris and Detective Gordon are talking to the co-pilot.

I hurry over to them. "Did you find her?"

Detective Morris shakes his head. "Not yet, but we're getting close. We just wanted to see you off and let you know that we've narrowed down our search. Oh, and the shrink is positive that Penelope won't hurt Rebecca after spending hours interviewing a few key witnesses."

"Then what the fuck are you doing here? I don't need your well wishes; I need you to find Becca!"

He nods. "We're actually on our way to Topanga; this was just on the way. By the time you land, I'm sure we'll either have her or be close."

Anna grabs my hand and squeezes it. I look at her, my temper is still flaring but I rein it in. "Fine. I'll call when we land," I say in a more level tone.

Both detectives nod and step aside. We head up the airplane's few steps and once I'm seated on the plane, Brad brings over a tumbler filled with scotch. I take it, suddenly feeling trapped and utterly helpless. I may never see Becca alive again. Worse yet, I may never see her *period*. Would this sick, twisted bitch show me the kindness of returning her remains so I could at least lay her to rest?

"They'll find her, boss man," Benny says as he takes the seat across from mine.

I swallow down some scotch and look out the window.

Anna walks over; her phone pressed against her ear but her hand is over the speaker. "Cory, its Chad Hightower. He says it's urgent."

"Chad Hightower?" I repeat as I look at her then at her phone. *Isn't he my neighbor?* I don't think I've spoken a word to him since the day I moved into my house.

"He's your neighbor," she adds.

"Right..." I'm at a loss as to why he would be looking for me. "Tell him I'm sorry for the media and thank him for his condolences."

She follows behind as I walk to the bar. "He said it's urgent, Cory, and that he'll just keep calling back."

Annoyed, I snatch the phone out of Anna's hand too roughly and tuck it against my shoulder while I pour more scotch into the tumbler. "Hey, Chad, I'm sorry for the media mess but—"

"That's not why I'm calling. Can you get some place alone?"

I finish pouring the scotch, set the bottle down, and grab the phone. "What?"

"Goddammit, walk your ass into the bathroom and lock the door. Make sure you have a pen."

My heart shifts into overdrive and I go on autopilot. I hurry toward the bathroom, only stopping long enough to grab a magazine.

"Cory?" Anna calls, but I ignore her.

I close the bathroom door and lock it. "What's wrong? Do you know something?"

"Are you alone?"

"Yes!"

He hesitates then whispers, "She called me."

"Who did? Becca?"

"No," he snaps. "Penny. She asked me to give you a message."

The tiny room sways, my heart rate pumping so fast that I'm scared I'm about to have a heart attack. "You know her?"

"No—well, yes, but it isn't how you think. She's blackmailing me, but we don't have time for that right now. Do you have a pen?"

"Yes."

"You need to take I-10 to 1 and then exit Tuna Canyon Road. Park your car on the corner of Tuna Canyon and Black Ridge. There's an empty lot there with a water tank. She said a phone would be waiting for you. Find it and wait until she calls."

"Okay, I—"

"You have to go alone, Cory. She'll kill Rebecca if she suspects anyone else."

I sob, suddenly so overwhelmed with relief that I hold onto the sink for support. "She's alive?"

"Penny said she is, and I made sure to ask several times, Cory. She's alive, so go, but...dude, just be careful. That chick is so nuts you need to realize that if you go, you and Rebecca might never come back."

"I know." I wipe tears out of my eyes. "I'll have my phone with me the entire way. Call me or Anna if you hear back from her."

"I will."

I end the call, drop the phone in my pocket, then rip the magazine page off and shove it into my other pocket. Anna and Brad are standing right outside the door.

"What happened?" Anna says.

"Is he okay? Did the media break into your house?" Brad asks.

I shake my head, pushing them out of my way as I hurry to the cockpit. I knock on the door, then push it open and quickly close it behind me so Anna and Brad can't follow.

"I need one of your cars."

They both stare for a moment, then the pilot finally says, "Ah...my keys are in my locker."

"What's the combo and what kind of car is it?"

The pilot shifts and pulls keys out of his pocket. "This is for locker one-oh-four. It's a Cadillac parked in the reserved spot on the other side of the hangar."

"Thank you," I say sincerely. "Can you keep my name on the manifest? I need the entire world to think I'm still on this plane."

He stands. "We will."

I turn to leave.

"Mr. Hudson?"

I look over my shoulder.

"Be careful. I hope you find her."

I look at him and the co-pilot and nod my thanks, and then I pull the door open. Everyone is crowding the doorway now. I try to push past them, but Josh grabs my arm.

"What's going on?" Anna asks.

I look at all their faces and yank my arm out of Josh's grip. "I have to go, and I have to go now, and I have to go alone."

"No," Brad says, shaking his head. "That's fucking suicide, Cory."

"What did Chad say?" Benny asks.

"I can't say, but I have to go. Stay with Rob—make sure everyone believes that I'm still on this plane." I head to the door, everyone following along.

They ask me a billion questions as I rush across the hangar and look for the locker room, but I don't answer them as I focus all of my attention on the pilot's locker. I unlock it, grab the keys, and rush toward the exit. Josh's imposing form steps into my path a second before I get to the doors. Will blocks the only other exit and crosses his arms over his chest.

"Get out of my way."

Josh shakes his head.

"Talk to us!" Anna whips me around, her strength surprising me.

"Fine!" I shake her off. "She's alive, but if anyone goes with me, she'll kill her."

"It could be a trap," Brad says.

"Or she could kill both of you," Benny points out.

"I know!" I start pacing. "Don't you think I don't fucking know that, but I have to go! If I can save her, then I don't care what she does to me—just as long as I can see with my own eyes that Becca's okay and then have the opportunity to get her back to safety."

"Even if it's only for a minute?" Anna asks.

I nod. "Yes, even if it's only for a second." I pull my cell phone out of my pocket. "When I get to the cabin, I'll call you and leave the phone as close to where I'm at. Once you get the call, get in touch with Detective Morris and have him track the signal."

Brad slaps my cheek a few times, then hugs me. "Be careful, kid."

Anna pulls me in for a bear hug.

I lean back and look at her. "If I don't come back, take care of him," I motion to Brad, "And take care of Rebel and Robbie."

She nods, tears streaming down her cheeks.

"Be safe, boss man," Benny says, tapping my arm.

I step away, looking at each of them for a moment before I turn. Josh and Will have gathered around the exit, but before I can tell them to get the fuck out of the way, they both reach into their jackets and produce their guns.

"Don't forget to take off the safety," Josh says.

"Keep one in your waistband and the other in your hand," Will advises. Then he reaches for his belt, removes a switchblade from a small pouch, and he drops it into my blazer pocket. "And if you get the chance, kill that crazy bitch."

"Thanks." I put one gun in my waistband, then pocket the other. I turn to look at Anna. "I'll call when I get there."

"Not so fast," Josh says. He holds his hand out. "Give Will the phone so he can download a tracking app on it while I get that cast off. It'll probably be better to have both hands free even if one of them is pretty much useless."

We all follow Josh back to the locker room, searching for something to help cut the cast off. When nothing useful turns up, we end up back on the plane, the pilot and co-pilot producing several tools to help. It takes some doing, but it finally comes off. Then everyone walks me to the exit and we say our goodbyes. The car is thankfully parked near the hangar and is on the opposite side of where all the reporters are. I start the engine and pull out slowly despite my anxiety, but I don't want to draw attention to myself. I dare one last glance at the door, everyone crowding around it to watch me off. I might not ever see them again—I know that—but I don't care. The only thing I care about right now is getting to Topanga and getting Becca to safety.

Chapter 38

Darryl

The joy of falling in love with someone over the span of a week is that you're always pleasantly surprised as you get to know the finer details. I already know that Chelsea is *amazing* in bed, but while Eric's faulty digestive system has him on the crapper, I'm quickly learning that my girl can have some wicked phone sex, too.

I look out the window and chuckle when she waves. She's standing a few feet away from her van while Jay is sitting in there waiting to record Cory's departure.

"Do you think you can hop that fence?" I ask her.

"Ah...I do believe that's unlawful entry."

I laugh. "I might have to cuff you and then frisk—"

Eric opens the door and drops into the car. "We've got a problem. Drive around back."

It's amazing how quickly a boner can deflate. "I have to go, babe. I'll be home right after I drop Eric—"

"No, you won't," Eric interrupts as he signals me to hurry. "When I got out of the bathroom, I caught sight of everyone walking *back* to the plane."

My brow arches. "Walking back? Is something wrong with the plane?"

He shakes his head while leaning out of the window. "Something's up—Anna was hysterical, and they all kept stopping to argue."

"Did you catch any part of it?" I ask after getting the car going.

"No, but Cory wasn't with them when the group made their way back to the plane." He points to a black Cadillac. "Tail that car."

My eyes squint a bit while I focus on the license plate. "Punch this in," I tell him. After reciting the license plate number, I glance over at him. "I guess your fucked up intestines have finally come in handy."

"Ha-ha." He hits a few more keys on the computer.

"Hey, is everything okay?" Chels asks.

I had totally forgotten she was on the phone. "I don't know. I'll call you back when I know what's going on."

"Okay, just be careful."

"I will." When Eric slaps the dashboard triumphantly, I quickly add, "I love you. I'll call soon."

"Yeah, okay," she says. "I love you too."

I end the call and look at Eric. "What is it?"

"I knew it!" Eric pivots the laptop so I can read the screen. "That's the pilot's car."

"So, who's flying the plane?"

"The pilot is. Cory is the one driving." Eric shakes his head. "I don't think he knew anything ten minutes ago because the guy was a wreck. That was too genuine, so maybe Penelope panicked when she thought he was leaving and contacted him."

I nod. "Call it in. We'll need back up if he does find her."

Eric snickers. "Yeah, I'm not messing with that chick again without the ATF heading the cavalry."

"Just make sure all those assholes keep their mouths shut. We don't need the media tagging along to fuck everything up."

"Does that include your girlfriend?"

I snort at that. "That especially includes my girlfriend. I don't want her anywhere near that crazy bitch."

Eric gets on the phone so I sit back and steer with one hand while trying to unsnap the annoying sling. I'm figuring I'll need both hands, along with my vest that's in the trunk, and my shotgun, and my extra ammo. But is all of that stuff enough to confront this woman? The game plan was to go to Topanga and wait until morning to start searching the area. Going on her turf at night, especially when we know that her fanatical father had a very good working knowledge of explosives that he passed onto his daughter, is risky.

Here's what I know, though. Cory Hudson is in love with Rebecca. I wasn't certain of that to begin with, but he's proven himself a thousand times, so he'll be stupid enough to do whatever Penelope asks to get her back. It's suicide, and he probably knows it. He just doesn't give a shit, and that alone makes this already dangerous situation explosive, pun intended.

When I veer onto I-10, Eric informs me that since the ATF already had men in the Topanga area in preparation for tomorrow, that they were already mobilizing and would get there before us.

That's comforting, so I sit back and relax for half a second before I spot the white news van a few car-lengths behind. I glance over at Eric. "You should call Monica. Tell her to give Levi a kiss for me too, but first, can you take my phone and call Chelsea and tell her to back off?"

He gives me that look, the one that says that he hates having to make the potential this-is-our-last-talk call. I don't blame him, especially now that I understand the sentiment, but with me it's worse because my girlfriend is stupid enough to follow me right into the danger zone.

Eric fishes my phone out of the cup holder and taps on the screen. "Hey, Chels, it's Eric. I'm on phone detail so hang on..." He taps the speakerphone button.

"Where are you going?" Chelsea asks.

"We got a lead. Can you just go home and wait—"

"Is that Cory in the Caddy?"

"No."

There's a beat of silence, then she chuckles and says, "Liar."

I grunt. "Go home, babe. Seriously...I don't want you to get hurt."

"Ditto, mister...besides, Jay is driving and he won't let this story go, so you're stuck with me."

"Dammit, Chelsea—"

"We'll stay a safe distance away. I promise."

I grind my teeth, then glance at Eric.

He shrugs. "It's her job, bro. You knew what you were getting yourself into just as much as she did."

"Shut up." I shake my head, then lean closer to the phone. "Just stay far the hell away from wherever you see us park so you don't get hurt, you got it?"

She once again falls silent. I look at the phone, wondering if the call dropped.

"Just be careful, Darryl," she finally says.

"I will—you too. I love you."

"I love you too," Eric says, then makes kissing sounds.

Chelsea laughs. "I love you both, so please, please, please be careful."

"We will," I say, wishing I had the use of both arms so I could slap Eric upside the head.

"Later, Chels," Eric says then ends the call.

"You're a jackass."

"I know, but you love me."

After dropping my phone into the cup holder, he reaches into his pocket and calls Monica on his phone. The car doesn't provide much privacy, but I tune him out as I start a pattern of looking toward the Caddy and then glancing in the rearview to make sure Chelsea is still close.

It's maddening.

I've never once hesitated to do my job, but right now, all I want to do is turn the car around and go home. It isn't because I don't want to help Cory and Rebecca, it's because it's the only way I can get that hardheaded girlfriend of mine out of harm's way.

Jesus, life was a lot simpler when I was single.

Cory exits the interstate and gets onto the Pacific Coast Highway. Once Eric ends his call, we drive in silence, lost in our own thoughts. Cory continues past South Topanga Canyon Boulevard, so Eric gets on the phone again because that's where the ATF was waiting for us.

We continue westbound for a few more miles. I slow down when the Cadillac exits Tuna Canyon Road and instantly realize that tailing Cory on this road could prove difficult. I can't lag behind so much that I miss if he turns off the winding road, but if I stay too close, he might become suspicious.

"Our guys are nearly at Tuna Canyon," Eric says, "and ATF is en route."

I nod, slowing down a bit so I'm not too close. Chelsea's van falls even farther behind, which is a relief. There aren't many streetlights so it's easy enough to maintain a visual of the Caddy's taillights, but the darkness leaves a lot of room for traps.

"What's the plan?" I ask when I lose sight of Chelsea's van.

"We just have to tail him then maintain a visual until everyone gets here."

That's not much of a plan, so I hope that deranged bitch doesn't kill Rebecca or Cory by then. Startled when I see brake lights, I slow down. Cory drives a little bit then hits the brakes again. He does this several times then turns on his left directional. Finally, he makes a left.

I keep driving along Tuna Canyon because turning off could potentially tip him off since the road is so isolated.

"He parked on the corner," Eric says. "Keep going."

Eric gets on his phone while I eye the rearview. "He's running across the street."

"What for?" Eric asks, turning around to look out the back window.

"How the hell should I know?"

I pull onto the shoulder, turn off the headlights, and then make a U-turn and park a little farther ahead so I have a visual on the parked Cadillac.

Eric calls to check the status of our backup, which only takes a second. "They're about a click away on Saddle Peak."

After removing my seatbelt, I lean forward and remove the sling. Eric and I do a quick ammo check then both get out and walk to the trunk. This might be our last chance to get ready, so we don our vest—the movement agonizing, but I force myself to ignore it. Then, like a well-oiled machine, we systematically get everything ready. When my cell phone vibrates, Eric and I get back into the car and close the doors gently.

I eye the caller ID then show it to Eric before I answer. "This is Morris."

"Detective Morris, this is Anna. Cory is at an intersection called Tuna Canyon and Black Ridge—"

"Slow down, Anna; I know where he is. Do you know why he's here?"

"Huh?" That completely throws her for a loop. "But, how...?"

"Never mind that for now," I say gently. "Can you tell me why he's here?"

"Yes. Yes. Of course," she stammers, still trying to catch up. "Chad Hightower called right before takeoff...I don't know what he said, but Cory left, saying he had to go alone or Penelope would kill Becca, but we made him promise to let us know where he ended up. He just texted me."

"So, he's going to exchange himself for Rebecca? Did he say anything else?"

"No, only that once he got to the cabin, he would call me and leave the phone somewhere, hoping you could trace the signal—"

"It doesn't work that way! We can triangulate an area from towers but—"

"We're sharing each other's locations, and his bodyguard put another tracking app that's linked to mine, for added info. I can see where he is right now."

Well that changes shit, doesn't it? "Okay, call me the second Cory calls you—use Brad's phone or whoever's, but try to keep him on the line while someone calls me, you got it?"

"Yeah, I will."

I end the call and look at Eric. "Well, he isn't as suicidal as I thought because he made sure we knew where he ended up, but he's ready to exchange himself for Rebecca. We just need to make sure we stay far away because if Penelope thinks he brought company, she said she'd kill Rebecca."

Eric nods and gets on his phone. I lean back in my seat, rubbing my stubble as I look for Chelsea's van. I don't see it, so I'm hoping she keeps her promise and stays far away, since I have no idea what this crazy bitch has in store for us this time around.

Chapter 39

Chelsea

I n keeping to my promise, I tell Jay to park a safe distance away from the swarm of police cruisers, ambulances, and ATF armored trucks that have converged at the base of the road that Cory and Darryl disappeared on exactly twenty-six minutes ago. Jay isn't too happy about that, so he took the camera and went up the hill to take some footage. Truthfully, neither am I, but I've had enough adventure this weekend, so I'll keep my promise. That doesn't help with my anxiety, though.

Will Darryl be okay?

I would feel better if he was still milling around the intersection with the other cops, but no, he and Eric went farther up the road with a small group of ATF and uniformed officers.

Why do I have to sit out on all the action and he gets to go? It seems grossly unfair that he can go in, guns blazing, while I sit here and twiddle my damn thumbs. Frustrated, I retrieve my tablet from my purse and start writing. Jay pulls open the door and gets into the driver's seat. He took the video camera and the Nikon with him, so after setting each down, he goes to work on pulling the memory card out of the camera.

"Okay, I got some shots of the entire chaotic scene and then a few of the police escorting the families out of their houses." He hands me the memory card. "They aren't taking any chances this time."

"Do you blame them?" I lift my laptop off the floorboard and pass it to Jay. "Let me finish this up."

He takes the laptop and starts downloading pictures. "Uh-oh," Jay says.

I look out the windshield, then at him. "What's wrong?"

"We've got company."

I turn and look out the back windows. A familiar white van is parking behind us. "How the hell did he know we were here?"

"I have no idea."

We wait in silence while Carson grabs his video camera, locks his van, and walks over to us. Of course, instead of walking to Jay's window, which would have been easier, he walks toward mine. I roll my eyes and lower the window.

"Jesus, what is going on here?" he asks.

"How did you know we were here?" I ask.

Carson shrugs. "I have my sources."

I look at Jay.

"Oh, hell no," Jay says while shaking his head. "It wasn't me."

"It doesn't matter how, because I'm here, so what's this all about?"

I contemplate lying so he'll get lost, but I need to give him a little credit. The man is annoying, but he isn't stupid, so Jay and I bring him up to speed.

Carson considers all of the information for a moment, then motions toward the woods. "What the hell are you guys doing here, then? With all the cops up at the intersection, we can cut through the woods totally unnoticed and film the rescue."

"Are you nuts?" I snap. "Do you have any idea how to maneuver through woods like these at night? There's wildlife and God knows what else in there—not to mention that no one even knows if Penelope lives here."

"And if she does, who knows what she has set up at this house," Jay adds.

Carson snorts. "Do you know how famous we'll all be if we record this?" He backs away from the window. "I'm going."

"You're an idiot," I say, though I'm slightly envious. The same thought of sneaking through the woods has crossed my mind, but I made a promise, and I really don't think the odds are in my favor, especially not in this outfit.

"Come on, Jay," Carson says, then walks around the front of the van.

Jay looks at me and sighs. I shake my head, but when Carson opens his door, Jay reaches for his video camera. Without a word, he gets out and makes sure he has everything he needs before he finally meets my concerned gaze.

"If it looks like too treacherous of a hike, I'll make sure we come back."

He slams the door, then gives me one final nod before he and Carson run across the narrow street and start up a hill. I watch them for a second, suddenly feeling torn between my promise to Darryl and my journalistic desire to get the best story.

When the guys disappear over the hill, I snatch the keys out of the ignition and hide them under the driver's seat. I grab the Nikon and loop the harness over my neck, then I reach into my purse and grab my notepad. Promise or not, my inner journalist beats out my inner girlfriend. I get out of the van and slam the door closed behind me, absolutely refusing to allow the story of the year to slip through my fingers.

Chapter 40

Cory

Why hasn't she called me yet? I make my tenth lap around the water tower and wonder if I should go back to the car. I parked it in someone's driveway, but I didn't have an option since Black Ridge Road is tiny—so small, in fact, that it doesn't even have a street sign. Thank God for GPS. The problem though is that I'm sure someone's bound to notice a strange car, though that might work in my favor because someone might call the cops. I texted Anna to let her know where I'm at, but God only knows where I'll end up. Tuna Canyon Road is dark and solitary. I've thus far only seen one car behind me, but it zoomed off when I parked. There hasn't been any traffic since.

This area is the perfect place for a nut-job to live.

When the phone rings, I startle and nearly drop it. I quickly right it and hit the accept key. "Hello?"

"Drive up Black Ridge. The road will end, but there's a dirt road. Two miles in, you'll come to a gate. It's unlocked. Park your car by the pine tree. There's an orange traffic cone so you know which one. Put the cone in the trunk then

strip—"

I jerk at that. "What?"

"I said strip! You can keep your briefs or boxers on only. Follow the path. It's about five miles. When you get to the cabin, stand in the spotlight."

"What?" I repeat, incredulous.

She hangs up.

Dammit. That means I'll have nowhere to conceal the guns, though I'm sure that's why she's doing it. I hurry to the car and start driving up the winding road. There aren't any streetlights this way—nor does it even register on the GPS—and the houses are fewer and farther between. True to her word, the pavement ends and turns into a dirt road. I drive slowly, the Caddy not really designed for the bumpy terrain.

The gate is open, but I slow down to look at the mailbox. *Well,* isn't that just my fucking luck that the address isn't on the box? I park the car by the tree, making sure to follow her instructions to an exception. I text Anna the information, then call her, leaving the phone on and tucking it beneath the cone in the trunk.

I can't take the guns, but I set them on the passenger seat and leave the car unlocked. If we do make it back here, I so don't need to be fucking around with keys or locks. With that thought, I leave the key fob in the cupholder and roll down all the windows just in case we need to make a speedy exit and have to jump into the car.

The switchblade is cumbersome, but I can fit it in my shoe. Not that I intend to do that with a five-mile walk ahead of me, so I keep it in one hand while I hold Penelope's phone in the other. Then I begin my journey. About two miles in, I consider running the rest of the way. I can cover three miles in about twenty-five minutes, but I decide against it, certain that I'll need all of my energy to get Becca and me to safety. Despite that, after another mile, I quicken my already fast pace.

I need to know that Becca is okay.

I'll play whatever role this bitch has in store for me—I'll pretty much do anything to keep Penelope distracted long enough so that I can get Becca to safety. Thankfully, the cabin finally comes into view. It looks normal—like a billion other log cabins I've seen in real life or on television—but this house isn't normal. The closer I get, the more I get a sense of...I don't know, but goose bumps erupt all over my body and I slow my pace. I kneel and put the switchblade in my shoe, and even though I'm not the praying type, I make the sign of the cross then look skyward. *Please, God, if you're there, help me and Becca get the fuck out of here.*

I shake my head, amazed that even in prayer, I can't contain my foul mouth.

Okay, rescind that. Let me keep it simple. *Help us.*

That's it. That's all I've got.

After taking a few calming breaths, I step under the beam of light coming from a sole wooden pole a few feet in front of the house. The phone rings.

"There are clothes on a chair by the door. Put them on, come inside, sit at the table, and place the phone beside your plate."

Once again, she hangs up before I can say anything.

I walk to the porch and climb the three stairs. After stepping out of my shoes, I pull on the jeans while eyeing the ankle-length work boots. Those are even better than my shoes, so I pull the long-sleeved shirt over my head, sit to pull the boots on, and then place the switchblade along my right ankle. It's not really warm enough for the cold-weather vest, but I put it on anyway, then walk to the door. I reach for the doorknob, my heart pumping so fiercely I can hear each beat as the blood slouches past my ears. This is it—my do-or-die moment.

I grip the handle and turn it. The anticipation of seeing what's behind this door scaring me more than I've been frightened before. I push it open slowly, a telltale creak causing my heart to race faster. Then my jaw drops. *No fucking way...*the room looks like it was taken straight from a *Better Homes and Gardens* spread, which for some reason is scarier than satanic symbols and macabre embellishments from the last house. The living area is to my left, decorated with pretty floral-patterned couches, curtains, and a ton of cheery ornamental items. A fire is burning within the huge fireplace. To my right is the dining area. Two places are set, and there are ten thin, white candles burning within elegant silver candleholders that are on either side of a bouquet of red roses.

Oh, Lord Jesus. This is worse than I could have ever imagined.

"Ethan, just close the door behind you and take a seat."

My eyes dart to a doorway just past the dining room table. I look outside, wondering if I should make a run for it—this shit is way too creepy for me not to think it—but I shove the thought aside and close the door. There's no way I'm leaving the looney bin without Becca.

I walk to the head of the table, figuring that since I'm playing the part of Penelope's boyfriend, I'm sure she'll want me to sit here. As I pull the chair out, Penelope steps into the dining room with a tray of food in her hands.

If I didn't know any better, I would think she was a vision of beauty.

Her long dark hair is curled loosely and pulled over her right shoulder. Her makeup is expertly applied to accentuate her light brown eyes, and she's wearing a sundress that's glued to all the right places, the apron cinched around her waist, emphasizing her hourglass figure. There's no denying it; Penelope Fitzpatrick is beautiful. Thankfully, though, I *do* know better, so I instantly recognize that her sundress looks a hell of a lot like one of Becca's and her hair is styled to match the way my on-screen girlfriend's hair is usually styled.

Beauty aside, this bitch is nuts.

Penelope smiles as she approaches. "I made your favorite," she says as she sets the plate before me.

I stare at the chicken Marsala for a moment, wondering how the hell she knew it's my favorite dish, but when I look at her, I suddenly realize that there probably isn't much she doesn't know about me, so I clear my throat and force a smile. "It looks amazing."

Her smile widens. "I'm so glad you like it." She pulls the phone out of my hand and drops it into her apron pocket. "I hope you're hungry. There's a ton of steamed rice and sautéed green beans. Oh," she places her hand on my shoulder and squeezes gently, "and I made a German chocolate cake for dessert." She moves behind me. "Here, let me take your vest. It's too warm in here for you to be wearing that."

My stomach churns from her touch, yet I lean forward. "Thank you."

She walks over and hangs it on the coat rack by the door, then excuses herself to the kitchen. I take the opportunity to look around, memorizing the layout of the land. There are three windows in the living room and two in the dining room. The front door has five deadbolts and a chain, which she's yet to lock, so it's a viable escape option. I can't see into the kitchen clearly, but there's a hallway directly ahead. All of the doors are closed, but I count three from my position.

Is Becca back there?

Penelope emerges from the kitchen, a dish filled with rice in her hand. She hurries off again, bringing out a dish filled with the green beans and a basket of bread. She meticulously places each dish, then hurries off again. On her final trip, she returns with two tumblers held in one hand and a bottle of scotch in the other.

"Eat up, silly. You don't have to wait for me."

She takes the seat to my right, serving scotch into both glasses. After setting mine right by my hand, she reaches for my plate and starts to serve me. "On my way back from the market today, I saw the cutest little kitten on the side of the road."

"Did you?" I say as I shift to try and get a better view into the kitchen.

"I did, so I stopped to rescue him because I knew that it would make you happy."

Really? Now I'm confused since I'm definitely not a cat person.

"He was the cutest little thing, Ethan," she continues, without skipping a beat. "It just breaks my heart that people can just toss them by a busy road." She finishes serving my food, then starts on hers. "I was in such a rush to get home to have dinner ready in time, but he came right to me, so it all worked out for the best."

"Oh?" I look around. "Where is he?"

"He's scampering around somewhere now. After I fed him, I let him go outside."

I take a sip of the scotch, not too surprised that it's the best damn scotch I've ever had. "Aren't you scared he'll get back to the road?"

She giggles. "Oh, no, silly; they all come back in the morning for their breakfast, so he'll follow the older cats. Besides," she says as she fluffs her napkin and sets it on her lap, "we're so far from the road that I'm not worried."

No shit. "That was some walk...you must own a pretty big chunk of land."

She cuts into her chicken. "Oh, yes, about twenty-five acres."

Isn't that fucking grand?

"Aren't you hungry?" she asks.

I want to vomit. Even the delicious aroma of one of my favorite meals is making me feel ill. I force a smile and shake my head. "I ate right before I came. I didn't realize you were going to make such an amazing dinner."

"Do you really like it?" she asks, leaning closer.

I nod.

"Well, I'll make sure to have your dinner ready by six every night. I'll always make your favorites so just put whatever you want on the list in the kitchen and I'll make it for you."

I point toward the kitchen. "That list...it's right in there?"

With chicken in her mouth, she just nods. When she's done chewing, she wipes her lips with the napkin. "It's been so long since you've been here, so I'm sure you've forgotten. After dinner, I'll give you a tour to refresh your memory."

"I'd like that."

She smiles. "Well then eat up, silly."

I set the glass aside and lift the silverware. The food is actually really good, but each bite settles in my stomach like a brick. After five pieces of chicken and a forkful of the rice and green beans, I push the plate away.

"This is delicious, I'm just a little—"

"Stuffed from earlier?" She places her hand over mine. "That's okay. We can save the cake for later. I'm sure we can figure out a way to work up your appetite." She giggles.

I throw up in my mouth a little.

She stands with her plate in hand. I stand and grab mine.

"I can do this. Why don't you enjoy your scotch and a cigarette? I'll grab them for you."

Penelope takes the plate out of my hand then rushes into the kitchen. Fed up with the act, I follow. She drops the dishes into the sink and turns, startling when she sees me.

"I just wanted to see where the list was," I say innocently.

"Of course!" She hurries to the cabinet and opens a drawer. When she turns, there's a pack of cigarettes and a lighter in her hands. "I'll get you an ashtray."

I shake my head. "I don't like smoking inside. Do you have some furniture on the back patio?" I ask, while eyeing the back door.

"Yes! I do." She walks over and hands me the cigarettes and lighter. "I'll get your scotch and meet you out there with an ashtray."

I watch her leave, her reaction so genuinely frazzled I suddenly realize *she's* merging realities. Yes. I'm currently wearing "Ethan Green's" outfit from my show, but that dinner was all me. Cory Hudson loves chicken marsala and scotch, and these are the kind of cigarettes Becca smokes, which I've inadvertently picked up smoking out of convenience. Which means that I may have a lot more leverage than I initially realized.

She stops short at the door, the scotch splashing out of the cup. "You didn't have to wait for me."

I plaster my million-dollar smile on and reach for my drink. "It seemed rude not to. Lead the way."

She smiles and nods. "There are only a few chairs outside, but we can go and buy whatever you want. The porch is big enough for a nice patio set."

I step onto the porch and look at the two plastic chairs. "Yeah, I might have to take you up on that offer since this shit kind of sucks."

Flustered, she hurries over and sets her empty glass on the banister, then runs to the chairs and dusts them off. "We can go first thing tomorrow, Ethan. I saw some nice stuff at Lowe's when I was driving by." She turns and looks at me. "Do you want me to go now?"

"Would you?" *Jesus!* That would be too fucking easy.

She scoffs. "No, no, it would be rude to leave you so soon, but I swear we'll go first thing in the morning."

Damn.

I purposely walk over and lean against the railing and light two cigarettes. I hand one to her, which she stares at for a moment before reaching for it.

"You do smoke, don't you?"

She nods, her body shaking from the force, yet she holds the cigarette between her thumb and pointer finger as if repulsed.

"Where's the bottle and ashtray?" I ask, just to see how far I can push my luck.

"Oh!" She searches for a place to put the cigarette, then finally turns and hands it to me. "I'll be right back."

Penelope rushes inside, throwing the door open so forcefully it bangs with a resounding thud against the wall. I turn and toss my scotch into the grass as I scope out the backyard, though the word forest seems more appropriate. There's no fucking way I can maneuver through that in the dark. Hell, I probably couldn't do it at high noon!

When I hear her running my way, I turn and lean against the railing again and take a drag off my cigarette. She returns with the bottle of scotch in one hand and an ashtray in the other.

"Great," I say as I set my glass beside hers. "Bring that over."

She places the ashtray and bottle on the banister, then reluctantly takes the cigarette I offer. I hold my cigarette between my lips and unscrew the cap on the scotch. After pouring some into each glass, making sure to serve more in hers than mine, I set the bottle aside and hand her the practically overflowing glass. "What should we toast to?"

She holds up her drink. "To us, of course."

I tap my glass against hers, then drain the entire contents. Once it's empty, I set it on the banister upside down.

Penelope is still holding her glass while eyeing mine.

I snicker. "Um, I'd like another drink..." I motion to my glass, then to hers. "Let's go."

"Right, yeah...of course," she whispers, still looking at my glass. She holds the glass higher and says, "To us."

The girl definitely takes it like a champ despite how difficult of a task it is for her. She chokes a bit when it's halfway down, but swallows the rest and turns the glass upside down and sets it on the banister.

"Right on!" I say.

She giggles and wipes tears from her eyes.

I turn the glasses right side up and serve another hefty amount. I hand her the glass, then motion to her cigarette. "You might want to flick that." I step closer to her. "Look, all you have to do is take a drag. It's like sipping out of a straw and taking a deep breath, like this." I demonstrate. "Then you exhale." This time I show her with my cigarette. After blowing out smoke rings, I motion to her cigarette again. "It's better than sex."

She giggles at that, but brings the cigarette to her lips. She takes a drag, but as novices will do, she coughs after inhaling, which leads to a hacking fit that causes her scotch to slosh out of the glass.

"Whoa," I say as I take the glass, "that's alcohol abuse." I set the glass on the banister, then pat her back. "Are you okay?"

"Yeah," she coughs but straightens up and laughs, "yeah, I'm okay."

"All right, try it again."

This time, she only coughs a little. I tell her to take a sip of her drink, then guide her to the stairs. I drop onto the bottom step and tap the space next to me. I need to kill time because I'm not sure how long it'll take Detective Morris to find the cabin. What if he goes the wrong way and I'm stuck here all night? That wouldn't be good, so my best bet is to keep Penelope entertained and keep her drinking. It may not be the best plan, but my alcoholism just might be my redeeming quality since there's no way she can out drink me.

I drop my cigarette in the ashtray and I walk over to grab the pack, lighter, and bottle of scotch before I sit beside her again. I motion toward her glass and wait until she drains it completely before refilling both, then I light two cigarettes. While she chokes on her second cigarette, I quickly pour my drink over the shrubs by the steps. A few minutes pass before she finally regains her breathing and finishes off her third glass of scotch. When she's done, she shifts closer and rests her head against my arm. "Won't it be awesome when it's finally just the three of us?"

My heart skips a beat as I serve more scotch into our glasses. "Three of us?"

She giggles. "Of course, now that you're here, we can go and get Eve."

I shake my head, desperately trying to figure out what the fuck she's talking about.

"Did you want to see pictures?" Penelope asks. "I keep tons for times when I can't get up there for a visit, and you haven't seen her in years."

When she looks up at me, I'm speechless, so all I can manage is a nod.

I follow her inside and watch as she pulls a scrapbook from one of the living room bookcases. Penelope pulls me onto one of the couches and opens the book so that one side is on my lap and the other is on hers. She points to a picture. "This was her first birthday party."

Curious, I lean closer and study the picture of a little brunette girl. There are a man and woman in the picture with the girl—the people looking a hell of a lot like the girl's parents. Beyond confused, I just continue to look at each picture that Penelope explains to me, then she flips to the final page. The little girl, who's about four or five years old at this point, is on a swing.

"We've missed out on so much of her life, but she's happy, and once we get her back, we'll make the perfect family."

I choke on my own spit, Penelope actually patting my back to help alleviate the coughing fit. Stunned, I finally shake my head then look at her; astonished that nature would allow *this* woman to have a child.

"Are you okay?" she asks.

No. I'm so far from okay that I just sit there with my jaw unhinged.

"Ethan?"

I stammer for a moment, then exhale slowly before I can look at her again. "Yeah...I'm fine. I could do with a drink though."

She sets the scrapbook aside and stands. I follow suit and we make our way back toward the kitchen. As she reaches for the doorknob, a thunderous roar reverberates through the house, the force of which rattles the windows and causes the ground to quake. I stumble a few feet and instinctively reach out to hold onto a counter.

"Jesus!" I say as I look around. "What the hell was that?" I glance in Penelope's direction just as her expression morphs into what I instantly recognize as fury. Instinctively, I take a backward step.

"Liar!" Penelope screams, her face contorting into a horrific grimace as she lifts a knife off the counter and runs toward me.

What the fuck just happened?

I jump back, barely avoiding her as I wonder why she's suddenly gone postal. She whips around quickly and charges again, swiping the blade crosswise. A searing pain radiates along my chest, but I don't have time to acknowledge the burning sensation because she strikes again. I jerk back, the knife barely missing me as I duck away from another attack. As she brings the knife around again, I kick her forearm. The blade clatters onto the ground and I run to tackle her. We slide a few feet along the wood floor, then I straddle her hips and grip her wrists. I bang both of her hands overhead, holding them down with one of mine. I squeeze my legs together to keep her still. Then I punch her with all my might, blood splattering out of her mouth.

"Where is she?" I grip her throat and apply pressure. "Where is Becca?"

"If you kill me," she manages, "you'll never find her. She'll die."

I release my hold on her neck.

"And if the police get here and take me away, I'll never talk."

"I didn't call the police! I swear—"

"Then who just set off the landmine?"

Huh? I stare into those light brown eyes and see within them a sense of truth. The crazy satanic stalker has landmines and she won't give Becca up unless I cooperate, so despite my better judgment, I stand and offer her my hand.

"You promised to let her go if I came. I'm here and I swear I won't leave. I'll stay here with you as long as you want me to, but only if you let her go."

"You swear?" She gets onto her feet. "You'll stay if I let her go?"

I nod. "Take me to her. Let me see that she's okay and then see her off and I swear I'll stay." At least long enough to slip away or, if necessary, kill her.

She seems to consider that, her attention focused on a nearby window. "Okay, but we'll have to wait until daybreak. I never venture out at night."

"What?" *Is the Princess of Darkness scared of the dark?* "Take me to her now or I'm leaving."

"I won't let you go, Ethan." She backs up, opens a drawer, and extracts a small handgun. "Even if I have to kill you again."

Again? "What?"

"Go!" She motions toward the hallway. "We'll pack up and stay in the tunnels until—"

A second explosion tosses me off my feet, my head cracking against the edge of the counter at the same time the windows implode. I collapse onto the floor, shattered glass raining down on me.

Penelope pulls me up and starts dragging me along as she runs to the master bedroom. Still dazed, I lean against the doorjamb and watch as she pulls her dress overhead, then dons jeans, a sweatshirt, and boots in record time. As she laces her boots and hurries to the closet, I examine the long gash running diagonally across my chest. It's bleeding pretty badly; so is the injury on the back of my head.

"Move away from the door," she orders, a machete now held within her grip. When I'm out of the way, she closes and locks the door, then she sets the huge knife onto the bureau so she can push the bed toward the wall. Without skipping a beat, Penelope flips the area rug back, exposing a trapdoor, and kneels to pull it open. She looks at me and motions for me to come closer. "Move it," she snaps.

I look at her, then peer into the darkness. I can't help but gulp even though I'm hoping those explosions mean that Detective Morris is close.

"Now, Ethan!"

I nod, and then I reach for the ladder, amazed that I'm so willing to descend into the ominous abyss with my crazy satanic stalker.

Chapter 41

Rebecca

I grip the gate and try to pull it open. "Hello?" I call out for what feels like the fiftieth time. After another minute of tugging, to no avail, I kneel and look at the lock. I wonder if I can pick it—not that I'd have any idea how to do that, but I can't just sit here. Whatever that loud, booming sound was hopefully means someone is on the way to rescue me.

I go to the bathroom and pull open every drawer, but I don't find anything I can use to pick the lock.

I go to the bathroom and pull open every drawer, but don't find anything I can use to pick the lock. *Dammit.* I'm sure psychogirl has tried every means of escape, but I refuse to just sit here. As peaceful as my sleep was, and as much as I want to go back to bed, I need to get out. Yet the bedroom doesn't turn up anything of use, so I place the lamp on the floor and drag the nightstand underneath the vent. Ignoring the pain in my heel and the aching throughout my entire body, I climb up and examine the vent. There are screws securing it into the cinderblock, but I slip my fingers through the grates and give it a good tug. It won't give.

Frustrated, I grunt, then step off the table. There has to be a way out of here. I go back to the bathroom, hoping I missed something that isn't obvious but that will help, but I stop short when I hear something. *What was that?* I quickly close all the drawers and cabinets, turn off the light, and hurry to the room. I close the door, leaving it open just a crack so I can peer at the gate. When silence ensues, I search the room for a weapon, just in case it's her. The lamp is the only thing I can use. It's plastic and looks pretty flimsy, but I'd rather have something than nothing. I hurry over, my hands shaking so badly I fumble the lampshade.

"Becca!" Cory shouts.

I whip around and look at the door. "Cory!" Then I tear through the room and nearly pull the door off its hinges in my haste. "Cory!" I grip the gate and press my face between the bars. "I'm in here!"

He pounds on the door. "Are you okay?"

"I'm okay!"

He doesn't say anything else that I can hear, but there's muffled voices on the other end.

"Cory?"

The lock disengages and the door opens. The light is so bright that I have to close my good eye and turn away from it.

"Becca! Thank God!"

He reaches through the bars and grabs my face. I flinch away even though I love the feel of his hand.

"Jesus," he whispers. He reaches his other hand through the gate and gently shifts my face toward him. "It's okay. I'm here."

I reach through the bars and wrap my arms around him, tears spilling onto my cheeks as I press my face against the bars and sob.

"It's okay, you're safe. She's going to unlock—"

"What do you mean *she?*" I lean back to look up at him, but when I catch sight of his bloody shirt, I press my hand against his chest. "You're bleeding."

He grabs my hand. "I'm okay. Listen to me, she's going to unlock the gate and let you out. Detective Morris is close—I don't know where, but stay on the path and get to the cabin. Make sure you keep shouting that it's you."

"What about you?"

"I'm staying—"

"No! Cory, you can't—"

"I'm staying! Run as fast as you can, find Detective Morris and get to safety."

"Cory—"

"That's enough," Penelope says, her voice causing goose bumps to erupt all over my body.

I grab onto Cory's shirt and pull him closer.

"I love you," he whispers, and kisses me through the bars. "Go."

He backs away, literally having to pry my hands off to do so, and then he hurries out of the bedroom. Penelope steps into full view with a flashlight held in one hand and a machete in the other.

"No funny business. I'm going to unlock the gate, then walk you out. When you surface, follow the path to the cabin." She shifts the flashlight to tuck it between her arm and torso. "Leave and never come back. I won't hurt anyone else if you all just leave us alone."

I study the flashlight, the long metal handle probably a good weapon if I could get my hands on it. "Okay. I'll leave."

"Back up," she orders. "You make one wrong move and I'll kill him right in front of you and then torture you for years before I kill you." She steps toward the gate. "Don't forget I know where your kids are."

My heart skips a beat as I tear my gaze off the flashlight and look at her.

She glares for a moment, then pulls the gate key from around her neck. "Walk straight to the stairs. Any funny business and I'll slice you in half."

When she unlocks the gate and steps away from the door, I walk to the gate. We stand off for a moment before she gives me a wider berth. I step through and take the lead, Penny right on my heels as I progress at a steady pace, all the while looking around for Cory. When I get to the ladder and step onto the first rung, Cory is still nowhere in sight.

"When you get to the top, reach in and I'll hand you a flashlight."

I nod and look around one last time. *Should I go?* I don't want to leave Cory here; God knows what this bitch will do to him, but what choice do I have? I'm in no shape to put up a fight and Detective Morris *is* here—or close. If I can get outside and find him, I can bring him back here to rescue Cory, and in the process, kill Penelope.

A part of me isn't happy with that, but in my current condition, that's my best option. I step onto the next rung of the ladder, but even with my heel cushioned in the sneaker, my wound, which is surely infected, is hurting badly. I move up to the next step with my left foot, then bring the right foot beside it, continuing my ascent in that manner until I'm to the top.

With the hatch open, I feel the cool night breeze. I'm nearly there—almost free—but I can't do it. I can't leave Cory here—not if I can do something so we can leave together. Penelope has the machete though, and even though she seems a bit out of it, I'm sure she's sharp enough to chop me into bits with no problem.

Almost as if he can sense my hesitancy, Cory steps into the living room. Our eyes meet and in a second, I know he wants me to get to safety and then bring back the cavalry. We both know I'm in no shape to pull off a rescue. I know that, but before I can convince myself to keep moving upward, I set my right foot onto the rung firmly and kick my left foot with all my might, catching an unsuspecting Penelope square in the jaw. She sails through the air, then falls, her head cracking against the side of the desk on her way to the floor.

Cory bolts into action. "Go!" he shouts as he runs to grab the machete.

I pull myself onto the next rung, completely forgetting about my heel until I shift my weight onto it. Pain shoots up my leg so fiercely that I lose my grip and fall backward. My scream ends abruptly when I crash onto the floor, my head bouncing against the cement several times. Black spots dance before my eyes.

Cory rushes over and pulls me into his arms just as another sharp pain spreads through me, this time originating in my lower abdomen. It knocks the wind from my lungs and tears blur my already fuzzy vision.

"Tell me where it hurts. What can I do?" he asks, clearly distraught, even though he's trying to maintain a calm façade.

"I'm okay. Help me up."

He stands with me in his arms. "Are you sure you can you stand?"

I actually chuckle. "I'm not dying here, so help me up. I'll stand and climb."

Cory walks to the ladder and sets me on my feet, but he never completely lets go of me. He helps me onto the first, then second rung, gripping my waist almost painfully to make sure I don't fall.

"What about Penny?" I wrap my arm around the rung and look down at him. "I'll be okay here for a second."

Cory looks down at her, then shakes his head. "She's out cold. I'll just lock her in once I get you outside." He looks up at me. "Go." It's an order that I won't argue against because the look of torment within his eyes is enough to get me moving.

With him right behind me, and with the knowledge that we're getting away, I move up the ladder as quickly as my aching body allows, which isn't too fast at all. When I get to the top, I grip the edge of the latch and use the last of my energy to pull myself out. I'm not sure how he does it, but Cory squeezes through the opening and helps me out the rest of the way, holding and shifting us so he catches the brunt of the fall when we tumble onto the ground. Pain floods through every nerve ending of my body for a moment, but as it recedes, I inhale deeply and revel in the smell of grass and fresh night air.

Cory gently shifts me over, but whereas I just lay there, my short energy burst fading, he quickly gets onto his feet, slams the latch shut, and spins the wheel to lock it. He locates a large rock and hits the metal wheel several times, then locates a large branch that he situates to hold the latch in place. Apparently satisfied with his handiwork, he drops beside me and gently pulls me into his arms. Despite the pain that causes, and despite his bloody chest, I press my cheek against his shoulder and sigh, beyond relieved that he's here and that we're both okay. We definitely aren't at our best—but at least we're alive.

He kisses the top of my head, then leans away. "The cops aren't far." He runs his fingers over my bruised and swollen cheek. "Can you walk?"

I nod, and then, for some reason, I think of *The Princess Bride*. "If you want, I can fly," I whisper, my British accent as horrible as ever. But instead of getting a kick out of the fact that I can quote a movie in the midst of this horror, Cory loses it and crushes me in an embrace.

Chapter 42

Darryl

Even though I was a good twenty-five feet away from the explosion, my ears are throbbing badly and I can't shake the high-pitched hum resonating in my head. Yet, despite the discomfort, Eric and I continue along the path toward Penelope's house, intent on finding our fallen comrade's foot. It's the least we can do since the ATF is making sure the house is free of explosives before we enter.

*Jesus...landmines...*I'm not surprised the crazy bitch has the property rigged, but I didn't think she'd have the bombs so close to her cabin. That first explosion was several miles away so we thought we were in the clear this close to the house—or so we thought until that poor officer stepped on the wrong spot. He didn't make it, but his family deserves to lay his *entire* body to rest, so I keep systematically sweeping my flashlight over the brush in search of his foot.

One of the ATF guys walks over. "They found it," he informs us.

"Good," Eric says. "Have they cleared the house yet?"

The guy shakes his head. "Not yet, but they radioed in that they're pretty sure Cory was in there. Unfortunately, it looks as if he and Penelope made a quick exit."

"Did we find out who set off that first explosion yet?" I ask while sticking my finger into my ear to give it a good shake.

"All of our guys are accounted for so the officers down at the roadblock think it might have been some reporters—"

"What?" My heart sinks. "Why do they think that? Do they know which reporters?"

The guy shrugs. "I'm pretty sure it was from one of the tabloids—"

"Entertainment Nightly?" I ask as I fish my phone out of my cargo pocket.

"Yeah, that sounds right," he says.

Fear, dread, and anger rip through me so forcefully that my fingers are shaking while I dial her number. "Did they find them? Was anyone injured?" I ask the officer as the phone rings.

He shakes his head. "Nope, and the captain said we aren't sending anyone in to find them until daybreak."

"What—" I nearly fall over with relief when she answers.

"Are you okay?" she asks.

"Are you?" I snap as I turn my back to Eric and the officer. "I told you to stay away from here, Chels—"

"I did. I'm standing at the roadblock watching them load someone into an ambulance and I thought it was you. I tried calling you a thousand times!"

Startled by the venom dripping off her words, I take a step farther away from Eric. "My phone is muted, but I have it with me. I want you to get in your van and leave, Chels. The bitch has this place rigged and I don't want you anywhere near here."

"I'm not going anywhere until I know this is over. Besides, Jay and Carson are off trying to get the film of the century and I won't leave without them."

Fuck. I rub my forehead then, in a gentler tone, I ask, "Chels, did they try to cut through the woods?"

"Yeah, why?"

"Nothing." I sigh. "Just stay with the cops down on the street —do not come up here, you got that?"

She grunts.

"I have to go. I love you."

"Darryl!" When I don't say anything, she huffs then says, "I love you too."

"I promise I'll keep calling or texting to let you know I'm okay when I can, okay?"

She sighs then says, "Yeah, okay."

When she hangs up, I shake my head. *Jesus.* It really was easier being single. I pull up my text messages and send her a text telling her I love her. It's the truth, and I realize I'm glad I'm no longer single; I just wish we weren't both involved in dangerous jobs.

"Is she okay?" Eric asks.

I nod. "She is, but I'm pretty sure Carson and Jay are the ones who set off that first explosion." I look at the officer. "We need to send people in there to get them."

He shakes his head. "The captain made it clear as mud that he wasn't risking any of our men for reporters who knew they shouldn't have trespassed." He starts walking toward the house. "They should have taken heed of all the warning signs."

I watch him walk off, understanding his sentiment. Cops and reporters are rarely on the same team. We try to solve cases while reporters undermine us at every turn, determined to get information to the public even if it hinders our cases. So, would I be so eager to send my brothers-in-arms out to find Jay and Carson if I didn't know them?

"My team just called the all-clear, gentlemen," an ATF officer calls to us.

We head over, Eric falling into step with me so he can pat my shoulder affectionately. "Lighten up, bro. She kept her word, so quit having second thoughts."

"I'm not...well, not about Chels. About her job—oh, hell, yeah."

"I get that. Remember how relieved I was when Monica decided to stay home after Levi was born."

"Yeah, but Monica's a nurse. At least you knew she was safe when she left for work."

He nods. "That's true, but you knew what you were getting yourself into."

I stop to glare. If he gives me another I-told-you-so, I'm going to hit him.

He chuckles, then taps my shoulder again. "Here's what you have in your favor: she and her family are obviously tight, and they probably hate her job just as much as you do, so maybe you have a chance of winning this fight if you play your cards right."

I consider that as we walk along. We reach the cabin and I've just climbed the first step when someone calls my name. It's distant, but definitely my name, and definitely a male voice. Eric and I turn and search around. Another shout drifts toward us, a little closer this time.

"That's Cory," I say as I pull my gun out of the holster and take a few steps toward the backyard. "Cory?" I shout.

When he calls my name again, his voice is faint, but it's definitely him.

"Cory!" I take a few more steps then turn to look at a nearby officer. "Get your guys to bring some lights out here!"

"Careful where we step," Eric reminds me.

"Yeah, no shit." I look at the ground then take another step toward the wooded area just beyond the mowed backyard.

An ATF officer drives his armored truck over and aims the headlights into the darkness.

"Cory, look for the lights, man!" I shout.

Several officers come over and form a line beside us, everyone shining their flashlights toward the wooded area. The officer in the truck honks the horn twice, then leans into it. My already tender ears aren't happy about that, so when I catch sight of shrubs shifting back and forth, I signal for him to let up on the horn. When it's silent, I take a small step forward. "Cory! Where are you, man?"

"Here!" Cory calls. A second later, he steps into sight;

Rebecca safely tucked in his arms.

"He's got her!" Eric slaps my arm.

"Son of a bitch," I say, just as relieved.

A loudspeaker crackles and screeches, then an officer says, "Just stay where you are, Mr. Hudson. There are explosives on the premises."

"I know," he shouts.

He gently lowers Rebecca onto a log and then sits beside her. On any other night, it might seem romantic, but even from this distance, I catch sight of his bloody shirt and Rebecca's battered face and cringe. *Damn, that crazy bitch sure didn't go down without a fight.*

"We're going to ask you to lie down behind that log, Mr. Hudson," the officer on the microphone says.

Then the explosive guys move closer and tell us to fall back because if something goes boom, they want the fewest amount of casualties as possible. I holster my weapon and turn. Eric falls into step with me and we've just taken a few more steps when a single gunshot pierces the night air. I instinctively duck and whip around just in time to see Rebecca Carter collapse onto the ground.

Fuck.

More gunfire erupts, coming at us in three-shot bursts, several officers toppling over in its wake. Eric and I dive behind a police cruiser and I peer around the bumper just as the ATF returns fire toward the tree line. Cory has since pulled Rebecca into his arms and he's taking cover by the log.

The barrage of bullets continues for what seems like an eternity. Then an officer calls a cease-fire and the woods, which a moment before had been ablaze with lights and a deafening clamor, falls eerily silent. Cory gets onto his feet, Rebecca's limp body in his arms. The officer on the microphone orders him to stand down, to stay in place until they can secure a safe path for him, but he doesn't listen. He beelines toward us and once he makes it to the armored truck, the SWAT team to my far left unleashes a fury of bullets into the woods to provide cover. I scramble up and grab the back of Cory's shirt to guide him toward the ambulance.

"She's still breathing," he informs us.

Eric takes the lead, disappearing around the trunk to pull the doors open. Cory and I are right behind him and the EMTs are suddenly there to pull Rebecca out of his arms. In less than a second, they have her on the stretcher and have cut open her sweatshirt to expose the bullet wound that practically tore off the side of her abdomen. They work quickly and meticulously. Once Rebecca is secure, one of the paramedics signals Cory to get into the ambulance.

"Mr. Hudson, let's go," the EMT orders after closing one of the doors.

Cory shakes his head. "Go. I'll be there soon."

"What the fuck are you doing?" I grab his arm and move him closer to the door. "You need medical attention and you need to be with her."

When he shoves me so hard I stumble backward and land on my ass, all I can do is sit in shocked amazement. When Eric grabs Cory and slams him against the closed ambulance door, I feel slightly vindicated. "Get in the ambulance, Mr. Hudson. That isn't a request. And the more time you waste arguing with us, the more time you're taking away from Rebecca's recovery."

He shakes Eric off. "I'll be there as soon as I can," he says to the EMT, then slams the other door closed.

I get on my feet and pull Cory back to the armored truck. "Cory, you're—"

"You either help me or you get the fuck out of here because I'm not leaving until I know Penelope is dead."

"We can't help you go after her," Eric says.

"Then get your men out of here and let me handle it. If she isn't already dead, then I can get her back into that cabin and finish off what you didn't."

I shake my head. "This is not the wild fucking west, Cory.

You can't just—"

"I can't what? There's no way I'm leaving here knowing that she's alive and that she'll just come back to finish what she started!" He looks at me, then at Eric. "She shouldn't even be here! I locked her in her bunker; so she's...don't you get it? She won't stop and *I* can finish this. Not you or these men. Me."

I look over at Eric; he shakes his head. I sigh because I know it's wrong, but what the fuck. I pull the gun from my holster and hand it to Cory. "With the amount of fire power they're throwing her way, there's no way she's still alive, but just in case she is, Eric and I will stay behind and we'll tell these guys to back off so that it looks as if they're gone. Are you sure you can get her back in the cabin?"

"I'm counting on it." Cory takes the gun. "There's a trapdoor in the master bedroom that has about a mile of tunneling that lets out into the woods. She'll take that back inside, so one of you needs to hide in the bedroom while the other hides in the kitchen. I'll sit on the back porch so she has a clear view of me."

I look over at Eric. He holds his fist out. "Winner takes the kitchen."

We rock, paper, scissor it. My rock breaks his scissors, so I take his spare gun, since Cory has mine. "Send me a message when she's inside and out of the room. Then we can both sneak up on her."

Eric nods, then holds his hand out to me. I give him a pound, then cover him while he hurries into the house.

"Get your guys out of here," Cory orders. "Trust me; if she's still alive, she'll come."

"This better fucking work, Hollywood," I say once Eric gets inside the cabin safely.

After taking a knife out of his boot and slipping it into his pocket, he tucks the gun into his waistband. "It will," he assures me, then walks toward the cabin, seemingly unfazed by Rebecca's injury, the oozing wound on his chest, or the barrage of gunfire.

Chapter 43

Penelope

He does love me! He must because, after everyone left, he stayed behind. He's even made himself at home, helping himself to a second bottle of scotch that he's been sipping on for thirty minutes while he smokes and looks up at the sky. He always did love stargazing, and I miss those times when he and I laid on the bed of his truck, wrapped in blankets, staring up at the constellations. It makes me long to be in his arms again, so after a thorough check of my surroundings, I shift away from the tree, grimacing as I move the arm that was grazed by one of many bullets fired upon me. I need to patch myself up, and then I need to make sure Ethan is okay, too. It doesn't appear as if he's taken the time to mend his injuries either, so I quicken my pace and double back to the tunnel.

I walk along the underground pipe with my flashlight off. I know these woods and this emergency route like the back of my hand so I don't need it. Thankfully, I'm just as familiar with the emergency escape route for the fallout shelter now too, otherwise I'd probably still be locked in there. I'm sure that stupid bitch was behind that stunt, because Ethan wouldn't have wanted me trapped in there. Why else would he have waited then?

When I arrive at the ladder, I climb up and unlock the hatch.

With my arm searing in pain, it takes monumental effort to pull the chains that shift the bed out of the way. Panting and winded from the exertion, I slowly lift the lid, the weight of the area rug sitting atop it making it heavy enough to wish I had gotten rid of it years ago.

My heart rate increases as I note that the master bedroom is open, the doorframe cracked where the police must have rammed it. I stay in place for a long moment, straining to listen for any clues that someone other than Cory is here. After another moment, I slide out of the opening, then get up and head into the bathroom. I pull open the linen closet, shift towels out of the way, and retrieve my Walter P99 from its secret compartment.

I check the bathroom, then the bedroom. With the coast clear thus far, I creep down the hallway, checking my old room and second bathroom, then I make my way into the kitchen. I ignore the mess and lightly tap on the windowpane of the back door so I don't startle Ethan. He looks over his shoulder but doesn't move otherwise, so I pull it open.

After tucking the gun in my waistband at the small of my back, I walk toward him slowly, attempting to gauge his mood. "Hey."

Without a word, he reaches for a second tumbler and serves scotch into it. He sets the glass on the step beside him, then lights a cigarette.

When he holds it out for me, I sit beside him. "No thanks," I say, but I lift the tumbler and take a sip, hoping that will appease him.

He takes a drag and finally looks at me, his eyes narrowing as he examines my face. "You got a pretty decent-sized bruise there," he says, then takes another drag off the cigarette.

I touch my nose. I'm pretty sure it's broken. That bitch definitely caught me off guard and she's hopefully dead now for it. "It'll heal," I say then take another sip of scotch. "How's your chest?"

"It hurts." He flicks the cigarette across the yard. "But I

figured that once you got here, you'd take care of it for me." He shifts to look at me. "You will, won't you, Penny?"

My stomach sinks for some reason, but I ignore it and nod. "Of course, I will. I'll do anything for you." I set the scotch aside and reach for his chest, catching the sudden change in his eyes a second too late.

I don't have time to avoid the knife that he plunges into my side. A scorching pain radiates from the entry point all the way to my back. Ethan rips the knife out and brings it down again. I reach for his hand to stop him, but he grabs a handful of my hair, pulls me against him roughly, and thrusts the blade into my gut. I push him away, but he only tugs me back toward him with greater force, the movement causing the blade to slide farther into my belly. The pain is so intense I can't breathe, and for a moment, black spots dance before my eyes.

He shifts his hand out of my hair to squeeze my neck. "How's that feel, Penelope?"

The rage in his eyes and menacing tone of his voice is more painful than the knife, more constricting than his grip. Tears blur my vision as I desperately try to hang onto consciousness and reach for my gun.

"Back away, Cory," someone shouts. "Let her go and we'll take her in."

Cory just yanks the blade downward, the searing pain multiplying a hundred-fold. I wheeze, then cough up blood. A man grabs Cory and pulls him off me. Without the support, I slide along the stairs and collapse onto the grass. Still wheezing and gagging on blood, I grab the bottom step and pull myself into a seated position. I look down at my stomach and instinctively cover it with my hand.

Amazed by his betrayal, I look at him. "Why?"

This close, I recognize the two detectives holding Cory at bay. "Are you...?" Cory stammers as he stops struggling against them to stare at me in utter disgust. "Just. Jesus. You really don't know how fucking nuts you are, do you?"

My heartache outweighs my physical distress, and in that instant, I know what I have to do. Because if I can't have him, then no one ever will.

I reach for my gun.

"Don't even think about it," Detective Morris says.

"Turn around nice and slow," Detective Gordon says.

Ignoring them, I wrap my hand around the pistol's grip and pull the trigger.

Epilogue

Cory

April is my least favorite month of the year, and it probably always will be. Years have passed since that fateful night, but the pain hasn't gone away. *Three years*...even with that much time, it hasn't eased the trauma of it all, or the nightmares. I still wake up in a cold sweat at least twice a week—the memory of everything I lost, of everything Penelope did, haunts me even on my good days.

Rebel pulls her hand out of mine, pulling me out of my musing. I watch as she slowly walks toward the gravestone, a single red rose held within her grip. Her long blonde hair blows in the breeze, reminding me so much of Becca. The older she gets, the more she looks like her, so even though I know I shouldn't favor her over Robbie, I do. She turns to look at me, those beautiful grayish-green eyes seeking encouragement that she's too proud to ever verbalize, so I nod. She walks the rest of the way and places the rose into the vase.

With his sister unable to see him—and subsequently tease him about being a baby—Robbie shifts closer and leans against me. I put my arm over his shoulders and pull him snuggly against my leg. He's my little shadow, and he's never once resented me the way Rebel has.

"Do I have to?" he asks.

I kneel beside him and shake my head. "If you don't want to, then you don't have to." He looks over at Rebel, then looks back at me. I chuckle because I know he's thinking that if Rebel is over there, then he should be, too. I ruffle his hair. "It's okay if you don't, Robbie." When he still appears unsure, I pull him in for a hug. "I love you, kiddo."

Robbie hugs me tightly. "I love you too, *Dad*."

He steps away and takes a deep breath. I hold still, wondering what he's going to do. Just when I think he's going to walk over, he shifts to lean against my bent knee and hands me the two roses he had picked from the bouquet. I take them and kiss his temple, even though I have no idea if that's the right thing to do or not.

Maybe I should bring them here more than once a year?

Parenthood is a funny thing. I never know what to say most times, but I've learned to go with my gut. That's why, when Robbie asked if he could start calling me dad a few months ago, I nodded and said of course he could even though it scared the shit out of me. Yet, it wasn't nearly as scary as when, later that day, Rebel walked right up to me and, in that stubborn-Rebel-like way, told me she refused to call me dad.

That crushed my heart in a way that defies words, but I nodded and told her I was okay with that too. I wasn't, but I didn't say as much, and I think she knew how much she hurt me. It was like a little victory for her, so on that long ago day, she walked off, her little shoulders square and her head held high as she made her way back to her room.

We never discussed it again, at least not until I started making plans to come here a few weeks ago. Out of the clear blue, she walked into my office without even knocking and sat on the desk. I set my paperwork aside and sat back in my chair, real relaxed like even though I wasn't.

Rebel looked right at me and asked if I thought her real dad would be mad if she started calling me dad. Always amazed that

I can maintain my composure when I'm just as confused as they are, I told her that maybe she should ask her dad what he thought about it. She considered that for a moment, then left, once again not mentioning it. But as I watch her place the rose in the vase and then sit by Rob's tombstone, I wonder if she's asking him now.

"Is she allowed to sit there?" Robbie whispers.

I nod while fixing his wind-blown hair. "Yeah, it's absolutely okay for her to be sitting there, but you don't have to if you don't want to."

Robbie shakes his head. "Can you put my flowers over there?"

"Of course, I can." I kiss his temple again, then rub his back gently.

Rebel walks back over and steps beside us. "I think he's okay with it," she announces.

"Are you sure?"

She shifts back and forth, doing what I like to call "The Rebel Shuffle." She does it when she's nervous or when she's lying. It's a dead giveaway that has led to more confrontations than I care to count or think about at the moment. The girl has definitely given me a run for my money.

"I'll tell you what," I say as I shift Robbie up so I can grab both of their hands. "You start calling me dad whenever you're ready to," I say to Rebel, "and I'll deliver your flowers until you're comfortable doing it yourself," I say to Robbie.

They both nod.

After kissing their foreheads, I point to the limo. "Why don't you guys go and check on your brother while I help Mommy up."

Rebel takes Robbie's hand and they start walking back to the car. Benny and Josh are waiting by the limo's door, and I know Darryl is nearby, probably up in a tree with some high-powered rifle. I never know exactly *where* he is, but I know I picked the right man for the job when I decided to hire permanent security staff members to act as my family's guardian angels. He already took a bullet for me once. I have no doubt he'll do it again.

I'm only glad that Darryl came as a matching pair, so I watch the kids until they're safely in the limo with their baby brother and Eric. Then I turn to look at Becca. Smiling as I walk over, I admire just how radiant she looks when she's pregnant. I set Robbie's roses into the vase on Rob's gravestone and offer my hand. "Have I told you how beautiful you look today?"

She scoffs at that. "Yeah, as beautiful as a beached whale." She takes my hand and stands. "I can't believe I let you talk me into this."

I rub my hand against her swollen belly and smile. The miracle of life still astounds me. Our daughter had survived with Becca through that entire harrowing experience with Penny. For that pregnancy, I had worried every day that Amanda would be somehow damaged from all of that trauma, but she had been perfect. Beautiful and perfect. For this pregnancy, I thought I wouldn't be worried at all. Our son was conceived in the love and safety of our home. Becca has had a perfect pregnancy and has been the picture of health. But I'm still worried. It's bizarre, but I would never let Becca know that. I would never worry her if I could help it. So I smile. "It's perfect now. We're totally balanced with two girls and two boys. You know I'm all about symmetry."

She laughs. "Well, I'm glad you're happy, because there's no way I'm doing this again."

I kiss her. "Agreed. Are you ready, or do you need a little more time?"

She looks down at Rob's gravestone and nods. "Would I be a horrible person if I said I'm good because I really need to pee?"

"No." I chuckle. "You would sound like you're seven-months pregnant, so I don't think anyone would be offended."

"Good, then let's go before I wet my pants."

I force my smile to stay in place, even though her words send a chill down my spine. The reminder, even though accidental, brings up images of her being tortured; of the scars that litter her body; of the memory of me coming so close to losing her. It never goes away—the horrors she had lived through. The smallest things remind me of it—that line especially, because I can remember the way her voice filled with disgust as she recounted how she smelled when she was finally able to relieve herself in that tiny, fortified bathroom.

Becca quickens her pace and asks Benny to get a move-on as she gets into the car. He and Josh hurry to the front of the limo while I climb into the back. Thankfully, it's a short ride to the Carters' house. Once we're on our way, I look at Eric. He's bouncing our son on his lap, but he still gives me that subtle nod to let me know that the Carters' house is secure and that Darryl is en route. He kisses the top of Jake's head, then sets him on his little feet.

Jake, who's my little clone, waddles over with that thousand-watt smile plastered on his little face that Becca and the media have dubbed "The Hudson." It melts my heart, yet there isn't a day that goes by that I hope little Amanda inherits Becca's looks instead of mine.

When the limo eases to a stop, Jake falls onto his hands and knees. Ever determined to walk, he grips Robbie's pant leg and stands. Robbie takes his hand and helps Jake make his way to us. I scoop him up and sit him on my lap. Robbie scoots over and rests his head against my arm. Rebel looks up from her tablet and eyes us. Becca signals her over, to which Rebel sighs and pretends that it's a major inconvenience to join us.

The limo is big, but with everyone sitting on the backbench, it's a little cramped. I shift Jake onto Becca's lap, then pull Robbie onto mine.

Rebel drops beside me and points to her tablet. "Can we go to your movie premiere?"

I look at Eric, then at Rebel. "Are you offering to be my date?"

She shrugs. "I had fun at The Oscars."

The Oscars had been a logistical nightmare. It was the first time Becca and I took the kids to a major event so I was more anxious about keeping everyone safe than I was about my best actor nomination. Though in hindsight, my anxiety over everyone's safety was probably the reason I wasn't the least bit worried during my acceptance speech; all my nerves frayed by the time they announced I won.

For that reason, I had planned to go to my new movie's opening night alone, since Becca is due right about that time and wouldn't feel up to making the trip. That was a perk in my mind, since Eric would have stayed at the house with them and Darryl would have been lurking in the background. But when I look into Rebel's eyes, I cave. "I'll tell you what. Mom will probably want to stay home to make sure everything is ready for when Amanda comes home, so you can be my date."

"Can I come too, Dad?" Robbie says.

Shit. I look at my little man and nod. "Of course you can."

The remainder of the drive encompasses Rebel and Robbie excitedly talking about our plans. I'm not excited. In fact, I want to keep them all locked up at the house because, at least there, I know they're safe. Becca, who has become scary good at reading my mind, squeezes my thigh. I look over at her and relax a bit when she gives me that cool-it-because-it's-going-to-be-okay look. *Will it though?*

Thankfully, I don't have to entertain that thought because we arrive at the Carters' house.

Eric gets out of the limo first, but Becca is a close second. She hands Jake over to him then hurries up the stairs, blowing past Darryl in her haste. I take Jake and wait for the kids before we head inside. Mr. and Mrs. Carter, along with Chelsea, Monica, Levi, Anna, and Brad, greet us in the foyer.

After quick hellos, Darryl, Eric, and I walk in the opposite direction while everyone else heads toward the kitchen—Josh dutifully following the crowd to the kitchen.

"How many men are on duty?" I ask Darryl as we head down the hallway toward the office.

"I have three other guys outside and it's all clear."

We step into the office and close the door. As always, Darryl hands me several manila folders. I take a seat on the corner of the desk and flip through a few pages. "What's the status on Eve?"

"Same," he shrugs, "I have new pictures if you want to see them."

I promised Becca I would stop looking at them last year. She insists that just because Penelope was a grade-A whack-a-doodle, that doesn't mean Eve will be one too. Unfortunately, I'm not as inclined to agree. "Is she progressing normally?"

"She appears to be like any other eight-year-old. As always, I have her most recent report cards and information regarding her adoptive parents."

I drop the files on the desk and shake off the temptation to look at the pictures. "Have you found out anything new on the girl who tried to raid the Oscar party?"

"After serving her the restraining order and speaking with her directly, I'm sure she won't be bothering you again." Darryl's tone conveys that he personally did the talking and that the girl definitely got the message. "We also completed background checks on all the cast and crew on your upcoming production."

Relieved about that, and about the clearance on my upcoming project, I nod. "How's our client list?"

Eric finally chirps in, since he's in charge of all the business aspects of Hudson Securities. "We have our usual ten and we just added on Ian Skylar."

My brows furrow. "Is that the guy who starred in that Indy film?"

Eric nods. "We have three bodyguards securing his set and rotating personal security while he finishes his current project."

There's a knock on the door, then it swings open. Becca, Monica, and Chelsea are standing just outside, their arms crossed over their chests.

"Dinner is almost ready," Becca says while rubbing her belly. "And your daughter is ready to eat."

I chuckle and nod. "We'll be right there."

The ladies head off, along with Darryl and Eric, but I stay behind. Becca is opposed to me walking around the house carrying a weapon, so I unlock the gun cabinet that Mr. Carter was kind enough to allow in his home. It seems the least I can do, given that he definitely wasn't happy about me and Becca being together at first. Not that I blame him. I mean, his son was killed because of our involvement, but he's smart enough to know that if he wants to remain a part of his grandchildren's lives, then he'll have to put up with me. So, while I don't think he'll ever approve of our marriage, he at least respects my insatiable need to keep them safe.

"You ready, sexy?" Becca asks as she steps back into the room.

"You didn't have to wait, babe." I pull my gun from the holster and place it in the cabinet.

"Oh, I did," she says as she walks over and lifts the files off the desk. "Otherwise, you would have gotten lost in work stuff and skipped dinner."

"You know, there are other things I could get lost in right about now."

When I kiss her neck, she giggles. "Oh, no, mister. Get your head out of the gutter and let's go. I'm starving and so is your daughter."

I groan, but then shift to kiss her belly. "Okay, but once we eat and get the kids to bed, you're all mine."

"Deal," she says, then kisses me in a way that definitely doesn't help her cause.

I slide her onto the desk, accidentally knocking over the files. I could care less about them. Unfortunately, Becca does, so when she pushes me back and looks at the paperwork all over the floor, I chuckle. "I swear I'll clean it up later..." But then I catch the look on her face and my laughter dies in my throat. I follow her line of sight and frown as I stare at a picture of Eve.

That little girl looks *too* much like her mother—the similarities so striking that it elicits a strong emotional response I know isn't right regarding a little girl. Yet, as much as I realize that Rebel is just a year older than this girl is, and that Eve doesn't deserve my scorn or hatred, I despise her...worse yet, *I fear her*.

Will she grow up to be as nuts as her mother? Is my family still in danger?

I don't want to hurt an innocent kid, especially since she never knew Penelope, or Ethan for that matter, because Penelope's parents had given the girl up for adoption when she was only one-day old. Yet I still wonder if the crazy coconut hadn't fallen far from the tree.

Becca slides off the desk, kneels to pick up the photo, and then studies it for a moment. I stand there, unsure of what to say. Pregnancy hormones can be a bitch, so I know to tread lightly when she hits her third trimester, but after another moment of staring, Becca sets the picture on the desk and smiles. "Come on. Let's go get some dinner?"

I study her, sometimes disturbed by how easily she can hide her emotions. "Yeah, just give me a minute."

"Okay. But don't be long." She leans up on her toes and kisses me. "I love you, Mr. Hudson."

"I love you, Mrs. Hudson."

I wait until she pulls the door closed before I start picking up the photos and reports. I'm nearly done when the door opens, Rebel poking her head around it. "Hey, Daddy?"

My heart skips a beat, but I calmly continue gathering paperwork. "Hey, princess. Is everyone waiting on me?"

She sighs then dramatically adds, "Yes. As always."

I chuckle as I stand and set the paperwork on the desk. "I guess it's rude of me to make everyone wait, huh?"

"Not really, but you know how nuts Mom gets when she isn't stuffing her face."

I laugh. "I do, but let's keep that a secret between the two of us."

She giggles.

I squeeze her hand, and force myself not to comment on the fact that she called me daddy. I'm elated about it, but I try to play it cool as we stroll along, hand in hand.

The dining room is abuzz with activity. Thankfully, the Carters don't mind my entourage because it's a rare day when we don't travel with our newly adopted family. Anna and Brad, along with Benny, Josh, and the newest members of the family, Darryl, Chelsea, Eric, Levi, and Monica, are always in tow. I love it, and I love having a real family. It's the best thing that's ever happened to me, so I'll protect it fiercely—at any cost.

* * *

Don't miss out on your next favorite book!

Join the Satin Romance mailing list
www.satinromance.com/mail.html

Acknowledgments

I wanted to take another moment to reflect on the serious nature of drug and alcohol addiction. In this book, Cory has an amazing recovery story, but that sadly isn't always the case. Addictions of any kind are messy and awful, and while some people may have happier or more successful journeys than others, there are also those people who lose their battles. It is tragic and it should never be the case.

If you are struggling with a substance or mental health concern, please know you are not alone and that there are people ready, willing, and able to help you at the Substance Abuse and Mental Health Services Administration (SAMHSA). They are available 24/7 at (800) 622-4357.

I also wanted to take a minute to thank everyone who helped me finish and edit this book. As we all know, this was a deeply personal subject for me, and I would have never completed it without the support of Nancy and Denise. Thank you for hating Cory's character so much that you encouraged me to finish the manuscript so I could redeem him. I hope I did him justice!

Lastly, another shout-out needs to go out to my trusted advisors, betas, and editors. Thank you, especially to Mike Lynch and Erin Winfrey for lending me your eyes. And last, but definitely not least, many, many thanks to Jeanne Covert for all of your amazing insight. I know this isn't Hollywood standard, but you helped me get it as close as the story would allow, so from the bottom of my heart, thank you!

THANK YOU FOR READING

Did you enjoy this book?

We invite you to leave a review at the website of your choice, such as Goodreads, Amazon, Barnes & Noble, etc.

* * *

DID YOU KNOW THAT LEAVING A REVIEW...

- Helps other readers find books they may enjoy.
- Gives you a chance to let your voice be heard.
- Gives authors recognition for their hard work.
- Doesn't have to be long. A sentence or two about why you liked the book will do.

About the Author

Winter is an award-winning author who lives in the moment and loves nothing more than being surrounded by her family, her fur-babies, and a ton of great reads! When she doesn't have her nose stuck in a book, she's usually thinking up far away, fantastical worlds or she's cooking up a storm in the kitchen! Professionally, she works at a library (because aside from writing, that's the best job in the world!), and academically, she's a proud geek and life-time learner who can't wait to finish her PhD soon! In her spare time, she is an avid reader of science fiction, fantasy, and paranormal romances, and she one day hopes to inspire young readers in the same way her favorite authors continue to inspire her today.

www.winterlawrence.com

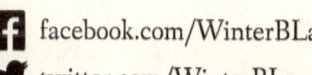 facebook.com/WinterBLawrence
twitter.com/WinterBLawrence
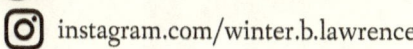 instagram.com/winter.b.lawrence

Also by Winter Lawrence

With Fire & Ice Young Adult Books

Eve 2.0: The Ultimate Gaming Series

Eve 2.0: Night Terrors

The Message on the 13th Floor

* * *

With Satin Romance

Nightmarish Dreams

www.ingramcontent.com/pod-product-compliance
Lightning Source LLC
Chambersburg PA
CBHW031055260626
47172CB00001B/76